Darcy and Elizabeth

A Promise Kept

Darcy and Elizabeth
A Promise Kept

A Pride and Prejudice Adaptation

BRENDA J. WEBB

DarcyandLizzy@earthlink.net
www.darcyandlizzy.com/forum

ISBN-10: 1530642639
ISBN-13: 978-1530642632
First Edition: March 2016

To my friend and editor, Debbie Styne, who inspires me to keep writing.

And to my betas: Kathryn Begley, Janet Foster, Wendy Delzell and Terri Merz, who worked tirelessly to correct my mistakes and to make this tale read better.

Without your help and support during the writing process, this book would have been so much harder to write. Thank you for being a part of my team.

Other Books by Brenda J. Webb

Available on Amazon.com

Fitzwilliam Darcy: An Honourable Man

Mr. Darcy's Forbidden Love

Darcy and Elizabeth: A Most Unlikely Couple

Chapter I

May 1817
Derbyshire

Hudson Hall, a stunning, three-storey, red-brick building, boasted over a hundred rooms on twelve thousand prime acres of English countryside. It had been built in the sixteenth century to showcase the Hudson family's legacy and was at its finest when filled to the brim with family and friends. Such was the case during the three-day foxhunt and ball that had just concluded. If there were any doubts the estate was still the centre of Derbyshire society, this event had put them to rest, for the most prestigious families in England had gathered once more to enjoy the fellowship of like-minded friends and associates. Still, as with all good things, the affair had come to an end with most of the guests having returned to their respective estates the day before.

Consequently, the hostess, Millicent, Countess of Markham, had begun to dread the loneliness that was sure to follow. The young widow of Lord Markham, who perished two winters earlier of influenza, was a beautiful woman with dark auburn hair, emerald green eyes and the perfect complexion of her Irish ancestors. Tall and regal like her father, she was the epitome of all that a man could wish for in a wife—that is, except for the one man who had been her obsession since the age of eight. That man, Fitzwilliam Darcy, still held a special place in her heart, though she suffered no illusions that he had ever thought of her as anything more than a good friend.

In contrast, Henry, the Earl of Markham, had come into her life as a lovely surprise the year she turned two and twenty. Never the jealous type, when they met he had guessed that she was besotted with his friend Darcy. A kind and gentle soul, it was he who taught her that the heart is capable of loving more than one person at a time, so long as it stayed true to just one. Gradually their friendship had developed into a strong and confident love, and his death had been devastating to her, as well as to their eight-year-old twins, Hugh and Katherine. In fact, Millicent still struggled to keep up the traditions of Hudson Hall—like the fox hunt—for their sake. After all, they would take their places in the *ton* soon enough. As an added benefit, with all the activity attending the festivities, she was able to forget for a short while that Henry was no longer there to enjoy them.

As yet another coach bearing a departing guest rolled down the long front drive, Millicent, or Millie as she preferred to be called, stood on the portico waving until the vehicle was entirely out of sight. Only then did she go back inside the manor and turn towards the library where the last of her visitors had congregated. These included her childhood friends, Colonel Fitzwilliam and Fitzwilliam Darcy, as well as the Barton twins, Lady Mary and Lady Carol, cousins of Henry's from Kent. The very plain spinsters, aged one and forty, had not visited since Henry's death and had only this morning decided they would stay another week. Their decision jeopardised her plot to convince Fitzwilliam to stay longer.

All of this was going through her mind as she reached the

library door and paused. Obviously the men and women had separated, for Richard and Fitzwilliam were across the room at the windows, whilst the sisters occupied a nearby sofa. Though the ladies were talking quietly, ostensibly to keep the men from hearing, Millicent could discern every word.

"While Colonel Fitzwilliam is amiable and quite the flirt," Lady Mary said, glancing wistfully in the direction of the tall, brown-haired man, "I overheard him tell Lord Wiggins that he would never marry, for the army was his family. And, as for Mr. Darcy, I fear he is a lost cause. He never pays the slightest attention to any woman."

"Any woman except Millie, you mean," Lady Carol whispered a bit too loudly. "I thought for certain he would make her an offer after her year of mourning was over."

"I did as well. Still, I have watched them carefully, and I have seen no real affection on his part. He treats her much as he does his sister. What is her name? I met her once in London, but the name escapes me."

"Georgiana."

"Ah, yes. That is it."

"I agree. It is a pity, for he and Millie make the perfect pair." Lady Carol lowered her voice again. "However, I must say that Mr. Darcy has certainly aged since we were last in his company. Perhaps he is ill, and that is why he has not acted."

Suddenly Mary noticed Millicent and stood to her feet. Carol followed her lead, and the two moved towards their hostess. Mary kept her voice low as she said, "There you are, dear cousin. Carol and I must return to our rooms to write Mother a note letting her know that we have decided to stay a while longer."

"Then I shall see you at tea?"

"At tea," the sisters echoed in unison as they quit the room.

William and Richard were so engrossed in their conversation that they took no notice of the ladies' departure. Consequently, in light of Lady Carol's remarks, Millicent took the opportunity to examine Darcy. For the first time she realised that the silver that once peppered his hair now completely covered his temples. Furthermore, the wrinkles across his forehead and around his eyes were more pronounced than ever. Still, there was no time to digest these facts before Richard's voice interrupted her thoughts.

"If you are still intent on leaving today, Darcy, I must check on Titan. He had a bit of a limp when I arrived, though he should be healed by now and ready to travel. If not, I shall see if the countess will let me borrow a horse and come back for him later."

"You know you have only to ask," Millicent said aloud as she began to cross the room towards them. "Anything I have is available for your use."

"Thank you, my lady," Richard said, bowing while at the same time sweeping his arm in a grand gesture.

Smiling, she stopped in front of him. "Old friends are like family. We share things without expecting thanks."

"Well then," Richard teased, "what say I borrow your favourite mare, Aello?"

This caused William and Millicent to laugh aloud, for everyone knew that no one but she rode that horse.

"Do not press your luck!" Millicent retorted. "You can be ousted from the family as easily as you were grafted into it."

"How quickly I am forsaken!" Richard exclaimed, chuckling along with them. Then, placing his hat on his head and giving it a tap, he added, "Now that we have that settled, if you both will excuse me, I shall see to Titan and return shortly."

William nodded and turned back to the windows. Millicent waited until the colonel was completely out of sight and then surreptitiously studied the man she had always loved, who by now was watching some horses frolic in a distant pasture. While his eyes were glued to the bucolic scene, he sipped a glass of brandy.

"A penny for your thoughts."

Sighing deeply before he answered, William said, "I was thinking of Georgiana and wondering how she is faring now that she and Lord Charlton have settled in Ireland."

"Are you worried about the marriage? I thought you approved of him."

"I had no choice but to approve. Though I was not a great admirer of his late father, I could find no evidence that the son was not a gentleman in every sense of the word. None of my friends had anything bad to say about him, either. Still, I tried to persuade Georgiana to continue the engagement another year, just to be certain. She refused."

"One and twenty is not too young to know your heart or to marry, Fitzwilliam, and, thanks largely to you, Georgiana has always been sensible."

"I suppose you are right."

Hoping to persuade him before Richard's return, she broached the subject of staying longer. "Can I not convince you to wait until the end of the week to return to Pemberley? With the children at their grandmother's estate, the house will be entirely too quiet after you leave."

Glancing at her sideways, William said, "I thought your cousins were staying."

"They are; however, they are not my idea of stimulating company. I fear that I shocked them when I chose to ride to the hounds alongside the men."

William could not suppress a grin. "Perhaps that is because a lady is expected to ride side-saddle."

"Then I suppose I am not a lady! And make no mistake—my cousins will lecture me about my misconduct until the day they leave." Then she grinned. "And you, sir, have managed to change the subject. Will you not at least stay long enough to see the children?"

"I cannot possibly stay. There are issues that require my attention at Pemberley."

"Why ever not? Lord knows you pay your stewards well to handle your estates. And you will just bury yourself in work at Pemberley—anything to keep from participating in the real business of life."

"I have no idea what you mean."

"I thought you abhorred deceit, Fitzwilliam! For years I have had to threaten to have Richard bring you against your will; otherwise, you would never have left your cave. Will you just admit that you enjoyed yourself once you arrived?"

"I was pleased to be in both your company and my cousin's, and I enjoyed participating in the hunt," William replied. Pensively, he took another sip of brandy before continuing. "I cannot say I enjoyed being on display again."

"What do you expect? You are one of the most eligible men in all of England and will always garner the attention of parents with unmarried daughters. And the widows cannot help but flaunt themselves at you, praying to catch your eye."

"I am only interested in one widow, and she will not agree to marry me."

Millicent turned to examine William's face for a certain truth. Not finding it, she walked over to a nearby chair and sat down. Wearily she said, "We have had this conversation far too many times."

"Just because I am not madly in love with you does not mean we would not do well together. My father was of the opinion that friendship should outweigh love when two people speak of marriage. He and Mother were only friends when they married."

"You were not formed for a marriage of convenience, Fitzwilliam, and marrying me would be exactly that. Besides, I am of the opinion that the heartache which permeates you so deeply is the result of an unrequited love."

William's brows knit as his voice rose. "As I have tried to tell you time and again, I have suffered no such heartache."

"I know you better than any woman alive—even Georgiana, I will wager—for she sees only her protective brother. This one thing I know for certain, after your trip to Kent five years ago, you returned a changed man."

William's lips curled sarcastically. "Pray tell me in what manner I changed."

"You were never sociable, but you became even more isolated—hiding even from me. Why else would I be forced to enlist Richard's help whenever I ask you to participate in some event?"

Unwilling to concede, William retorted, "I will not argue with you over something that you have imagined."

"I imagined it? What about Richard? He agrees with me."

"Because of your influence, Richard has turned into a worrying woman, too. If I am less *sociable*, it is merely that my responsibilities have increased every year."

"Look me in the eye and swear that you are not pining over a woman."

Steeling himself to answer without betraying his emotions, he said, "I am not," and he added almost too quickly, "I have simply been busy."

"If I did not know you so well, I would never guess you are lying."

William set his now empty glass on a nearby table. "Think what you will; you always do. I shall return to my room and see if Adams has finished packing, for I should like to leave in an hour or so."

As he walked towards the door, Millicent's sentimental heart prodded her to reconsider if she could be wrong.

"Fitzwilliam, may I make a proposal?" William stopped to look over his shoulder, his expression puzzled.

"I am listening."

"It is no secret that my children still need a father's guidance, and they adore you. And, you know how I feel about you...how I have always felt about you."

"I would treat Hugh and Kathy as though they were my own," William said, his voice more hopeful. "And you know that I have always admired you."

"I do not doubt that you would be a great father. However, we both know that, though you admire me, you are not *in love* with me. There is a big difference."

"But, I—"

She raised a hand to silence him. "It would crush me if we were to marry, and afterward you were thrown into the company of this woman...the one you still love. And, for the sake of argument, suppose she were available."

"What utter nonsense! Once married, I would never break my vows."

"Which is precisely why I propose that we enter into an agreement that, for the period of one year, we shall spend more time in each other's company. Not so much as to raise suspicions, but enough to determine if this is truly what we want. No one is to know, not even Richard."

"I will do as you ask, but, whether you wish it or not, we may raise expectations if we are seen together more often."

"We shall use the children as our excuse. You have promised each of them a pony and jumping lessons, so that is reason enough to spend part of the summer at Pemberley, and we are always in Town at the same time each winter. Since you are normally my escort and always take the children riding and skating, we have only to extend our stay in London to be in each other's company more often."

"I see your point."

"Fitzwilliam, look at me," Millicent said. Light blue eyes focused on hers, and her heart clenched. "During this year, I implore you to contemplate what it is you desire."

"I asked you to marry me; does that not signify my desire? Do you think me a deceiver?"

"I trust your sincerity, and I am convinced that you actually believe this is what you want. Still, not being in love with me—the way a man should love the woman he marries—can leave you vulnerable to another."

"If I refused to act on an attraction, what would be the harm? Besides, you would never know."

"Believe me, I would."

William took a ragged breath. "I fear you are determined to find a reason not to accept my hand."

"You may be right. Still, these are my conditions. If you agree, then one year from today we shall meet again to make a determination. At that time, either of us may decide we were foolhardy to have ever considered such a union, and we shall remain good friends." She smiled wanly. "None of our family or friends will be the wiser, so we may change our minds without fear of scandal."

"I do not need to wait. I know what I want. Nonetheless, if it will convince you, then I will agree."

"Excellent. Now, swear to me that there will be no hard feelings if either of us reneges."

"I swear."

Millicent stepped forward. As she placed a kiss on his cheek, she secretly prayed, *Lord, let him truly fall in love with me.*

"And I swear."

Pemberley
Two days later

As he descended the stairs towards the foyer, Richard marvelled once more at the luxurious surroundings. The beauty of the manor house was such that it never failed to amaze him, and halfway down the grand staircase he stopped to stare at the scenes from the life of Julius Caesar painted on the ceiling.[1] Though Matlock Manor was magnificent, Pemberley was even more so, and it never ceased to take his breath away when he stopped to admire her. At that instant, voices from below caught his attention, and he hurried on expecting to find his cousin. He was not disappointed. William, who was just leaving the dining room, had stopped to talk with the butler. As he approached, he could hear their conversation.

"Thank you, Walker. Please tell Mr. Sturgis to meet me in my study within the hour."

"Yes, sir."

As Walker stepped away, he spotted Richard. "Good morning, Colonel."

"Good morning, Mr. Walker. Please send a footman to the stables, and tell them to have Titan saddled. I plan to ride in a few minutes."

"Very good, sir."

Turning back to William, Richard noted that he was holding an express post in his hand. "Bad news?"

"I have no idea, though I am almost afraid to open it," William answered as he walked in the direction of his study. Entering it, followed closely by Richard, he shut the door soundly and went directly to his desk. While he sat down, Richard remained standing.

"You, afraid? I do not believe it. Who is it from?"

"Charles."

"Bingley?" Richard asked. William nodded but made no move to read the letter. "Come now, it cannot be that bad." Grabbing the missive, he declared, "Let me read it first."

William offered no protest, so he began and, after a few seconds declared, "Well, will wonders never cease? Mr. Bingley requests the honour of your presence at Canfield Manor. Isn't that his estate in Richmond?"

"Let me see that!"

William took the paper a little too forcefully, his conduct leaving Richard puzzled. As he watched his friend devour the letter, he ventured, "I often wondered what led to the demise of your friendship. All you said after that summer was that you would no longer be welcome at Netherfield. I supposed that it was because you had refused to marry that odious, persistent sister of his. What was her name?"

"Caroline."

"Yes, that is it! I can no longer stomach the name, for it brings back visions of that irritating creature. I certainly understand your desire to escape—"

"Richard, you are mistaken as to why Bingley and I are no longer friends."

"Will you enlighten me? After all, it has been five years, and whatever happened affected you greatly."

"You have been listening to Millie too much."

"I realise that she is relentless where your welfare is concerned, but she is right about that one thing."

William sighed. "If you must know, I will tell you...but only you. Swear you will not reveal what I am about to say to anyone, most especially Millie."

"It will be difficult, but I swear."

"When Bingley left Netherfield, it was because I had persuaded him that Miss Bennet did not care for him as he cared for her. Afterward, Miss Bennet came to London and called on his sisters. Caroline was unkind and unceremoniously sent her away. She told me of Miss Bennet's visit only because she felt I was an ally in her campaign to separate them, and she knew I would keep the secret."

"Were you an ally?"

"I suppose I was at the time."

"I cannot believe you would be so unkind as to make him think her heart was untouched or to keep Caroline's secret. Obviously, Jane Bennet loved him, for they are still happily married—at least according to the gossip at Cheapside."

"How would you know the gossip at Cheapside?"

"One of my sergeants has a sister who is married to a merchant. His warehouse is next to Bingley's. Whenever we travel together, he talks incessantly. He is worse than any woman. But, back to my question—how could you stoop so low?"

"I was acting out of concern for Bingley. I believed Miss Bennet was only bending to her mother's will to marry a wealthy man. However, when I was at Rosings, I had opportunity to speak with her sister Eliz...Miss Elizabeth Bennet. She informed me of my error in judgement, and when I returned to London, I confessed everything to Charles. He broke all ties with me."

If the slip of Elizabeth's Christian name piqued Richard's interest, he let it pass. "So, Bingley would not forgive? That does not sound like the man I knew."

"He forgave me. It is just—" William struggled for the right words. "A few months later, after he and Miss Bennet were married, I received a letter in which he broke off all contact."

"Whatever for? You did the honourable thing by confessing."

"By then he had learned of my insults to Miss Elizabeth, and since he was now a member of the family, he did not wish to expose her to my company."

Richard shook his head in dismay, stood and walked over the liquor cabinet. Pouring himself two fingers of brandy, he tossed it down before enquiring, "How did you manage to insult her?"

"I asked her to marry me."

Having just poured another glass, Richard whirled around, the brandy sloshing from side to side with some staining his uniform. William opened a desk drawer and threw him one of the serviettes he kept there. As Richard wiped the brandy from his clothes, he squeaked, "You did what?"

"I asked Elizabeth Bennet to marry me."

Sinking down in the nearest chair, Richard let go a low whistle. "I thought that was what I heard. But...but you did not marry."

"She refused me. In fact, she said I was 'the last man in the world she could ever be prevailed upon to marry.'"

"Then you should be thankful! Obviously she is not of sound mind. More importantly, why in the world would you ask for the hand of someone so far beneath you?"

"Why do you say that she was beneath me?"

"You talked of nothing else when you first returned to London from Netherfield, which I admit should have been a warning. You ranted on and on about her relations—simpleton of a mother, out-of-control younger sisters and a father too lazy to correct them."

"I had forgotten that I told you."

"Darcy, you can have your pick of the most eligible women in England—the cream of society. Why choose her?"

"In society's eyes she might be beneath me, but in every pertinent way, she is by far my superior." William turned to gaze out the windows. "Still, it was for the best that she refused me. Her personality was too lively to waste on someone of my—" He hesitated. "What shall I call it? My *stick-up-the-arse* manner?"

"You do yourself a disservice, Cousin. You are not as bad as that."

"Really? I was called that and worse at Cambridge. You should remember. You took it upon yourself to defend me often enough."

"You are merely taciturn, which is an accident of birth and not your fault. And, after your father's death you had to raise Georgiana, manage Pemberley and worry that every woman you met was just after your fortune. In my opinion, that would make anyone more reserved."

"Elizabeth Bennet was definitely not enamoured of my fortune...or me."

"Then she is a fool."

"On the contrary, she was the most intelligent woman of my acquaintance." William smiled wanly, rose and walked over to pour himself a glass of brandy. "However, there is no need to discuss her any further. By now, she is likely married with several children holding to her skirts." He took a large swallow of the caramel-coloured liquor and winced as it burned his throat. "I cannot fathom what Bingley wants with me after so long a time."

"What does that last line of his letter mean—I need to collect on your promise?"

"I wrote Charles after he broke off our friendship and promised that if he should ever need me, he had only to ask."

"Ten to one, he wants to borrow money."

"I do not think so. Over the years, I have asked my vendors in the warehouse district about him. By all reports, he has done well. He has expanded to two warehouses, and he owns a large estate in Richmond as well as the townhouse in London. It appears he is well situated."

"Looks can be deceiving. You know that."

"I do."

"Do you wish me to accompany you? I have to be in London next week."

"I would appreciate the company to London, though I feel I should meet with Bingley alone."

A knock at the door signalled Mr. Sturgis' presence and Richard stood. "I shall get moving, for Titan needs his exercise."

"Shall I join you after I am done with Sturgis?"

"If you are not too long in coming, for I would love a chance to beat you in another race."

"Over my dead body!"

"I can arrange that!" Richard barked a laugh at the startled look on the steward's face as he passed him in the doorway.

Leaning in, he whispered to the servant, "You never heard me say that."

William tried hard to keep a straight face.

Chapter 2

Richmond
Canfield Manor
Three days later

As his coach neared the front entrance of the handsome, grey stone manor that was now Bingley's home, William pictured the last time he had been there with Charles. Back then, his young friend had been as excited as a schoolboy, unable to stay seated in the coach as he moved from window to window, exclaiming over first one aspect of the estate and then another. Having decided it was time to be a landowner, he was so exuberant that William had a hard time convincing him to rent an estate in lieu of buying one. In that way, he had reasoned, Bingley would have opportunity to see if the estate and the neighbours suited before making a purchase he might later come to regret.

At that time, Canfield Manor belonged to an old classmate of William's from university, Lord Norton, who had inherited it upon the death of his grandmother. He happened to mention to William that he was considering renting the manor; therefore, he and Bingley had driven to Richmond to inspect it. As was his habit, immediately upon seeing the property, Charles had declared that it was everything he wished for in an estate. Nevertheless, not long after their visit, Norton changed his mind, and Bingley had settled on renting Netherfield Park instead. The die was cast when Charles met the Bennets, which led to the demise of their friendship and initiated the misery that had been William's constant companion ever since.

With the recollection of Netherfield, Elizabeth instantaneously appeared to be sitting across from him in the coach. It was a cruel twist of fate that manifested whenever he was alone. Filling the emptiness of the vehicle, as well as his longing heart, one impertinent eyebrow rose in question as she slowly smiled. It was an expression he had often seen directed his way when she stayed at Netherfield after Jane fell ill. At the time, he thought that she was being flirtatious, only to learn later that that was not her intent in the least. Suddenly, William's heart began to beat rapidly, just as it had that morning when he considered the possibility of seeing her again. Taking a ragged breath, he closed his eyes and whispered encouragement to his beleaguered soul. *In all likelihood, she is married to that Lucas boy and lives in Hertfordshire. There is no earthly reason to think that she may be here today, of all days.*

Just then, the driver began to guide the coach around the huge circle in front of the manor, and in only seconds, the weary team was being pulled to a halt. The sudden stop caused William to pitch forward. Jostled from his vision, he grabbed an overhead strap to keep his seat and peered out of the window. A footman was hurrying down the steps towards the vehicle, while behind him an older man, obviously the butler, stood at the open front door.

The footman opened the coach door, and William exited the vehicle, donning his hat as he did. When he looked back at the front door, Jane Bingley stood beside the butler. She smiled, though she did not appear to be happy. Instantly, he wondered at the reason for Charles' absence.

"Thank you for coming, Mr. Darcy," Jane said softly, shading her eyes with her hand as she followed his progress up the steps. "I hope your trip was pleasant."

As he neared his hostess, William noted that she was just as beautiful as when he had last seen her, despite the fact that she was obviously with child.

"It was pleasant enough, thank you."

Her eyes followed his to her swollen belly, and Jane addressed the butler. "Mr. Goings, please see that Mr. Darcy's luggage is taken to the guest room we have prepared for him."

The balding, rotund man nodded to her and then to William before rushing down the steps to supervise the unloading. Jane swept her hand towards the open door. "I am afraid that Charles is not well enough today to greet you himself. Please allow me to direct you to him."

Strangely, William felt that he should not enquire about Charles' health, so, without a word, he followed her inside the manor. As the housekeeper took his hat and coat, across the marble foyer two young maids reached the last steps of one of the matching staircases. In one maid's arms was a ruby-cheeked child with ginger hair, while a similar little girl of about four years clasped the hand of the other servant. Both children fa-voured Charles, though it was obvious from the colour of their hair alone that he was their father. At the sight of Jane, the eldest let go of the maid's hand and ran towards her mother with her guardian on her heels.

"Mama! Please, may I see Papa?"

Jane waved the maid away and squatted to embrace the child. Meanwhile, the youngest struggled to be set down. "See Papa!" she parroted her sister.

The maid fought to control her wiggling charge until Jane proclaimed, "You may let her come." Instantly, the child joined her sister at her mother's knee.

"Now, what has your aunt been teaching you? Young ladies do not raise their voices," Jane said serenely. "Especially not while in company." At the mention of company, two sets of dark blue eyes peered around Jane to look at Darcy.

"Mr. Darcy, this is our daughter Grace Elizabeth," Jane said gently pushing the oldest forward. The four-year-old did a passable curtsey, causing William to bite his lip to keep from laughing.

"And this," Jane said, bringing her youngest forward by the hand, "is Marianne Jane." The smaller child immediately turned to hide her face in her mother's skirt.

"It is a pleasure to meet such beautiful young ladies," William said, bowing slightly. The older child turned as crimson as Charles always did whenever he was embarrassed.

Jane leaned down to speak to her children. "After Papa meets with Mr. Darcy, you may see him; but for now, Jenny and Cora have graciously agreed to take you to the stable to see how much the new baby ducks have grown. I expect you to mind, and if you do, you may each have a chocolate biscuit when you return. Would you like that?"

"Yes, Mama!" excited voices echoed in unison.

Jane stood erect and smiled apologetically at the maids. "Please, continue with your outing."

"Yes, ma'am," the maids murmured. Then, each taking the hand of a child, they started towards the back of the house.

Jane waited until they were completely out of sight before saying, "I apologise for the interruption. The girls are without their governess this week, and they know the maids will not uphold her high standards."

"There is no need to apologise. Your children are very well mannered, especially given their ages."

"How kind of you to say. Now, if you will follow me, I would like for you to see Charles before he grows tired. His energy lags as the day wears on."

Unable to keep from glancing over the interior of the house as he followed Jane up the grand staircase, William noted that not much had changed since his last visit. However, he had little time to dwell on that fact, for suddenly they were on the second floor, and Jane picked up her pace. She continued swiftly down a hallway, only to stop abruptly in front of one particularly ornate door. Taking hold of the door handle, she paused. William felt her anxiety as her troubled eyes met his.

"I shall leave you and Charles alone, as that is his wish. However, should you get the impression—" Her voice cracked, and she stopped to recover her composure. When she began again, her eyes brimmed with tears. "Should you feel that Charles needs assistance, please do not hesitate to ring the bell on the table by his bed. I shall be waiting in the sitting room next door, and I will hear it."

William was taken aback at her words and actions. "Forgive me, if it is not my place, but is Charles—"

"You must ask that of Charles," Jane interrupted. "He would rather explain everything to you. I am sure that you understand."

Without awaiting his answer, she opened the door and walked straight towards a large bed in the centre of the room where her husband lay propped up on several pillows. A man, obviously Charles' valet, held a cup from which he was drinking.

"Please leave us, Bartlett," Charles said weakly.

"Very good, sir."

The valet, a grey-haired man of about fifty, hurried to set the cup on a tray on a nearby table. Nodding first to Jane and then to William, he exited the bedroom. With his departure, Jane leaned down to place a kiss on her husband's forehead, then stepped back so that he could clearly see William. Charles held out a much too thin hand.

"Darcy! Thank you for coming so swiftly."

The cheerfulness of Charles' greeting belied his appearance, for William had never seen him look so ill. Forcing a smile, he gripped his old friend's hand. "It has been too long, Charles."

"Yes, it has! And I suspect you have been hiding in Derbyshire since last we met, for I have not seen your name mentioned in the papers in years."

"You know me, Charles. I am not one for making the social circuit."

"You never were. Have you married?"

"No."

"A pity."

At that point, Jane said, "I shall leave so that you may talk freely. Please do not overtax yourself, Charles. You know what Mr. Clark said about rest."

Charles smiled lovingly at his wife. "I shall behave, Janie. I promise."

Seemingly appeased, Jane forced a smile and addressed William. "Dinner is at eight, but since Charles has been ill, I have had a tray sent up here so that we may dine together."

"Please do not alter your plans for my sake. I should enjoy eating in my room tonight so that I may retire early. I plan to return to London in the morning. That is, if Charles and I have concluded our business."

"Thank you for being so understanding," Jane replied. Then, with an anxious glance at her husband, she walked to the door.

As the sound of the door's click signified her departure, William could remain composed no longer. "I am not going to mince words, Charles. I am shocked to see you so thin and pale. What in the world has happened?"

"You remember the influenza epidemic of two winters past?" William nodded. "When it swept through London, I was caught there when the roads were closed to keep it from spreading. Mercifully, Jane and the children were not in Town. I came down

with the dreaded disease, and had it not been for the quick thinking of my staff, I would likely have died. I was one of the first
admitted to the hospital, and they got the malady under control
before it got the better of me. Still, I have not been completely
well since."

"I am so sorry to hear that you have been ill. How well I remember the epidemic. It took a good friend's life—Lord Markham."

"I remember reading of his death in the papers. Many people
died, so I have no reason to complain, though my lungs were
weakened. I still suffer with a persistent cough, and a trifling cold
can turn serious in mere hours. Still, I felt well enough to return
to work and, until a few months ago, kept the hours that I did
before I was stricken."

"What happened a few months ago?"

"Out of the blue, I began having stomach pains so severe I
could not keep anything down. The stress of this new ailment
served to exacerbate my cough."

As if to testify to the truth of his words, a wracking cough
overtook Bingley, requiring William to retrieve the cup of tea
that Bartlett had set aside. As he held it for Charles to take a sip,
he asked, "Does your physician think the two are related?"

"The local physician in Richmond exhausted all his theories
months ago. That is when I asked Mr. Grantham for his opinion."

"I am glad you sought him out. I trust Grantham, for he has
been my family physician for years."

"I remembered. That is why I sent for him."

"And what was his conclusion?"

"He is still uncertain as to the source of my stomach problems,
though he has prescribed different draughts in a bid to find one
that works. However, he is adamant that the best hope for my
lungs is a warmer climate. Did you know that he has a clinic in
Spain? He wants me to settle there while they work to determine
the cause of my current distress, and he is certain that the warm-

er climate will allow my lungs to heal entirely."

"I have heard of the clinic. Several members of White's, or their relations, have been residents of the facility—to their betterment, they claim." Charles nodded, so he continued. "Then, you have decided to sail for Spain?"

"I do not think I have a choice at this point."

"Did you ask me here because you wanted me to accompany you?"

"No. Only my valet will accompany me; even Jane and the children will stay here." Charles sighed raggedly. "We had a stillborn child last year...a son. It was so devastating to us both that I would never chance having Jane travel in her condition."

"I am so sorry for your loss. I never knew, or I would have written you."

"I believe that, and I appreciate your kind words."

"Still, Charles, I must be honest. I cannot help but feel that it would be very hard on Mrs. Bingley to be separated from you, especially now that she is with child."

"But it would not be *as* dreadful if you are available for counsel and to protect her and the children in my absence." Seeing William's brow furrow, he hurriedly continued, "What I want to do is to give you the legal power to handle my business and personal affairs whilst I am away."

"What about the members of your own family? I heard that a cousin joined you in the warehouse business. Will he not resent me for taking over that responsibility in your absence?"

"David Howton is my only living cousin and a partner in my business. I agreed to that, not because I thought him a good addition, but because his mother, my favourite aunt, asked me to help him. I sold him a third interest in the warehouses, his portion to be paid monthly from his salary."

"And, has it been paid off?"

"Only about half has been paid." Charles took a deep breath

and let it go loudly. "I do not mind saying that I quickly became disappointed with his work habits."

"What do you mean?"

"I continued to conduct acquisitions and sales, while he was to supervise our employees and keep the ledgers regarding inventory. When I returned to work after the influenza, it was evident that he had not recorded anything in the ledgers in months. His greatest achievement seems to be his ability to charm the ladies, though Jane cannot abide to be in his company. As for having other family who can help, Caroline is still a spinster, and Louisa's husband drinks more than ever."

"Cannot Mr. Bennet be of service?"

"You really have buried yourself in Derbyshire if you have not heard."

"Heard what?"

"Jane's father and mother died soon after she and I married. They were staying with friends when their cottage caught fire. No one escaped."

"I had no idea." Seizing the opportunity to learn more, William ventured, "Are none of Jane's other sisters married?"

"Darcy, I called on you because you promised to help me. I trust your judgement above anyone else's, but if you are not willing to keep your promise, pray say so now."

"I intend to keep my promise, but need I remind you that I have never managed a warehouse?"

"It is no different than managing Pemberley." When William did not reply, he added, "Though I cut ties with you, I never stopped caring for you like a brother, and I do not think you stopped caring about me."

"I have not."

"Then why are you hesitating?"

"When you broke off our friendship, you said it was because you feared being in my presence would upset Miss Elizabeth.

Will it not upset her to see me now?"

"To be honest, so much has transpired in her life since you and I cut ties that I feel your presence is no longer an issue."

Darcy's heart sank at his old friend's candour. Still, he had no time to dwell on the reasons he was now insignificant to Elizabeth's wellbeing, for Charles had begun another fit of coughing. William helped him take another drink of tea.

As the cough abated, Charles pleaded, "I trust you, Darcy. You are an honourable man and capable of great compassion. Should I not recover, I know you will take diligent care of my family. Will you not agree?"

"Stop talking nonsense, Charles. Of course you are going to recover."

"Let me be frank, my friend. Both of my physicians say there is a chance that I may not live, but I intend to fight as hard as possible. In any case, I want to leave someone in control who I know will not take advantage of my Janie."

William's resolve crumbled at the expression on Charles' face. "When do you want me to start?"

"I sail for Spain in a little over a week."

London
Darcy House
Two weeks later

As William and his London steward, Mr. Perry, poured over the first of many stacks of ledgers for Bingley's warehouse, Mr. Barnes appeared in the open study door. Taking in the chaos of papers and books strewn over every possible surface, the butler temporarily forgot his purpose in coming. Only the sound of William's voice snapped him back to attention.

"Yes, Barnes?"

"Excuse me, sir, but there is a Mr. Howton here to see you."

William had wondered how long it would take for Charles' cousin to search him out. When he visited the warehouses after receiving the legal papers from Bingley's solicitor, the foreman, a Mr. Dabney, had reported that David Howton had left for Liverpool the week before, ostensibly to collect merchandise. When pressed, he admitted that he had no idea where the man was staying in Liverpool or when he might return. He did say that, as far as he knew, Howton resided at Bingley's townhouse when he was in London.

William had left word with both Mr. Dabney and with the servants at Bingley's townhouse that Howton was to call on him as soon as he returned. That meant that if he was just now calling, the buying trip must have taken all of three weeks to complete. Eager to take the measure of Charles' cousin, he asked Mr. Perry to wait in his own office while he talked to the man. As the two passed in the doorway, Perry made no attempt to acknowledge the visitor.

Howton stepped into Darcy's study with an unassuming manner. He was not at all what William expected, for he looked older than Bingley and did not favour him in the least. Of average height with brown hair and eyes, he was a nondescript fellow. Walking straight towards him, Howton leaned over the desk and stuck out his right hand.

"It is good to finally meet you, Darcy. My cousin has always spoken highly of you."

Bothered by the *assumed* familiarity of addressing him by his surname, William did not stand. Instead, as his eyes bored into the man, he laid down the pencil with which he had been making notes in the margins of a ledger, and shook the outstretched hand.

"Bingley warned me that you could be very charming."

"He is too kind."

"I think not," William replied. Then he waved his hand towards the chair Perry had vacated. "Please, have a seat."

Howton sat down and looked around, spying the books strewn here and yon. "May I enquire as to what this is all about? I have just today found out that Charles actually sailed to Spain two weeks ago. He said he was considering it the last time we talked, but I assumed I would be notified when he had made up his mind."

"He left it to me to notify you."

"I see. Still, as his partner, I expected to be in charge of the business should he leave, so why have you collected all the ledgers?"

"You are the *junior* partner. Charles appointed me to take his place whilst he is unable to function; and, as for the ledgers, my steward and I are going through them to familiarise ourselves with the business in hopes of determining why it has been losing money. Mr. Perry is an excellent bookkeeper."

The smile left Howton's face, but just as quickly reappeared. "I am sure that you will find everything in good order. I have done my best to keep things as organized as Charles had them before he took ill."

"I have to ask. With money so tight, is a three week trip to Liverpool worth the expense, or do you stay with friends while you are there?"

William watched Howton's smile disappear entirely. "No. I have no friends in the area. I lodged at the main hotel. As it happened, one of the ships I was to have met was delayed. I thought it best to wait in Liverpool rather than risk having our shipment waylaid by another warehouse owner."

"Hmmm." William was not convinced. "What was so valuable that you thought it worth waiting nearly a month?"

"Coffee...and tea!" Howton's cravat suddenly felt tight, so he ran a finger underneath it. "You have no idea how hard it is to purchase good tea or coffee. If we were not there the very minute it comes in, some unscrupulous competitor might attempt to buy it right out from under our noses."

"I thought you had contracts to purchase tea and coffee before the shipments ever left foreign ports."

"We do! Still, nothing is guaranteed if we are not there to take custody. Also, we buy other supplies on the spot and extra tea and coffee if they should become available."

"Why would such sought-after goods become available?"

"Often small warehouses contract for merchandise, but cannot afford to pay for them once they arrive. In such cases, we can negotiate for those goods at reduced rates."

"I see. Then as I go through these ledgers, I should expect to see entries where some merchandise is purchased at lower than contract prices."

Howton stood to his feet and began to pace. "To be honest, I have not had an opportunity to buy any lower priced items of late. And, being so busy since Charles became ill, I may have forgotten to record everything purchased or sold in the last few months."

"But you just said that I would find everything in good order."

Howton forced a smile. "As I said, I have done my best under the circumstances. The truth be known, Charles has no earthly idea how much money I have saved us by buying diligently. Poor fellow has been so muddle-headed of late that I tried not to bother him with facts and figures. If you should find anything in the books that does not make sense, just ask me."

"I shall. And, let me assure you that I am not bothered by facts or figures."

Howton's face dropped. "Then I shall leave you to it. If you need me, you know where to find me."

As Charles' cousin swiftly headed to the door, William called out, "Mr. Howton?" He stopped and eyed William warily. "Am I to assume that you are still residing at Bingley's townhouse?"

"Yes. My cousin graciously offered me the use of his house when I first moved to London. My cousin, Jane, prefers Richmond, I suppose, for she hardly ever visits, and Charles often said that he enjoyed my company when he was in London. For that reason, I never moved."

William appeared to be considering that explanation, so Howton asked, "Is there anything else you wish to say before I leave?"

"Yes. I want every expense and purchase or contract from this day forward to be submitted to me, via Mr. Perry. He will be helping with this task until Charles is well. Is that understood?"

Howton's eyes narrowed. "I understand completely."

Chapter 3

London
Darcy House

As William descended the grand staircase for the trip to Richmond, it dawned on him that he was not dreading this trip as he had the one only a few weeks ago. No doubt the fact that Elizabeth was nowhere to be seen when he was last at Bingley's home added to his sense of wellbeing. It had taken years for him to overcome his ardour for that lady, and it simply would not do to add fuel to waning embers. No, given a choice in the matter, he would never again knowingly put himself in her company.

Barnes stood at the bottom of the stairs with his hat and coat. As he approached the butler, the servant asked, "Do you expect to return today, sir?"

"I do. It is only about an hour's drive. Given that I have only to pick up the household ledgers and go over a few things with Mrs. Bingley, I should easily return this evening."

"You do realise that it has begun to rain."

"I had not."

"It is merely a steady drizzle at this point."

"Good. Barring any storms, you may expect me back in the late afternoon."

"Very good, sir."

Barnes looked as though he wanted to say more, so William obliged. "Is there something else?"

"If you do not mind my asking, how is Mr. Bingley faring?"

The entire house was aware that a post from Spain had arrived the evening before, so William was not surprised. "He arrived safely in Spain. Mr. Grantham's associate is optimistic that with rest, plenty of sunshine, and natural remedies, Bingley may recover completely. For now, all we can do is wait and pray."

Barnes nodded. "You can be assured that the staff is praying for Mr. Bingley. He is well thought of by every member of this household."

"I never doubted that," William replied as he took his hat, donned it, and turned so that Barnes could help him with his great coat. "I, too, pray that Mr. Bingley will be restored to health quickly."

With that said, William walked towards the back door, intending to depart for Richmond via the alley behind his house. The second he went through the door, however, he was confronted by someone rushing up the gravel path, head down against the rain. When the man looked up, William recognised Harold Smith, the son of Bingley's solicitor, who had joined his father's company a short while ago. He sighed in resignation. The young man was very talkative, and he did not wish to be delayed. An enormous grin split Smith's face as he joined William under the awning that sheltered the back door.

"Mr. Darcy! Thank goodness you are still here! I had planned to travel to Canfield Manor via horseback, but thought better of it when the rain began. Then father mentioned that you said that you were going today, so I hurried here to beg a ride."

"I do not mind your company, Mr. Smith, but why in the world are you making the trip?"

The younger Smith patted his coat. "I plan to deliver Mrs.

Bingley's copy of the recorded agreement between you and her husband."

"There is no need for you to travel so far. I have authority to accept legal papers on her behalf, and I will gladly see that it gets to her."

The cheeriness left Mr. Smith's face. "This is true, but I really wanted to make the trip myself." At William's raised brow, the young man rushed to explain. "You see, I met the governess for Bingley's children when I accompanied my father to call on Mr. Bingley several months ago, and, to be truthful, I am besotted with her."

Remembering that feeling all too well, William's heart clenched. "Does the lady return the sentiment?"

"Not yet, but she will," Smith declared confidently. "I intend to pursue her until she accepts my hand."

William motioned towards his coach. "Then, let it not be said that I delayed true love."

Canfield Manor
Jane's bedroom

"Thank you for offering to chaperone the girls today, Lizzy. I did not want them to miss the celebration of Lady Celeste's birthday, but I am too tired to attend."

Elizabeth sat down on the side of her sister's bed, reaching out to brush some curls from her forehead while surreptitiously checking for a fever.

"That is understandable, given your condition, but you owe me no thanks. With Jenny's help, I shall have no problem taking them all." Elizabeth's smile faded. "Are you sure that I do not need to send for the physician?"

"I am merely tired, Lizzy, not sick. To be truthful, I miss Charles terribly, and I fight so hard not to let the girls see me morose; however, the effort takes its toll. Every so often, I think I shall scream if I have to smile one more time. Just being away from the children for a little while should help to restore both my patience and my strength."

Elizabeth squeezed Jane's hand. "That is good to hear." Then in a bid to lift her sister's mood, she giggled. "I must admit that I am as eager as the children to see what Lady Needham has amassed to entertain her daughter's peers this year. I predict there will be as many adults at Warrington Park as children, for word has spread of the extravagant entertainment she has provided in the past."

"I do not see how the countess can best what she staged last year," Jane stated. "What with ponies to ride, china to paint, clowns, actors presenting plays, and more food than I have ever seen in one place, I do not think it possible."

"We shall see," Elizabeth said, rising to her feet. "I shall provide you with a complete description once I return. Promise me that you will rest while we are away."

"I promise that I shall lie here until Mr. Smith arrives and lie down again after he leaves."

Jane dared not mention that she was expecting Mr. Darcy, as well. Though she hated misleading Lizzy, recollection of her frame of mind the summer that she and Charles married made her determined to hide that man's involvement in their lives for as long as possible. For that was the summer Lizzy had returned from Kent a wretched imitation of the sister she knew. Nothing Jane said could compel Lizzy to disclose the source of her misery until word that Lydia had eloped with George Wickham reached Longbourn.

Only a catastrophe of that magnitude had the power to prompt Lizzy's confession, and, through copious tears, she revealed that Mr. Darcy had exposed that vile Wickham's lies while they were both in Kent. Moreover, she admitted that Mr. Darcy had proposed marriage, though he cited their family's many failings and flaws during his poorly executed offer—an offer she rightly refused. Concerned that being thrown into his company again might be awkward for her sister, she spoke to Charles about the situation soon after they had married. That resulted in Charles breaking all ties with his friend, and, until he had fallen deathly ill, Fitzwilliam Darcy had never been mentioned again.

"Father or son?"

Lizzy's question brought Jane's attention back to the present. "Pardon?"

"Who is coming? Herbert Smith or Harold Smith?"

"I understand that it is the son."

"Excellent. Perhaps he will think I am away by design."

Picturing the brown-haired, blue-eyed gentleman, Jane said, "Oh, Lizzy, why do you say that? He seems such a pleasant young man, and it is clear that he likes you. I do not know why you will not give him the time of day."

"It is NOT the time of day that he wants, Jane! I have tried to discourage him in every possible way, but he still follows me around like a puppy whenever he is here."

"You cannot deny that he is amiable and handsome."

"As I have said too many times, I am not looking for a husband. Besides, I am six and twenty, and he is merely a boy."

"He is two and twenty. That is not a great difference in age."

"Please. I do not wish to hear anything more about Mr. Smith."

"If that is how you feel."

"It is!" Lizzy retorted, turning on her heel. "Now, I shall collect Emily, Gracie and Marianne, and we shall be on our merry way!"

"Tell my daughters that they are to mind you," Jane called after her.

Elizabeth stopped in the doorway to smirk over her shoulder. "They always mind me. They ignore you and Charles because you spoil them."

With that, she laughed and exited the room. The sound of her laughter faded the farther she went down the hall. Jane smiled. It was true.

On the road to Richmond

During their journey, Harold Smith chatted animatedly and nonstop, a behaviour that reminded William greatly of Bingley. Moreover, he was about the same age as Bingley was when they met; thus, it was inevitable that whilst the solicitor chatted incessantly, William's mind flew to the first time he had seen his former protégé. It was during his final year at Cambridge that he stepped in to defend an immature, newly-arrived student against several peers who were ridiculing his connections, or lack thereof. Being grateful, Charles Bingley had eagerly subscribed to his benefactor's advice and had followed his counsel without question for years afterward—even to the point of quitting Netherfield when William suggested that Jane Bennet's feeling did not match his own. That unpleasant incident, however, turned out to be the last time Charles listened to his counsel.

William held no ill will towards Bingley for what had transpired; he blamed only himself. And he suffered no illusions that, had health not dictated, his old acquaintance would never have contacted him.

Having paid no mind to his passenger's wordy conversation, William had no idea that Smith had stopped talking to address him—at least, not until a heartfelt apology penetrated his musings.

"I repeat, sir. If I have offended you, I apologise."

William had no option but to confess. "I am afraid that I have been woolgathering. I have no idea what you might have said to offend me."

"I was speaking of the woman I adore, and I asked if you had ever been in love. I apologise for asking something so personal. It is just—well, a man of your age is likely to have had much more experience in matters of courtship and marriage than I."

For a split second, William felt insulted, though just as swiftly he shrugged off the unintended offense. *To a man of his age, I must appear ancient.* For unknown reasons, William decided to be uncharacteristically forthright.

"Once I thought I was in love, but the lady did not return my affection. So I am afraid that I am no expert on the subject."

"I am sorry if my question stirred any regret. I may well be chasing a dream by pursuing Mrs. Gardiner, but I simply must. I intend to do all I can to win her trust and, hopefully, her heart."

William tried to remember where he had heard that name before. "Mrs. Gardiner? Is that the governess' name?"

"Yes. She is widowed, according to Mrs. Bingley, and not keen on remarrying."

"Why would Mrs. Bingley reveal something so personal to you?"

"In hindsight, I believe she surmised that I had developed a fondness for her governess, and she wished me to know the woman's circumstances in order to spare my feelings if they were not returned."

"It has always been Mrs. Bingley's nature to be kind."

"I agree." Pulling a small book from inside his coat, Smith held it out. "I observed that Mrs. Gardiner reads a great deal and most often enjoys poetry; thus, when I saw this book in a shop window, I purchased it."

"You do know that a gentleman does not give gifts to a woman if they are not engaged."

"I am not that foolish, sir. My hope is to leave it where she will find it after my departure. My name is written inside, you see." He opened the cover to show William. "In this way, she will know that we have similar tastes."

"Do you like poetry?"

"Not a great deal, but since she obviously does, I am determined to acquire an appreciation for it."

William sighed. "May I offer a word of advice?"

"By all means."

"Be truthful and forthcoming, no matter the subject. A relationship based on half-truths is as vulnerable as one based entirely on lies. Accept the woman you love for who she is, and ignore those things that do not matter—such as her lack of fortune or connections and her family's idiosyncrasies; for, if the truth be known, you might find those attributes, or worse, in your own family. Otherwise, true love may slip through your fingers with life-altering consequences."

Smith's brow furrowed. Obviously, Mr. Darcy was speaking from personal experience, for few ladies of his sphere had any connections, much less fortunes. Still, the counsel about being truthful would apply to people of all stations. "I shall keep in mind all that you have said."

Almost immediately the coach entered the huge ornamental gate that announced the boundary of Canfield Manor, while a servant occupying the guardhouse waved them on. Both men fell silent, each contemplating the issues of love from different perspectives.

Harold Smith had never actually considered that a man of Darcy's rank might face any difficulties with matters of the heart. After all, did not wealth and position mean he could have his pick of any woman he wished? Still, he was not ignorant of the fact that marriages among the *ton* were, for the most part, arranged. Out of the blue it dawned on him that if he were equal in rank to his host, then marrying Mrs. Gardiner might be out of the question. Unsettled at the thought, he breathed a prayer of thanksgiving.

Lord, it is times like this that I am thankful to not be among the wealthy and titled.

Canfield Manor
Jane's bedroom

Though Jane dearly longed for sleep, it would not come. Whenever she closed her eyes, fear overwhelmed her. It was difficult being with child and having Charles so far away, with his very life hanging in the balance. Still, the carefree days of leaning on her father or her husband for support were over. It was up to her now if she was to remain sane, and she was determined that she would. She owed that much to Charles and the children.

Thoughts of the children brought to mind Lizzy's tease about spoiling them, which made her smile anew. Ever since her sister had come to live with them, insisting on earning her keep as the governess for their daughters, the girls' manners had improved, as had Grace's numbers and letters. Not only was Lizzy an excellent teacher, but Jane's children loved her, as did the other child in the house, three-year-old Emily.

Though Lizzy loved Emily as her own, she was not. Instead, conditions beyond her control had left the girl in her care after her mother's death. Fear gripped Jane again as visions of a tall, humourless, flaxen-haired man she and Charles had met once in London came flooding back. That man was Emily's father, and she would never forget the evil look in his impossibly pale blue eyes. She shivered. His image brought to mind the evening Lizzy had arrived on their doorstep with Emily wrapped in a blanket. Until that moment, her sister had kept the gravity of her employment situation a secret, and there was nothing she and Charles could do then but hide her and the baby.

The worst part was having no indication whether Emily's father cared enough to search for his daughter—that, and the fact that if she were found, her parentage would be indisputable. The child was the very image of her father, a man Lizzy once declared was not the kind of person one wished to oppose. Though still very vigilant, over time her sister had relaxed her guard somewhat, beginning with visits to their sisters' homes and then neighbouring estates on special occasions—such as today.

Jane sighed from the weariness of it all. The past five years had been a whirlwind of difficulties, beginning with Lydia's elopement with Mr. Wickham. That debacle had ended with her death during childbirth, mercifully taking the child with her. Escaping the gossip regarding their youngest daughter was the stimulus that had sent her parents to visit friends outside of Hertfordshire and, ultimately, to their deaths. Then, without warning, Mr. Collins had arrived at Longbourn's doorstep ready to claim his inheritance, leaving her remaining siblings homeless. Being a kind man, Charles had offered to take them all in, but each had balked at the idea of imposing on the newly-married couple.

In quick succession, Mary had accepted the hand of the newly appointed vicar in nearby Compton, whilst Kitty married their Uncle Phillips' law clerk, someone who was twice her age. John Lucas, as expected, offered for Lizzy, but she refused, saying that he was too much like a brother. Soon after, she took a position as a companion to the mother of one of Aunt Gardiner's friends, though that job ran its course in less than a year with the lady's untimely death.

Lizzy had spoken very little about her next position, which was as governess to a boy of four named Nicolas. She did say that the parents, a Count and Countess Van Lynden, were well connected and, if memory served, one of their fathers had been a diplomat from the Netherlands and the other a trusted aid to King George III years before. Lizzy had shared this bit of information with her only to emphasise the family's significance and to explain their insistence on privacy. A year later, after the birth of a daughter, Count Van Lynden had banished his wife to an obscure estate in Scotland along with the little girl, whilst he and the boy stayed in London. Lizzy had accompanied her mistress.

Suddenly, the sound of coach wheels on gravel caught Jane's attention, and she rose from the bed. Walking over to one of the many floor-to-ceiling windows, she pulled back a rose-coloured silk curtain. Mr. Darcy's coach was circling the drive. *He is early!*

Rushing to a gilded mirror on the wall, Jane began smoothing the few curls that had escaped her bun. Then realising that there was no one arriving that she cared to impress, she quit and headed towards the door. Someone was knocking before she got there.

"I am coming."

Exiting the coach, William found it odd that no one was waiting to greet them. Nonetheless, by the time he and Smith reached the top step, a footman came rushing out the front door, followed closely by the butler and then Mrs. Bingley. Seeing that the guests had already exited their coach, the footman sheepishly stopped in his tracks and took up a position next to the door.

"Mr. Darcy, Mr. Smith, welcome to my home," Jane Bingley said in her usual genial manner. Before either man could reply, however, she looked upward and gasped, her hand coming to rest over her heart. "Oh, my word!"

Concerned, William stepped forward. "Is something the matter?"

"For...forgive me," Jane sputtered. "I did not mean to frighten you. It is just that the children accompanied their governess to a birthday party at Warrington Park—a *lawn* party. Had I known the weather was going to take a turn for the worse, I never would have allowed them to go."

William peered in the direction Jane was looking. The clouds there had thickened and were getting dark. "I would not worry prematurely; all we encountered on the trip here was rain."

"But my children—"

"Surely the hosts will be sensible enough to gather all of the children inside if need be."

Jane murmured, "I suppose you are right."

Trying to lift her spirits, William teased, "On occasion, I am."

Jane smiled, lifting her chin bravely. "I understand that you want to return to London today, so please come inside, and let us get started."

"That is my desire. Still, the best-laid plans of mice and men—"

Harold Smith interrupted, "Often go awry."[2]

They were all laughing as they entered the house.

Chapter 4

Canfield Manor
The library
Several hours later

Harold Smith's spirits had plummeted the second that Jane disclosed that the children and their governess were elsewhere. Though he pasted on a smile in hopes of masking his disappointment, he was certain from Mr. Darcy's expression that he was not fooled. It had taken only a few minutes to present Jane Bingley with the agreement between her husband and Darcy and to explain it to her. When she had no further questions, there was nothing left for him to do. He had planned to flirt with Mrs. Gardiner whilst their hostess and Darcy conducted business. Alas, those plans had certainly *gone awry.*

An hour later, Smith was standing at one of the large windows in the cavernous library, holding back a heavy drape so that he could keep watch on the lengthy front drive. Barely conscious of the muffled voices discussing household accounts somewhere in the room, he watched silently as once-distant clouds moved in their direction, turning from gray to black as they came. He hoped against hope that the changing weather might bring Mrs. Gardiner and her charges back early, fearing at the same time that Darcy might notice the ominous clouds gathering and decide to leave ahead of them; thus, he said nothing about what was happening outside.

"Mr. Smith? Will you not join us for a cup of tea?" As she was speaking, Jane Bingley walked towards him, so Smith let go of the drape. "Surely you must be famished if you have not eaten since morning. We have sandwiches, cakes and rolls."

He turned to her with an innocent expression. "A cup of tea sounds wonderful."

Heading towards the serving cart where a maid was already pouring a cup of hot tea, he noted that Darcy still sat at a table piled high with ledgers, folders and other paperwork. "From the looks of it, you may need to stay longer than you planned, Mr. Darcy. If so, please do not think that I shall mind."

William rose to his feet and stretched. Then, he walked to the cart, addressing Jane. "I am beginning to think that I may need to take the ledgers with me to London, Mrs. Bingley, for my task is taking much longer than I expected. That is, if you do not mind."

"Given Charles' handwriting, I do not wonder at it taking so long," Jane said, smiling wanly. "I have no objections to your taking them, but I fear you may find more entries needing interpretation. My husband's handwriting was never elegant, and I fear it deteriorated even more after his illness."

William took a cup of tea from the maid, nodding his appreciation to her as he answered Jane. "Since you have so kindly translated a goodly portion of his script, I believe I shall be able to decipher the rest."

Wishing to change the subject, Smith, who was now at a table laden with trays of food, declared, "Come, Darcy. You must sample these cinnamon rolls. They are heavenly."

"I am well aware of their allure. I had several during my last stay."

"I had forgotten that you were here before."

After everyone had finished eating, Jane addressed William. "Shall we continue our examination in hopes of getting finished? Or are you still of a mind to take everything to London?"

"I think it best if I—"

Without warning, a thunderous boom shook the entire house. It began to rumble slowly through the manor from front to back, rattling glasses, china and windows as it went. The windows shook so terribly that, for an instant, Jane feared they might break. As soon as it passed, she hurried to the windows, throwing back a curtain and gasping at the sight. Coming towards her, William reached the window just as another thunderous boom clapped and then reverberated throughout the manor. Lightning began to illuminate the sky incessantly, with one particularly large bolt striking a tall oak not a hundred yards from the house. A huge limb crashed to the ground, and Jane began to weep, bringing even Mr. Smith forward to assess the damage.

William pulled an initialled handkerchief from a pocket inside his coat. Offering it to Jane, he said gently, "Please try to be brave. In your state, it simply will not do for you to become distraught."

"He is right, you know," Smith agreed.

Jane took the proffered gift and began dabbing at her eyes. "I...I shall try."

Like a tale from a penny novel, the storm intensified. One clap of thunder was immediately answered by another, each harder and more pronounced than the last. The house trembled with each deafening round, while the constant flash of lightning gave evidence of the storm's fury without. Raging winds blew small limbs and leaves across the manicured lawn as the rain continued to increase. Suddenly, the tall statues that stood on either side of the front steps became invisible.

Mesmerised by the display, everyone startled when the door

to the library flew open. Bursting into the room, the housekeeper stopped in her tracks and wrung her hands as she searched the room for her mistress. Fearing that she would frighten Jane even more, William walked towards her, shaking his head ever so slightly from side to side.

"Yes, Mrs. Watkins?"

The elderly woman saw the resolute look on that gentleman's face. "I was wondering what we should do about the children, sir."

"There is nothing any of us can do at present but wait and *try not* to panic," William replied. Surreptitiously, he tilted his head in Jane's direction, praying the woman would take his meaning. "Nothing good comes from being too frightened to act, should it becomes necessary."

"Mr. Darcy is correct," Jane said, turning away from the window. "There is nothing we can do at this point, other than to pray that they are all safe."

William was about to suggest that Jane go upstairs and rest while he watched for the children, when the butler suddenly appeared in the doorway. His face was shockingly white.

"A carriage is coming."

Disappearing as quickly as he had come, Jane hurried after him. "We have to get everyone safely inside."

William and Mr. Smith were right on her heels, and the three gained the foyer just in time to see a footman go through the open front entrance carrying a large umbrella. As they gathered at the threshold, a flash of lighting revealed the Bingleys' carriage racing down the drive and soon after the umbrella turned inside out.

William stepped back inside the foyer. Addressing the fearful butler, he ordered, "Fetch our greatcoats! We shall use them as shields against the rain."

By the time Mr. Mercer and a maid returned with their coats, the Bingleys' carriage had stopped at the bottom of the steps. It appeared that the driver had his hands full keeping the horses from running wild, and, recognising the danger to the occupants of the carriage, William donned his coat and was the first one down the steps. Opening the carriage door, his gaze fell on four-year-old Grace, who was nearest the door. Realising that she might not hear him over the din of the storm, he held out his arms and mouthed, "Come."

Immediately the child fell into his embrace, and he clasped her to his chest, covering her entirely with his coat. Hurrying up the steps and into the foyer, he had barely set her on the floor when Jane rushed to embrace her. Turning, he almost collided with Smith, who was now coming through the door.

"I have Marianne!" the solicitor shouted. "Go help the others!"

Hurrying back to the entrance, William watched as a footman who had swung one heavy greatcoat over the shoulders of a very frightened maid, helped her manoeuvre the last slippery steps to the top. Then, as they both rushed across the portico towards him, the servant shouted, "Mrs. Gardiner is still in the carriage."

While removing his own coat to use in the same manner, William was astonished to see a petite woman, wearing only a cloak against the rain, exit the carriage as it rocked precariously back and forth with every shift of the horses' feet. As soon as she had cleared the vehicle, the driver let the frightened creatures have their heads, and they rushed towards the stables, leaving her exposed. In the blink of an eye, a strong gust of wind ripped the bonnet from her head, sending it bouncing across the drive. At once, a profusion of long dark curls escaped the pins in her hair and covered her face. Spellbound, William stood frozen in place until the wind whipped the cloak aside, revealing that she held a small child in her arms. Immediately he raced down the steps.

Wrapping his greatcoat around them, William employed a steadying arm about the woman's waist as they started up the steps. Water rushed down the steps in torrents, and, when her footsteps faltered, he swept woman and child into his arms and carried them inside. After setting the lady on her feet, he was employing both hands to remove the heavy rain-soaked coat from off her shoulders when her head came up. Instantaneously, he was lost in a pair of ebony eyes, the same eyes that still haunted his dreams. *Elizabeth.*

Suddenly Jane was beside them, motioning for a footman to take the coat from his hands. As the servant obliged, she chatted nervously whilst William and Elizabeth stood rooted to the spot, staring mutely at one another.

"Mr. Darcy, you certainly cannot return to London under these conditions. If you and Mr. Smith will wait in the library, I shall have rooms prepared so that you may change clothes and rest before dinner."

Still unable to speak, William watched as Jane took the child from Lizzy's grasp and handed her to a maid. "Come, Emily, sweetheart. Cora will take care of you while I help your mother to her room so that she may change into something dry."

Mother. The realisation that Mrs. Gardiner was, in actuality, Elizabeth, and that she had a child, pierced William's heart. Still, he could not help glancing at the child as the servant carried her away. Her hair was flaxen, and her eyes the lightest blue. It struck him that she looked nothing like her mother and images of all the light-haired men he had ever known crossed his mind. *Stop it! You will drive yourself mad.*

Most of the uproar created by the circumstances ceased with the departure of the children and their maids upstairs. Only William and Smith were left in the foyer with Jane and Elizabeth.

"If you will excuse us, gentlemen," Jane said, taking her sister's elbow and leading her towards the stairs. "Lizzy needs to change clothes."

When the solicitor came forward to stand beside him, his curiosity was so palpable that William could feel him straining to keep silent. Still, he said nothing as they watched the sisters ascend the grand staircase. Once Elizabeth reached the top of the stairs, she turned to look down from that vantage point. Emotionless, she sought William's face and held his gaze for several seconds, then disappeared down the hall. The second she was out of sight, Smith could restrain himself no longer.

"Sir, you led me to believe that you did not know Mrs. Gardiner. Was that merely a ruse?"

Annoyed at Smith's attitude, William snapped, "I knew her only as Elizabeth Bennet, and not very well at that."

"Bennet? Then, she is—good Lord! Why did Mrs. Bingley not tell me the governess was her sister?"

"You shall have to ask her."

Smith had witnessed the shocked expressions on the faces of both Darcy and the woman when the coat was removed.

"Forgive me, but from the way Mrs. Gardiner reacted, I would wager that she remembers you well. Were you...that is to say—am I to believe that you were never more than acquaintances?"

Reminded of his ill-fated offer for the lady, William took a deep breath and let it go slowly to keep from exploding in anger. "*Acquaintances* is a fitting description of our relationship. In truth, I do not believe I ever knew her."

Turning on his heels, he walked towards the library. Fortunately for Harold Smith, he did not follow, for William was in no frame of mind to be questioned further about Elizabeth. Nor did he intend to resume work on the household accounts. Having spied a liquor cabinet in the room earlier, he hoped brandy might calm his wildly beating heart. Walking directly to the cabinet, he poured two fingers of the liquor in a glass and tossed the entire thing down in one gulp, wincing as it burned his throat.

What ghastly luck! Just when I have finally gained control of my life, you appear! Downing the contents of an additional glass, he began to pour still another. *Very well, Elizabeth, you leave me no recourse! I shall keep to my room tonight and leave first thing in the morning.*

Unfortunately, just as with Mr. Smith, William would soon find his carefully made plans were about to go awry.

In Elizabeth's bedroom

The moment the door was shut, Jane began unbuttoning her sister's wet gown and apologising profusely as she worked.

"Oh, dearest! Can you ever forgive me for exposing you to Mr. Darcy? I know how much you despise him. That is why I had Charles break off all contact with him after our marriage, so that you would not be thrown into his company ever again. I want you to know that I was greatly upset when Charles decided to leave him in charge of our well-being whilst he is in Spain, and I tried to convince him that it was not a wise decision. Still, he would not listen."

Lizzy's gown slipped to the floor, and Jane began to untie her stays, all the while talking so rapidly that she was almost breathless.

"Whenever I tried to explain, Charles kept repeating, 'I believe that Darcy is the best man for the job.' Naturally, at length I had to acquiesce. Still, I did my best to keep the two of you from seeing one another while he was here. You were to be at the birthday party. How was I to know that the weather—"

"Jane! Pray, stop!" Elizabeth's plea caused her sister to stop midsentence and to watch as she turned to face her. "I suppose I am just too weary to make sense of what you are saying, so let me ask the questions, and you may answer them."

Jane nodded nervously.

"Why is Mr. Darcy here?"

"When Charles realised that he would have to travel to Spain to recover, he insisted on sending for that gentleman to handle the warehouse and our estate. I tried to remind him that he promised not to bring Mr. Darcy into our homes ever—"

Elizabeth interrupted, "All these years he never visited because of me?"

"Yes. When you told me of his hateful offer, I resolved that you would never be subject to his company ever again, at least in my homes."

Elizabeth sighed. "I should have told you everything then, and maybe all of this could have been avoided."

"Whatever do you mean?"

"I admit that immediately after he made me an offer, I was upset and hurt, but, with time, I came to realise that Mr. Darcy was not trying to be unkind so much as he was being truthful. Look at what happened to Lydia because our parents let her go unsupervised."

Sinking down into a wooden chair, Elizabeth began to remove her wet boots. "If I was distressed for so long, it was because I was coming to terms with my prejudices. I realised that Papa had made me think I was clever at sketching the character of others, while my time in Kent showed me how far off the mark I was. I believed Mr. Wickham's lies, for he had all the appearance of goodness, while Mr. Darcy—" Elizabeth seemed unable to continue.

"Then...then, you did not despise him?"

"No, not then and not now."

"You mean to say that I had Charles break off their friendship because of a false assumption, and still he agreed to help us?"

"I am sorry that I never explained fully. I apologise."

Jane sighed heavily. "No need to apologise. What is past is past. However, have you considered that Mr. Darcy has never married? From the odd way he acted today, could it be that he still thinks of you with regret?"

Elizabeth shook her head resolutely. "If you believe that, it is because you did not see the expression in his eyes when he removed the coat. For a moment, I thought I would be physically ill, for he looked just as he did the day I rejected him. You see, it was raining that day as well, and he and I were both soaked to the bone.[3] I intended to wound him with my refusal, and obviously I hit the mark. It was evident from the hurt in his eyes that he has never forgiven me."

"What did you say that was so dreadful?"

"I said that he was the last man in the world I could ever be prevailed upon to marry."

"Oh, Lizzy, you did not!"

Elizabeth nodded uncomfortably. "Odious words, once spoken, are not easily forgiven or forgotten, especially by one undeserving of them."

Suddenly everything made sense. "Oh, my word! You did not hate Mr. Darcy; you were in love with him...and you are still."

"I am not!" Elizabeth protested. Seeing Jane's look of disbelief, she tried to explain. "To be truthful, I regretted my refusal almost immediately, but I was too proud to admit it. Fortunately, the events of the last five years have freed me of my feelings for Mr. Darcy. I am sure he has moved on with his life, just as I have. And now that I have Emily, I do not intend ever to marry."

"Emily needs a father as much as any child."

"Unfortunately, she has a father—an evil man who will destroy anyone who stands in his way should he ever decide to look for her."

"But, if you were married, your husband could protect you both."

"I have not told you everything about Lord Van Lynden's wickedness, but suffice it to say that I will not put another person in danger. Should he ever find Emily, I shall have only one alternative. That is to go back for her sake."

"You once said that he made unpleasant advances towards you whenever his wife was not present."

"I stayed with the family only for Lady Van Lynden's sake, for his attentions made me very uncomfortable. Still, if it comes down to it, I would return as Emily's governess, for I will not be separated from her."

"Oh Lizzy, I pray that he never finds you. I cannot abide the thought that you or she could be under that man's control."

"Neither can I." Elizabeth shivered and walked over to the dresser. Opening a drawer, she pulled out a dry gown. "Please help me into this. I feel as though I could sleep until morning."

"You may take a nap, dearest, but you most certainly cannot miss dinner! I am not going to try to entertain both Mr. Darcy and Mr. Smith when you are the one they are both expecting to see."

"Jane, I cannot—"

"I will not be gainsaid. You insist that you are no longer in love with Mr. Darcy."

"I am not."

"Nor do you wish to have Mr. Smith's regard."

"Heavens, no!"

"Then, there is no reason for you to be affected by their company. You have only to let Mr. Smith know you are just not interested, and he should withdraw his attentions."

"And Mr. Darcy?"

"In light of the fact that I misinterpreted your feelings, separating him and Charles erroneously, I wish him to know that *both* of us are grateful for his assistance."

"Assistance? He is being paid for his services, is he not?"

Jane folded her arms. "It seems you have not learned your lesson on sketching character, Lizzy! Charles wanted to pay him, but he would not hear of it." At the bedroom door, she hesitated before going out. "In light of all that he is doing for our benefit, it would be thoughtful if you tried to make amends for thinking unkindly of him. I intend to do the same."

"I am not sure that is possible. He once told me that 'his good opinion, once lost, was lost forever.'"

"I believe you quite capable of making him form a new opinion of you, if that is what you desire." When Elizabeth did not answer, she added, "Furthermore, I wish you to wear the yellow gown that Charles and I gave you for your birthday."

"But that gown is too fine for a governess."

"You are first and foremost my sister, not the governess. Please do as I ask, just this once."

Without awaiting an answer, Jane went out the door.

Chapter 5

Canfield Manor
That evening

Early on, Jane decided that dinner would be served in the family dining room, a much smaller venue, which held a round table that could accommodate four or five people. Her intention was to have her sister sit on her right and Mr. Smith on her left, which would place Mr. Darcy across from her and next to Lizzy. This, she hoped, might inspire conversation between the two. Nonetheless, when Mr. Mercer went to that gentleman's room to announce that dinner would be served shortly and that everyone was convening in the drawing room, William pleaded exhaustion and requested a tray be sent to his room. Against proper etiquette, and her character, Jane sent Mr. Mercer back to William with a personal request that he join the party downstairs instead.

As the dinner hour neared, she headed to the drawing room, praying under her breath that Mr. Darcy's good manners would cause him to act more graciously than she. Still, gaining the room, she found only Mr. Smith and Lizzy, each having a glass of wine. She stood in the doorway long enough to observe that her sister seemed bored with the solicitor's endless chatter. At length, he seemed to become aware that the object of his affection was looking over his shoulder, and he turned to greet her.

"There you are, Mrs. Bingley! I was just saying to Mrs. Gardiner that it appeared that she and I might be left to dine alone." Behind his back, Lizzy rolled her eyes. "Not that I would mind, for I find her company fascinating."

Jane tried not to laugh as Lizzy made yet another face. "I assure you, Mr. Smith, that that would never happen."

"Well, I, for one, would not be surprised if Mr. Darcy did not join us tonight. Men of his age tire easily, and, what with the storm, each of us had a draining day."

Jane took exception to his insinuations. After all, Charles was only a few years younger than Mr. Darcy. Still unsure if that gentleman would join them, she declared confidently, "He seemed no more affected by today's circumstances than you."

As Lizzy grinned at her uncharacteristic boldness, Jane glanced at a gold-plated clock that sat on the mantle. "Besides, it is not quite time to dine."

A footman came forward with a tray holding a single glass of water. Jane smiled her thanks, took the glass and brought it to her lips. Just as she did, William entered the room.

Seeing Lizzy's eyes go wide, Jane turned and was immediately struck by how handsome Mr. Darcy was in his black coat and breeches, stark white shirt and cravat with a diamond stickpin, and a teal brocade waistcoat. The grey in William's hair made him look even more attractive than the first time she and Lizzy had met him in Meryton. Glancing to her sister to gauge her reaction, Jane bit her lip so as not to smile. For someone who had just vehemently denied being in love with the man, Lizzy seemed unable to tear her eyes away from him.

"I am sorry to be late," William said to Jane. "It took me longer to dress, since I brought no valet."

"A valet is a luxury someone such as I can only dream about," Smith said, a little too mockingly. "I imagine that for a man used to being attended, dressing yourself is an ordeal."

Darcy shot him a sharp look. "I assure you that I travel quite often without a valet. I merely strained my shoulder during a fencing match last week and have found it difficult to raise my arm overhead ever since. Had I known I would be staying overnight, I would have made arrangements to bring my valet."

"So," Smith crowed with a smirk, "you were injured attempting to fence?"

"No. Actually, my opponent tripped, and I endeavoured to break his fall."

Apparently determined to chip away at Mr. Darcy, the solicitor enquired, "If you do not mind me asking, are you ranked?"

"Though I do not visit London as much as in the past and, thus, do not fence as often, I still hold the record for the most wins ever at Angelo's."[4]

Smith swallowed hard. William's answer had silenced him quite handily.

Jane stepped forward. "Thank you so kindly for joining us tonight, Mr. Darcy. Please forgive me for not realising that you might need assistance. Charles' valet accompanied him to Spain, but one of our footmen fills in for Bartlett whenever he is away. I am sure he would have been only too glad to be of service."

William smiled at Jane warmly. "Please do not concern yourself over something so trivial. I managed, even if I was a bit slow."

Mr. Mercer appeared in the door at that very moment. "Dinner is served."

Though it may have seemed to others that William was not conscious of Elizabeth's presence, he most certainly was. The second he had spied her in the drawing room, he began to regret bowing to pressure and joining the others. She looked stunning in a low-cut, yellow sarsenet[5] gown, embroidered with white roses along the hem, the bodice and the sleeves. A white silk rose adorned her dark hair, which was swept atop her head, leaving a few long curls hanging over one shoulder. By the time dinner was announced and Jane asked him to escort her sister, William was so flustered that it took all his strength not to stare at her décolletage.

Once Elizabeth was seated and he had taken his place at the table, William ran a finger under his cravat in hopes of loosening it, for the room had suddenly become unbearably hot. Regrettably, it was not long afterward that Mr. Smith broke away from a myriad of questions from Jane to address Elizabeth. Unfortunately, the issue that he put forward made William's temperature soar even higher.

"Mrs. Gardiner, I could not help but notice that you seemed to recognise Mr. Darcy after he rescued you from the carriage; however, on the trip here, he gave me the impression that the two of you had never met."

Elizabeth's face flushed and noting that, William glared at Smith. Feeling compelled to ease her mind about what he might have said, he declared, "It is no great mystery, Mr. Smith. As I explained to you *when you asked earlier*, I did not know the lady as Mrs. Gardiner. I knew her as Miss Elizabeth Bennet."

Elizabeth's eyes flicked to William. "That is correct. We met just before my sister married Charles. Mr. Darcy and Charles are good friends, and he was my brother's guest at Netherfield."

"But you looked so—" Smith seemed to search for a word. "*Shocked* is the only reasonable description of your expression. Surely if Mr. Bingley and he are good friends, you have seen him often enough so as not to be shaken to find him here."

"You forget, sir, that I was married. I did not live near my sister during that time."

"Then your reaction is understandable," Smith said. "If I may change the subject, I am familiar with a Gardiner who owns a warehouse in London. Was your husband kin to him by chance?"

Obviously surprised that Smith had so easily made the connection, Elizabeth began to stutter, "I...we..."

Jane rushed to explain by reciting the story concocted by their aunt and uncle to explain Lizzy's present situation. "Lizzy's husband, John, was a distant cousin of our uncle, Edward Gardiner, who is the proprietor of Gardiner's Warehouses in Cheapside."

At least the part about being a cousin was true, though the elderly bachelor had conveniently died of old age about the time his identity was needed. Having no relations other than the Gardiners, there was no one to question their version of his life.

Hoping to thwart further questions, Jane quickly added, "John owned a small business in Wales. He and Lizzy resided there, and Charles and I persuaded Lizzy to live with us after his death."

William's brows furrowed. "He died of influenza whilst living in Wales?"

"Yes, the same epidemic that struck Charles also took his life," Jane replied guardedly.

William turned to Elizabeth. "I have a small estate in northern Wales. By any chance was your home in the north?"

Elizabeth looked uncomfortable. "No, we lived in Cardiff."

William instantly went silent, and the remainder of dinner was relatively uneventful. Other than Mr. Smith extolling his love of reading and asking Lizzy pointed questions about what subjects she most enjoyed, there were no other discussions.

Early on, Jane had lost hope of William and Elizabeth having a private conversation as long as Mr. Smith was present; thus, when dinner was finished, she suggested that they all retire. No one objected, though it was clear from his frown that Mr. Smith would have liked to spend more time with her sister.

Daylight found Mr. Darcy and Mr. Smith on the road to London. The younger man had wished to say goodbye to Mrs. Gardiner, but his companion insisted on leaving. Thus, as the vehicle made its way back to Town, Mr. Smith was uncharacteristically silent, incapable of thinking of anything save how to see Mrs. Gardiner again. Mr. Darcy was thinking the exact opposite.

For far too many years, that gentleman's nights had consisted of reliving Elizabeth Bennet's stinging refusal, and last night that dream had returned with a vengeance. It tortured him, leaving his heart raw, and motivated his desire to leave without as much as a farewell. In the end, the fact that Elizabeth had not returned from a walk by the time the coach was ready to leave resolved the issue.

Later, as the coach settled into an easy sway due to the smoother roads closer to Town, William laid his head back against the padded seat and wearily closed his eyes. All at once his agreement with Millicent came to mind, and he realised that this was the first time he had thought of her in days. Their pact to spend more time together had brought serenity back to his soul and sleep to his tormented nights.

Father always maintained that marriages were meant to unite suitable friends, not those with uncontrollable passions. Could I trade peace of mind for the passion of loving Elizabeth again?

He concluded that he could not.

Darcy House
William's study

Richard stood at the door of his cousin's study for some time, marvelling at how diligently he and Mr. Perry worked on the piles of papers and ledgers covering the desk. Wordlessly, each flipped through a ledger, making notes in the margins and on a separate sheet of paper. Finally, he could stand the silence no longer.

"Mr. Barnes said that I would find you in this mausoleum, Darcy. According to him, this mission of mercy for Bingley takes up the majority of your time now. In fact, years from now, I would not be surprised to find your lifeless body at your desk with those exact ledgers under your head."

William looked up and smiled, motioning the colonel into the room. "And what of Mr. Perry? Will he be here as well?"

"Of course! Perry is nothing if not loyal. He will expire in that chair and most likely be found having slumped to the floor."

Chuckling at his employer's cousin, the steward rose and addressed William. "I shall continue with this ledger in my office, sir."

"Thank you, Perry."

Nodding to the career officer as he passed, Perry exited and then closed the door. Richard took his vacated chair.

"I assumed that you had gone through all the ledgers by now—business as well as personal."

"I might have accomplished that if Bingley's handwriting had been better, especially in regards to those items that concern his estate."

"Good Lord! I had forgotten how illegible his script could be. But why would he keep the estate ledgers? Is that not a steward's job?"

"I learned that his steward died last spring and was not replaced. I suppose Charles felt he could save expenses by not hiring a new one."

"Did your trip to Canfield Manor uncover any avenues whereby you could cut expenses there?"

"Actually, Charles has done a fine job of keeping the estate expenses under control. I could find nothing to recommend, other than the addition of two guards. Though the servants are loyal, there are no men at Canfield that I would trust to protect the family."

"Will you call on Hartley and Boggus?" Richard asked, referring to the retired Bow Street Runners that William used whenever he needed extra security.

"I will. Or, I should say, I have already. The minute I got home I had Barnes send for them. They are on their way to take up positions at Canfield Manor as we speak."

"What did Mrs. Bingley have to say about the guards?"

"Per Charles' instructions, I have the final say. Still, I explained to her that I wanted men at Canfield that I could trust to keep them safe—good, decent men who would look out for her and the children as they would their own family. And, being former army officers as well as Bow Street Runners, I felt confident they could handle any situation. In the end, she seemed appreciative."

"And, pray tell, how will she pay the guards' salaries when her income is steadily dwindling? Did that not worry her?"

"Charles requested that his wife know nothing about the decline in their income."

"But how can that help to—"

William interrupted, "Mrs. Bingley is with child, Richard! I will not have her worrying about anything, save her husband. I intend to fund the guards."

"And will you fund the current shortfall?"

"If necessary." William shrugged. "I have the means, so it is no great sacrifice."

Richard held William's eyes until he looked away. "You are withholding something, and you know I will goad you until you tell me everything. Begin with when you left for Richmond and keep talking until I tell you to stop."

Used to his cousin's persistence and knowing that, in the end, Richard was the only one he had to confide in, William began to recite all that had happened during his trip to Canfield Manor. By the time he had finished, a big smile covered the colonel's face.

"You mean to tell me that Elizabeth Bennet is presently the

governess for Bingley's children and that you are now in charge of her welfare as well as Mrs. Bingley and her children?"

William nodded mutely.

"How rich is that?" Richard said, his laughter filling the room. "She threw you over and married some *nobody*, and now she is under your care. How mortifying that must be!"

"I am glad that you find it all so very amusing!" William snapped. "Frankly, I find it impossible to fathom why Charles did not tell me that Eliz...Mrs. Gardiner would be my responsibility in addition to his family."

"And she has a child, you say?"

Again, William nodded.

"It occurs to me that Charles was likely so afraid that you might refuse that he conveniently left out that bit of information."

William rose and walked over to the windows, staring at the scene outside for what seemed a long time. Richard waited until he was ready to speak.

"There is something else that I found unsettling."

"After hearing that you are now responsible for Elizabeth Bennet, I could never conceive of anything more preposterous, so just tell me. I could never guess."

"Correct me if I am wrong, but during the influenza scourge two years past, was it not one of your duties to station men at various checkpoints to keep the populace from entering or leaving the most affected areas or crossing the borders to Wales and Scotland?"

"Your memory serves you well. It was my responsibility to keep the larger pockets of infection quarantined and to keep the borders closed."

"And, if I am not mistaken, you told me afterwards that Wales was totally untouched, save for a town in the northern part that bordered England. You believed those few cases were the result of people trying to flee Liverpool."

"This is true. It was the town of Hawarden."

"Then I have to wonder why Mrs. Bingley and Mrs. Gardiner both maintain that her husband perished from influenza whilst living in Cardiff."

Richard's brows knit. "There is no possible way that he contracted influenza in Cardiff."

"I thought the same."

"So, knowing how your mind works, what are you going to do about this ruse? Confront the lady?"

"I will do nothing. I merely wanted to confirm my suspicions. I have no desire to know why she and Mrs. Bingley went to the trouble of concocting the story."

"Are you not the least bit curious? If they have lied about that, what else is a lie? Did Miss Bennet even have a husband? Is her child a—"

"Stop!" William exclaimed, visibly agitated. "I will not delve into her motives."

"What a relief that is to hear! Your weakness for that woman was almost your undoing."

"Do not be so melodramatic!"

"I am being frank. I feared what would happen if you were to—"

"You may rest easy. I do not intend to be drawn into her affairs, past or present."

"Good. And, speaking of the present, I ran into Millie on Picadilly Street. She was at Hatchard's bookshop and—"

"Since when do you frequent Hatchard's?"

"I do not. I was on my way to Hawkes to acquire a new uniform."

"That makes more sense."

"To get back to what I was saying, Millie asked me to remind you that you are to be her escort tomorrow."

"I had no idea that she had returned to London. Moreover, I know nothing about what is taking place tomorrow."

Richard picked up a stack of unopened letters on the edge of his cousin's desk. "What is all this?"

"My personal correspondence. Perry does not handle that. I do."

"Well, if you actually *opened* your personal correspondence, you might know what is happening tomorrow."

William waved a hand over his desk. "As you can see, I have been busy."

Richard held one envelope to his forehead, closed his eyes and pretended to read what was inside. "Lord and Lady Matlock request the pleasure of your *impressive, imposing, inspiring, notable, majestic* company on the—"

"My cousin, the clairvoyant!" William declared irritably. Rising, he leaned over his desk to grab the letter from Richard before sitting back down.

"What you are holding is your invitation to attend a dinner party honouring Lady Marjorie Darlington's engagement to Lord Morgan."

Sorting through the other letters, Richard held up another. "This is from Millie, most likely informing you that she is returning to Town."

"Enough!" William said. "I shall go through the rest tomorrow."

"Cousin, I know you are drowning in responsibilities now that you have taken on Bingley's duties, but you cannot shirk family duties, like Mother's soirées, when she knows you are in Town. She does not ask for much, but she does insist on your attendance when you are here."

"Why must I honour Lady Marjorie? I never cared for her, and I cannot abide Lord Morgan. He is a womanising gambler who should have married twenty years ago, or at least before he was too old to father children."

"He is four and sixty and, from the rumours at Boodles, is still quite able to perform."

"Just because he can, does not mean he should," William said, tossing the invitation from his aunt on the desk.

"Come now, Darcy! Lady Marjorie spent years on the shelf waiting for an offer from you. The least you can do is wish her well."

"I never gave her any encouragement."

"I am very aware of that. Still, Mother expects you to attend, and so does Millie."

"And so I shall."

Richard stood. "Then my mission here is accomplished. I shall now go visit my family. Never fear, for I will return in time to dine with you."

"I have to wonder what your parents think of the fact that you rarely stay with them when you are in London."

"Mother knows why, and Father suspects. He and I get along much better when I am not under his roof. I am too old to take orders, and it keeps the peace between us."

William shrugged. "I am all for keeping the peace."

"Dinner is still at eight?"

"At eight."

William could not help but smile as Richard donned his hat, touched the brim as a salute, and marched out of the room. Only his cousin had the ability to make him laugh when he was at his lowest, and William counted himself fortunate to have such a man for a friend, as well as a member of his family.

While these thoughts swirled in his head, the steward knocked on the now open door then peered inside. "Are we ready to continue?"

"Yes."

As the steward came forward, William asked, "Perry, would

you say that I neglect my personal correspondence?"

The look on the steward's face was all the answer he required. "Forget that I asked."

Canfield Manor
That same day

When Elizabeth went for a walk, she tried to clear her mind of every thought, save the beauty of her surroundings. Given the opportunity, she employed the exercise twice a day—a short turn about the gardens at dawn when the children were still asleep, and one in the afternoon when they were taking a nap. Jane objected to her long, solitary walks on the grounds that they were dangerous and had only taken a slightly softer line after being convinced that the walks rejuvenated Elizabeth's soul. Still, worried that an accident might befall her sister, it had taken a solemn promise not to be gone for more than an hour and a half to dispense with the requirement that a footman follow her every footstep.

Though Elizabeth kept to the gardens in the mornings, she favoured jaunts in the woods in the afternoons, most often heading straight to a certain large, flat boulder that jutted from a cliff next to a small lake. This, in her opinion, was the perfect place to ponder all of the things she kept secret—especially from Jane.

Reaching the rock today, she sat down and pulled a notepad, a pencil and a book, *Poems* by John Donne, from a small bag. The book was one of the few tomes she had purloined from her father's library right out from under Mr. Collins' nose the day he arrived unexpectedly to take possession of Longbourn.

The remembrance made her smile. She had relied on the fact that the rector would never miss a single work of poetry. After all, he frowned on everything except books of sermons. She had been right. Collins never mentioned the books when he accused the sisters of taking items that he felt he should have been his—including a rickety footstool that Kitty used to climb into bed each night. Each rescued book now served as a bittersweet reminder of the hours spent debating with her father over what an author may have meant by a certain passage. The remembrance was overwhelming.

Oh, how I miss you, Papa!

Later, having tried to read the same page several times without comprehending a word, Elizabeth gave up. Laying the book aside, she removed the thin shawl from her shoulders and formed a makeshift pillow. Then, rolling onto her stomach, she crossed her arms over the pillow and laid her head down on them. The warmth of the smooth rock seemed to penetrate all the way to her bones, and she closed her eyes. Not having slept at all last night, she was fatigued and might have rested, had not an image of Mr. Darcy's doleful eyes suddenly appeared before her. Immediately propping up on her elbows, Elizabeth tried to vanquish all thoughts of him by concentrating on what was happening on the water below. A brood of ducklings had followed their mother across the lake and were just below her perch, so she leaned over the edge to watch them until they were completely out of sight.

When there was nothing entertaining left, she glanced at the book again, groaning aloud with frustration. Compared to what was secreted in the pocket of her gown, poetry held no allure. Sitting up, she searched for the handkerchief she had spotted that morning in Jane's hand, while recalling how she had teased her about it.

"Whose handkerchief do you have, dear sister? From what I can see of the initial, it cannot possibly be Mr. Bingley's."

Jane had blushed, unfolding the handkerchief she had plucked from a table in the library. A perfectly stitched letter D revealed the owner.

"You are correct. Mr. Darcy lent me this when I began to cry because you and the children were still out in the storm. I intend to have it washed and ironed, and then return it to him."

Taking the cloth from her sister's hand, she had quipped, "I shall see to it. You have enough to worry about."

Suddenly the shell with which she had shielded her heart all these years splintered. Returning Mr. Darcy's handkerchief had never been her intention, and Elizabeth brought it to her nose, closed her eyes and inhaled. The faint fragrance of soap and sandalwood still lingered in the weave, and she went limp with relief. Then, she began to sob as memories of her first and only dance with that gentleman flooded her, a stark reminder of how shamefully she had treated him at the Netherfield ball for Wickham's sake. Thrusting the treasure back into her pocket, she tried to recover her composure by scolding herself.

Why torture yourself! He left without even saying goodbye. Is that not enough to convince you that you are the last woman in the world he could ever be prevailed upon to marry?

The use of her own detestable words caused the tears to flow again, and she roughly brushed them from her cheeks with the back of her hands. The only man she had ever loved was now in control of her family's very existence and, though he despised her, he was so honourable that he was willing to help her as well as Jane. Unfathomable! Elizabeth felt that she could not bear it if he were to learn of her regrets on top of it all.

Glancing up at the sun, she realised that it was time for her to return to the manor. By the time she reached the gravel path that threaded through the garden to the back entrance, Jane's shadow filled the doorway. Pasting a smile on her face, Elizabeth waved.

Chapter 6

London
Matlock House
The dinner party

The soirée in honour of Lady Marjorie had gone just as planned. Lady Matlock had outdone herself with the elegant decorations, and more than one hundred of the *ton's* finest had wined and dined on the best food and drink available. After supper, as the guests reassembled in the ballroom to dance to the music of the preeminent ensemble in London, the hostess surveyed the crowd from her vantage point, a slightly raised platform at one end of the room. The raised area featured a three-sided screen painted with an oriental scene and several comfortable tall-back chairs, as well as numerous tall, potted plants in huge containers on each side. No one dared occupy the area, however, without an invitation from the countess, for she resided over it as though it were her throne.

"Well, my dear," Lord Matlock said as he stepped onto the stage next to his wife. "You have done it again! No one in London can match your flair for entertaining, and from the talk at White's today, scores were still hoping for an invitation as late as this afternoon."

"Thank you, Edward," the countess replied. "I could have invited a good many others, but I do not care for the attitude of those with newly acquired wealth. They think they should be routinely welcomed at every event in Town." Her brows knit. "Which reminds me, do we know a Caroline Bingley? I got a letter yesterday from someone by that name. She practically begged to be included tonight, even mentioning that her brother was a friend of our nephew, though I have no recollection of the name."

"Bingley?" Lord Matlock said, his hand coming up to clasp his chin. He rubbed one finger across his cheek in concentration. "Oh, Bingley! Is that not the name of the young man that Fitzwilliam befriended at Cambridge and promoted for years afterward?"

"Good heavens, you are right! We invited Mr. Bingley to a dinner party, at our nephew's insistence, and that horrible sister of his accompanied him—without an invitation, I might add. She hung onto Fitzwilliam's arm all night, which made me physically nauseated." Lady Matlock shuddered at the remembrance. "But he has had nothing to do with those people for years. Why should she write to me now?"

"Fitzwilliam did mention to Richard that he was going to assist someone named Bingley by overseeing his estate and business while the man is ill. I had not put the two together until now. Perhaps Miss Bingley thought this a clever time to insinuate herself back into our nephew's company again."

"I cannot understand why Fitzwilliam feels he must be of assistance to everyone who asks. He certainly has enough responsibilities just managing Pemberley."

"He is a grown man, Evelyn. It is his decision to make, which is fortuitous. He has not relied on my advice in years."

"Well, you should be encouraged that he has taken your advice concerning one thing, howbeit a few years late."

"And, pray tell, what might that be?"

"I do believe he has realised it is time to marry and provide Pemberley with an heir."

"Whatever gave you that idea?"

"Have you not noticed how besotted he is with the Countess of Markham?"

Lord Matlock looked about the dance floor until he found his nephew and the lady in question. They were easy to locate because William was taller than most of the men, while the countess commanded everyone's attention in a dazzling gown of blue satin and lace. For a short time, he watched them go through the steps of a dance. Then he replied, "Besotted? I cannot agree. He looks at her as he always has—as a friend, nothing more."

A slight smile crossed Lady Matlock's face as she watched the same couple. "You are wrong, but then all men are imperceptive when it comes to matters of the heart. There is something entirely different about both of them tonight. I would not be surprised if an announcement is not imminent."

Her husband smiled, shaking his head. "I may not be perceptive, but I do know that Fitzwilliam does not act like a man who is besotted; however, knowing how you ladies love to speculate, I shall not try to dissuade you."

Lady Matlock laughed, and he held out a hand. "Would you do me the honour, my lady?"

Playfully, she dropped a small curtsey. "I would be delighted."

As they made their way to the dance floor, they passed William and Millicent, who were so deep in conversation that they took no notice of his relations.

Almost the entire conversation between William and Millicent this evening concerned the newly-engaged couple. Millicent loved to tease William about Lady Marjorie, for she knew how doggedly that woman had pursued him—not that she had been any more determined than the debutants and widows who had preceded her. Provoking William in order to hear him deny any interest in other women was a boost to her self-esteem, though this night her teasing led to something unexpected.

In reply to yet another taunt, William said without thinking, "I doubt they will find lasting happiness, given the circumstances. Lord Morgan seems pleased, but it is obvious that Lady Marjorie is not in love, except perhaps with his fortune. It is a business transaction...a convenience, nothing more."

Millicent felt as though a bucket of cold water had been tossed over her. She asked guardedly, "So...so you believe that the chances of Lady Marjorie being happy with Lord Morgan are slim because there is not equal affection?"

Totally unconscious that his words echoed Millicent's justifications for refusing his offers in the past, William continued to pontificate. "It has been my observation that people who marry for convenience are more miserable, in due course, than had they stayed single, especially when they realise the enormity of what they have given up for the convenience."

As he continued to talk of the pitfalls of Lady Marjorie's decision, Millicent considered challenging him. In the end, however, common sense prevailed.

Is this not the very reason you insisted on waiting a year—to help him discern his true feelings? If you point out his every inconsistency, he will only guard his words more carefully the next time.

Though she was shaken to the core, Millicent smiled. "I see your point. Obviously, Lady Marjorie is not enamoured with his handsome face."

Her quip elicited a laugh from William, followed by an incredible smile. At that instant, he looked so very handsome that she forgave him for not being in love with her yet. Putting her hurt feelings aside, she determined that she would make the most of the rest of the evening.

After all, at this moment, I am the envy of every woman in the room, if not all of London. Perhaps, with luck, one day I will no longer have reason to envy the woman who still possesses his heart tonight.

London
Bingley's townhouse
Two days later

Bingley's staff in London had long since been cut to the bone, with the butler and housekeeper, Mr. and Mrs. Carson, oversee-ing fewer maids and footmen each month. It all began when Mrs. Bingley quit frequenting London after Mr. Howton moved into their townhouse, and it accelerated when Mr. Bingley's health deteriorated. If not for his ill-mannered cousin, the long-time servants firmly believed that their employer might have already sold the house. Still, that man seemed no closer to finding his own lodging than when he arrived in Town.

Howton, who behaved as though *he* were the master when Mr. Bingley was not about, acted even worse once his cousin had become so ill that he stayed in Richmond. From then on, he invited men of questionable means to the house for cigars, brandy and cards, leaving the entire house in total disarray when they departed. In the Carsons' opinion, the men who propped their feet upon Mr. Bingley's furniture and depleted his stock of fine cigars and imported brandy looked as though they would be more at home in the Mint[6] than in Mayfair. Fortuitously, after Mr. Darcy was appointed to run the warehouses, their detestable presence had stopped at once.

As if Howton's disrespect for Charles Bingley was not vexing enough, his sister's arrival in Town was even more so. Without a word of warning, Caroline, her sister, Louisa, and Louisa's hus-band had arrived a few days earlier, even though Mr. Bingley had specifically banned Miss Bingley from his homes after she had had some particularly harsh things to say about Jane Bingley's sister. The Hursts were still welcome, as long as Caroline was not with them. Still, once their brother was out of the country, all three descended upon the townhouse as though he had never made any such pronouncement.

With their arrival, Mr. Howton had transformed into the epitome of a gentleman, putting his best foot forward. Not so Miss Bingley, who had not been in residence for a full day before several of the maids had threatened to resign. It had taken Mrs. Carson speaking to Mrs. Hurst to settle the matter. Though things improved, Caroline Bingley still appeared to be on the verge of an outburst at all times, which kept all the servants on edge.

The dining room

This morning the conversation at the table was quieter than usual. Mr. Hurst was busy eating, as was his wont, while Louisa nibbled on a piece of toast and covertly watched her sister peruse the newspaper. Suddenly, Caroline flew into a rage, wadded the news into a ball and tossed it across the room. Louisa cringed at what she knew would come next.

"I cannot believe that I was not invited to Lady Matlock's dinner party!" she declared angrily. "There are people listed at that party whom I have never heard of in my life. I keep up with the *ton!* I know who is important and who is not. Who does Lady Matlock think she is, inviting insignificant people while ignoring one of her nephew's best friends?"

"The grand dame of London society, I imagine," Mr. Hurst said dryly, though his eyes never left his plate. "And I doubt she considers you a friend of Fitzwilliam Darcy, much less a *best* friend."

Her brother hardly ever deigned to comment, but when he did, his words hit their mark. Caroline gave him a wicked glare.

"I was speaking to Louisa. What business is this of yours?"

"You made it my business when you convinced me that you had an invitation to her soirée; otherwise, I would never have deigned to stop in London. Charles will hold me responsible, for he specifically said that you were not welcome in his homes ever again."

"Given his current circumstances, I think we can safely say that Charles was not in his right mind when he said that. And for your information, I never pretended to have an invitation!"

Louisa could stand her sister's lies no longer, for it was she who had convinced Bertram to defy Charles just this once. "You made a show of addressing a letter to Lady Matlock, inferring you were answering an invitation to a dinner party."

"If you had the wrong impression, that is hardly my fault," Caroline whined. "You have no idea how difficult it is to meet suitable men now that you and your husband stay in the country year round. I counted on the fact that, since Mr. Darcy has relented and is helping Charles, the Matlocks would be aware of our present closeness."

"Why are you still aiming for a man of the *ton?*" Hurst asked. "You should settle for an equal. Take Howton for example. I am sure your dowry would tempt him."

"Good heavens, no! Besides the fact that he is not attractive in the least, I will never marry a man without a title unless he is as wealthy as sin."

Louisa interrupted. "Mr. Hurst is right. You should aspire to marry a man in our sphere. And if that was *not* a reply you sent to Lady Matlock, then you displayed despicable manners by corresponding with someone whom you had no right to address."

"I have every right! I was a guest in her home once. Surely you remember."

"I remember that you were not invited the night you accompanied Charles, nor were you ever invited afterward."

Caroline stood. "Humph! You are just as contrary as your husband. I shall not sit here and be insulted."

As she exited the room, Mr. Hurst declared to her, "We are leaving in the morning. I suggest you see if one of the maids whom you have been so unkind to will be willing to pack your trunk. Otherwise, you will have to do it yourself."

Caroline slammed the door and leaned against it. Seething, she considered what to do next. Deciding that a glass of brandy might help to clear her mind, she headed to the library, where Charles always kept a stocked liquor cabinet.

David Howton, who had broken his fast hours earlier, happened to be in the library at that very moment. He paced steadily, for that exercise helped him to think more clearly. It was a habit formed from years of plotting how best to take advantage of others and, on occasion, how to get out of scrapes with the law. After being summoned by Mr. Darcy, his habit had increased markedly. The thought of facing that man again gnawed at his soul. He was certain that Darcy or his steward would uncover the shipments that had been paid for but never delivered to the warehouse or recorded in inventory. He simply had to devise a plan to escape the consequences.

If Charles survived to learn of his misdeeds, Howton had no doubt that his mother would intervene on his behalf. But would Charles listen to her or to Mr. Darcy? He had no desire to end up in prison, should she be unsuccessful. Moreover, there was always the chance that the doctors might discover the source of Charles' stomach ailments. That would shed new light on the depths of his depravity. Should that occur, there would be no escaping a charge of attempted murder. And should his cousin die...

How ironic that my life could hinge on your survival, Bingley!

Suddenly Howton knew what he must do—quickly dispose of all the stolen goods, take the money, and to sail to the Americas—but he had to have more time! Even if the men he had hired to sell the merchandise worked twice as fast, it would take several more weeks. For now, he needed to create a diversion to take Mr. Darcy's mind off the warehouse. But what?

That thought had no more than formed when Caroline Bingley hurried into the room and rushed straight to the liquor cabinet. As evidenced from the evening before, her lack of control where drink was concerned was unmistakable. It had taken Louisa to quiet her incessant prattle by forcing her to retire for the night; thus, Howton was not in the least surprised at the size of the brandy she poured or how quickly she drank it. Totally oblivious to his presence, Caroline began to pour another.

If I am fortunate, she will be in her cups soon. Then, I may be able to prod her into revealing a secret about Bingley's wife or her sister, both of whom seem to set her tongue wagging. I need some-thing—anything—to use as bait for Darcy.

As Caroline drank the second brandy, Howton called her by name.

Startled, she jumped and then tried to compose herself. "Mr. Howton, forgive me. I was so intent on...er, calming my nerves with a bit of brandy, that I never noticed you."

"No need to apologise, I assure you." Then his brows knit in what he hoped was a sympathetic expression. "Is there some-thing the matter? May I be of service?"

"It is only that my brother Hurst has upset me once again with his hateful attitude. He has no earthly idea how I suffer because Charles would not hear the truth." Warily she glanced towards the open library door. "Forgive me. I should not have voiced my grievances to you."

"Nonsense! We are cousins, and I care about you, even if we are seldom in each other's company. Why not tell me what you said to Charles to make him so angry? Perhaps when he returns to London, I can intervene on your behalf or at least help him to see your side."

The liquor had begun to take effect. "You are too kind. What say we walk in the garden in case they look for me? It would not do for anyone to overhear our conversation."

Howton held out his arm. "As you wish. May I escort you, dear cousin?"

Less than an hour later, Howton had his ammunition. According to Caroline Bingley, Mrs. Bingley's sister, Elizabeth Gardiner, was an unmarried woman raising a bastard child. That was enough to stir up a firestorm of controversy.

All he had to do now was convince Mr. Darcy that someone was targeting that lady with either intent to harm her or the child, or, at the very least, to expose her secret unless they were paid a fair sum to keep silent. A gentleman as honourable as Darcy would drop everything and rush to protect Bingley's sister's reputation. That was the key! Now, what to do first?

I know! Caroline mentioned that Jane Bingley still has two sisters residing near Meryton. I shall send a man there to ask questions about the Bennets, Elizabeth Gardiner in particular. That should fire up the gossip mills, and the news should reach Jane Bingley in a matter of days. Meanwhile, I will write an anonymous letter threatening to reveal Elizabeth's secrets. One of my associates can mail it to Canfield Manor, so the servants here will be none the wiser.

For the first time in weeks, David Howton smiled. *Thank you, Cousin Caroline. You may have caused Bingley a lot of trouble in the past, but you were my guardian angel today.*

Darcy House
William's study
The same day

Richard reached into one of several crates on the floor, grabbed a ball and began tossing it into the air. "What is all this?"

William sighed, never looking up from the letter he was writing. "Have you forgotten your childhood already? Those are toys."

"I can see that! But why have you purchased Hudson's entire stock?" he asked, chuckling. Squatting to examine several dolls, wooden building blocks, still more balls and a boat with a sail, he added, "Need I ask who the lucky recipients will be?"

"They are for the children at Canfield Manor and for Hugh and Kathy."

"Millie mentioned that she and the twins are to be at Pemberley in two weeks. She said that you promised the twins new ponies and to help with their riding lessons. Can you do all of that and still handle Bingley's affairs?"

"I have no choice. I promised Hugh and Kathy, and I will not break my word to either them or Millie. I have set up a household budget for Mrs. Bingley and sent her a copy. It is generous, so I do not think she will have any trouble implementing it. And Mr. Perry is willing to help her, as well as handle all of Bingley's ledgers until I can hire another steward."

"How much more will you have to pay him for that?"

"I will pay him well enough."

"Is there no end to your generosity?"

"*Richard.*" William dragged the word out as a warning.

"This time I am not teasing. How in the world can you fund another estate? There has to be a limit to how much one man can do."

"Perry and I have discovered a number of irregularities in the books at Bingley's warehouses, including missing and incomplete shipments. Frankly, I think his cousin has been selling items surreptitiously and pocketing the money. After I have had time to meet with Charles' employees, I will bar Howton from participating in the business while we continue our investigation. If I am right, with him out of the way, the profits should right themselves."

"Who will take charge then?"

"Mr. Dabney, Charles' foreman. He had been in charge of scheduling the employees before Howton arrived, as well as advising Charles what goods were needed. I intend to increase his salary and have him keep the inventory. Mr. Perry will still pay the employees and order and pay for goods, just as he is doing now. Of course, I will assist as needed."

"But Howton owns a third of the company. Can you legally suspend him? And what will he live on while you investigate?"

"He would be foolish to threaten me with legal action, especially if I am right. I will allow him to continue to live at Charles' townhouse, and he will get a stipend until I have all the facts. If I can prove what I believe to be true, I will delay pressing charges until Charles tells me his wishes; after all, the man is his cousin."

Richard shook his head. "Just another disaster to add to your worries."

"I can use your help."

"What can I do?"

"Find two more men I can trust as much as Hartley and Boggus. I intend to put one at each warehouse, just in case Howton decides to challenge my decision or Mr. Dabney's authority."

"That will not be a problem. When do you want them?"

"Yesterday."

Chapter 7

Canfield Manor
One week later

As William waited in the library for the butler to locate Jane Bingley, he perused the titles on a bookcase that covered the entire west wall. Impressed with the collection, he surmised that the estate must have come with the furnishings, since everything seemed much as it was when he and Bingley toured the house years ago, and a well-stocked library was not one of Charles' priorities. Then, too, Lord Norton had deliberated renting the property because he had two other estates, so William felt reasonably certain that the man would not have taken the majority of the books with him when the estate sold, if any.

Caught up in his observations, William was unaware that Elizabeth had entered the room behind him. Since she was not expecting him to be at the Bingleys' residence that day, she did not see him either, and turned in the opposite direction. Even so, he was alerted to her presence when she began humming a tune he remembered from his childhood—*Lavender's Blue.*[7]

The minute he spied her, his breath caught. Only once had he seen her hair in its present style—at a picnic Charles had hosted at Netherfield. The sides were pulled up and tied with long, pink satin ribbons, the ends of which were now entwined in the dark curls that cascaded down her back. As his eyes followed her lithe frame across the room, he was tortured by thoughts of how it would feel to replace the ribbons with his fingers. Thoroughly dismayed at the path his thoughts had taken, William tried to picture Millie's hair worn in the same fashion, but could not.

In Elizabeth's hands were several books, and, once she reached a small, round table, she laid them there. Then she walked down an identical wall of bookshelves until she found a library chair. Sliding this object along the floor until it was where she wished it to be, she flipped the chair over, revealing four built-in steps. Then, taking the top book from the stack, she lifted her skirts and put one dainty foot on the bottom step. Since she wore simple slippers and no stockings, William had a good view of her left ankle and leg clear to the knee. Instantly aware that he should have announced his presence before now, his heart began to race. Still, in light of the circumstances, he was incapable of speech.

Unfortunately, Jane Bingley chose that moment to rush into the room. "Mr. Darcy, I had no idea you would come today! It was only yesterday that I sent the express."

At the sound of Jane's voice, Elizabeth's head swung around. Finding William staring in her direction, she dropped her skirts and lifted her chin, giving him a stern glare.

Thoroughly embarrassed, William turned to Jane, stuttering a reply. "I...I was preparing to leave for Pemberley, but your letter gave me the impression that you were frightened; thus, I came here first."

By then, Elizabeth had walked towards them. Jane's eyes went wide when she realised that her sister had heard everything. Before she could speak, however, Elizabeth said impatiently, "You were frightened, Jane, yet you did not think to tell me?"

Jane's hands flew to her face, and she began to cry, and Elizabeth pulled her sister into an embrace, patting her back.

"Please do not cry, dearest. I was only wounded that you did not feel that you could confide in me. I want to know when anything is amiss. In your condition, you should not carry burdens alone."

"It is not that I felt I could not confide in you. It is just—" Jane stopped to pull a handkerchief from her pocket and dab at her eyes. Looking from her sister to William, she said, "Let us sit down, and I will tell you both what has transpired."

Minutes later, Jane had shared a letter from Kitty that had arrived a week earlier. That letter had informed her that a strange man had been seen in Meryton asking about the former occupants of Longbourn. More particularly, he had visited that property and spoken to Mr. Collins, presenting himself as an old friend of Mr. Bennet. Upon being informed of the calamity that had befallen their parents, he enquired as to whether the daughters were all well. He also wanted to know whether they had married and where each lived. Only the arrival of Charlotte Collins from a quick jaunt into Meryton cut short the rector's long-winded recitation of each sister's fate before he got to Elizabeth. Charlotte, being more wary than her husband, had informed Kitty of the man's inquisitiveness the next day. Nonetheless, by the time Kitty asked for the man's whereabouts in the village, he had slipped away.

Already planning a visit, the following day Kitty travelled to the nearby village of Compton where James Parton, Mary's husband, was the vicar. Immediately upon arrival, Kitty informed Mary of the strange man in Meryton. Consequently, Mary related a similarly odd occurrence. It seemed that a stranger had come by the parish in search of counselling only the week before, and his conversation had swiftly moved from his own concerns to assertions that he knew Mary's father years ago. When he enquired as to how the sisters had fared since their parents' untimely deaths, the vicar mentioned that Kitty had married Harvey Thomas, a law clerk, and still lived in Meryton. When he asked about Elizabeth specifically, Mr. Parton became suspicious and sent him on his way.

Once Jane had finished reading, the room was eerily silent. The look on William's face was enough to convince her that he was contemplating the situation before commenting. Elizabeth, however, had no such reluctance and attempted to make light of it all.

"Surely asking about our family is scarcely a reason to think that anyone means to do us harm? On the contrary, Papa had many good friends from university, and upon hearing of the circumstances of his death, why would they not profess an interest in our welfare?"

Jane was about to answer, when William retorted, "I am afraid that I cannot agree, Mrs. Gardiner. One incident may be logical. Two is suspect."

Apparently still angry that he had not made his presence known earlier, Elizabeth snapped, "Mr. Darcy, you may be in charge of all our finances, but you are not in charge of my life! Surely I have a right to live without fear of every person who asks after me."

"Lizzy," Jane said, "you have no right to talk to Mr. Darcy in that manner."

William held up a hand. "Please. Let her say what she wishes; that is her prerogative."

"I wanted to spare you the worst of it, Lizzy, but I see that I simply cannot," Jane said wearily. "Mayhap you will change your tone after hearing this." Reaching into her pocket, she withdrew another missive. Holding it out to William, she said, "This arrived yesterday morning and was what prompted the express."

William took the paper, his brows furrowing as he read what was written thereon. *I know the secret about your sister and that child.*

Seeing his expression darken, Elizabeth asked, "What does it say?"

Looking up, he locked eyes with hers. "Do you not think it time I was told the truth?"

Not able to meet his gaze, Elizabeth looked away.

"He has earned the right to know, Lizzy."

For a time it seemed she would not reply. Then, taking a deep breath and sighing loudly, Elizabeth said, "I am not Mrs. Gardiner; in fact, I have never been married. Mr. Gardiner was the deceased cousin of my relatives in Cheapside, raised from the dead to make me a legitimate widow."

When he was a boy, William had fallen from the hayloft onto a small pile of hay. The impact had forced the air from his lungs, and he remembered thinking he would die before he could catch another breath. Elizabeth's confession caused much the same effect, rendering him mute.

"I...I know you must think me a—" Looking up to see the odd expression on William's face, she did not finish.

"And Emily is not her natural daughter," Jane interjected.

With Jane's proclamation, William's eyes closed in relief. *The child is not hers.* Trying to collect himself, he coughed as if to clear his throat. "I must know everything about this situation in order to protect you."

"You were hired to protect my brother's family. You are not obligated to protect me or—"

"Lizzy, please!" Jane exclaimed. "Go and pack yours and Emily's clothes while I explain everything to Mr. Darcy."

Stunned, Elizabeth stammered, "Are...are you asking me to leave?"

"I have no choice," Jane said, becoming teary eyed. "If you stay here, whoever wrote the letter *will* find you."

"But where can we go? I cannot take Emily to London. There are too many prying eyes in Cheapside. And, other than our sisters and their families, we have no other relations."

"Pemberley." All eyes came to rest on William, who added, "You shall stay at Pemberley. Who would suspect that you are in Derbyshire? Charles and I have not been close in years. Only my relations and yours know that I am handling his affairs, and we can make certain that they tell no one."

Elizabeth dropped her head, her voice now a whisper. "I cannot impose."

"You must!" Jane insisted. "If only for Emily."

"What of you? I cannot leave you—not in your condition and with Charles in Spain."

"Kitty will be only too glad to stay with me until the baby is born. She stayed with us when I was expecting Marianne and was very helpful."

William broke in. "I will leave Hartley and Boggus here for protection. In addition, I shall have Richard begin an immediate investigation. With any luck, we may be able to figure out who mailed this note."

"See, it is all settled," Jane said, placing a hand on both her sister's shoulders. "I shall rest easier knowing that you are safe at Pemberley."

Elizabeth smiled wanly. "You know that I cannot refuse you, but I shall expect a letter from you every day. If not, I shall return on the next post coach."

The sisters hugged, and, with a last puzzled glance in William's direction, Elizabeth left the room.

"Please be seated, Mr. Darcy, while I tell you how Emily came to be with Lizzy." A half-hour later, William knew all that Jane did about Emily's father. "If Lizzy comes to trust you, I have no doubt that she will tell you more about Lord Van Lynden. She said that she had not shared the half of what happened with me because she wanted to spare me the worst."

"You truly believe this man is capable of great evil?"

"I do. Seldom have I seen so callous a soul as the day I looked into his lifeless eyes. It frightened me exceedingly, and from that day on, I feared for Lizzy's life. Now I fear for Emily's as well. If he were to return to England—" Jane could not continue.

William patted her hand. "Please know that I shall protect Elizabeth and the child with my life, if necessary."

"I never doubted that. Charles would never have placed my life or the lives of our children in your hands if he had not trusted your heart. Let me take this opportunity to thank you for all that you have done and are proposing to do for my family."

"I have no doubt that Charles would have done the same for me, if the circumstances were reversed." William stood and stretched. The morning had barely begun, and he was already exhausted. "There are miles to go before we reach the first post inn tonight. We must be on our way."

Jane stood. "I shall go up and hurry them."

"Before you do, would you send a footman for Hartley and Boggus? I mean to speak to them before I leave. Moreover, I would appreciate a pen and paper. I wish to send a letter today to my cousin, Colonel Fitzwilliam."

"Everything you need is in those drawers," Jane said, pointing to a small writing desk almost hidden behind the door. "And I shall see that the guards are summoned."

"Thank you."

Moving to the table, William sat down. According to what his cousin had told him, Richard was due a leave, which would give him ample time to investigate the source of the letter, in addition to Lord Van Lynden's whereabouts, if he were so inclined.

By the time the former Bow Street Runners appeared, William had finished the letter and sealed it. Handing it to the butler who had shown the men in, he said, "Please see that this is posted today."

"I would be pleased to, sir."

William trained his eyes on his employees. "Sit down, gentlemen. I have a great deal to tell you in a short period of time."

On the road to Pemberley

Sharing the coach with Mr. Darcy proved a humbling experience for Elizabeth. Not only had he been kind enough to insist that she accompany him to his ancestral home for her own safety, but he was very kind to Emily. Right after she, Emily, and the maid, Cora, were seated in the coach, he had entered, taking the seat across from them. Almost immediately, he exited the coach, saying that he had forgotten something. Ordering a footman to hand down a large satchel strapped to the top of the vehicle, he took several items from it and then handed the bag to a footman who had come back down the steps with Jane.

As Jane was peering inside the satchel, William remarked, "Just a few things to cheer the children."

"Oh, Mr. Darcy!" she exclaimed, her face aglow. "You are entirely too generous. But, on behalf of my children, I thank you."

Good-naturedly brushing her remarks aside, William re-entered the coach. Laying some items on the seat, he held out a doll to Emily. Big blue eyes turned to Elizabeth as if asking permission to accept the prize.

Elizabeth smiled. "You may."

Immediately, the blonde-headed child took the doll, closing her eyes as she hugged it to her chest. Elizabeth's heart swelled to see her so happy.

"Do you have something to say?"

"Thank you, sir," Emily said. "I am certain I shall love her."

It was the first time William had heard the child speak, and he noted how mature she sounded for her age.

"You are most welcome."

His eyes flicked from her to Elizabeth, and, for a fleeting moment, he saw something different in her expression. Was it regard? *Surely not! Most likely it is only gratitude.*

"I have saved a set of coloured blocks and a ball for you to play with when we get to the inn. I do not think they are well-suited for the coach."

This made Emily smile, and, out of the blue, she slipped off the seat and moved to sit next to him, leaning her head against his arm in a sweet gesture. Unsure how Elizabeth would feel about that, William slipped an arm around the child's shoulder before glancing at her.

"I believe you have made a friend for life," Elizabeth said, smiling.

"I am glad. One can never have too many friends."

It was not long until the movement of the coach rocked the child to sleep, so William pulled her legs up onto the cushion, letting her head fall into his lap. Despite the ruts in the road, Emily slept soundly until they reached the inn. William picked her up and brought her inside, her head on his shoulder with her eyes still closed.

Suddenly the innkeeper rushed out of a door, taking his place behind the desk and breaking the spell. "Mr. Darcy, sir, I was beginning to wonder if you would arrive tonight."

"We had a stop to make first and got behind in our schedule. I wonder if you have another room I may rent."

"Oh, sir, I fear that that is impossible, for all are now occupied. If only you had been here earlier."

"I understand. It is not your fault. I shall just have to sleep in the stable with my men."

"I do have a few cots that can be added to the suite you rented, if that will suffice."

Not wishing to bring more attention to their unconventional sleeping arrangements, William acquiesced. "Please have two cots brought up, then."

"Right away, sir!"

In the end, Elizabeth, Emily and Cora took the bedroom, with Cora sleeping on a cot. William tried to sleep on one of the cots in the sitting area but was too tall. Thus, after they parted for the night, he contorted his body to fit on the small sofa. In the morning, Elizabeth almost laughed aloud when she found him asleep with his head on one arm and knees hanging over the other. Only the realisation that he suffered for her sake caused her to keep silent. Closing the door, she waited until he knocked, so as not to embarrass him.

The rest of the trip was spent in the same manner—William sleeping in whatever position he could manage. This caused him to be so tired that he fell asleep as often as Emily once the coach began to move. The child insisted on sitting next to her new friend, so inevitably they would end up with William asleep against the corner of the coach and Emily stretched out on the seat cushion, her head in his lap. The sight never failed to cause a lump to form in Elizabeth's throat, and by the time they reached Pemberley, she was certain that she could never think ill of that gentleman again.

Pemberley
Three days later

It was growing dark by the time William ordered the driver to stop at the highest point of the road leading through the woods to Pemberley, asking Emily if she would like to see his home from this vantage point; naturally she agreed. Elizabeth followed the two of them out of the coach, curious to see the property that Caroline Bingley had always touted as *the finest estate in all of England.*

Astounded by what she saw, when asked what she thought, Elizabeth was too stunned to answer. Having toured many grand estates with the Gardiners when just a girl, she was used to ostentatious displays. Pemberley, however, fit its surroundings as though it had always been a part of the landscape. Caught up in the view, it had taken William asking twice to gain her attention.

"It...it is lovely," was all she managed to murmur before they re-entered the coach.

If Mrs. Reynolds or Mr. Walker were surprised to see the master return with an unfamiliar young woman and child in tow, they were too practised to let it show, especially in front of the myriad of maids and footmen now lining both sides of the steps. Only a quick exchange of glances acknowledged the implications of the circumstances, before each focused on greeting the master. Thus, when William escorted Elizabeth up the front steps with Emily in her arms, one would have assumed from their expressions that it was commonplace.

"Mrs. Gardiner, allow me to introduce Mrs. Reynolds and Mr. Walker, my housekeeper and butler," William said. "Mrs. Gardiner is Mr. Bingley's sister. She and her daughter, Emily, will be our guests for the summer."

Already surreptitiously studying Elizabeth, the long-time housekeeper nodded, a slight smile her only expression. "Welcome to Pemberley, Mrs. Gardiner. I hope you and your daughter find your stay here pleasant."

Elizabeth's heart had begun racing the moment the coach stopped in front of the manor house. Pemberley looked even more striking with closer inspection, and the numerous servants standing on the steps furthered the idea that she was completely out of her element.

"Thank...thank you. I am sure I will," she sputtered.

Immediately upon entering the foyer, William began issuing orders. "Please prepare a suite for Mrs. Gardiner, placing Miss

Emily in the adjoining bedroom. Have a footman bring Georgiana's childhood furniture from the attic and exchange it for the furniture in there."

Turning back to Elizabeth, he said, "If you like, a small bed can be placed in your daughter's bedroom for Cora. Since Emily is familiar with her, perhaps that will help her to adjust to Pemberley more readily."

"I should like that very much."

He addressed Mrs. Reynolds again. "As time permits, open the nursery and do whatever is necessary to refurbish it. As I remember, it proved very useful when bad weather prevented outside activities when Georgiana was small."

"Sir, it may be tomorrow before all the bedroom furniture is in place. It must be found, cleaned, polished and a suitable mattress located."

William glanced to Elizabeth with a slight smile. "I am certain that Mrs. Gardiner will not mind sharing a bed with her daughter tonight. They have shared a bed at every inn from London to Pemberley."

Mrs. Reynolds' eyebrows rose as the idea of just where each had managed to sleep came to mind. Nonetheless, she quickly composed herself. "If you will wait in the drawing room, Mrs. Gardiner, I shall have a room ready directly." Addressing a maid, she said, "Maggie, will you escort Mrs. Gardiner to—"

"I shall be glad to do it myself after I have spoken with one of the footmen," William said. Then he enquired of Elizabeth, "Do you mind? This will only take a moment."

"No, not at all."

As he walked out the front door, Elizabeth watched the housekeeper issue orders to various maids and footmen regarding rooms and trunks. After the foyer was empty of servants, Elizabeth began examining the splendour of her surroundings. Though the estate was magnificent, the grounds were nothing compared to the interior of the house. As her eyes moved from one exquisite furnishing to the next, they were drawn by several large mirrors and paintings up a great expanse of wall to the painted ceiling three stories above. She was unable to tear her eyes away from that display.

William walked back into the foyer just in time to hear her say, "Look up, Emily! See the beautiful paintings?"

The child obliged, her head nodding in agreement at the splendour. Overwhelmed with the notion that, except for his arrogance, Elizabeth might have been his wife by now, this child their own, he stopped mid-step. Only an enquiry from Emily brought his thoughts back to the present.

"Are you hungry, Mama?"

Elizabeth chuckled, for this had always been her daughter's way of saying that she was. "I am. Are you?" Emily nodded vigorously.

William came forward. "May I?" He reached out for Emily, who fell into his arms willingly as he said, "Please follow me to the drawing room. The sofas there are comfortable whilst you wait for your rooms to be readied."

His long stride took him across the foyer quickly, and Elizabeth hurried to catch up. As she did, she heard him say, "Miss Emily, if I am not mistaken, this is the day that Cook makes her famous gingerbread. If I can persuade her to accommodate us, would you care for some tea and a gingerbread biscuit while you wait?"

More nodding ensued, causing Elizabeth to say, "Thank you for thinking of us. I know that I could use a cup of tea."

"If at any time you wish for something, you have only to ring for a maid."

Just then they reached the drawing room, and William set Emily on her feet. Pulling his father's watch from an inside pocket, he flipped the lid back. "It is not as late as I thought. Dinner is at eight, so after you have something to eat and are settled in your rooms, there will be plenty of time to rest before we reconvene in the dining room."

"If you do not mind, I should like to eat with Emily tonight. She is used to eating with Grace and Marianne in the nursery, and I do not want her to feel abandoned."

"Why do we not all eat in my sitting room tonight?"

"You...you want to do that?"

"I would not have asked otherwise."

How could she refuse?

"Then I...Emily and I accept your kind offer."

It was much later before Mrs. Reynolds had an opportunity to catch the master alone. After dinner he had gone to his study to read all of the notes made by his steward, Mr. Sturgis, whilst he was away. It was Mr. Darcy's habit to make sure he knew everything of importance before he retired. The housekeeper wondered at his being able to sleep a wink after filling his mind with all those worries; still, she had given him an hour to go over the list before asking the questions that she knew would plague her own sleep.

At her soft knock on the door, he called, "Come!"

Taking a deep breath, she opened the door and walked straight to his desk. He looked so much like his father that, for an instant, she almost broke into a smile. Nevertheless, she caught herself and waited for him to look up.

"Yes, Mrs. Reynolds?"

"It may not be my place to ask, but is the Countess of Markham still scheduled to visit Pemberley?"

"Yes. She, her aunt and her children are to arrive in less than a sennight. Why do you ask?"

"I have to wonder, sir, what that lady will think about Mrs.

Gardiner being in residence. I need not remind you that it is highly improper for a single gentleman to host a lady with no chaperone."

"You are correct. I do not need reminding," William said dryly. "The majority of Lambton and, dare I say, most of Derbyshire, will never know she is in residence, much less without a chaperone, if our servants are discreet."

"I wish it were that simple. I stress to all our servants that we do not tolerate gossip at Pemberley, but even the best of servants may talk if they believe their master has broken with decorum."

"I assure you that I have NOT broken with decorum."

"What about Mr. Gardiner? Why is he not here?"

"Mrs. Gardiner's husband is dead. She is a widow."

A hand came up to cover her heart. "Oh, my word. Are the two of you—"

Frustrated, William said a little too harshly, "There is no *two* of us." Then, he stood and began to run his hands through his hair. "I suppose Walker is as concerned about this matter as you."

"He is. I passed him on my way here."

"Please fetch him then. I had rather not repeat myself, and I suppose now is as good a time as any to tell you both what has happened. The safety of Mrs. Gardiner and her child will depend upon the three of us."

"As you wish."

By the time that William, Mrs. Reynolds and Mr. Walker retired, none was able to sleep. Theories of what might be needed in order to keep Elizabeth and Emily safe swirled in their heads, keeping them awake. As a result, the next day found each of them tired and on edge, though they tried not to let it affect their interactions with their guests.

Chapter 8

Pemberley
Two days later

William had ingratiated himself to Emily on their first full day at Pemberley by taking her to the stables to see the four new ponies he had purchased. There was a pair of taller blacks with white stockings, presents for Hugh and Kathy, and two much smaller ponies—one brown, one white. The solid white one quickly became Emily's favourite because it was the shortest, so William set her on the mare, and a groom led the pony around the paddock while he walked alongside. Once they had done a number of laps, he motioned for another groom to take his place while he crossed the paddock to speak to Elizabeth. She had been watching with fearful eyes from her perch, feet planted firmly on the bottom rail of the fence, arms resting on the top. Drawing near, William struggled not to smile, for her bottom lip was caught between her teeth—a gesture she often employed when she was worried.

"I think your daughter would like a pony of her own, and I should like to give her one. What say you?"

"I do not wish Emily to be afraid of riding, as I am, so I feel somewhat obligated to accept; however, I will agree only if you will promise to teach her to ride safely."

"I shall gladly supervise her lessons, but Mr. Wilson is far better at teaching children to ride than I," William said. "He has more patience."

"Mr. Wilson?"

"My livery manager." Elizabeth nodded and William displayed a devastatingly handsome smile. "However, if your wish is for Emily not to fear something, then you must not fear it, either."

Immediately, her dark eyes fixed on his blue ones. "You...you want me to ride?"

"I wish you to be a good example. Why not overcome your fear of horses while Emily learns to ride? Tomorrow is as good a day as any to start."

"But...but, I have no riding clothes."

William's gaze moved slowly from her head to her toes and back, causing her to blush. "My mother's riding habit is packed away, and with a few alterations, I feel certain it will fit you. It is practically new, for she ordered it the summer before she became pregnant with Georgiana. Once my sister was born, mother never recovered sufficiently to ride again. After...after she died, my father could not bear to part with it; I suppose because it reminded him of the last joyful summer with his wife."

"Oh, I could not possibly—"

"Contrary to his reason for keeping the habit, clothes are not meant for keepsakes; they are meant to be worn. Besides, if you had known my mother, you would know that she would be so pleased you have gotten some use of it. Mrs. Reynolds is a magician with needle and thread and can make alterations very quickly, and altering mother's habit will give us time to have another one made especially for you."

Elizabeth made no comment on his last remark, although she had no intention of letting William purchase clothes for her. "Very well, Mr. Darcy. If Mrs. Reynolds can work magic, I shall give riding a try tomorrow."

The next day

The day to test her mettle had arrived, and Elizabeth looked beautiful in Anne Darcy's burgundy riding habit. Though it was too tight through the bosom, it fit well enough elsewhere after Mrs. Reynolds took four inches off both the bottom of the jacket and the skirt. Upon seeing Elizabeth in the habit, tears had filled the housekeeper's eyes, for she well remembered seeing William's mother in that particular outfit.

William found himself too tongue-tied to do more than whisper, "It fits you well."

Later, as Emily skipped ahead of her to where William stood talking to a groom at the paddock fence, Elizabeth caught sight of a grey horse that most likely had been saddled for her. The steed was the same colour as the beast that had thrown her as a child, breaking her arm, and though she vowed not to show any fear, a lump formed in her throat.

William picked up Emily and led Elizabeth inside the paddock and over to the grey. "This is Belle. She is the gentlest horse in our stable."

She? The demon horse had been a stallion. A bit of relief swept over Elizabeth.

"I assure you that she is also the slowest," William added, chuckling as he handed her a riding crop. "If you do not keep after her with this, she will stop and graze whenever the mood strikes."

A heartfelt smile greeted his assertion, and for a brief moment William was rendered powerless. Quickly recovering, he sought to hide his discomfort by reaching into a pocket and bringing out a small apple. "Feed Belle this and she will follow you anywhere."

Elizabeth took the apple, placed it on her open palm and held it out. The mare gently nibbled the apple from her hand and began to devour it.

"Me, me!" Emily exclaimed, clapping her hands.

William set the child on the ground, took her hand and led her over to the white pony. Removing another apple from his pocket, he squatted beside her and demonstrated how to offer it to the animal safely.

Afterwards, as she stroked the pony's head, William asked, "We have yet to think of a name for this little girl. Do you have any ideas?"

Emily's brows knit seriously. "She is white, so I think she should be named Snow."

"Then, Snow she shall be." William said. Emily turned to smile at Elizabeth, who nodded her approval.

Lifting the bright-eyed little girl again, William walked over to place her atop his stallion, Zeus. "I will have Mr. Wilson search for a saddle to fit Snow, but until I find the right one, will you ride in front of me?" Emily nodded, causing William to smile broadly. "I knew you were a brave girl the first time I saw you."

As Emily beamed, William motioned for the livery manager to come forward. "Stand here with Miss Emily while I help Mrs. Gardiner mount Belle."

"I shall be happy to," Mr. Wilson replied, winking at the child.

Returning to the grey, William was pleased to see Elizabeth stroking her head, howbeit a bit timidly. "Now, let us get you on horseback."

Taking the horse's reins, he led Belle over to a set of wooden steps next to the fence and motioned for Elizabeth to step up on them. She did as instructed, finding that she was now at the perfect height to mount the horse. William handed her the reins, and she took them in addition to taking hold of a large section of the horse's mane—something her father had taught her. After settling herself in the saddle, William pulled the horse forward enough that he could adjust Elizabeth's leg around the pommel. At length stepping back, he seemed pleased.

"Do you wish for me to go over the basic tenets of horseback riding?"

"No. I have always been capable of riding, if compelled. I just did not care to ride after—" She glanced to make sure that Emily was not listening. "After I broke my arm when I fell off a horse."

Instantly, William's face sobered. "The woman I came to know in Hertfordshire could never be intimidated by any creature for long. I am confident that you will do well, Miss Eliz...excuse me, I meant to say Mrs. Gardiner."

"Since we are now friends, please call me Elizabeth...at least when we are not in company."

He smiled. "If you agree to call me William, when we are not in company."

"William," she repeated. "It suits you. Moreover, whenever I hear Fitzwilliam, I think of your cousin, the colonel."

"My mother said that is precisely why she called me William. However, I think it best if we continue to address each other formally when we are in company. I fear there may be speculation as to the nature of our relationship, and I do not wish to lend any ammunition to the fray."

"I agree," Elizabeth said, her smile fading. "Please allow me to apologise. I never wished your reputation to be tarnished for my sake."

"Let me worry about my reputation," William said, giving her a wink.

Her eyes followed him to Zeus, and he mounted the stallion in one fluid motion. Though he had always looked impressive on horseback, when he slipped an arm around Emily and pulled her close to his chest, the gesture touched her deeply, and for a moment, what might have been crossed her mind.

Suddenly, Zeus began to trot towards the paddock gate. "Follow me!" William called over his shoulder.

To set her in motion, Mr. Wilson slapped Belle's rump, which snapped Elizabeth out of her reflections. Pushing all her traitorous desires to the recesses of her heart, she reminded herself why they resided there in the first place. *He and I were never meant to be. Not then, and certainly not now.*

Fortuitously, as the mare began trotting after the black stallion, Elizabeth was forced to focus on all her father had taught her regarding staying in the saddle, and not on her heartache.

They had not ridden far when they came upon a narrow gravel and dirt road. William turned Zeus down the road, and soon they went through a wooded area. After a mile or so, the road ended at a meadow of roughly five acres, surrounded by forest. In the middle of the meadow was a handsome, two-storey greystone house, about half the size of Longbourn. As they drew closer, Elizabeth noted that the road was now more densely covered with gravel and the lawn was manicured, with flowers, shrubs and trees planted in an orderly fashion.

Reaching the structure, William dismounted and set Emily on her feet. Straight off, she ran towards the flowerbeds, whilst he walked over to help Elizabeth from the mare. Once on her feet, Elizabeth stretched and bent over as if to touch her toes.

William tried not to smile. "Sore?"

"A little. But I am sure that by tonight I shall rue the day that I let you talk me into riding again."

A loud guffaw filled the air. "That is unfortunate, for I wish to do this every day."

"I do not think my body will ever adjust to riding horses, William."

The sound of his name on her lips gave him pause. Unable to reply, awkwardly he turned to look in the direction Emily had gone. In that instant, a man came around the side of the house behind William. Roughly five and forty, he was wearing dirty clothes and holding a hunting rifle in the crook of his arm. Startled, Elizabeth gasped, causing William to turn completely around.

"Mr. Darcy, sir. I was not expecting you. When I heard the horses, I thought I should check. One cannot be too careful."

"I appreciate your diligence, Mr. Parker," William replied. Tilting his head towards Elizabeth, he added, "Mrs. Gardiner and her daughter are our guests, and I wished to show them Rosehill."

Touching the brim of his hat and bowing slightly, Parker said. "I am sure you will find it very agreeable, ma'am." Then, addressing William, he said, "If you have no need of me, I shall get back to my work. The boys and I are thinning the shrubs next to the house in the back."

William's practiced gaze settled on the house. "I have not been here in a long while, but I notice that the windows need caulking, not to mention a fresh coat of paint."

"I have already ordered the paint. My sons and I plan to caulk the windows in a few days; we shall paint them afterward."

"As usual, you have anticipated my concerns. Thank you. You may go now."

"Very good, sir." With another nod and bow, the man disappeared around the corner as quickly as he had appeared.

"You have a superior eye," Elizabeth said. "I would never have noticed the caulking around the windows had you not mentioned it."

William shrugged. "Once one is in charge of an estate, one notices everything—especially what needs repairing. It comes with the responsibility."

By now Emily was coming towards her mother with a disheveled bouquet of lilies—most with hardly a stem attached.

"For you, Mama!" she announced proudly, holding the flowers

out to Elizabeth.

"Why, thank you," Elizabeth said. "They are beautiful." As the child ran back to pick more flowers, she called after her, "This is plenty, Sweetheart. Leave some so that the yard will still look lovely!"

"I will, Mama!" she called, though she did not look up as she picked another handful. "But first I must pick Mr. Darcy's flowers!"

William's lips pursed as he tried not to laugh. Seeing the loving way that he was observing her daughter, Elizabeth said, "You have been so kind to Emily...to us both. How can I ever repay you?"

Uncomfortable with her praise, William murmured, "Just seeing both of you safe and happy is payment enough."

Suddenly Emily was back, shyly holding flowers out to William. He took them. "They are lovely. Thank you." Then, squatting beside her, he asked, "Do you want to know a secret?" Emily's head bobbed up and down. "No young lady has ever given me flowers before. You are the first, and I shall always remember this moment."

Emily's hands went around his neck in a hug. Then, hastily pulling back, she placed a quick kiss on his cheek before suddenly becoming shy. Retreating to Elizabeth, she clasped one of her legs, leaning into her skirts as though to hide.

Touched more than he wanted to show, William rose and began to busy himself by tying up the horses. The manoeuvre did not fool Elizabeth, but still she changed the subject.

"The house is unique—smaller than Pemberley, but almost as beautiful. Does anyone reside here?"

"I am the only one who has stayed here since my parents died. It was once the dower house, though if one believes the household records, it has not been used in that capacity for over a hundred years. Pemberley is so large that, more often than not, when the heir would marry, the new mistress would simply join him and his parents in the manor house. Of course, if the new mistress and the former mistress did not see eye to eye—"

"She could be banished to here!" Elizabeth said with a chuckle.

"Precisely!"

"Is it locked, or may we see it?"

"It is always kept locked, but I have a key, as does Parker."

Taking a small ring of keys from a pocket in his jacket, he used one to open the door, then pushed it wide for her to enter. The sun streaming through the opening illuminated the foyer, and, taking Emily's hand, Elizabeth stepped just inside. Immediately, she was in awe. Though it may have been much smaller, it was as elegantly decorated as Pemberley itself.

"No servants reside here permanently," William began to explain, "other than the groundskeeper, Mr. Parker, and his wife and two sons, who occupy a cottage at the rear of the property. However, once a week Mrs. Reynolds sends several maids here to do a thorough cleaning." He laughed. "She says it takes very little effort to keep it clean if I stay away. She claims I am untidy!"

One of Elizabeth's eyebrows rose along with the corners of her mouth. It was an expression he adored. "Do you agree with her?"

"I suppose I do. After all, I am a man."

A thought came out of the blue. *You are most definitely a man.* Colour rising, aloud she chose to repeat what he had once said to her at Netherfield. "Are you not being too hard on your own sex?"

William's smile waned. "Would you be any less brutal?"

Her heart challenged her to confess everything. "I am reminded, William, of how cruelly I once treated you. Please believe that I shall never be that foolish again."

An endless string of emotions played across his face, the last being uncertainty. When she realised that either he had not grasped her meaning or her opinion of him no longer mattered, Elizabeth's spirits fell.

A persistent tug on her hand bade her look away, and she followed Emily's finger to a picture on the wall. "Mama, is that Rex?"

Determined not to crumble beneath her disappointment, Elizabeth focused on the framed charcoal drawing of a dog. It was the same breed Charles kept for hunting, including Emily's favourite, Rex. The picture stood in stark contrast to the formal portraits on the rest of the walls. Picking Emily up, she walked over to read the artist's signature.

Knowing he would be unmasked, William said, "I fear that is one of my earliest efforts. Mother insisted that I sign it and she had it framed. Of course, she praised all my efforts, good or bad."

Elizabeth studied the details of the drawing. "I cannot believe you drew this. It is very, very good."

He chuckled. "You could pretend less amazement."

"But I am amazed. I would never have dreamed—" She faced him. "You do realise that you draw remarkably well."

"That is kind of you to say. I suppose that is why my father never encouraged me in the arts or hired tutors."

"Are there others?"

"Yes. When she was alive, Mother insisted on hanging those she had framed in this house. So, you may find one or more in every room."

Elizabeth set Emily down. "Come, let us play a game and see how many of Mr. Darcy's drawings we can identify." Then she smiled at William. "You may follow us if you like, but you may not give us any hints."

Not surprisingly, what was supposed to be a short turn about the house took more than an hour, and it was almost dark when they returned to Pemberley. Later, after they had eaten dinner, Elizabeth returned to her dressing room to find a hot bath awaiting her. There was also this note.

I had always considered Rosehill a place to be alone. After today, I shall never think of it in that manner again.
William

Now it was Elizabeth's turn to be uncertain. Was William suggesting that he liked her company, or company in general? Too fatigued to ponder his meaning, she slipped into the bath and began to re-read the letter from Jane that had been waiting when they returned to the manor.

Dear Lizzy,

Another letter has arrived from Charles, and he is in much better spirits. Thank God his lungs are responding to the drier air and the sunshine, and he coughs much less. Strangely, he has not been sick to his stomach since he sailed from England. I pray that that continues, too.

Kitty has been here three days already, and while I dearly love her, she is clearly not as diverting company as you. Still, she is a great help with the girls and has tried to keep up the lessons that you began. Do not tell her that I said as much, but your position as governess is in no danger! Gracie and Marianne miss you and Emily very much and asked that I tell you so in this letter. As for Mary, her last letter states her family is in good health. She asked me to send you her love, as does Kitty. I have written to our Aunt and Uncle Gardiner. When I hear from them, I shall pass along their news.

You may not believe this, but Mr. Smith rode all the way here without announcing his plans beforehand. Per our agreement not to tell anyone but family where you are, I would not reveal your whereabouts. He was so upset that he turned right around and rode back to London. The last thing he said was that he planned to ask Mr. Darcy where you had gone. I have to wonder if he will put two and two together when he finds that gentleman is no longer in London either. Surely not.

I received three letters from you in one day, so do not worry if you do not get one from me every day. Most likely they will come in bundles, just as mine have. I miss you and Emily so much, Lizzy. Nonetheless, please know that having you safe is a burden off my shoulders. Tell Mr. Darcy that I shall be eternally grateful for his kindness.

I shall close this letter so that I may post it today.

Your loving sister,

Jane

Smiling, Elizabeth dried herself, put on her nightdress, slipped the letter under her pillow and lay down beside Emily. Even though Georgiana's childhood furniture had been moved into the adjoining bedroom two days ago, Emily still came to her bed to sleep. Looking at her sleeping child, Elizabeth's heart swelled with love. Still, she vowed to make her sleep in her own bed tomorrow, lest sleeping with her became a habit.

The next morning

Though she was sore, Elizabeth had every intention of riding. In the past few days at Pemberley, she had almost forgotten that the proposal at Kent ever happened, as well as the whole turmoil with Emily's father. Her child was already quite attached to William and seeing the two so close was a balm to her battered soul. At times she found herself praying that her stay might never end. In more rational moments, she accepted what must be. One such moment had occurred when she overheard two maids discussing an expected guest—the Countess of Markham—just before going downstairs to break her fast.

They had not gone very far on their morning ride before a rain shower forced the three of them to take shelter in one of the many barns dotting the property. Thrilled to have an opportunity to play in the hay, Emily was doing just that by the time William walked over to help Elizabeth from Belle.

A strong wind had preceded the rain, causing the combs in her hair to loosen and curls to frame her face. Most of the rest had escaped the bun and now cascaded down her back. William was spellbound, and it took all of his strength not to react when he placed a hand on either side of her waist, and she leaned towards him. As this was happening, her foot caught in the stirrup, and she pitched forward. To keep his balance, William pulled her to his chest and slowly released her to slide down his body until her feet touched the ground.

Each affected by the other's proximity, neither thought to break the embrace. Staring mesmerised into each other's eyes, a cry from Emily caused them to step awkwardly apart.

"Mama, look!"

Fearing what she may have found, Elizabeth rushed towards the child, who was standing atop a haystack in the corner. In a hollow in the back of the stack lay a calico cat with four kittens—each a different colour. Eagerly, Emily started towards them.

"No, Sweetheart," Elizabeth said. "They are newborn and not to be handled yet. Leave them alone, and in a few weeks they will be big enough for you to touch." Elizabeth patted the hay. "Meanwhile, sit here and watch them."

"Yes, Mama."

Elizabeth and William walked back to the open door, where Elizabeth pretended to be enthralled by the rain. In truth, her mind was on what had occurred only minutes before. Chilled by the misting rain or perhaps his nearness, Elizabeth crossed her arms and rubbed them with her hands. William removed his coat and placed it over her shoulders.

"Thank you," she murmured.

"Think nothing of it." Then, seemingly out of the blue, he declared, "I must confess that when you agreed to come to Pemberley, it meant a great deal to me, especially in view of our shared past."

She had closed her eyes briefly with the joy of his pronouncement, but opened them to reply, "If we are confessing, I must tell you that I have loved every second of my stay. Not only is Pemberley a veritable paradise, but I am free from having to look over my shoulder every minute. I have you to thank for that."

"You are free to stay as long as necessary. I will not have your life, or Emily's, in jeopardy."

"I appreciate your kindness, William." She turned to face him. "But I fear your future wife will not wish to share Pemberley with me."

"My future wife?"

"I was not trying to eavesdrop, but this morning the maids preparing the room across the hall talked a bit too loudly. They mentioned that a widow, the Countess of Markham, and her children were expected tomorrow."

William sighed raggedly. "I should have told you before now, but I feared you might believe you were intruding by being here. The countess is someone I have known since I was a boy. With her marriage, her late husband, Henry, became a good friend as well. His passing left a large void in her life, as well as the children's. I felt that a visit here might be beneficial for them."

Elizabeth was not so dim-witted as not to know the significance of a widow bringing her children to a single man's home for the summer. "I...I cannot but fear that my presence here will wreak havoc with your plans."

"My *plans* are to present each of her children with a new pony and to have my livery manager instruct them in how to take jumps. I have known the twins, Hugh and Kathy, since their birth, and I am quite fond of them."

She smiled bravely. "How old are they?"

"Eight years of age."

"I do not doubt that they adore you, for Emily does already."

"I am most fond of Emily, too."

Just as quickly as it had come, the rain suddenly stopped. Feeling a bit out of sorts now that Elizabeth had brought up Millicent, a subject he had avoided thinking about all week, William suggested they return to the manor.

"I think we had best head back to the stables. For, while the rain has lifted, more ominous clouds are gathering in the distance."

As they made their way to the stables, it was not lost on William that the *gathering clouds* were an omen of what was to come when Millicent arrived. With no guile on his part, he had fallen as deeply in love with Elizabeth as before. Torn between his agreement with Millicent and not knowing Elizabeth's heart, William was at a loss for how to proceed. In the end, he concluded that all he could do was pray that God worked the matter out according to what was best for all concerned, for he did not have the foggiest idea what that might be.

The Countess of Markham's coach arrived at Pemberley to find no one about, save a footman. Wanting to surprise William, Millicent had left Hudson Hall a day early, and she expected him to be eagerly awaiting her arrival. As she stepped from the coach, followed by her aunt and the twins, Mrs. Reynolds rushed out onto the portico, wiping her hands on an apron.

"Forgive me, Countess Markham. I was in the stillroom[8] checking the progress of the rosewater when a maid rushed in to tell me that your coach had arrived," the housekeeper declared as she came down the steps.

Millicent smiled at the elderly servant she had known most of her life. "It is no great matter, Mrs. Reynolds. I am a day early, after all." She turned to her aunt. "I believe you know my aunt, Lady Foggett."

Mrs. Reynolds smiled and nodded. "I do. Mr. Darcy is so pleased to have all of you visiting with us at Pemberley."

"Where is Mr. Darcy?"

"I am afraid that he is riding at the moment, though we do expect him back in time for tea. If you will allow me, I shall see that you are settled in your rooms straightaway. That will give you an opportunity to wash off the dust from the road and change clothes, if you so desire, before he arrives."

"That would be lovely," Millicent said. Then, turning to her aunt and children, she said, "Let us hurry. Mr. Darcy will be back before we know it, and I would like to make a good first impression."

After getting settled in her room, Millicent could not relax for want of seeing William. As a distraction until he arrived, she threw open the French doors of her sitting room and crossed the balcony to the wrought-iron railing in order to view the breathtaking landscape. Closing her eyes, she took a deep breath of the fresh air and let it go leisurely. When she opened them again, she was startled to see three people coming up the gravel path from the stables— a dark-haired woman and a man holding a child. Suddenly, it dawned on her that the man was William. Stepping back into the shadows near the house, she watched the scene undetected.

William was clearly as comfortable with the little girl as she was with him. That, in itself, was telling, for he did not relate easily to children, not even to Hugh and Kathy, whom he had known all of their lives. Millicent's breath caught as he stopped and faced the woman. Never had she seen him look so unguardedly at any lady, much less smile so warmly. Clearly, whatever the conversation, they were both engaged in it.

Her hand flew to her heart. *Have I lost him before the year has begun?*

Deciding she would not give in quite so easily, Millicent vowed to learn all there was to know about the interloper. Studying the lady more closely, she realised the riding habit she wore fit poorly and was years out of date. Her hair, which must have been fashioned into a bun earlier, had lost most of its pins and was now untamed.

She looks almost wild. William would never approve of Georgiana making such an exhibition!

There was no time for further examination as the couple had walked on and were instantly lost behind some trees. Rushing back into the bedroom, Millicent addressed her lady's maid. "Mrs. Dowd, I should like for you to re-style my hair into something more elaborate, and I wish to wear a more elegant gown than this for tea."

"Do you mean you wish to wear the silk?"

"Yes, my blue damask will do nicely. It may be too fussy, but I wish to remind Mr. Darcy why he invited me to Pemberley."

"Yes, my lady."

Chapter 9

Pemberley

William tried not to show his annoyance when, upon returning to the manor, Mrs. Reynolds informed him that the Countess Markham's party had arrived a day early. He had relied on having one more night to think of the right words to tell Millicent why Elizabeth and Emily were at Pemberley. Faced with doing so straightaway, his mind went completely blank. Thus, while he changed clothes, William made the decision that it was best *not* to face Millicent or her formidable aunt, Lady Foggett, across the dining room table. Instead, he would have Mrs. Reynolds serve tea on the terrace.

Having already made plans to escort Elizabeth to tea, in less than an hour, they walked out on the terrace to find Millicent and her aunt already seated. At the sight of Elizabeth on William's arm, Millicent's eyes narrowed whilst Lady Foggett gasped loudly enough to be heard. Mrs. Reynolds was still there, directing two maids on the correct placement of trays of tea, biscuits and cakes, which did provide a brief reprieve. Still, after the servants had all disappeared, there was nothing left but for William to make introductions.

"Lady Millicent, Lady Foggett, may I introduce Mrs. Elizabeth

Gardiner? She is the sister of a long-time friend of mine, Charles Bingley of Canfield Manor in Richmond. She and her daughter, Emily, are our guests for the summer."

The great ladies merely stared speechless. Undaunted, as Millicent's eyes bore into her, Elizabeth met and held her gaze.

"Mrs. Gardiner, may I introduce Lady Millicent, Countess of Markham. We have been friends and neighbours most of our lives, and her late husband, Henry, was a good friend of many years." Glancing to the frowning woman seated beside her, he added, "And this is the countess' aunt, Lady Foggett of Perryton Park, Sussex."

Elizabeth had noted the exchange of frowns between the elegantly clad and coiffed ladies; nevertheless, she curtseyed. "I am pleased to meet you." This was acknowledged by a curt nod of the countess' head.

Millicent immediately turned to William. "Charles Bingley? I do recall hearing the name, though it has been years since last you mentioned him."

Her pronouncement caused William to do something that he had always abhorred—he lied. "Though we have not been in each other's company in the last few years as much as I would have liked, we have kept in touch."

Seemingly stunned, Elizabeth was staring open-mouthed at him when the countess addressed her.

"I do not recall him ever mentioning you, Elizabeth," Millicent said, her tone surprisingly civil despite the frown on her face. "You do not mind if I call you Elizabeth, do you?"

Elizabeth's courage rose. "You may if you wish, Countess."

"Good. Now, do tell me how you first met Fitzwilliam. He is too gentlemanly to speak of *all* of the women he knows, much less how he met them."

William gave up all attempts to smile, his lips settling into a thin line.

Elizabeth answered, "I met Mr. Darcy approximately five years ago. He was visiting my brother at Netherfield. I believe Charles wanted his opinion on whether to purchase the property."

A knowing look spread across Millicent's face. "Netherfield? That is in Hertfordshire, is it not?"

"It is."

"I do remember Fitzwilliam speaking of his visit to Hertfordshire a few years back." Her eyes settled on William, though she continued to address Elizabeth. "As I recall, he visited Hertfordshire that spring and shortly thereafter, Kent. Have you ever been to Kent, Elizabeth?"

"Yes, a dear friend of mine married the vicar at Hunsford, Mr. Collins, and I visited them that same spring."

"Collins? Is that not Lady Catherine's vicar, Fitzwilliam?"

By now the hair on the back of William's neck was standing up. "Yes, it is." Quickly he tried to steer the conversation in another direction. "Where have you hidden Hugh and Kathy? I am anxious to see them again."

"Surely you realise they are too young to join us for tea. The trip was tiring, so I had refreshments sent to their rooms and instructed them to rest afterward. I plan to have them greet everyone and exhibit in the music room after dinner." Then, reaching over to place a hand on William's arm, she gave it an intimate squeeze. "Be assured that they are as eager to see you as you are them. They dote on your attention. I suppose that is only natural, since Henry's early death deprived them of a father."

Before William could reply, Lady Foggett croaked, "And your husband, Mrs. Gardiner? Will he not miss his child if you dally all summer at Pemberley?" The tone of her voice oozed contempt. "Perhaps he may come to fetch her."

Elizabeth well remembered the expression now on William's face. She had first seen it at an assembly in Meryton when her mother crowed about his income being *ten thousand a year.* Hoping to quickly defuse the situation, she replied, "I fear that that would not be possible. My husband died of influenza two years ago."

Feeling more sympathetic after that revelation, Millicent declared, "Then I fear we have something in common. My Henry died of influenza during the same scourge." Turning to Lady Foggett, she said sweetly, "Aunt, we must allow Elizabeth to enjoy her tea without fear of being subjected to an inquisition."

"I was hardly the one conducting an inquisition!" Her aunt sniffed.

The rest of tea was spent in relative peace as Lady Millicent and William carried the conversation. They talked of people and events they held in common, which served to highlight what Elizabeth already knew—she was not a part of their sphere. When tea had concluded, the countess pointedly asked William to escort her through the gardens.

No doubt, Elizabeth thought as she returned to her rooms, *to discuss my presence at Pemberley.*

Once in her sitting room, she went through the French doors onto the balcony, determined to enjoy what little sunshine had finally broken through the clouds. Praying that the bucolic view might lift her spirits, she took a seat in a chair facing the pastures in the distance. Nonetheless, laughter from somewhere below acted the siren's song, willing her to search the gardens for the source. Regrettably, the moment she spotted William on the walk below, the countess stood on tiptoes to kiss his cheek. Closing her eyes against the scene, Elizabeth reminded herself of what any sensible person would know.

No single man invites a widow and her children to his home for so long a stay, unless as a prelude to a proposal of marriage.

A small voice tried to create doubt. *Then how do you explain your situation? Are you not a widow with a child? Yet he is not courting you.*

Elizabeth lifted her chin defiantly, hoping to silence the interloper. *My visit was inspired by William's compassion, not his love. If I am to repay him for his kindness, I must keep to myself and let nature take its course.*

The garden

William and Millicent walked for several hundred feet down the gravel paths that wound through the picturesque gardens of Pemberley with hardly a word spoken, save speculation about the weather. Though that was not out of character for the gentleman, it most certainly was for the lady.

In truth, the countess was attempting to come to terms with the different aspects of Fitzwilliam that she had seen today. Thoroughly suspect of the dark-haired beauty who looked so comfortable on his arm, Millicent recalled the unguarded smiles he directed Elizabeth's way and how he instantly changed the subject when Kent was mentioned. Artifice had never been part of Fitzwilliam's nature and to see it now was disconcerting.

Unable to keep silent any longer, she said, "Fitzwilliam, you must know why I asked you to take a turn about the gardens."

"I think I do," he answered dolefully. There was a long pause before he spoke again. "I...I have no way of explaining Mrs. Gardiner's presence here without revealing secrets that I swore never to share with anyone."

"Have I ever given you reason not to trust me?"

"I trust you implicitly." William sighed heavily. "And, I know there should be no secrets between us."

"You are correct. There should not be."

"Promise me that you will keep it confidential."

Millicent's curiosity rose, along with a fear that she might learn more than she wished to know. Still, she stopped and stood on tiptoes to kiss his cheek again. "I thank you for your trust.

125

You have my word that I will keep anything you tell me private."

"Shall we have a seat on the swing, then? It may take a while to relate all that has transpired."

Millicent agreed, and they made their way to a white swing hanging under the largest oak tree in the garden. Subsequently, half an hour later William had told her everything that had happened since he took charge of Bingley's affairs.

"My word, Fitzwilliam! What an impossible situation! A blackguard cousin stealing the very livelihood out from under Bingley's nose, and some unknown person threatening to expose Mrs. Gard—" She stopped abruptly. "I suppose I should say Miss Bennet."

"You and I must still refer to her as Mrs. Gardiner when speaking in front of others. Being a widow defers speculation about her daughter, and if someone is looking for her or Emily, it will not do to have rumours swirling about Lambton or, God forbid, all of Derbyshire. And she has agreed that you may call her Elizabeth when you are in each other's company, so that is settled."

"Will you tell her that I know everything?"

"Yes. It is only fair that she knows who has been trusted with her secret."

"I am very sorry for her, Fitzwilliam, but I am also sad for you. I do not think you could have found any more trouble had you tried."

William shrugged. "I did not foresee any of this when I agreed to help Charles, nor could he have dreamt it. Still, he would have done whatever it took to take care of my family had the situation been reversed. I can do no less."

"Of course."

From what little she had seen of his interaction with Elizabeth, in addition to the fact that he had changed the conversation when Kent was mentioned, Millicent was almost certain that this lady was the reason for his despondency all these years. Yet

William had not mentioned their history during his explanation, and for an instant, Millicent considered forcing him to deny that Elizabeth was the one who had broken his heart. Only her better judgement kept her from doing so.

At this point, it seems he is only interested in helping Elizabeth and her daughter escape Lord Van Lynden. If I force a confession, Fitzwilliam may perceive me as a jealous shrew or, even worse, a threat to her safety and side with her against me. I shall simply have to wait and see how things unfold.

Dinner turned out to be harder for Elizabeth to bear, simply because it lasted so much longer than tea. She was beginning to wonder if she had the fortitude to remain a guest at Pemberley if doing so meant watching William and the countess act so familiar. Just as at tea, their discussions were of people and places she did not know. And though, on occasion, William attempted to include her in the conversation, she knew that she added nothing of value to the exchange. Eventually, she became as silent as Lady Foggett, who made no attempt at conversation and obviously took great pleasure in examining her.

Later, in the music room, the countess asked William to turn the pages while she played the pianoforte. It was such a picture of domestic harmony that unbidden tears filled Elizabeth's eyes. Only the steady glare of Lady Foggett, sitting directly across from her, kept them from falling. Still, the absolute worst part was seeing how fond the countess' well-mannered children—a sandy-haired duo with freckled faces—were of William. She could not fault either child for loving him; after all, Emily had known him only a few days, and she did. Moreover, it was clear that William delighted in the twins' musical proficiency—one on the pianoforte and one on the harp. Seeing all of this brought Elizabeth a new pang of conscience.

How can I hope William will care for me again when he obviously loves those children and they him?

By evening's end, Elizabeth had resigned herself to the inevitable—William and the countess would marry. It was at that point she learned a hard new truth—the loss of one's hopes and dreams the second time was much more excruciating than the first.

The next day

When dawn broke, an unexpected visitor arrived—Colonel Fitzwilliam. William was already in his study, having slept very little, and was surprised but pleased when his cousin stuck his head in the door.

"Darcy, ole man! What in the world are you doing in here? With the lovely weather this morning I would have thought you were already riding."

"Since Mrs. Gardiner came to Pemberley, I have been riding with her and her daughter, which necessitates that I ride much later than usual. Might I ask what brings you to Derbyshire?"

A big grin crossed the colonel's face. "While I am on leave, I can be wherever I please. And today it pleases me to be here."

"You did not reply to my last letter, so I hoped that you had taken leave. I very much need your expertise."

"I am here to help, though it seems you may need more assistance than even I can provide."

William's brows furrowed. "How so?"

"I can only imagine having Mrs. Gardiner at Pemberley did not sit well with Millie." Seeing William's surprised look, he added, "Mrs. Reynolds told me that she arrived early."

"And why, pray tell, would Millie mind if I invited Mrs. Gardiner to Pemberley?"

"Come now, Cousin! We both know that she has had her

sights set on you since before you entered Eton. Only Henry had the charm to divert her goal whilst he was alive. Frankly, I cannot fathom why you and she have not reached an understanding since he has been gone these two years."

If he had not met Elizabeth again, William might have confessed that he had tried to convince Millie to marry him; however, he was so confused about what he desired at present that he was unable to make sense of it, much less explain it to Richard.

"At present I have too much on my mind to consider something as significant as marriage. *And* I would appreciate it if you would not bring that subject up again."

Richard saluted. "As you wish, Commander. I shall not mention marriage." Then, he grew more sombre. "Still, it is my opinion that Millie will be jealous. After all, Mrs. Gardiner is the woman who broke your heart and sent you into the abyss of despair."

"Must I keep saying there was no abyss, no despair? And, though I felt that I had to tell Millie all that occurred to bring Mrs. Gardiner here, she does not know that I once offered for the lady, and you shall not tell her!"

"I should like to be a fly on the wall when she learns the truth, and she will eventually. Why not confess now and save yourself a world of trouble?"

"I have my reasons. Please honour my wishes."

"I have no choice but to honour your wishes, for you hold all the cards." Richard laughed aloud at the fierce look directed his way. "How I would suffer if I could not stay in your excellent homes, ride in your first-rate coaches and partake of your expensive cigars and brandy. Not to mention, receive superior service in all the shops by brandishing your name."

"So this is why you associate with me?"

"Not entirely, Cousin. You know that I am fond of your sparkling wit and personality."

As William tried not to smile, Richard grew more sombre. "I

do bring some news that I fear will dampen your spirits."

"About Charles' warehouses, or have you found the letter writer?"

"It concerns both. My associates have verified that Howton diverted merchandise from Bingley's business to a rented warehouse not three blocks away. Moreover, they have identified and are watching six men who helped him to steal and dispose of the goods. Now all we need is Bingley's permission to have them all arrested. Until we do, I suggest that, for now, you refrain from asking Howton to stay clear of the business. Let him think that we do not suspect him."

"As you wish. I explained what we suspected in my last letter to Charles and am awaiting his reply to act."

"Excellent. According to my sources, the warehouse holds enough goods to last only a few more weeks. Once it is empty, there is no telling where the rats will slink. We may not be able to find all of them if we do not move soon."

"And the source of the threatening letter?"

"The Carsons were able to describe Howton's cohorts, for he often hosted them at the townhouse for cards. One of the men in his employ is a thug named Carney. He is easily recognisable, for he has fiery red hair and freckles, which fits the description of the man who was in Meryton, as well as Compton, in the weeks before Mrs. Bingley received the letter. What is more, the proprietor of a pub in Cheapside said that once, when Carney was drunk, he bragged about being paid good money to frighten some ladies in Hertfordshire."

"Howton is responsible? But how would he know anything of Mrs. Gardiner's history?"

"Guess who was in residence at Bingley's townhouse just before the letter was sent?" As William's eyebrows rose in question, Richard declared, "Caroline Bingley."

"But I thought that Charles—"

"Banned her from his houses? He did. But with Bingley out of the country, Caroline must have felt brave enough to defy him. Did Charles tell you why she was banned from his homes?"

"No."

"The Carsons said that after Mrs. Gardiner came to live with her sister and Bingley, Caroline told everyone who would listen that she did not believe for a minute that Elizabeth Bennet was a widow. Caroline maintained that she was a whore who had borne an illegitimate daughter before returning to her family in shame."

"She always hated Elizabeth."

Ignoring the slip of the tongue regarding her name, Richard continued. "In any case, I believe the letter sent to Canfield was meant as a diversion. Howton wished to take your mind off the investigation, and it worked. You were instantly caught up in helping Mrs. Gardiner."

William leaned back in his chair, propping his elbows on the arms and tenting his fingers under his chin. "I fear I may have underestimated Howton, for that does make perfect sense."

"I believe it does. And there is one other piece of bad news."

"Things cannot get much worse, so just come out with it."

"Leighton is back in Derbyshire."

William groaned and began to massage his forehead with his fingers. "What happened to that wealthy widow in Ireland—the one who had buried two husbands already, owned three estates and had enormous breasts? I thought they were soon to marry."

"My brother has not said, though I suspect, as with all his amours, the novelty has worn off. In any event, he is at Matlock, and my parents will be arriving in less than a sennight. As customary, Mother wishes to pretend he is a contributing member of society by hosting a ball to celebrate his return."

"Why, pray tell, did he return to Derbyshire? Why not London? That town holds all the vices he admires—gambling, drink and loose women."

"The widow with the large breasts is presently in London. Word is that she is nursing her injured pride at her uncle's town-house. And you know how little civility there is between my brother and Lord Franklin. I should not be surprised if the man calls Leighton out for wounding his niece's pride."

"With all the liquor your brother imbibes, he has long since lost his edge with sword and pistol. Perhaps that is why he is hiding in Derbyshire. It would behove him to behave if he wishes to keep topside of the ground a while longer."

"I could not agree more."

"If your mother happens to invite me, I shall just have to invent an excuse not to attend."

"I wish you luck. Mother will invite you and Millie. And Millie will expect you to escort her. My only purpose in letting you know was to give you time to compose yourself. It is clear he and you are like oil and water."

"As I recall, so are the two of you."

"We are. But I make sport of his insults, whereas you take them seriously. The last time you were in each other's company, I thought you were going to call him out."

"I did not appreciate what he had to say about Georgiana's husband, that is all. As long as he keeps a civil tongue in his head, there will be no problem."

"I understand and agree wholeheartedly, but he will likely say something just as off-colour the next time you meet, so be prepared."

"Perhaps, given my present state of mind, you had best warn Leighton, not me."

"I intend to do just that. Now, what say we both go to the dining room to see what delicious foods Mrs. Lantrip has prepared?" William's eyebrows rose. "Mrs. Reynolds also told me that you had not yet eaten."

William stood and walked towards Richard. As they left his study, he ventured, "Mayhap you should pay my housekeeper a stipend to keep you informed of all my doings."

"I have tried, but she loves me too much to take even a farthing in payment."

"So, with no incentive in the least, she tells you everything."

"Exactly."

Just as Richard and William sat down to eat, Millicent entered the dining room, so they both rose from their chairs.

"My goodness, Richard, I did not expect to see you today! Good morning! And a good morning to you, Fitzwilliam! Please, sit down while I help myself."

As they did just that, William said, "Are the children awake?"

"They are so excited about the new ponies that they were up before daylight; presently they are in their sitting room preparing to eat. By the way, I met Elizabeth in the hallway upstairs, and she said that Emily has a slight fever, so they will not be coming downstairs today."

William and Richard exchanged wary glances. "Perhaps I should see if she wishes for me to send for the physician," William ventured.

"There is no need. Mrs. Reynolds asked, and Elizabeth said that her daughter will be fine with a little rest."

William did not want to raise Millicent's suspicions, so he nodded mutely.

Richard changed the subject. "Well, I cannot wait to see the new ponies, either. Hugh and Kathy ride so well that learning to jump should present no problem, especially under Mr. Wilson's tutelage. That man is a genius when it comes to horses."

"He is that," Millicent said as she sat down with a plate of food. "I well remember watching him teach Georgiana to jump.

Though I had been jumping for years, I learned even more by watching him instruct her."

"I am blessed to have him in my employ," William declared, standing and dropping his serviette as though he had finished eating. Then he made a show of checking the pockets of his coat.

"What is the matter, Cousin?" Richard said chucking. "Lost your spectacles?"

"I do not wear spectacles, as you well know. It seems that I left my father's watch upstairs. I feel lost without it, so I shall go fetch it." Instantly, he disappeared.

Millicent stared at the door through which William had gone. "It seems to me that Fitzwilliam is acting rather oddly."

Richard knew to weigh his words carefully. "Whatever do you mean?"

"I cannot put my finger on it, but he has definitely changed since he was at the foxhunt."

"Darcy said that he has told you what he encountered since taking on Charles' responsibilities."

Millicent nodded. "Yes, he did."

"Well, if I had as much riding on my shoulders, I might act a bit oddly, too."

Millicent smiled half-heartedly. "Of course. That must be it."

Upstairs

William knocked on the door of the sitting room in Elizabeth's suite. Cora, the maid from Canfield Manor, opened the door and, seeing who it was, turned to her mistress with a quizzical look.

"It is alright, Cora. He may come in."

Elizabeth, who was sitting in the window seat, had been reading to Emily, whom she held in her lap. As William came into the room, the child slipped off her mother's knees and ran towards him. William stooped down to catch her in his arms, and, as he stood, she slipped her arms around his neck and laid her head on his shoulder.

"I came to see how you are faring," he said into her fine, blonde hair. Then, his eyes questioned Elizabeth, as he added, "I hoped to find you much better, for the saddle we purchased for Snow is to be delivered this afternoon."

Emily pulled her head back and looked into his face. "Mama says I have a fever, but I do not feel sick. Please, can I ride Snow today?"

By then Elizabeth was coming towards them. Her hair was completely down, and she was still dressed in her nightclothes, covered by a gold, embroidered dressing gown to preserve her dignity. As she got closer, she nervously pulled the belt tighter. Mesmerised, William could do nought but stare.

"I...Emily had a fever when she awoke. Though it has since subsided, I feel it is best that she stay inside today."

Recovering his senses, William smiled wanly as he addressed the child. "Your mother knows best, Miss Emily. Hopefully, you will be well enough tomorrow to try out the new saddle."

"But...but I want to ride today," she whined, sniffling.

William's eyes focused on Elizabeth as he answered. "I know, Sweetheart, but sometimes we cannot have what we desire. All we can do is trust God to provide us with what He feels is best."

Elizabeth reached out to take her daughter from his arms. "Come, Emily. I am certain that Mr. Darcy is anxious to get started with the riding lessons for Hugh and Kathy. If you continue to improve, later we shall sit on the balcony and watch them from here. Would you like that?"

Emily had met the twins briefly the day before. Her head bobbed up and down at the prospect of watching their lessons.

William brushed a silky lock of blonde hair from Emily's forehead. "I shall check on you again later. Promise me that you will be a good patient so you may get well quickly."

"I promise."

With that William left the room, closing the door solidly behind himself. Once in the hallway, he paused and leaned back against it. Emily did not seem ill. Had Elizabeth simply invented an excuse to avoid being with him and Millicent? Since he had no way of discerning if this were the case, he headed back downstairs to face an inquisitive countess.

The twins had taken to the new ponies readily and, in mere minutes, were taking the smaller jumps effortlessly. William was pleased and watched for the majority of the first lesson, only returning to his office when notified that his steward had some pressing issues and wanted to speak to him. Millicent, of course, wanted to wait until they were completely finished, so Richard stayed with her.

As the twins made yet another circle around the enclosure used for jumping, Richard remarked, "I cannot believe that Hugh and Kathy are eight years old. It seems only yesterday they were beginning to walk."

"Since I have had the children, time seems to pass so much faster."

"And tall! Your children are much taller than most are at this age."

"Well, their father and all his relations are tall, and I am not a petite person!"

"I think you are the ideal height. I like a woman whom I can look in the eye—especially if we are dancing."

Millicent laughed. "You always know how to make me smile, Richard. If one were to listen to you, I have always been perfect."

"Not perfect," Richard teased. "But close enough." Out of the blue his true feelings surfaced, and his expression grew sombre. "Millie, may I be frank?"

She turned from following her children's activities to give him a puzzled look. "I was of the opinion that you always were."

"I have not been completely frank with you regarding Darcy for some time. That is because I did not want to hurt your feelings."

"Of course I wish you to be frank with me, Richard. Say whatever is on your mind."

He took a deep breath and ploughed ahead. "Why do you long for Darcy when you know he will never think of you as more than a good friend? Why settle for less than a man who will love you with his entire heart, like Henry did?"

"Has Fitzwilliam told you he is not in love with me?"

"You know he does not discuss matters of the heart with me. But he is honest to a fault, and, if you ask him, he will not lie." Millicent was silent, so he continued. "I do not say this to disparage my cousin. He is a good and decent man, and if all you require of a husband is friendship, then he will do splendidly. I merely want to remind you that you have other options."

"Such as?"

Richard wanted to shout that he loved her—had always loved her—but he feared his confession might be seen as a joke, so he spoke in generalities.

"There are many amiable men available whom you may have not considered. Second sons like me, for example. Most women overlook me because they have their hearts set on Leighton and his title, not realising how cruelly he would use them should they marry."

Apparently totally unaware that Richard was championing himself, Millicent teased, "Whoever marries you will definitely get the best of the Fitzwilliams. And, moreover, they will never lack for entertainment with your quick wit. That is for certain."

Just then Mr. Wilson interrupted, wishing to discuss the children's progress with their mother. As she walked away, Richard chastised himself for saying what he had to Millie.

She has never thought of me as anything more than a friend. The thing I must do is keep silent and not make a fool of myself.

Chapter 10

Pemberley
Several days later

If Elizabeth harboured any hope that the countess' visit was simply a result of her long-standing friendship with William, those hopes were dashed when he divulged that he had told that lady everything about her reasons for being at Canfield Manor, and now Pemberley. The fact that he would not keep it secret from Millicent, more than anything else, convinced Elizabeth he planned to marry the woman. Thus, from that point on she tried to prepare her heart for the inevitable by staying clear of the couple. She did this by focusing on Emily during the day and retiring shortly after dinner.

The saddle purchased for Snow worked very well, and Emily took to riding eagerly. So Mr. Wilson divided his time between instructing Emily first thing each morning while Hugh and Kathy rode with their mother and William, and working with the twins once they returned. Though William never failed to ask Elizabeth to join them, she insisted on staying with her daughter. Still, every time he rode off, surrounded by his future family, she died a little bit more.

Unbeknownst to her, Richard suffered similarly. After his talk with Millicent, he was even less inclined to watch her fawn over his cousin, so he turned down every invitation to join them as well. Ostensibly, his motive in staying behind was to keep Elizabeth company; however, not knowing that the colonel had no designs regarding the woman he loved, William became suspect of him. Therefore, among the adults at Pemberley, Millicent and her aunt were the only ones truly happy with how events had worked out.

On one particular afternoon, the weather was so beautiful that William scheduled tea on the terrace again. Everyone had been served, and the conversation was proceeding harmoniously when Mrs. Reynolds suddenly appeared at the French doors. Uncharacteristically, she was wringing her hands.

"Yes, Mrs. Reynolds?"

"Sir, the Earl and Countess of Matlock have arrived. In fact, they are presently in the foyer."

William's head swung around to Richard. "Why would they veer so far off course instead of going straight to Matlock?"

Very deliberately Richard stood and set his cup down on a glass-topped table. "I suppose we shall not know the answer to that unless we ask."

William had just risen from his chair when Lady Matlock suddenly marched onto the terrace. She was followed by her husband, who held back, as if reluctant to intrude.

"Mother! Father!" Richard declared a little too earnestly. "What a pleasant surprise. I did not expect to see either of you until the ball for Leighton."

"Humph!" the Countess of Matlock sniffed, looking past him to the only person present she did not know—Elizabeth. "I imagine that none of you expected me to learn your secrets so quickly."

"Secrets?" William said, trying to contain his rising temper.

"Do not feign ignorance, Nephew," the countess declared, turning on him. "I am here because a report of a most alarming nature reached me last evening. It was said that you escorted an unmarried woman—one with a child, no less—to Pemberley. Though I thought it must be a scandalous falsehood, I instantly resolved to set off for this place to have the report contradicted."

William was livid, though he tried not to show it as he turned to address the others. "Mrs. Gardiner, Lady Millicent, Lady Foggett, will you please excuse this intrusion? My relations and I shall remove to my study to discuss this further."

"No," Elizabeth said, causing every head to turn in her direction. "This concerns me, and I have a right to defend myself."

"She is right, Fitzwilliam," Millicent interjected, quickly turning to Lady Foggett. "Aunt, if will you please excuse us, I shall join you shortly." After her aunt had exited the terrace, Millicent added, "Since I had a hand in bringing Elizabeth to Pemberley, I intend to stay as well."

Hearing this bald-faced lie, William and Elizabeth exchanged guarded looks. Still, there was nothing to be done but to go along with the countess' claim, so William turned his attention to his relations. "Do you intend to stay the night? If so, Mrs. Reynolds will have rooms prepared."

Lord Matlock glowered at his wife. "It was never my intent to stop here in the first place. Come what may, I intend to make Matlock by nightfall."

"As you wish," William answered. "If we are all intent to take part in this discussion, there is no need to remove to the study, so please be seated. Mrs. Reynolds, please fetch some fresh tea. I fear mine has gone cold."

The housekeeper bobbed a curtsey, and as she rushed away, William spoke. "Now, Aunt, I should like to know where you heard such a report."

"Where I heard it is hardly the issue," Lady Matlock exclaimed. "What is important is that you explain your behaviour. Why would you do something so foolhardy and completely out of character?"

Millicent broke in. "It is my fault. When I learned from Fitzwilliam that Elizabeth was now a widow and living at Canfield Manor, I begged him to bring her to Pemberley when he returned. We have not seen each other in many years, and I wished to renew our friendship."

Lady Matlock did not look convinced, and she refused to acknowledge Elizabeth. "Obviously, you and she are not of the same station, Lady Millicent. Tell me how the two of you formed a friendship."

"Of course. Several years ago, Fitzwilliam invited Mr. Bingley to Pemberley. Elizabeth was staying with her sister, Mrs. Bingley, at the time, so she accompanied them. Henry and I were already visiting with the children, and she and I became fast friends. Is that not true, Elizabeth?"

Having no choice but to agree, Elizabeth lifted her chin confidently and replied, "Yes, it is."

"Well, if someone had bothered to inform me of the nature of her visit, I might have had the opportunity to contradict the rumours that are likely entertaining London as we speak."

"Never mind that, I should like to know who told you," William insisted.

Lady Matlock huffed, "Very well. My personal maid was at the confectioners' shop to pick up an order of caramels for this trip. She swore that she was not trying to eavesdrop, but two men seated at a nearby table were speaking loudly enough for everyone to hear. Knowing that you are my nephew, when your name was mentioned, she took note of what was said. The gist of the conversation was that you and a woman had mysteriously disappeared—you from London and she from Richmond—and were seen travelling together."

"And did your maid happen to recognise the bearer of such gossip?"

"She claimed never to have seen them before. However, another man stopped by their table, and he addressed the younger man as Mr. Smith."

Shaking with fury, William closed his eyes. No doubt the love-struck solicitor had decided that he had spirited Elizabeth to Pemberley even without proof. Even worse, he was not gentleman enough to keep his conjectures to himself. He would address that later.

"When Millicent asked me to invite Mrs. Gardiner to Pemberley, I saw no reason to refuse. There is nothing more sinister involved, Aunt."

"What single man in his right mind would host two widows and their offspring simultaneously—not to mention that one travelled with you without a chaperone?" Lady Matlock replied. "When this news spreads, it will create a scandal."

"Mrs. Gardiner had a maid with her," William declared.

"Hardly a proper chaperone," Lady Matlock said. Then she addressed Millicent. "I know that you and Fitzwilliam are very fond of each other, my dear. Why not announce your engagement? That would put a damper on all the innuendoes which are sure to follow."

Not waiting for Millicent's answer, William jumped back into the fray. "I will not be a slave to what the *ton* thinks, Aunt!"

"Just like a man!" Lady Matlock declared. "Your reputation will not suffer as theirs' will." William was too incensed to answer as she continued, "Announcing your engagement would put any gossip to rest. All I ask is that you consider it."

Having had her say, she was headed towards the French doors when she suddenly whirled around. "I forgot to say, Nephew, that you and the countess will both receive an invitation to the ball I am having for Leighton. I expect you to attend."

Instantly Millicent exclaimed, "Please, you must invite Elizabeth, too!"

Lady Matlock, an authority on protocol, lifted her chin to study Elizabeth. She realised it would be best to destroy the mystery regarding this young woman by letting society see that she was not of their sphere. "Mrs. Gardiner shall receive an invitation, too."

Before Elizabeth could voice an objection, William's aunt disappeared out the door, followed by her husband, then Richard and William. Her mind was swirling with all that had occurred when Millicent spoke, startling her from the trance.

"I hope you do not mind my little white lie," she said. "I did not want you, or Fitzwilliam, to suffer his aunt's disapproval. She can be quite formidable when she wishes. I felt it better to tell her we are friends, and that your visit was my idea."

A bit dazed, Elizabeth nodded. "I do not mind if it helps Will— Mr. Darcy. But why did you insist that Lady Matlock invite me to the ball? I have no gowns suitable for such a soirée, nor do I relish being put on display for the amusement of the *ton*."

"You will learn that the best way to meet gossip is directly," Millicent replied. "The *ton* thrives on mysteries, rumours and innuendoes. They will lose interest once the truth is made abundantly clear. And as for the proper attire, let me worry about that."

"I suppose I have no choice."

"You do not," Millicent said, chuckling. "What say you and I take a stroll about the grounds before the children wake from their naps?"

When William and Richard returned to the terrace, there was no trace of the ladies. Seeing that they were alone, Richard said circumspectly, "I do not know about you, Cousin, but I am not looking forward to Mother's ball."

"Neither am I. I wish Millie had not said anything about inviting Mrs. Gardiner, for I wished to keep her presence at Pemberley a secret."

"It makes me ill to think what Leighton will do once he sees her. You know how he enjoys preying on young widows, in addition to kidding you about preying on them."

"If Leighton knows what is good for him, he will leave Mrs. Gardiner alone."

"When has Leighton EVER known what was good for him?"

"Perhaps, then, it is time he found out."

Annan, Scotland
Sagewood Manor
That same day

By the time the coach halted in front of the once beautiful facade of Sagewood Manor, storm clouds were gathering. Strong winds sent leaves scurrying across the ground, and flashes of lightning illuminated the deteriorating structure as an elderly servant, lantern in hand, ran down the front steps. Fearful of his master's displeasure at seeing his estate in this condition, the long-time butler, Wilhelm Lothar, prayed for time to make excuses before Lord Van Lynden entered the premises. He reached the coach just as that man stepped out.

"Lord Van Lynden, I am pleased to see you, sir," Lothar said nervously. "At the same time, I am surprised, since it was only yesterday that I received your letter and—"

Van Lynden waved his hand in dismissal. The long-time servant went silent. "Never mind, Wilhelm. When no one met me at the docks in Edinburgh, I took it as a sign you had not received my letter in sufficient time to send a coach; thus, I had to hire one, as you see."

"Sir, you should know that the house is not in good repair.

I wrote to you at the last address I had, explaining that all the servants deserted when we could no longer afford to pay them. I tried to carry on, but I fear that my declining health did not permit me to keep the estate running as it had before your departure."

Van Lynden shrugged. "At least Sagewood still belongs to me. The funds you hid in Edinburgh will allow me to live comfortably and reimburse you for your efforts, as well as your loyalty. And the next time I leave England, you shall come with me."

"I did nothing to garner praise, your lordship. Still, I look forward to going back whenever you do. I may have resided in Scotland all these years, but my heart was in Rotterdam."

"Spoken like a true Dutchman! Thanks to you, I did not end up penniless, even if my life is in shambles. You see, my father is dead and our business is in ruins. All thanks to that bastard Castlereagh."[9]

"Allow me to say I was saddened to read of your father's death. I worked for him the better part of my life, and he was always good to me, just as you have been."

Van Lynden, who had begun taking the steps two at a time, halted. "You read of his death?"

"Yes. I received a letter, apparently mailed just before you were—" The old man went silent.

"Sentenced to prison," Van Lynden finished. The servant nodded, so he continued. "I worried that the whole sordid mess would be published in the papers here."

"Not that I ever saw, your lordship. I read the Edinburgh papers left at the local inn and the ones from London whenever my cousin sends a package. To my knowledge, it was not mentioned in either of them. I would never have known if not for your letter."

"If that is true, it is a stroke of luck. I have some goals that would be hard to achieve if my misfortunes were well-known in

England. As for prison, three years in that hellish place seemed more like thirty. Nonetheless, I never let them break me, and my solicitor was finally able to convince them that I had no part in the attempt to stop that ghastly treaty. When they set me free, those fools had no idea that I was the mastermind."

"I am sorry, your lordship, but my mind has been so addled that I do not recall the name of the treaty, much less the details."

"It was called *The Eight Articles of London*[10] when signed in July 1814. Then, in August, Viscount Castlereagh and Hendrik Fagel signed the formal treaty, which awarded our ancestral homeland to William I of the Netherlands. Moreover, it no longer permitted Dutch ships in the slave trade in British ports and extended restrictions on a ban on involvement in the slave trade by Dutch citizens. All of which put the nail in the coffin for my country and my livelihood."

"I...I had no idea."

Van Lynden had reached the front entrance by then, and, without stopping, he marched into the dimly-lit manor. Reaching to take the lantern from Lothar who came in behind him, he held it aloft. White muslin covered all the furnishings, casting large shadows on the walls. A thin layer of dust floated in the air, most likely dislodged by their footsteps.

"I found several ladies in the village willing to clean the master bedroom by promising payment as soon as you arrived. They washed and changed the bedding as well; so at least your rooms should be liveable."

"Thank you for accomplishing that with such little notice. Since the house is in such disrepair, if the women wish to continue working here, inform them they will be well compensated. I wish to hire enough servants to run the house, for I intend to make use of it until the purpose for my return is satisfied."

"Yes, my Lord."

"Wilhelm, just before I left England, I received word from you that my wife died. What happened to the girl?"

Wilhelm's eyes got large. "I...I do not rightly know."

Van Lynden's voice now reflected irritation. "What do you mean you do not know?"

"For several months before her death, Lady Van Lynden had me ship various crates to the Countess of Willingham's estate. On the day she died, I had taken a wagonload of crates into Gretna Green to meet a post coach. Upon my return, I discovered that she had passed. Still, it was not until the next morning that I realised that the nanny and the child were missing. I searched for them for several weeks, but it was almost as if they had vanished into thin air."

"Were the child's belongings shipped to her grandmother's estate as well?"

"I cannot say. Due to the circumstances, I was afraid to disturb anything; thus, I immediately locked all the family rooms."

"No one has entered them since?"

"No, sir. Not even to clean."

"When this happened, how many servants were left?"

"Only the cook, a maid and a footman, as well as Mrs. Graham, the housekeeper."

"Did you question them?"

"I did, but one and all denied any knowledge of what had happened to the two of them."

"Where is Mrs. Graham now?"

"She said she was going to live with her daughter."

"Do you know the daughter's name and where she lived?"

"I cannot recall for certain—Harrison, Harrington—something of that nature. And, if I remember correctly, she lived in London."

Lord Van Lynden sighed. "There is no time to dwell on these things tonight. Is it possible to heat some water so that I may wash off the dust of the road?"

"It is. I shall start a fire in the kitchen and put on some water.

Then I shall fetch a young man who still resides in one of the tenant houses. He helps me on occasion. I am certain he will be glad to carry the water upstairs to make a penny or two."

Van Lynden reached into his pocket, bringing out several coins. He handed them to the groundskeeper. "Keep the shillings, and pay the man whatever you think is fair. Tell him there is more where this came from, if he wants a steady job."

"Yes, my Lord!"

With that, Mr. Lothar departed. Left to himself, Van Lynden glanced about the house, and a scowl crossed his face.

Well, Margaret, have you managed to defy me even in death? It would be in your nature to send what I need to complete my task to your simple-minded mother. Van Lynden scratched his chin as he considered the possibilities. *I suppose if the moneybox is not upstairs, I shall have to make a trip to Eagleton Park.*

Shrugging in resignation, he began up the stairs, holding the lantern higher to light the way.

London
Cheapside
A warehouse

As Mr. Howton surveyed the motley group now assembling in the rented warehouse, he weighed for the hundredth time what price he might pay for cheating them of their share of the profits. Based on the fact that it was he who would have to sail from England or face prison, and each of them could carry on their lot as swindlers and thieves, he felt more than justified. Still, he was uncertain if any would pursue him in order to collect their share. Truth be told, he figured they would not have the means, even if they had the desire.

While he waited for the last man to arrive, an unbidden smile crossed his face as he reflected that, had the law suddenly appeared and arrested the lot, the majority of crime in Cheapside would cease immediately. His mirth was short-lived, however, for the straggler walked in, taking his place on one of the remaining crates, and Howton assumed a more sombre mien when he began to speak.

"Let me congratulate you on a job well done. We have contracts for most of the merchandise still here. Only sales of fabrics, household goods and blacksmith supplies are wanting, so please concentrate on finding buyers for these. I anticipate having all the payments in hand in just over a fortnight. This means you will be paid shortly thereafter. As in the past, I shall send a messenger when we are next to meet. At that point, all distributions will be made."

A burly man with stringy brown hair spit on the floor. "Since you are no longer going to need us, how do we know you will not take the money and leave?"

"Have I not always been very generous with you?" There were murmurs and nods of agreement. "Why would I suddenly change?" Then Howton's expression changed to a slight smile. "Besides, I am certain that one or more of you would track me down if I tried such a thing." His reply seemed to satisfy the men, for it produced a round of laugher.

"Now, remember to be careful. Mr. Darcy is suspicious and probably has men watching all the warehouses in this area. Make the transfers at night, and be certain that you can trust the merchants you are supplying."

After this word of warning, the meeting concluded, and everyone left but Howton and Carney. As Howton entered the office of the warehouse, Carney followed him.

"Do you need me to make another trip to Meryton or mail another letter?"

"No, Mr. Carney. I believe that our efforts alarmed Mr. Darcy well enough. My contact at Canfield Manor tells me that he was so frightened for Mrs. Bingley's sister that he took her to Pemberley when he returned. We may have put off his interference altogether."

"That is unfortunate, for I quite enjoyed dressing up in fancy clothes and acting the part of a gentleman's old friend. And I would have relished seeing that one sister again—the one married to the parson. I think that she liked me, for she gave me a sweater against the cold. Of course, that was before her husband asked me to leave."

"Get that idea completely out of your head! I do not need your presence in Meryton traced back to me."

"Whatever you say, gov'ner."

With that, Carney left the office, and Howton took a deep breath and let it go shakily. *I shall be so glad to be free of your kind, Mr. Carney!*

Chapter 11

Derbyshire
Matlock Manor

The party from Pemberley departed in ample time to arrive at the Matlock estate early on the afternoon of the ball. This was calculated to give the ladies plenty of time to rest before having to dress. Elizabeth had tried, yet again, to avoid attending, saying she did not wish to leave Emily. Yet even with William's insistence that Elizabeth's presence at Pemberley should be kept secret, Millicent would not hear of her staying behind. She argued that gossip had likely spread throughout Lambton already concerning Mr. Darcy's *guests,* and if Elizabeth was introduced as her good friend, it would leave little room for scandal or speculation. Not one to be thwarted, she had had her way in the end.

Richard had opted to ride his horse, leaving the seat next to William free, so the countess chose to sit beside him. This forced Elizabeth to watch as that lady whispered privately to him and patted his arm knowingly throughout the entire trip. If William seemed a bit put off by Millicent's actions—not smiling and rarely replying—Elizabeth felt certain it was only because he had an aversion to public displays of affection.

Once they arrived at the manor and were greeted by Lord and

Lady Matlock, they were immediately shown to their rooms. For Elizabeth, this meant occupying a bedroom next to the Countess of Markham in the family quarters because, as Lady Matlock explained, all the guest rooms were assigned to friends who were expected later. As Elizabeth took in the extravagance of her surroundings, she felt like a fish out of water. There was no doubt in her mind that Pemberley was just as luxurious, but it felt more like a home and less like a showplace. In fact, everything about Matlock Manor proclaimed status, and for a brief moment, she regretted not having accepted Millicent's kind offer to have her maid rework one of her gowns for the ball. Instead, Elizabeth maintained she would wear the one that Jane and Charles had gifted to her. Then, as usual, she came to her senses.

In truth, the ton would not approve of me even if I wore a gown of spun gold with the crown jewels.

After being confined to the room for almost an hour, Elizabeth was bored. Eager to explore the gardens she could see through the windows and after checking to be certain that no one was about, she slipped out of the room and hurried down a set of stairs at the far end of the hallway. She had hoped it would lead to the rear of the house, and fortuitously, it did. She was able to avoid everyone, including all the servants, save for one footman who stood at the rear entrance. He only nodded and opened the door as she approached. Relieved to have escaped discovery, she hurried down the gravel path of the garden until she felt secure among the large shrubs and trees that dominated one particular section.

The gardens were expertly laid out, and the farther she walked, the more the anxiety that had plagued her since leaving Pemberley began to dissipate. Happening upon a maze—a challenge she had always enjoyed—she entered it. Before long, she discovered that the path she had taken led to a large circular space featuring a tall, stone fountain. It was fashioned with a large bench where one could sit down; thus, Elizabeth took a seat and playfully ran her fingers through the water. Oblivious to any danger, she closed her eyes and took a deep breath of air.

"What luck finding you here! And entirely alone, at that."

Startled, Elizabeth jumped to her feet, her hand covering her heart, which by now was beating like a drum. A man having the same dark blond hair and brown eyes as Colonel Fitzwilliam stood at the entrance to the circle, arms crossed as though he was securing the only way out. Stouter and shorter than Richard and not nearly as handsome, Elizabeth knew instantly that it was the Viscount Leighton. Richard had mentioned his brother only once in her presence, but his disdain for the man had been clearly evident. Considering the viscount's present posture, she was beginning to understand why.

Gathering her courage, she stood as tall as possible. "Sir, you startled me. I did not realise you were following me."

His loud guffaw was even more intimidating. "So, you do not think I was merely taking the air and innocently happened upon you in here?"

"I do not."

Realising that, more than likely, she had heard Richard speak of his reputation, since his brother was currently staying at Pemberley, Leighton's eyes darkened, and he took a few steps forward. "I like a woman with passionate views, one not easily cowed."

"I am not intimidated by anyone, male or female, titled or no," Elizabeth declared more boldly than she felt. "Now, if you will excuse me, I will return to my room."

He stepped closer, his gaze now settling on her bosom. As Elizabeth's face crimsoned, he declared, "Come now, Mrs. Gardiner. You *are* Mrs. Gardiner, are you not? My mother has talked of nothing but you since she returned from confronting Darcy. Allow me to introduce myself properly, I am the Viscount Leighton."

The sound of twigs breaking underfoot caused both of them to look towards the opening of the maze where the Countess of Markham suddenly appeared.

"Ah, there you are, Mrs. Gardiner!" As she walked past Leighton, Millicent lifted her chin while simultaneously giving him a look of displeasure. "When I discovered that you were not in your room, I made it my duty to find you, my dear. We must start dressing for the ball if we are to be finished on time."

"The ball is not for hours, Countess," Leighton countered, his irritation evident. "There is no need to rush Mrs. Gardiner inside; she and I were just getting acquainted."

"In a secluded garden? I think you know better than that, naughty boy!" Millicent exclaimed as she began to escort Elizabeth away from the viscount. "You will have ample opportunity to get acquainted with Mrs. Gardiner at the ball."

The viscount chuckled as he watched his prey being led away. *You are a fool, my dear Millicent, if you think Darcy is not bedding that woman. That prig would never risk his reputation for someone so far beneath his station if she were not satisfying his lusts.*

He followed behind them from the maze, enjoying the movement of their hips as they walked. *Patience, old boy.*

The Ball

Elizabeth's first thought upon entering the ballroom was that she had neither seen so many people gathered for a ball, nor had she seen so vast a dance floor. The assemblies at Meryton were crowded, but only because the rooms were so small. Having never seen Pemberley's ballroom, she had no idea how it compared, but this room dwarfed Netherfield's, a ballroom she had considered extraordinarily large. In addition, every woman in attendance looked as though she had just stepped out of the pages of

La Belle Assemblée.[11]

Richard must have felt her tremble as she nervously clutched his arm, for he gave her a reassuring smile and then leaned close to say how lovely she looked. Appreciating the gesture, Elizabeth smiled warmly back at him, though in her heart, she wished it had been William offering the compliment. Looking about until she found that gentleman, she noted that he seemed oblivious to everything except Millicent, who stood beside him keeping up a steady conversation.

Having already endured many introductions by Lady Matlock, who repeatedly presented her as the Countess of Markham's dear friend, Elizabeth was thankful when the band finally struck a chord. Almost everyone assembled prepared to dance, including William and Millicent. As she watched the man she loved escort the countess to the dance floor, an unintentional sigh escaped. Richard, who had also been following that couple as well, heard and responded.

"Mrs. Gardiner, would you care to dance with a man who has two left feet?"

Elizabeth chuckled. "I see no such partner available, but I would love to dance with you."

Richard took her hand, and they advanced towards the dance floor. "Oh, you will see him soon enough!"

Elizabeth could not help laughing at his tease, and, as it happened, they passed William and Millicent on the dance floor that very second.

William's heart had almost stopped the very moment she descended the grand staircase wearing the same simple, yellow gown she had worn at Canfield Manor, the only change being the yellow roses interspersed in her silky, upswept hair. Wearing a single strand of pearls with matching earrings that Millicent had insisted she borrow, the effect was spellbinding. That effortless ensemble showcased Elizabeth's natural beauty, directly contrasting with those who wore copious amounts of jewels and elaborate gowns to gain notice.

Upon hearing Elizabeth's laugh and seeing her so relaxed on Richard's arm, William's heart ached. He had no grounds on which to object, for he could not think of an honourable way out of his agreement with Millicent, and, even if he could, he was not certain Elizabeth would welcome his pursuit. Thus, he agonised over her growing closeness to his cousin, as well as Millicent's rapidly changing posture. Since meeting Elizabeth, the countess had begun to cling to him whenever they were in company, especially Elizabeth's company. This brought to mind someone he had always loathed: Caroline Bingley.

"Fitzwilliam," Millicent said for the second time. When he still did not answer, she said more loudly, "Fitzwilliam!"

Having circled yet another couple, as dictated by the dance, Millicent's voice finally snapped him from his reverie. Wondering if he had made a misstep, he sputtered, "Yes...yes?"

"Obviously your mind is occupied elsewhere. If I were not certain, I would think you were counting the steps, though I know perfectly well that you could perform this dance in your sleep."

"I beg your pardon. I was wool-gathering. I have a lot on my mind."

Taking his hand, Millicent drew him towards the French doors. "Come. Let us take the night air. It may help to clear your head."

Obediently, William let her lead him onto the terrace, where he lifted his head to the starry sky, closed his eyes and took a deep breath.

"Is that better?" He nodded, though his eyes stayed closed. "Now that we are alone, I have a question to ask."

William's eyes flew open, and he cringed while awaiting the

question.

"What do you think of your aunt's suggestion?"

"Suggestion?"

"That we announce our engagement."

"As I remember, it was your proposition that we take a year to decide if marriage is what we truly want."

"Not exactly. I knew all along what I wanted, but I thought it best that you wait a year to make sure that you knew your heart."

"And now you think I should decide immediately?"

"Only if it would deter a scandal."

"Have you any evidence that a scandal is brewing?"

"No. It is just—"

William interrupted. "I am much too busy handling Charles' affairs to give proper attention to all the social aspects of an engagement, should we decide in favour of one. For now, I think it best we keep to our original plan."

"I suppose you are right."

"I am." With that, William took another deep breath and let it go slowly. "We had best return. I want to keep an eye on Leighton, for he fancies that all widows are fair game, and that will include Mrs. Gardiner."

Millicent had kept secret Elizabeth's earlier encounter with Leighton, fearing William might confront him before the ball. Given his current frame of mind, she felt certain she had chosen the right course. Even if afterwards she suffered his wrath for not disclosing the incident sooner, the ball could proceed without disruption.

As these things were going through her mind, William offered her his arm. Gladly wrapping hers around it, she smiled up at him as though she had not a care in the world.

A good while later, after having danced with Richard, Lord

Matlock and several of the Matlocks' acquaintances, Elizabeth found herself observing while others danced. Standing next to Lady Grambling, one of Lady Matlock's friends, she noted that William and Millicent were talking with a couple on the other side of the ballroom while Richard was on the dance floor with his mother. Grateful to sit out this set and not have to make small talk, Elizabeth found herself under a steady barrage of questions from Lady Grambling. She managed to answer most of the queries so vaguely as to render them ineffective, but she was no longer willing to suffer her interrogation.

"Please excuse me, Lady Grambling. I see someone that I know from Hertfordshire, and I wish to greet them."

Immediately disappearing into the crowd, Elizabeth headed in the direction of one of the entrances to the ballroom. Noticing a small alcove to one side that was filled with several tall, potted plants, she decided that would be a good place to survey the room without being observed. Fatefully, as she headed towards the alcove, Viscount Leighton caught sight of her. Full of brandy and bravado after several rounds of cards, he had left a group of willing admirers specifically to look for Elizabeth. Now stalking her, he almost ran into the Countess of Markham, who was waiting for William to return with a cup of punch.

Unable to resist taunting her, he leaned in to whisper in her ear. "I always believed you were one of the few women of the *ton* with some intelligence." Millicent silently lifted her nose in disdain. "But it is apparent that you believe Darcy is not sharing his bed with Mrs. Gardiner, which proves you are as dim-witted as the rest."

"You are a drunken fool!" the countess hissed through clenched teeth.

"I may be in my cups, but I am no fool! Nor am I blind, like you. If you wish to know the truth, keep a close eye on Darcy."

The viscount walked away, leaving Millicent fuming and

fighting a scowl as she glanced around. Having Elizabeth at the ball was supposed to squash any rumours that Fitzwilliam was interested in her, and Millicent was not about to let the *ton* think she was remotely worried.

Leighton sidled up to Elizabeth from between two large planters. "Mrs. Gardiner, what a shame that we have both been so busy that we have not had time to share a dance."

Jumping at the sound of his voice, immediately Elizabeth's stomach began to churn. "Once again you have managed to startle me, sir. Do you make it a habit to creep up on people?"

"Perhaps if you were not so elusive, I would not have to act so stealthily. Now, as I was saying, we have not shared a dance, and I would like to rectify that." He bowed with great finesse. "May I have this dance?"

Elizabeth wished to decline, but knew that was out of the question. After all, the ball was in his honour and refusing her hosts' son would be taken as an insult, not to mention that she would have to refuse all future dances.

"Of course."

Lamentably, the minuet, quadrille and cotillion had already been featured, so the band began to play a waltz. Though her skin crawled at the thought of dancing in such close proximity to the viscount, there was no going back.

"What luck!" Leighton declared as he escorted her to the floor. "Waltzes provide a more intimate opportunity to get to know one another." Once he had halted, he pulled her as close as possible. "Do you not agree?"

Trying to resist his iron grip was impossible, and Leighton began to twirl Elizabeth about the dance floor. That, in addition to the liquor on his breath, turned her stomach. Refusing to look at him, she fixed her gaze somewhere over his shoulder.

"It is not necessary that we know each other. I am to return to my sister's estate very soon, and I dare say we shall never meet again," Elizabeth managed to say.

The viscount laughed scornfully. "Do not count on it, Mrs. Gardiner. I am determined to know you more intimately, even if I must go to the ends of the earth in order to find you."

Infuriated, Elizabeth repeated something she had overheard Richard tell William. "Just as you travelled to Ireland in pursuit of your last conquest? You will only be wasting your time."

The viscount's steps slowed as his mien darkened. He hissed under his breath, "Are you so dull as to think that because you are my cousin's whore he will marry you? Once that self-righteous fool and the Countess of Markham marry—and mark my words, they will—he will toss you aside like a filthy rag. When that happens, I may well be the only man in England who can keep you in the same style as Darcy. Think about that before you speak so conceitedly!"

Elizabeth stopped, jerked her hand from his grip and stepped back. "You are not only inebriated, you are delusional."

As she walked away, the viscount's expression grew fearsome. Fearing someone had witnessed his humiliation, sniggers nearby reinforced his mortification. Thoroughly embarrassed, he waited until Elizabeth had passed through the doors to the terrace before starting after her.

William, cup of punch in hand, was threading his way back to Millicent through the crowded assembly when he caught sight of Elizabeth's argument with Leighton. Earlier he had made certain that the cad was in the card room and had assumed that he was still there. Cursing under his breath for not keeping a better watch over Elizabeth, when she exited the ballroom with the viscount following, William knew he must act fast.

On his way to the French doors, he handed the cup of punch to the first lady he encountered. "Here is the punch you requested, madam."

That lady, a recent debutant, thanked William profusely. Nonetheless, he was already out of the ballroom by the time she realised that he was not going to slow down. Reaching the terrace, he ran down the steps to the gravel path. With no glimpse of either his love or his cousin, William's heart began to race, and he picked up his pace. He had gone approximately one hundred yards when the path divided. Hearing a noise to the right, he rushed in that direction. Rounding a curve, he caught sight of Leighton. He had Elizabeth by an arm and was pulling her inside a large, white gazebo. Though she fought valiantly, he was able to accomplish his task and immediately pressed her against one of the structure's posts to forcibly kiss her.

"Let her go, Leighton!" William shouted as he closed in.

Caught up in his assault, Leighton suddenly found himself jerked around to face William. With no time to react, a rock-solid fist immediately connected with his jaw, and he fell backwards, his head hitting the floor with a sickening thud. Seeing that he was not going to fight, William was quickly at Elizabeth's side. Holding to the post and trembling like a leaf, silent tears had begun down her cheeks.

William settled for gently touching her hair. "Do not cry, Elizabeth," he whispered. "He shall never touch you again; I swear it on my life."

Inexplicably, Elizabeth turned into his embrace, and, unable to resist, William enveloped her in his arms. He felt her shoulders shaking as the tears increased, and he rocked her, soothing, "All is well, dearest. All is well."

Out of nowhere, Richard appeared. He had been observing the dance when he saw Darcy abandon the cup of punch and stride purposely from the room. Knowing how easily the relationship between his cousin and his brother could ignite, he presumed Leighton was the motivation. Providentially, he had arrived in time to see William throw the first and only punch. Giving the loving couple a moment's privacy, he stooped to check on his sibling.

"It seems you still possess a deadly right hook, Cousin. He is unconscious."

Elizabeth was drying her tears on a handkerchief that William had produced from his pocket when Richard addressed her. "Mrs. Gardiner, please allow me to apologise for my brother's behaviour. I know my apology cannot erase his cruelty, but I am very sorry."

Elizabeth nodded, dabbing at her eyes. "You are not to blame, Colonel. I...I believe the fact he had too much to drink is mainly at fault."

"Unfortunately, I cannot agree. My brother has rarely been held accountable for his actions, and that is the basis for his lack of moral fibre."

William stepped forward. "Let us get Leighton out of here before someone comes along."

"If you will throw him over my shoulder, I will take him into the house through the back entrance. I doubt he will awaken until morning, but I shall post a guard to alert me if he should."

As William began to assist, Richard said to Elizabeth, "I suggest that you return to the ball as soon as possible."

As the colonel disappeared into the darkness, William once more fixed his eyes on the woman he loved. Desiring nothing more than to gather Elizabeth in his arms again, he fought that temptation in order to encourage her spirits. For, in spite of all that had happened, it was imperative that she return to the ball.

Lifting her chin with two fingers so that their eyes met, he offered her a slight smile. Praying that she could read in his eyes how he felt about her, he murmured, "The Elizabeth Bennet that

I met in Meryton once said that her courage always rose with every attempt to intimidate her."

She could not help but smile at his quote. "I fear that *that* Miss Bennet may have been exaggerating."

"I do not believe that for a second. I believe that she is a very courageous woman who can overcome anything, if she puts her mind to it."

With that, she smiled wholeheartedly. Having accomplished his goal, William grew sombre again, taking both of her hands in his. "Elizabeth, when we return to Pemberley, you and I need to talk." Seeing her ebony eyes fill with apprehension, he hurried to explain. "There is absolutely nothing to fear. It is just that I need to—"

Suddenly, Millicent walked up the steps to the gazebo, causing William to let go of Elizabeth's hands and step back.

"Elizabeth!" she exclaimed. "When I realised that you were not in the house, I hastened to the gardens in hopes of finding you here. Are you well? You look as though you have seen a ghost."

William answered for her. "Elizabeth is well. Being drunk, as is his usual wont, Leighton tried to assault her. Richard and I stepped in to stop him, and at present he is being carried to his room, unconscious."

"What in the world will the Matlocks say when they hear of this?"

"I shall tell my aunt and uncle the truth. As for the guests, since the house is bursting at the seams, I doubt many will miss Leighton. Most likely they will think that he is simply in another room. Now, would you be so kind as to accompany Elizabeth back to the ball? I mean to check on Leighton to be certain he does not disturb anyone else."

"Of course," Millicent said, wrapping an arm around Elizabeth's waist. "You poor thing! Let us go back inside before the gossips empty the ballroom to search for both of us."

Millicent's presence in the garden was not happenstance. Though she knew Leighton was in his cups, she could not dismiss his taunts about Fitzwilliam's feelings for Elizabeth. Nor could she look away from the drama that played out right before her eyes shortly thereafter. For, just as the viscount had predicted, Fitzwilliam looked every inch the jealous lover as he pursued Elizabeth and Leighton from the ballroom. She had trailed after him, taking care to avoid the areas lit by torches, and had been able to disappear into the darkness near the gazebo.

Exceedingly worried after seeing the fury in Fitzwilliam's eyes as he followed Leighton from the ballroom and the devotion he displayed when he comforted Elizabeth, still she told herself that he was only being compassionate. After all, Elizabeth was under his protection and would be as long as he was obligated to Bingley. Clinging to that notion, she held her head high for the balance of the evening.

As for the viscount, William had been correct. The party was so large that he was not missed, save by several of the gaming crowd to whom he owed money and by his parents. Consequently, the soirée held for the honourable Viscount Leighton went down in the annals of society as a roaring success. That is, if one overlooked the black eye and bruised cheek the honouree sported for the next several weeks or the fact that he refused to leave his rooms until the party from Pemberley had departed the premises the next morning.

Chapter 12

Surrey
Eagleton Park

The trip from Scotland to Eagleton Park had been long and arduous for that august estate was reachable only by less travelled roads and some that were no longer well maintained. If there was a positive side to Lord Van Lynden's visit, it was that he learned that his late wife's father had died six months earlier and her mother shortly afterward. This left the estate in the hands of a distant cousin, a young man of four and twenty who had previously resided in Ireland. Fortuitously, the new earl had no knowledge of the animosity that characterised his relationship with Margaret's parents and had no reason to mistrust him. Thus, Van Lynden had no trouble regaling him with a revised version of history.

"Let me see if I understand," Lord Willingham said. "You contend that your father's death is the reason you have been away all these years."

"In part. My late father, Baron Johan Van Lynden, was taken ill when he returned to Rotterdam on business. He was a diplomat when he met and married my mother and decided to reside here once his diplomatic mission was complete. This necessitated his travelling to and from Rotterdam quite often to manage his shipping business, and he was there when he took ill."

"Your father was a baron? Then you are now Baron Van Lynden?"

"No. My father was the last to hold the title. Our lands were forfeited in the various treaties formed with Germany, France and the Netherlands in the last few years, and the title disappeared along with our property."

"I see. Was any of your family with your father when he died?"

"No. I was his only child, and my mother died when I was twenty. You may have heard of her, Lady Martha Turnbull? She was the only child of the Earl of Chesterfield."

"Of course," Lord Willingham said. In truth, he knew very little about the English aristocracy.

"In any event, I rushed to the continent to be with Father when he became ill. Unfortunately, having always been an outspoken proponent of South Holland's independence, once I set foot in Rotterdam, I was arrested and not allowed to see my father before he died. I was held as a political prisoner without a trial. It was only in the last month that my solicitor managed to clear me of all charges, and I was released."

"What a horrible ordeal! Not only to be held without trial, but to miss your father's last days and return to England to discover that your wife is dead and your daughter missing."

"And Lord and Lady Willingham also died in my absence." Van Lynden hoped his artificial expression of sadness looked convincing. "I was very fond of them. Save for the fact that I have a son who needs me, I might not have survived the shock."

"Where is your son?"

"He is still in Holland, safe amongst my relations. I hope to be reunited with him once I find my daughter, Ingrid."

Apparently impressed with the man and his quest for answers, the new Earl of Willingham gave him permission to inspect some crates that the housekeeper said had been shipped from Scotland shortly before his cousin Margaret's passing. The servant maintained that her master had expected his daughter's imminent return; thus, he had the crates taken directly to the attic upon their arrival to await her inspection. Later, after word of his only child's death and granddaughter's disappearance, he and Lady Willingham had been too sick and distraught to bother with them. Thus, they remained in the attic intact.

When he began going through the crates, Van Lynden was optimistic. Yet his efforts proved futile, for the contents consisted mainly of Margaret's personal items, family heirlooms and a small portrait of Nicolas, which he seized. One crate actually held a few children's clothes, clearly those outgrown by Nicolas, and several toys. However, the money box[12] that he secretly sought was not amongst the contents. Frustrated, he enquired if the housekeeper or butler had any knowledge of the children's nanny, a woman he believed had absconded with his daughter. They pleaded ignorance, and when he boarded his coach for the trip back to London, Van Lynden was no wiser than when he had arrived.

Watching the coach slip out of sight down the lengthy drive in front of the manor, Mr. Adcock and Mrs. Kennedy stayed on the portico long after their new master had gone inside.

Looking about furtively, the butler said, "Do you think that blackguard will find the little girl, Mrs. Kennedy?"

Hand shading her eyes against the sun, the housekeeper answered without bothering to turn to address him. "I pray he does not, for the child's sake as well as Miss Bennet's."

"I have often wondered if the child is still with her," Adcock said. "After all, it takes courage for a single woman to raise a child, much less one not of her own flesh. She could easily have given her to a couple who had no—"

"I believe Miss Bennet had the courage," Mrs. Kennedy interrupted, irritated at her colleague's insinuation. "The letter I read was written by a woman with conviction. I am just thankful you and I went through the crates after Lord Willingham died. Otherwise we would not have discovered the missive, nor would the mistress have known before her passing that her beloved granddaughter was not only safe, but being reared by a good and decent woman."

"And Van Lynden would have found the letter," Mr. Adcock added. "Still, men like him, those with resources that you and I can only dream about, have ways of discovering things. They can hire investigators. I cannot help but worry what could happen should he locate them."

"On her deathbed Lady Willingham asked me to pray that Van Lynden never set foot on English soil again. I am relieved she is not here to see this day."

As the coach passed entirely out of sight, the two servants went back inside, silently vowing to pray even harder for Lady Willingham's grandchild and the woman who had taken her into her heart.

Accompanying Van Lynden on this trip was one of his cohorts in the original plot to undermine the treaty between England and the Netherlands—John Guthrie, a fashionable Londoner of six and twenty. Guthrie fancied himself an anarchist, when, in fact, he was a ne'er-do-well who used his late father's fortune to dabble in such pursuits after his mother grew too ill to notice or object. It had been easy for Van Lynden to locate Guthrie on his way through London, for that gentleman still resided in Mayfair. Moreover, he knew just where to find the other men involved in the 1814 plot—Klaus Jansen, Peter Visser and Jann Bakker, all of whom were Van Lynden's compatriots. Each held a low-paying position as a master of music or art and, being strapped for cash, was eager to join another scheme to kill Viscount Castlereagh. Not only did they despise the viscount for ending South Holland's bid for independence, but getting paid well to ensure his demise meant they could leave behind their tedious occupations and return to their homeland as wealthy men.

Acting the part of his friend's valet while at Eagleton Park, Guthrie had to keep his opinions to himself; however, now that they were alone, his frustrations poured out.

"What rotten luck to come this far without finding the moneybox or learning anything about the nanny! Let us hope our friends in London had better luck in locating Mrs. Graham."

Face set like flint, Lord Van Lynden continued to stare out the window as he answered Guthrie's outburst. "Never doubt we shall find both the nanny and the box. It is just a matter of time."

Secretly, Van Lynden was not overly confident. When his original scheme to kill Castlereagh had been aborted by that man's sudden departure for France and his father's subsequent death, he had thoughtlessly stuffed his plans for the attack into a ceramic money box given as a gift to his youngest child, fully intending to carry out the deed later with said information. It was only after his departure from England that he realised the peril of someone else opening the box. As it was, that item held a small drawing of the configuration of Castlereagh's townhouse in London and a key, both provided by a disgruntled servant. In addition, the names and addresses of all involved in the original plot were listed on the back of the drawing. Potentially incriminating if it fell into the right hands, Van Lynden was determined to get it back.

Matlock Manor
Lord Matlock's study
The morning after the ball

As the men entered the study, the atmosphere there grew tense. Leighton's lack of self-control infuriated everyone. Darcy especially seemed to have had his fill of his cousin's behaviour.

As a rule, Lord Matlock never drank before noon, but today seemed just the occasion to ignore that principle. Heading straight to the liquor cabinet in the corner, he tried to recall the arguments he had formulated last night to calm Fitzwilliam. Unfortunately, his mind went blank.

"Brandy, anyone?" he asked, pouring the caramel-coloured liquor into a glass.

Both Richard and William declined, instead heading directly to the chairs in front of the earl's desk. Meanwhile, Lord Matlock crossed the room, drink in hand, and had no more than taken his seat behind the large mahogany desk than William began to speak.

"Uncle, I have neither the time nor the patience for small talk this morning. I shall get straight to the point. I had hoped it would not come to this, but apparently Leighton did not believe I meant what I said after he disparaged Georgiana's husband at her wedding. I will no longer suffer him attacking or demeaning members of my family or those under my protection. He leaves me no choice but to issue a challenge as soon as he recovers from his present stupor."

Lord Matlock glanced to Richard, pleading for help with his eyes. "I realise Leighton was out of control last evening. Still, I believe I can make him listen to reason."

"You have not been successful in the past."

"I have never had to step in decisively. What's more, you know your superior skill with sword and pistol would render him defenceless in a duel."

"Like the women he molests?"

The earl studied the top of his desk. "I will not defend his actions; he behaved like a barbarian." He met William's eyes. "Still, he is my son, and it is my duty to make him see reason. Besides, the law is clear concerning duels. Your aunt and I could not bear to see you prosecuted as a result of his appalling behaviour—no more than we wish to see our son killed."

"I would gladly suffer prosecution to save another woman from his brutality."

"Your selflessness is admirable, but I do not believe anyone has to be killed or prosecuted."

"Remember this," Richard said, "if you kill my conniving brother in a duel, the reason you took action will stand a greater chance of becoming common knowledge. Do you want to risk bringing Mrs. Gardiner's name into a scandal of that magnitude?"

Richard's logic cut through William's resolve. "Very well!" he exclaimed, angrily coming to his feet. "But I leave it to you, Uncle, to make certain Leighton understands that the next time he touches or dares to insult Mrs. Gardiner, he will find himself facing me across a field of honour. I shall not hesitate again for any reason."

"I will see that he understands," Lord Matlock replied solemnly.

After William walked stiffly out of his study, the earl dropped his head in his hands and began to rub his eyes. Then, looking up, he addressed Richard. "While I do not condone Leighton's actions, I cannot understand why Fitzwilliam feels obligated to defend the honour of Mrs. Gardiner."

"Surely you know Mrs. Gardiner is under his protection until Bingley returns from Spain."

"I had forgotten. Still, Fitzwilliam will spread his chivalry too thin if he is not careful. In any case, I am relieved he conceded this time, and I am determined to do all in my power to rein in your brother—for society's sake, as well as his own."

"And just how do you plan to do that? Leighton has kept his own counsel for many years now."

"Yes, and he may decide to continue. However, your mother and I have the power to decide whether he inherits a large, thriving estate or one that is greatly reduced. Moreover, for the present, I intend to trim his allowance until it barely covers the necessities."

Richard chuckled. "Not having the money to fund his lavish way of life would hamper his ability to impress the ladies."

"That is not my concern. He should have married years ago. Perhaps this will force him to grow up, and he will find a decent woman and make her an offer."

"One can always hope."

"I have not said anything to you before, but last year I amended my will. You will now solely inherit all of your mother's assets—your grandmother's estate in Essex and the one in Scotland, which belonged to your great-grandmother, in addition to her dowry and all wealth she brought into the marriage. I am also gifting you the estate in Wales, which my uncle left to me. It is not as grand an estate as Matlock, but it makes a tidy profit each year."

Richard looked stunned. "I do not know what to say."

Lord Matlock patted his son's shoulder. "Say nothing, Richard. You deserve it. You have always displayed a sense of responsibility and duty that has made both your mother and me proud." Then he sighed. "Should Leighton defy me and keep to his present behaviour, we may covertly transfer more bonds and stocks to her estate. There is a good chance that if your brother does not conform, he will inherit Matlock Manor and the house in London, only to discover he lacks the funds to run them."

"Matlock Manor could be lost?"

"No. If Leighton cannot maintain either property, he must first give you the opportunity to purchase them for a fair price, established by our solicitors and with the counsel of your mother. And, make no mistake—you will have the funds with which to do so, though you may have to sell the smaller estates in your power."

Richard let go with a long whistle. "I have no desire to usurp Leighton's role in the family, but I would like to see him change. He would be a fool to keep to his present course with such dire prospects hanging over his head."

"Let us pray he listens before it is too late," Lord Matlock said. Then, his expression softened, and he slapped Richard on the back as they began towards the door. "You had better hurry. As eager as Fitzwilliam is to get as far away from here as possible, he may leave without you."

"That is not possible! I told Darcy's driver not to leave until I gave him permission, or he would answer to me personally once I returned to Pemberley."

Chuckling, the two exited the study and went in the direction of the foyer. There, Elizabeth and William stood next to each other, strangely quiet, while Millicent and Lady Matlock conversed about the latter's next ball, which she was planning for London.

As they approached the others, Richard gave his father a surreptitious wink. "I feared you might have left me behind, Cousin."

"I might have," William huffed, clearly agitated, "had not Mr. Cleary noticed the traces were twisted. He is seeing to them now, though I do not know why he did not notice before he brought the coach around."

"A shame," Richard said solemnly. "One simply cannot find expert help these days."

No one noticed the earl struggle not to laugh, for by chance, Lady Matlock resumed her conversation with Millicent, and being hard of hearing, she commanded everyone's attention.

A misting rain fell steadily, so Richard rode in the coach instead of astride his stallion. He took the seat next to his cousin, which left Millicent no option but to sit across from the men. This, and the fact that she was beginning to question William's feelings for Bingley's sister, curtailed her usual talkative nature. Elizabeth was quiet, too, for she was lost in the memory of being in William's embrace and contemplations of what he meant by saying they had to talk. For a while the colonel attempted to cheer everyone with small talk, though no one seemed remotely interested in furthering the conversation, least of all William. Unbeknownst to the ladies, that gentleman's sullen expression and behaviour was a result of the meeting just concluded with Lord Matlock.

Due to the deafening silence, Millicent and Elizabeth each settled into a corner of the coach, closed their eyes and tried to nap. Richard and William stared aimlessly out opposite windows; though, before long, William's attention was drawn back to the women. Covertly studying them in earnest, he pondered what drew him to Elizabeth but not to Millicent.

Millicent, tall and slender with dark red hair and green eyes, had a typical Irish complexion and a straight, patrician nose. Although no longer a debutant, she was still so handsome she often attracted more attention in a ballroom than the current year's collection. From childhood she had been schooled in the management of an estate and the rules of the *ton*, and, for the most part, she followed those rules staunchly, never acting impulsively. Though she had a sense of humour, she was mostly predisposed to a serious air.

Elizabeth was the opposite—petite and voluptuous with almost black hair and eyes and a ready smile. Her complexion was rosy and included a sprinkling of light freckles across her small, upturned nose—a result of not following the edict that all proper ladies were supposed to wear bonnets. As if to emphasize her opinion on the matter, as soon as the coach began down the drive at Matlock Manor, Elizabeth had immediately removed the bonnet she had donned solely in regard for the Matlocks and was now bareheaded. William understood she was not flaunting tradition merely to be disagreeable, for once in Meryton he had heard her say that she was determined 'to act in that manner which will, in my own opinion, constitute my happiness.' It was an attitude he secretly found refreshing.

As these thoughts swirled in his head, the answer became suddenly clear. Not only had Elizabeth captured his heart, but her own *joie de vivre* had awakened something in him which he once feared lost forever—the sheer joy of being alive. The thought of losing her a second time caused his heart to burn in his chest, and he immediately began to plan how to tell Millicent she had been correct. Though he had always denied it, Elizabeth had owned his heart since the summer of 1812.

Having decided on a course of action, William was very pleased when they reached Pemberley while it was still daylight. Thinking of nothing save clearing up any misunderstandings between him and Elizabeth before either went to sleep, he was all anticipation by the time he stepped from the coach and helped Elizabeth to the ground. Little did he know that finding time to speak to her before she retired would not be as easy as he had hoped.

Chapter 13

Pemberley

If William had known the many trials that awaited him at Pemberley, he might have reconsidered having his driver urge the horses to get home early. From the instant he exited the coach, Mrs. Reynolds, Mr. Walker and his steward, Mr. Sturgis, all requested a conference as soon as possible—even before he had washed the dust off or changed clothes.

Mrs. Reynolds wished to inform him that she had just dismissed a popular maid and a footman, who had been caught together in a compromising situation. William had only to reassure her that he supported the decision, before she returned to her duties. Mr. Walker wished to request immediate time off to travel to Liverpool in order to see to his brother, who had been hurt in an accident. His appeal was handled swiftly, with William granting Walker all the time off that he felt he needed, with pay.

Mr. Sturgis' issue was not as easily settled. It involved a dispute between two tenants, each of whom claimed ownership of a calf. The disagreement came about because both had cows that gave birth on the same day in a common pasture. Sadly, one of the calves died shortly after birth, leaving one tenant to accuse the other of substituting the dead animal for his. Their dispute swiftly progressed to fisticuffs, frightening not only their families, but the surrounding tenants, as well. Sturgis had warned them twice that Mr. Darcy would not tolerate such behaviour, but tempers still ran high, and they had another argument that morning. Thus, knowing his master was to return that day, the steward had required both men to come to the manor house. Having been kept waiting for hours by the time the coach pulled to a stop, William felt duty-bound to hear their case straightaway, and he resolved the dispute by donating a calf to replace the one that died. Still, by the time all was settled, William had just enough time to bathe and dress before dinner.

Later, when Elizabeth entered the dining room in an unadorned but stunning blue sateen gown—another gift from Jane—William's patience was put to the test. She looked so lovely that it reinforced his desire to speak to her that day. Still, it soon became apparent that, with the exception of Lady Foggett, who had remained at Pemberley with the children, everyone was weary from the trip. That fact permitted Millicent's opinionated aunt to carry most of the conversation throughout dinner, a feat she had no difficulty accomplishing.

Afterward, in a bid to keep everyone from retiring, William asked Millicent to exhibit on the pianoforte. She declined the request, saying she was too weary and wished to retire straightaway; thus, his plan to speak to Elizabeth whilst the others were distracted by the music was thwarted. Lady Foggett, Elizabeth and even Richard followed Millicent's lead and went directly to bed after they finished eating, leaving William staring at a sea of empty chairs.

Not surprisingly, midnight found William unable to sleep. Sitting on the balcony outside his bedroom, clad in nothing but an unbuttoned shirt and breeches, he was finishing off the last of a bottle of French brandy under a full moon which bathed Pemberley in a light akin to dawn. Despite the current tranquillity, William noted that dark clouds were gathering in the distance, signalling an approaching storm. So far, he had managed to keep thoughts of Elizabeth at bay by watching several cats on the yard below who were hunting prizes only they could see. Nonetheless, the second the animals ran out of sight, Elizabeth consumed his thoughts once again, stirring his blood in a less than gentlemanly manner. Having exceeded his self-imposed limit on alcohol, which undermined his struggle against the yearnings of his heart, he reluctantly capped the decanter and set it back on a table. Then, leaning back in the oversized chair, he lifted his bare feet to rest on the top rail and closed his eyes. It took less than a minute to realise that the only way to occupy his mind was to immerse himself in a book. Moreover, a sudden burst of wind made it clear it was time to vacate the balcony.

Standing, he was turning to leave when he caught sight of a speck of white through the trees. Steadfastly focusing on the object until a stronger gust shifted the limbs impeding his view, he was rewarded by the sight of a woman in a white gown on a nearby balcony. Quickly calculating the number of balconies between his and the one in question, William's heart soared to realise it had to be Elizabeth. Without waiting, he rushed through his bedroom to the door that led into the hallway.

Opening it as silently as possible, he glanced both ways. Seeing no one about, he rushed to the door of the room that divided Emily's bedroom from her mother's. With another quick glance to either side, he tried the knob and was relieved to feel it turn in his hand. With his heart beating like a drum, he stepped inside. A lone candle burning on a shelf illuminated the space, and through the window he could see Elizabeth standing by the balcony railing with her back to him. Throwing caution to the wind, he entered her bedroom and crossed to the French doors that opened onto the balcony. The sight of the wind tossing her long ebony locks about instantly immobilised him. Elizabeth must have sensed his presence, for she turned to face him.

Wearing only a lace shawl over a thin, silk nightgown, she immediately covered her neck and shoulders with the wrap. Still, she could not stop herself from shyly taking in William's state of undress. Her eyes travelled slowly from his bare throat to the fine, dark hair that covered his powerfully built chest and abdomen, and still further to where it disappeared inside his breeches. The inspection ignited an unfamiliar fire within, and Elizabeth found herself willing her knees not to buckle.

William stepped forward. "Please, do not be frightened, Elizabeth."

"I...I could never be frightened of you. If it appeared so, it is simply because I was just praying that—" Her words stopped mid-sentence.

William stepped closer. "You were praying?"

"I was praying—" Struggling to continue without crying, she took a ragged breath. Her next words were barely audible. "That, if it be God's will for you to marry the countess, He would help me to conquer my feelings, for I have loved none but you."

William briefly closed his eyes before rushing forward to draw Elizabeth into his embrace. Laying his head atop hers, he murmured, "My dearest love, do you have any idea how I have hungered to hear you say those words?"

Clasping her more tightly, he placed two brief kisses in her lavender scented hair. "What fools we have been, you and I. We could have been married all this time."

"But...but, what of Millicent?" Elizabeth asked, pulling back to look into his eyes. "It is obvious that she is in love with you, and I know in my heart that you care for her."

"I do care for Millicent, but only as a cherished friend."

"Yet clearly she is here because she has expectations of marriage."

"If you promise to listen and not hate me afterward, I shall try to explain."

"I vowed to hate you once before, and it proved impossible." Elizabeth's eyes softened as she lovingly smoothed a strand of silver-tinged hair from his forehead. "No matter what you tell me, I shall never stop loving you."

With a hopeful smile, he began. "When we parted at Kent, it was as though the door to my heart had slammed shut. I was certain then I would spend the remainder of my life alone, and I buried myself in my duties. It was only after my sister became engaged that I began to once again consider marriage. I had long wished to have a child—an heir. With Henry's sudden death, Millicent was in need of a father for Hugh and Kathy, and it made perfect sense that we should marry, for we have known each other all our lives. She refused my offer many times, saying she believed the source of my misery was unrequited love. Consequently, just before I went to Canfield Manor, she and I entered into an agreement. We vowed to spend more time in each other's company for a period of a year, which she felt would give me time to determine if I truly wished to marry her."

"I see," Elizabeth responded, her voice trembling slightly. "May I ask when you changed your mind?"

"It was after you came with me to Pemberley. Just being in your presence again proved conclusively what Millicent had wisely tried to make me understand—that I love her, but I am not *in love* with her. I am in love with you. I have been all these years."

Her eyes grew shiny with fresh tears as he gently ran two fingers along her perfect jaw before lifting her chin. "I thank God that He sent you back to me," he whispered. "You are the only woman I have ever desired." Brushing a soft kiss across her lips, he added, "I have loved only you."

He captured her mouth again, this kiss quickly intensifying from innocent to torrid as she began to respond passionately. And once her delicate fingers slid up his naked chest to loop behind his neck and entwine in his hair, the last of William's vaunted control fragmented. Urging her lips to open, his tongue slipped inside, finding and teasing her own. Tightening his embrace, one hand threaded into her silky, dark hair, whilst the other slid down to press her hips to his.

A strangled moan escaped Elizabeth's throat, bringing William back to his senses. Quitting the kiss, leaving them both breathless, William smiled sheepishly. "Forgive me, my darling. Your kisses make me forget everything that I hold dear."

Pulling her back into his arms, he was content just to hold her. After a short while, Elizabeth murmured, "I pray that Millicent will understand that neither of us meant to hurt her."

"In her heart, she will know this is for the best. After having known the love of a man like Henry, who adored her, she would have been wounded that I could not offer her the same devotion."

"When will you tell her?"

"I cannot go through another day acting as though I do not love you. As observant as Millicent is, she will likely know what I plan to say before I begin. She has always known me better than I know myself."

Elizabeth's expression became serious. She reached up to caress his face. "I long to know you just as intimately, William."

"And so you shall," he replied hoarsely, following this pronouncement with another ardent kiss.

The kiss soon became as volatile as the one previously, and it took all of Elizabeth's strength to pull away. "I am at your mercy, my love; your kisses leave me powerless."

William stepped back, offering her a tortured smile. "In the morning I shall explain to Millicent that I love you. Then our engagement will be announced—a *very* short engagement. We shall be man and wife before a fortnight has passed."

"So soon?"

A slight smirk crossed his face. "If tonight is any indication, it may not be soon enough."

Elizabeth blushed, but did not reply. Immediately William became circumspect, smoothing some ringlets from her face, whilst staring at her so intently that she felt her face crimson once more. Just as she was about to speak, he drew a blue ribbon from her unkempt hair and placed a demure kiss on her forehead.

"Until tomorrow, my heart."

Before she could reply, he disappeared into the house. At that moment, a tremendous clap of thunder shook the manor, and Elizabeth looked up.

How symbolic that the earth moved the moment you kissed me, Fitzwilliam Darcy.

Immediately, the rain began in earnest and she rushed inside.

The next morning

The sun had dried the shallowest puddles of water in the garden by the time Cora entered Elizabeth's bedroom through the sitting room door. Drawing the drapes, and in the process rousing her mistress, the maid set about straightening the room.

"Cora, why did you let me sleep so long?" Elizabeth asked, stretching as she sat up. "Emily must be eager to ride her pony."

The young maid smiled. "Miss Emily is just now eating, ma'am. She and I had quite the time while you were away. She must have been exhausted because she did not wake as early as she normally does. And, since she slept late, I waited a little longer to wake you."

Elizabeth's thoughts immediately flew to William. "Is Mr.

Darcy already at the stables?"

"No, ma'am. Word downstairs is that Mr. Darcy is not here."

Elizabeth sat up straighter, her brows furrowing. "Not here?"

"No ma'am. When I went to fetch a tray of food for Miss Emily, I heard Mrs. Lantrip tell another maid that an express rider arrived in the middle of the night. It seems that Mr. Darcy and Colonel Fitzwilliam left shortly thereafter on horseback."

"Did she mention where he was going?"

"If she said, I did not hear."

Extremely concerned, Elizabeth stared blankly into space. She knew William well enough to know it was not in his character to change his plans at the last minute or to leave without saying a word.

Cora noted the expression on her face. "Are you well, Mrs. Gardiner? You look pale. I could send for Mrs. Reynolds if—"

"I am well, Cora," Elizabeth interjected with a smile to calm the servant. "It is only that I am surprised to hear Mr. Darcy left in such a hurry. I pray it was nothing serious."

"I dare say you will know the reason soon enough," Cora added, a twinkle in her eye. "According to all the upstairs maids, Lady Foggett knows everything that happens under this roof. No doubt she will tell you exactly where Mr. Darcy is once you go downstairs to break your fast."

Elizabeth tried to hold back a smile. "Cora, you do realise that you should not say such things about the countess' aunt."

"No disrespect intended," the maid replied unfazed. "Would you like me to help you dress now, or should I come back later?"

"Please give me a few minutes to wake up first."

"Then I shall see if Miss Emily is finished eating and ready to be dressed." With that, Cora exited the room.

Sliding off the bed, Elizabeth scoured the floor for the slippers she had rid herself of last night. As she was doing this, she spied a paper on the floor near the head of the bed, just inside the door that led into the hallway. Picking it up, she immediately noticed that her name was written on the outside in William's elegant script. Sliding one finger under the flap to break the seal, her heart raced as she began to read.

My darling Elizabeth,

I apologise for leaving without a proper goodbye. It could not be helped. I received word only this morning that Charles' cousin has purchased a ticket on a ship to the Americas. It sails in a sennight, and my sources in London wish me to have him arrested in Charles' stead.

Know that I will return as soon as possible, and when I do, I shall take care of all that we discussed last night. Try not to worry. I hope to be back shortly with a special license in hand.

I love you,
William

While his declaration of love made her smile, the prospect of being without William for an entire week made her heart ache. Still, knowing the news could have been worse, Elizabeth folded the missive and went towards the dresser where she kept her personal items. Secreting the letter inside a small jewellery box, she first closed the lid and then the drawer. Resolving to stay busy so that the time would pass swiftly, she began to fashion her hair. Before long, Cora returned to help her dress, and she went downstairs to break her fast.

The stables

As Elizabeth and Emily entered the paddock, Mr. Wilson walked out of the stable leading Snow. Walking the pony over to the excited child, he lifted Emily onto the saddle, and, in no time at all, her blonde curls were bouncing up and down as she trotted Snow around the enclosure.

"That little lassie has the perfect seat," the livery manager said to Elizabeth as he watched Emily make circle after circle. "Seldom do I see one so young ride so effortlessly."

Elizabeth beamed. "She does look as though she has always ridden, thanks to you."

"I can take no credit. Miss Emily has excellent instincts. She learned to make Snow comply with her wishes faster than any child under my instruction. You have a very smart little girl, if I say so myself."

"Thank you, Mr. Wilson. I could not agree more."

Suddenly, Millicent and her children could be seen galloping down the path from the fields, having gone on their early morning ride without William. Seeing Elizabeth, the countess waved, and in a short while, she had dismounted and handed off her horse to a groomsman. Hugh and Kathy kept riding until they entered the area where all of the jumps were situated. While the twins began taking the jumps, Millicent walked towards Elizabeth with a wide smile on her face.

"Good morning, Sleepyhead! I see that you finally decided to wake up and join us!"

Elizabeth smiled sheepishly. "Cora was supposed to wake me; instead, she let me sleep late."

"That is just as well. With Fitzwilliam and Richard away, there is little here to entertain. My aunt is not amusing in the least. I can attest to that!"

Elizabeth laughed but decided it best not to mention anything about the information in William's letter.

"Mrs. Reynolds allows that their departure was the result of that awful situation at Mr. Bingley's warehouse. You do know that his cousin has apparently been robbing him blind?"

Elizabeth nodded, for William had apprised her of his suspicions.

"Now it appears that awful man has decided to take off for parts unknown, leaving Fitzwilliam no choice but to go straight to London to sign a warrant for his arrest." She sighed loudly. "I have to wonder if Fitzwilliam would have taken on Bingley's responsibilities had he known all the work that would be involved." Millicent caught her mistake and added, "I am sorry, Elizabeth. I did not mean to imply that he regrets helping you."

"There is no need to apologise. I have often wondered the same thing."

Millicent quickly changed the subject. "Has Emily told you what she and my children did to occupy themselves while we were at Matlock Manor?"

Elizabeth looked puzzled. "No."

"Well, it seems that Mrs. Reynolds organised paints and easels so the children could paint. In fact, she left everything in the conservatory so they can indulge in that activity whenever they like. My Hugh has a talent for drawing, and he drew a horse he wishes to finish with oil paints. Why do we not join them today? Though I do not claim proficiency, I love to dabble in watercolours—flowers being my favourite subject."

"I am certainly not proficient," Elizabeth said, keeping a sharp eye on Emily whilst they talked. "However, I confess that I do love to try my hand from time to time."

"Excellent! You and I shall compete to see who is least likely to be employed as an artist!"

By that time, the children were ready for a respite. They were informed that lemonade and tea were being served on the terrace and returned to the house to rest and partake of the refreshments.

Chapter 14

Pemberley

Elizabeth could not hold back a smile as she made her way to the conservatory, for, whenever the rain kept her from her usual walk around the grounds, the variety of tropical plants, trees and flowers in that special place made it possible to imagine that she was in a garden, and not trapped inside the house. Moreover, the scent of the various offerings therein was intoxicating. The room was sizeable, accommodating not only vegetation, but several strategically placed settees and chairs where one could relax, have a cup of tea or read a book. Her favourite spot was a settee almost hidden from view amongst the citrus trees.

Reaching the conservatory today, she noted that several pieces of furniture had been moved to accommodate three easels where Emily and the twins were already busily painting. Millicent stood watching them, one hand clasping her chin as though deep in thought. Spying Elizabeth, she smiled and waved her forward.

"I was waiting for you, Elizabeth. If you will supervise the children, I wish to check on the maids I sent to locate two more easels a half-hour ago. I cannot imagine what is taking so long. I know that Fitzwilliam has an art studio. I saw it years ago, though I cannot recall just where. Surely there are extra easels there."

"I really do not have to paint," Elizabeth said. "I would be content just to watch."

"Nonsense! How else will you and I become proficient artists if we do not practice?"

With a hearty laugh, Millicent was out the door before Elizabeth could reply.

Just before reaching the end of the hall, Millicent heard women's voices. Being the curious sort, she stopped to listen and recognised the maids in question. Unable to discern exactly what was being said, she crept closer and peered around the corner. A maid was leaning an easel against the wall next to an open door, and from her vantage point she immediately recognised the exposed room as William's art studio.

"I told you to wait out here!" The older woman hissed as she reached to shut the door.

"I only meant to help you, Martha; it seemed you were struggling to move it."

"I apologise for being so sharp," the older one said, sighing heavily. "Mrs. Reynolds was clear. Only I was to go inside to fetch the easel."

"I am shocked that she trusted you to do that," the younger maid, Clara, declared testily. "When I think of how often I have been told none of us are to go in there, not even to clean; well, it is a miracle she let you in."

"Mrs. Reynolds had no choice. She has someone in her office, and the countess wanted the easels now."

"You have worked here many years. Has it always been locked?"

"No," Martha said, her expression becoming puzzled as she tried to recall the circumstances. "It was about five years ago, just after the master returned from a trip. He was terribly moody; you might even say withdrawn. He had always spent a good deal of time in the studio, but he practically lived there then, even having his meals served on trays. Once I went in to clean and came across him asleep on the sofa. About three months later, out of the blue, he walked out of the studio and, to my knowledge, has not gone back inside. That is when the door was locked, and we were told never to clean it again."

"And you never asked why?"

"I do not pry into matters that are not my business. You will learn to do the same if you want to stay employed at Pemberley."

"Well, to my way of thinking, the least Mrs. Reynolds could have done was send a footman to help you with this heavy thing."

"All the footmen, except those at the front entrance, are in Mr. Walker's office. I imagine they are getting an earful about the recent firing."

"I was shocked this morning when Mrs. Reynolds said that Florence would not be back. She was hired after I was."

"Florence was caught breaking the rules once before and got a warning. She knew what would happen if there was another mistake."

"Still, it makes me want to be more cautious. I need this job."

"Speaking of which, if we want to stay employed, we need to get this easel to the countess. We can worry about the other one next."

Each maid grabbed a side and picked it up. They took several steps before Clara exclaimed, "Wait!" Setting her side down, she said, "Are you not going to lock it?"

Exasperated, Martha eyed the closed door. "I left the key lying on the table." Then she shrugged. "We will not be gone long, and everyone will assume it is locked."

That being said, the maids again began to carry the cumbersome easel in Millicent's direction. Thinking quickly, she assumed a regal air, lifted her head and walked around the corner, almost colliding with them.

"There you are! I see that you have found one. Still, we will need another."

"We can only manage one at the time, my lady," Martha replied.

"Of course. When you reach the conservatory, please tell Mrs. Gardiner that I left something in my room and will return as soon as I locate it."

Without waiting for a reply, she walked on. Then she stopped and turned to address them again. "Oh, I forgot. My children are complaining of thirst—the conservatory is easily warmer than the rest of the house. Would you please fetch some lemonade for them before you bother with the other easel?"

"Yes, ma'am," they replied in unison.

As soon as the maids turned the corner, Millicent rushed to the door of the forbidden room. Her curiosity piqued, she was eager to discover what William might want to keep hidden. Stepping inside, she closed the door and leaned against it. The room appeared the typical art studio; the shelves that lined the wall on her right were stacked with paints and brushes of every description, as well as coloured pencils and charcoals too numerous to count. In the middle of the room stood a freestanding bookcase with every imaginable book referencing the art of drawing, sculpting and painting. On the left side, a sheet was draped over items sitting on the floor and propped against the wall.

Hurrying there, she lifted the sheet to discover several landscapes in various stages of completion. Disappointed, her eye followed the wall down to where two folded easels were propped, as well as a dozen or more blank canvases. Suddenly, she caught sight of what was hidden by the free-standing bookcase—a square table, splattered with flecks of paint in various colours. It sat right in front of the windows, and next to it stood an easel covered in cloth.

As quickly as possible, she was at the easel jerking off the cloth. The thin layer of muslin floated to the floor along with a cloud of dust. It unveiled a portrait so well executed that it left her breathless. Striking ebony eyes were showcased in a charcoal drawing of a woman of approximately one and twenty years. She wore only a simple muslin gown and a slight smile. Hair—dark, long and curly—spilled almost to her waist. Regardless of the fact that she was older now, Millicent had no trouble recognising the subject. *Elizabeth!*

Immobilised, when a noise brought her back to her senses, Millicent was unsure of how much time had elapsed. Quickly concealing the portrait with the muslin and the items on the floor with the sheet, she headed to the door, opened it and peeked into the hall. Seeing no one, she rushed out, closing the door just as the maids rounded the corner.

Pasting an innocent smile on her face, she said, "I found what I was looking for upstairs and am now eager to begin painting. Have you finished with the easels?"

"The refreshments took us away from that task, my lady, but we are on our way to fetch the last one."

"Excellent!" Millicent said.

As she walked in the direction from which the maids had just come, she did not look back. Had she done so, she might have seen the puzzled expressions on the faces of the servants, who watched her until she was completely out of sight.

"That is strange," Clara whispered. "No one would pass this way if they were going to the conservatory. And she was right beside the door. Do you suppose she went inside?"

"I had the same thought," Martha replied. Quickly opening the studio door, she surveyed the contents. "Nothing looks amiss. In any case, it is not wise to point the finger of suspicion at your betters. And do not say anything to Mrs. Reynolds. Should she get wind of it, she will blame you as sure as me."

"You need not worry. I know when to keep things to myself."

The farther she walked, the more Millicent's carefully constructed facade began to crumble. Since arriving at Pemberley, she had ignored her intuition regarding Fitzwilliam's feelings for Bingley's sister. Nevertheless, given the passion visible in his drawing of a young Elizabeth, there was no denying that he was deeply in love with her when it was drawn, and he likely still was. All that remained in question was what she would do with that knowledge. The quiet voice of her conscience encouraged her to be selfless and inform him that she would no longer hold him to their agreement. But having loved him for most of her life, she was reluctant to so easily give up the dream of being Fitzwilliam Darcy's wife.

I shall just forget I ever saw the drawing. After all, it was done many years ago. And, though he may still care for her, Fitzwilliam may also have realised Elizabeth cannot possibly manage his estates or rear his children to enter society as well as I. Yes! That is likely why he has said nothing to me about ending our agreement.

Satisfied the matter was settled, Millicent picked up her pace. Walking into the conservatory, she found Elizabeth already painting. Pasting on a faux smile she went over to observe.

"You have been keeping secrets, Elizabeth."

Elizabeth turned, one eyebrow raised in question. "How so?"

"You said that you were no artist, but I beg to differ! At least you are capable of painting a tree which looks like a tree and not a bush."

Both women laughed and Elizabeth resumed painting. Soon Millicent joined her, and they spent much longer than they had planned enjoying that activity. In fact, Mrs. Reynolds announced tea before either of them knew it.

London
Darcy House
Several days later

William's study was filled with cigar smoke, as well as conversation. Not only were Mr. Browning and Mr. Whitaker—Bow Street Runners hired to watch Charles' warehouses—in attendance, but also present were three sergeants—Tiller, Hannah and Combs— who had once served under Richard. After several minutes spent in private discussions over brandy, the last of Richard's comrades rapped on the door, and when Lieutenant Sprague stepped inside, William began to explain why they had been summoned.

"Gentlemen, this morning I received and signed the warrant for Mr. Howton's arrest. Immediately afterward, I was informed he had vacated Bingley's residence last night, taking his clothes and personal items. According to the housekeeper, Mrs. Carson, he was there when she retired, but his room was empty this morning. Moreover, one of the footmen was missing a uniform, which explains why Sergeant Tiller did not follow him when he left the house."

"I regret that he managed to slip past on my watch," Sergeant Tiller replied.

"It could have been any of us," Sergeant Hannah interjected.

"What is done, is done," Richard interrupted. "What is important is that we locate him before he boards that ship. Once on board, there are too many places a man can hide."

"Do you think he became aware of our presence?" Mr. Whitaker asked.

"Though it is possible, I think not," Richard replied. "His ship sails in four days, and he has yet to meet with his men to divide the spoils. My guess is that he wants to leave England with all his ill-gotten gain; thus, he is trying to avoid his cohorts from now until the ship sails. In any event, his whereabouts are currently unknown, and it is your job to find him and, if possible, his associates. Before you leave this morning, Mr. Browning will assign each of you an area to focus on. Please canvass the pubs and inns in your assignment. I also asked him to share his experience on how to do that more efficiently." Richard motioned to one of the men. "Mr. Browning, if you will begin."

Browning stood and cleared his voice. "The most important thing to remember is to fit into your surroundings. Never wear service uniforms, old or new. You should choose clothes that are old, ragged and even a little dirty. A bit of mud on your face could not hurt, for thieves and beggars rarely take baths. Get a room in your assigned area. The locals are more inclined to talk to you if they think you are one of them. Mr. Darcy has generously given each of us a hundred pounds to loosen tongues, so keep your eyes and ears open, and if you come across a credible lead, do not hesitate to pay for information."

"If we look just as poor as they are, will they not wonder how we have so much money?" Sergeant Combs enquired.

"They will assume you got it the same way they would have—you stole it."

"All good advice," Richard declared. "Now, are there any more questions or suggestions?" When no one spoke, he added, "Then, be on your way. Take caution, and stay in touch with your partner. The men we seek have nothing to lose, for prison or a rope awaits if they are caught. They will not hesitate to kill you if cornered."

The meeting having concluded, Browning handed out their assignments, and the men filed out of the room, leaving William and Richard alone. Once the door was closed, William wearily sat down behind his desk.

"You and I need to discuss the letter I received from Mr.

Grantham early this morning."

"I intended to ask you how Bingley is faring. From your expression, the news cannot be good."

"On the contrary, Charles is greatly improved; that is not the problem."

"Oh?"

"Grantham is convinced that, in addition to Charles' lung problems, he has been poisoned. He writes that he suspected as much from the beginning, due to the stomach ailment and other symptoms; however, his first objective was to get Charles' lungs healed so that his body could fight the effects of the poisoning. Most likely the poison used was arsenic, for there is still a high level of that substance in his blood even after all these weeks."

"My money is on Howton!"

"He would have had the opportunity, since they lived and worked so closely together; however, even after Charles returned to Richmond, his health continued to decline, which can mean only one thing."

"Howton had help inside Canfield Manor," Richard retorted. At William's nod he began pacing the room. "He must have bribed one of the servants who travelled to London with Charles, which casts doubt on his valet and the footmen."

"The Carsons told me after Jane stopped coming to London, Charles no longer accepted invitations to soirées and dinner parties, and his valet no longer made the trips to Town."

"That leaves the footmen," Richard declared. "And they would have had easy access to Charles' food and drink."

"I agree."

"What is your plan? Will you alert Mrs. Bingley?"

"I do not wish to frighten her, so I will write to Mr. Boggus and Mr. Hartley, informing them of what we suspect and asking them to keep a closer eye on Mrs. Bingley and the children. I shall also ask them to ferret out any gossip amongst the servants. Meanwhile, you and I will inspect Howton's room at the townhouse, as well as the warehouse office. With any luck, we may find evidence to connect Howton to the poisoning. Otherwise, we have another mystery on our hands."

"When do we start?"

"I sent a note to Mrs. Carson directly after I received her missive, asking her not to disturb the room. Hopefully, it arrived in time. Meanwhile, Mr. Barnes was instructed to tell the livery to saddle our horses directly after the meeting, so I suspect they will be ready shortly."

William stood, walked over to the windows and reached into his pocket to retrieve Elizabeth's ribbon. As he stared listlessly at it, Richard walked up behind him.

"What is that you have, Darcy? A blue ribbon?"

Instantly it went back into his pocket. "It is nothing."

"Darcy, is there something you are not telling me? You seem upset by more than just this ordeal with Howton."

"I was optimistic that Charles' cousin would keep to his usual habits until I could sign the warrant and have him arrested, along with his cohorts. I was thinking with my heart, I fear, for I planned to return to Pemberley in a sennight or less. Now, I have no idea how long it will be until I see—" Abruptly he stopped.

Richard ventured, "See who, Cousin?"

Ominously, William began to run his fingers through his hair. "There is something you should know. I was going to tell you— tell everyone—once we returned to Pemberley. However, this whole matter with Howton has mushroomed into more than I ever anticipated."

Richard's heart began to pound. "Tell me what?"

"Elizabeth and I are to be married as soon as I return to Pemberley with a special license. I sent word to my godfather the minute we arrived, asking him to procure one and have it delivered to me here."

"You actually petitioned the bishop?" Richard said, his brows furrowing in concern. "Does the need to act so swiftly mean that Mrs. Gardiner has been compromised?"

William faced him, even more irritated than before. "It means that we do not wish to wait any longer to be man and wife. We have been in love with one another since the summer of 1812, though we were both too proud to admit it."

"What do you propose to tell Millicent? You do know that she fancies herself in love with you, and bringing her and the children to Pemberley made it appear that you were getting serious about marriage."

"I never meant to hurt her or the children, but I cannot give up Elizabeth. I will simply tell Millicent I finally realised what she has been saying all along. Though I love her, I am not *in love* with her. I am in love with Elizabeth."

"I wish you luck, but I am not certain you will be able to dissuade her. Once Millie makes up her mind, she is not easily dissuaded."

"I am aware of that, but, in this case, she will have no choice once I marry Elizabeth."

"Well, at least that will force her to face the fact that she needs a man who can offer her more than friendship. She deserves to be loved as Henry loved her."

"I could not agree more." Suddenly Mrs. Barnes appeared in the open door. "Yes, Mrs. Barnes?"

"Sir, your horses are out front."

London
Guthrie's townhouse

John Guthrie's residence was still one of the finest Mayfair had to offer, though he cared little for wealth and status these days. More interested in political matters, he was convinced that Lord

Van Lynden held the secret to ridding England of the Viscount Castlereagh, whom he held responsible for England's decline on the world stage—a decline strictly of his own imagination. Had his father still been alive, he would have coaxed his son from this delusion, just as he had all the others. But alas, he was not. That, and the fact that his mother's mental decline meant that she no longer wielded any influence, gave Guthrie free reign to right any perceived wrongs using his fast shrinking wealth.

Entering the library this day, he was delighted to see all his associates in one place. He smiled confidently at those with whom he had chosen to ally himself—Lord Van Lynden, Klaus Jansen, Jann Bakke and Peter Visser. "It is good to have all of you under my roof. Please, have a seat."

Van Lynden sat down. "It is good to have such a nice roof over my head. My townhouse was sold before I left England, and without your hospitality, I would be forced to reside in an inn."

"There is plenty of room for everyone here, if any of you would like to reside here."

"It would draw too much attention," Van Lynden declared, as though it were an order. Seeing that no one was going to challenge him, he continued. "Since John and I were unsuccessful at Eagleton Park, I am hoping that one of you had better luck in locating Mrs. Graham."

The three men, all employed in London, exchanged satisfied looks. Seeing this, Van Lynden said, "Do not keep me waiting. Did you find her?"

Peter Visser replied, "I was hired two weeks ago to teach violin to Lord Jackson's daughter. It was only after you left London that it dawned on me the housekeeper at that residence is a Mrs. Graham. She is not very sociable, so I had had little interaction with her and barely remembered her name."

"She is the Graham we are looking for?"

"She is, but let me explain how I know. That old hoyden barely acknowledges me when I come through the door, so I knew I would get no information from her. Still, I was walking towards the servant's entrance when I overheard her arguing with a young woman about money. The young woman referred to the housekeeper as her mother and, since she is evidently short of funds, I reasoned that for a few farthings she might be willing to talk. I managed to get her name and address from one of the maids who fancies me."

"From the look on your face, I gather she was happy to cooperate," Van Lynden replied.

"Yes. Thanks to her mother, she was very familiar with the nanny, whom she readily admitted absconded with your child. Her name is Elizabeth Bennet, or I should say that was her name. She calls herself Mrs. Gardiner now."

"Elizabeth Bennet. Yes, that was the name," Van Lynden said solemnly.

"Oddly enough, she said her man had recently been paid to go to the village of Meryton to harass what few relations Miss Bennet—er, Mrs. Gardiner has left in that area."

"Who hired him, and to what purpose?" Van Lynden asked.

"She said she could not remember, but I suppose she just wants more money. But she said Carney—that is what she calls him—would be around on Sunday to see his children, and she would get the information from him."

"Tomorrow is Sunday. We shall be waiting when he arrives and ask him directly. With a little luck, by this time tomorrow we will know exactly where to find her."

Smiling now, Lord Van Lynden stood and held up his glass. "A toast, gentlemen! To finding the money box so that we can kill that bastard Castlereagh before the month is out."

All the men stood and raised their glasses to cheers of "hear, hear!" Then one and all downed the contents.

Chapter 15

London

The small dwelling housing Mrs. Graham's daughter and her family was located in the warehouse district next to a livery stable. The stench emanating from that establishment made the place intolerable, so when Lord Van Lynden and Guthrie arrived on Sunday to speak to Mr. Carney, they insisted on going to a nearby pub to conduct business. Consequently, by the time the proprietor placed three glasses of ale on the table, Carney was eager to fleece the elegantly dressed gentlemen in exchange for what little information he had or could concoct.

"My woman said you asked about the lady I was hired to frighten." He took a big swallow of his ale. "If you want my help, it will cost you."

Van Lynden's expression hardened. "You need not worry. If your information helps us locate the person we are looking for, you will be well rewarded."

The criminal did not look convinced. "Got any samples of what you consider a fair reward?"

Van Lynden reached into his coat and threw a shilling on the table. Carney slipped the coin into his pocket. "That will do for a start. What do you want to know?"

"I am looking for my children's former nanny. When she worked for me, she was called Miss Elizabeth Bennet. I understand she may be going by Mrs. Gardiner now."

"I was hired by a man to frighten a Mrs. Gardiner's relations. He did mention that she had been a Bennet before she returned to Richmond to live with her sister."

"What was the man's name, and why would he wish to frighten her?"

"I do not know if I can trust you with that information. You might be tempted to rat on me, and I could end up in prison."

Van Lynden leaned forward. "I can assure you that I have no intention of passing along to the authorities anything you say. In fact, I may be interested in hiring you to help me find Mrs. Gardiner, but only if I can trust you to keep your mouth shut."

Carney's eyes went wide. "Just to find her, nothing more?"

"Nothing more."

"How much are you willing to pay?"

"One thousand pounds once she is in my hands," Van Lynden said, throwing two more shillings on the table.

The thief's eyes lit up. "We have a deal!"

"Now, as to my earlier question—"

Carney interrupted. "His name is Howton. He hired me and my mates to steal goods from Mr. Bingley's warehouses, and then we sold them ourselves. After Howton came under suspicion for the thefts, he decided to give the man who was conducting the investigation something else to focus on. So, he had me frighten Mrs. Gardiner, who is the sister of Bingley's wife, by going to her family in Meryton and asking questions. He wanted them, and her, to think that I was looking for her."

"Who is investigating the theft?"

"Some gent I never heard of before. Fitzhugh...Fitzgerald...I can't remember his Christian name, though I do recall his surname—Darcy."

"Fitzwilliam Darcy. He should be well known to you, if only because of his fortune." Van Lynden took a sip of his drink. "A formidable opponent, I dare say. I met him years ago."

"I know of him," John Guthrie added. "He is not a sociable man in any sense of the word. Rather dull, if you ask me."

Ignoring his remark, Van Lynden continued. "What damning information did Howton have pertaining to Mrs. Gardiner?"

"I was not told. My job was just to question her relations—make them think I was searching for her."

"And did it work?"

"Howton was pleased. According to him, Darcy took Mrs. Gardiner to Derbyshire for her protection. In any case, the questions ceased."

"Do you know if Mrs. Gardiner had a child with her?"

"No."

"It seems I must question this Howton fellow myself. Where can I find him?"

"I wish I knew where that blackguard is now. He was supposed to give my mates and me our share of the loot this week. Instead, he moved out of his house without so much as a word."

"In that case, I may have to proceed without his help. I would like you to accompany me to Derbyshire. When can you leave?"

"Give me until tomorrow. I have an idea where ol' Howton is hiding, and I intend to get my share of the money now. That way I will be free to go with you."

Van Lynden threw several coins on the table to pay for the ale. Then he quickly wrote Guthrie's address on a piece of paper. "Be at this location tomorrow, prepared to travel to Derbyshire, if you wish to earn the thousand pounds. Come in the back gate and make sure you are not followed."

"I can do that, my lord!" Carney boasted. "Just you hold your coach until I get there."

"Do not be too late, Mr. Carney."

Lord Van Lynden and Mr. Guthrie quit the pub without look-ing back.

"What in the world prompted you to hire that man? He is not one of us, and with his attitude, he is liable to get us all killed," Guthrie asked as soon as both were seated again in Van Lynden's carriage.

"Someone has to take the blame for Castlereagh's assassina-tion. He will lead me to Mrs. Gardiner, and after we have the money box, he will help our men eliminate the viscount. Regret-tably, he will be mortally wounded and left for the authorities to discover. In his possession will be evidence to explain why he wished to kill the ambassador. It will all be very logical. You know how the magistrate loves to boast of solving crimes quick-ly? I intend to give him the opportunity."

Guthrie smiled. "That is brilliant! I confess that I would never have thought of leaving someone behind to blame."

"Over the years, I have learned that it pays to be thorough."

"Do you think Carney will actually come tomorrow?"

"Mr. Carney impresses me as the kind of man who will move heaven and earth if there is easy money to be had."

"What use will he be to you in Derbyshire?"

"Carney will deliver a letter to Mrs. Gardiner at Pemberley, Darcy's estate."

"Why not confront her yourself?"

"If I were to arrive there, it would appear I wanted a confron-tation. And while I am not afraid of him, if I ever have to face that gentleman, it will be at a time and place of my choosing. For now, I hope to spur Mrs. Gardiner to leave the estate on her own, without raising suspicions."

"I see," Guthrie said, though his expression did not match his words.

"I do not think you do. I have thought of nothing but killing Castlereagh these last four years, but I cannot afford to bring attention to myself. Once we have the money box, there is nothing to stop us from finishing off the ambassador."

"What do you plan to do with Mrs. Gardiner and the child after you have the box?"

"I have not decided. I do remember finding Miss Bennet, or whatever she calls herself now, remarkably pretty. We shall see if time has dimmed her beauty. As for the child, I will take her back to Holland, if for no other reason than to appease my relations. They believed me when I said I was devastated by the loss of my wife and child, and retrieving the girl will likely cement their good opinion of me. After all, once we do away with Viscount Castlereagh, I will need their help to hide."

"I aim to take my mother to visit her brother in Ireland just before Castlereagh is killed. I believe a year spent away from London will be sufficient. And, since you intend to blame everything on Carney, I may be able to return even sooner."

Lord Van Lynden did not reply. He was of the opinion that all of those involved, save himself, would likely be caught and hanged. Of course, it was of no concern to him. Each one involved knew the risk and had freely chosen to join his efforts to rid the world of Castlereagh. That was sufficient to allay his conscience.

London
Darcy's carriage

"Cousin, I think we have our evidence!" Richard declared. "The powdered substance in that envelope in Howton's room at Bingley's residence still had enough green particles to be identifiable, and the emerald green paint[13] drying in the tray in the warehouse office would convince any jury that it was Howton's source. Moreover, that is not even taking into account the copy of the report warning of the dangers of poisoning from the use of this paint which you found lying on his desk. Though most people disregarded the warning when it was issued, I recall General Lassiter ordering our building repainted because he believed it posed a danger."

"I remember reading of it as well. I had wallpapers removed from two rooms as a result."

"I suppose the paint would take years to do its work, though if you dried it and created a powder, as Howton did, it could more easily be ingested and wreak havoc faster."

"I believe Mr. Grantham would agree with you. Still, I am sending the powder to his associate's office to be analysed. I do not want any surprises when Howton goes to trial."

"Speaking of a trial, I got a note from Mr. Browning this morning. He thinks he knows in what area Howton is hiding, and it is only a matter of time until he is arrested."

The carriage slowed as they neared the front of Darcy House. William glanced at the top of the steps. "Perhaps they have him already. Browning is at the door."

Richard leaned over to look out the window. "That was fast."

The moment the carriage stopped, William was out the door with Richard close behind. As he neared the Bow Street Runner, William had only enough time to nod before the front door flew open to reveal Mr. Barnes. Seeing the master, he stepped aside to let them enter. Everyone filed inside, handing their coats and hats to him.

"We shall be in my office, Barnes. See that we are not disturbed."

"Yes, sir."

By the time that Mr. Browning had completed his report,

Richard was pacing the room. "So you followed Howton from the pub and through an alley where you were hit from behind and knocked unconscious?"

"Yes, Colonel. Since Howton was not carrying anything, I assumed his ill-gotten gain was wherever he was staying. I followed him, hoping to discover where that might be. He turned down an alley near the docks, and I waited until he was halfway down before entering. The next thing I knew Mr. Whitaker was calling my name, and I had this awful lump on my head."

As if to be sure he had not imagined it, Browning's hand came up to rub the knot. He grimaced.

"By the time I had regained my senses well enough to stand, Whitaker and I headed in the same direction he had gone. At the end of the alley, we noticed that a crowd was gathered outside a door about two hundred yards to the right. Talk was that someone had been killed only moments ago, so we rushed over to see if it was Howton. The magistrate, Mr. Langley, had been only four streets over when the murder occurred, so he was already on the scene by the time we arrived. Recognising us, he allowed us inside the building. Howton was lying in a pool of blood on the floor of a small bedroom. Whatever property he may have had was long gone, as there was nothing in the room—not in the dresser drawers, under the bed, or in the closet. I did, however, find this lying on the floor."

Browning held out a piece of paper, which Richard took. The colonel kneaded his chin with one hand while he studied it. "Strange. This address is in Mayfair. Since most likely Howton's men caught up with him before we could, perhaps this will provide a clue."

"I agree," Browning said. "Whitaker and I decided to conceal the address from Langley. We assumed you would still want the others arrested, and we can be more effective without him and all his men descending on that address. It is best that whoever killed

Howton thinks he got away with it."

"I agree," William said. "And, yes, I want his cohorts found and arrested. With any luck, we may be able to return at least some of Charles' money."

"Where is Whitaker?" Richard asked.

"I left him and the others searching the area where we found Howton."

"We have to consider that perhaps only one of the men Howton cheated did the deed. The others could be looking for the killer to get their part," William added.

"Anything is possible," Browning said. "After all, there is no honour among thieves."

Pemberley

Even though the children kept them busy, days passed so much more slowly for Elizabeth and Millicent now that William and Richard were no longer in residence. On this particular morning, Millicent appeared especially eager to have Elizabeth keep her company.

"Why do you not ride with me today, Elizabeth? The children are lost in their own world, and I am left to ride alone. Mr. Wilson is always with Emily. Surely you trust him to take care of her?"

The livery manager, who was helping Emily onto Snow, stopped to hear Elizabeth's reply. Seeing that he was awaiting her answer, Elizabeth tried to appear confident of his care, even though she was not eager to leave her child.

"It is not Mr. Wilson's responsibility to watch Emily."

"That makes no sense. No matter how you frame it, he is watching her whilst he instructs her in riding. I dare say that you will not be missed," Millicent added with a smile.

"I do not mind, Mrs. Gardiner," Mr. Wilson interjected. "I will stay right with Miss Emily while you ride. That is, if you wish to accompany Lady Markham."

Elizabeth had no alternative. "I suppose, then, you may have my horse saddled."

The livery manager called for a nearby groom to fetch Belle, and in no time at all, Millicent, Elizabeth and the twins were trotting down the trail leading to the pastures. When they entered the pasture, as usual, Hugh and Kathy began to gallop ahead. Millicent kept her horse to a trot to accommodate Belle's slower gait, and concentrating on riding, neither spoke until they came upon a small stream that meandered through the pasture.

Hugh and Kathy had already dismounted to allow their ponies to drink and were sitting under the shade of a large tree. Millicent and Elizabeth did likewise, though they chose a different tree for their shelter. The sun was already high, and the heat was becoming unbearable, so Millicent reached into a pocket and pulled out a handkerchief. She used it to mop her brow.

"I think we shall have to return earlier than usual. Today is the hottest it has been all week, and I fear I shall need a large glass of lemonade for refreshment."

Elizabeth smiled. Though she was an excellent horsewoman, Millicent did not spend as much time out of doors as she.

"Why are you smiling?" Millicent teased. "Is it because the heat does not affect you?"

Elizabeth laughed. "I confess that I am used to walking several miles a day...or I was, before I came to Pemberley. I have always been a walker, no matter what season of the year. So I suppose the summer heat does not affect me as much as it might others."

It was now Millicent's turn to laugh. "Others? Like me, for instance?"

"Yes."

Though she still kept the secret of Elizabeth's portrait, the notion that she might be keeping two star-crossed lovers apart bothered Millicent more than she wished to admit. In fact, night terrors had begun to plague her—terrors in which Fitzwilliam announced he was leaving her for Elizabeth. Each one battered her shaky resolve, and twice she had almost asked Elizabeth about their relationship. Only the fear of knowing the truth held her back.

Last night's dream, however, had been worse than any previous one. And this morning when Emily asked Elizabeth when Mr. Darcy was coming home, she knew it was time to learn the truth. Consequently, she asked Elizabeth to join her on her morning ride, knowing that when Hugh and Kathy returned to Pemberley for their jumping lessons, they would have privacy.

Presently, the twins remounted and galloped back to the stables. Elizabeth watched them ride away. "I am amazed that your children are so self-sufficient, Millicent. Nothing seems to frighten them, and they ride like little soldiers."

Millicent, who had stood to see her children off, shaded her eyes with a hand when she answered. "Their father wanted them to be independent, so he insisted they not be spoiled. Both could sit in a saddle by the time they were two years old, though we made them ride with us."

"They are very polite and mannerly, as well. So many children are not these days."

"Yes. They are good children, even if I say it myself."

"You have every reason to be proud."

"As do you. In my opinion, Emily has those same qualities."

"Thank you."

Millicent cut her eyes to Elizabeth, who was still watching Hugh and Kathy in the distance. "Elizabeth, I have wanted to ask you something ever since the day we met."

Elizabeth's brows knit. "Then why not ask me now?"

"I wish to know what happened between you and Fitzwilliam in Kent five years ago this summer. And please do not try to convince me that you had nothing to do with his melancholy all these years. I know better."

Elizabeth's heart sank. Would William be upset if she confessed to Millicent? After all, he was supposed to break the news of their future marriage before he left. In addition, she had no earthly idea how much the countess knew at this point.

"You look as though you are debating what to tell me. If it is too painful to discuss, I will understand. It is only—" Millicent could not go on and turned to and face the creek.

Touched, Elizabeth walked over to put an arm around her waist. "Tell me, please."

"I think it is evident why I was at Pemberley for the summer—a widow with young children in tow. However, what was supposed to be a joyous season of getting to know one another better turned completely on its head with your arrival."

"May I ask in what manner?'

Suddenly no longer able to refrain from doing so, Millicent began to share from her heart. "Only weeks before I came to Pemberley, Fitzwilliam was very attentive to me. I thought he had finally made up his mind about what he wanted out of life. When he returned to Pemberley with you, however, his entire demeanour had changed. I saw a side of him I had never seen before, and I have known him most of my life. With time, I began to believe that there was more to his devotion to you than any perceived duty to Charles Bingley."

When Elizabeth did not reply, she continued. "I believe I deserve to know the truth. Will you tell me what happened that affected him so profoundly?"

Reluctantly, Elizabeth acquiesced. "Mr. Darcy and I were at odds from the moment we met in Meryton. I thought him haughty and proud after he declined to dance with anyone save Mr. Bingley's sisters at our local assembly.

Afterwards, it was easy to believe the lies that George Wickham spread about him."

"I am familiar with that scoundrel. Wickham tells lies to make himself seem a saint and Fitzwilliam a villain."

"Sadly, most of Meryton believed his lies, just as I did. It was only much later, after Wickham lured my youngest sister into an elopement that I saw the truth."

"I am most interested in what happened at Rosings later that summer, for he was an altered man once he returned from there. Was it while you and he were there that Wickham's elopement with your sister became common knowledge?"

"Unfortunately, I did not hear of that until I returned home from Kent."

"Then what happened at Kent that was so devastating?"

"Mr. Darcy proposed, and I...I refused him."

"You did not!"

"I did. I said that he was the last man in the world I could ever be prevailed upon to marry."

Millicent was stunned. Rendered speechless for a time, when she spoke again, her voice was barely audible. "I cannot imagine any woman refusing Fitzwilliam, much less someone—" She hesitated. "Forgive me, but, in truth, you are far beneath his station."

"At the time I did not care. I blamed him for separating my sister from Mr. Bingley and for ruining Mr. Wickham's life. My goal was to wound him as deeply as I believed he had wounded Jane."

"Well, that solves the mystery. No wonder he had been so miserable. He is so principled that hearing those words from someone he cared for would have been devastating."

"Remembering that time has been very painful. With my sister's elopement, I finally saw the treasure I had refused. I am not speaking of his wealth or position...but the honourable man that is Fitzwilliam Darcy."

Millicent was genuinely touched. "I witnessed Fitzwilliam's pain; I can only imagine how you felt once you knew Wickham's true nature."

"Not a day has passed that I have not regretted my actions."

"Has he told you he still loves you? It is evident to me he does."

Elizabeth turned to face Millicent. "I confess he told me just before he left for London, but he also said he loves you very much and does not want to hurt you."

"I believe you," Millicent said with a wan smile. "Fitzwilliam and I have been friends far too long for one of us to hurt the other intentionally."

"He said you would always be the best of friends."

"Now, it is time for my confession. I have always known Fitzwilliam loved me, just not in the way a man should love the woman he intends to marry. Yet, even after I realised he was genuinely in love with you, I would not give up my goal. I am very ashamed. I let my desires override what I know is best for Fitzwilliam. I shall ask his forgiveness when next we meet, just as I am asking for your forgiveness now. I pray, with time, we can be good friends."

Elizabeth leaned in to give Millicent a hug. "Love makes fools of us all. I cannot blame you for loving him, so there is nothing to forgive."

Millicent reached for Elizabeth's hand. "Thank you." Then smiling, she added, "Come. There is something you simply must see at Pemberley."

Elizabeth looked puzzled as Millicent led her towards the horses. "It is time you knew the full depth of Fitzwilliam's love for you."

Chapter 16

London
Guthrie's Townhouse

As John Guthrie and Lord Van Lynden waited in the library for Carney to arrive, the housekeeper appeared. "Sir, would you care for more tea?"

Guthrie looked to Van Lynden, who had been reading a book. That gentleman shook his head. "No, thank you, Mrs. Southard."

The servant returned to her duties.

"It looks as though Mr. Carney has thought better of joining you, Van Lynden."

"I never expected the man to be on time. Those of his ilk do not concern themselves with being punctual," Van Lynden said. Then, glancing to a gilded clock on the mantel over the hearth, he added, "He should be here ere long."

"You have more confidence in him than I. Are you certain you do not want me to go with you to Derbyshire? I would not trust that man enough to close my eyes for a nap in the coach."

"No, I need you here. Someone has to keep abreast of the ambassador's schedule, and you are the only one in our group who is a member of White's. There you can hear the news before the papers even print it. I am hopeful Castlereagh has no cause to leave England on the spur of the moment as he did last time."

A soft cough alerted them that the butler was standing at the door. "Mr. Guthrie, sir, there is a questionable man at the back entrance. He says his name is Carney, and he is supposed to meet you and Lord Van Lynden here."

"Thank you, Haggard. Please show him in." As the puzzled butler went to do as he was told, Guthrie spoke. "Your insight never fails to amaze me."

Before long, Carney strode into the room with the butler on his heels, calling, "Sir...sir!" When the ill-dressed stranger did not halt to be announced, the servant threw up his hands in frustration.

"Never mind, Haggard," Guthrie said, amused at his butler's discomfort. The servant stiffly bowed and quit the room.

Carney stopped in the middle of the library. Slowly he turned in a circle, eyeing the expensive silver, crystal and gilded items in the massive room with an expression much like that of a child in a confectionary shop. Whilst this was happening, Van Lynden noted the fresh scratches and bruises on the man's face.

"Did you make certain you were not followed, Mr. Carney?"

Carney's observation came to a halt. "I am not a dullard. I slipped into a cart full of hay one of your grooms was bringing through the back gate. I dare say he did not see me get in or out of it, so how could anyone else?"

"Excellent. From the damage to your face, I imagine you caught up with Mr. Howton."

Carney's expression grew menacing. "What do you mean?"

"It appears you have been in a fight."

Not one to trust anyone, Carney lied. "I was in a brawl, but not with Howton. I never caught up with that scoundrel. Besides, one of my friends said he has sailed from England already. That leaves me no choice but to work for you; my children have to eat. "

Van Lynden stood. "Then, if you are ready to accompany me to Derbyshire, we really should leave. I wish to make Lambton in less than three days time, if possible."

"You will wear your horses out at that pace."

"Horses are of no consequence."

As Carney followed Van Lynden out the back of the townhouse and into a coach with no crest, a single thought crossed his mind. *I doubt very little is of consequence to you—least of all what happens to me. That is why I will be keeping an eye on you, too, Van Lynden!*

London
Darcy House
William's study

Richard, who had been out of the house all morning, had barely taken a seat when William spoke. "Have you heard from Sergeant Hannah? What has he learned about the address Browning found on the floor next to Howton?'

"Give me a chance to breathe, Darcy, before bombarding me with questions!" Richard said, propping his feet on the end of his cousin's desk. He almost laughed aloud at the expression of irritation which crossed William's face. "I thought the address seemed familiar, and I was right. It belongs to John Guthrie. You remember him—the one who sees a conspiracy around every corner. His theories started a good many arguments at White's, or they did when he was a regular visitor."

"I vaguely remember your father and some of his friends making sport of him at White's, but that was years ago. I cannot remember when I saw him last."

"I cannot, either. Still, Browning and Whitaker think it is best if we watch his house and not make a move too soon. If he was involved in Howton's death, the others who stole from Bingley may come there at some point. Let them think they have gotten away with murder. With any luck, they will get careless."

William slammed his fist down on the desk. "I despise all this waiting!"

Exhausted from watching his cousin brood about circumstances beyond his control, Richard declared, "Then let us go for a ride in Hyde Park. Titan is ready for a good workout. What about Kronos?"

William threw down on the desk the pen he was holding and stood, raking his hands through his hair. "I am not in the mood!"

Richard watched him take up guard at his favourite spot. "You have been in a foul mood since you realised you would not be returning to Pemberley as soon as you wished."

William dropped his head in his hands. "All these years I yearned for Elizabeth to care for me and now that she does, we are separated by one man's greed. I am not a young man anymore, and I am finding it hard to control my disappointment. In fact, had I caught up with Howton first, I might have strangled him with my bare hands just for being the one thing keeping us apart."

"No, you would not. You are too honourable, whereas I would have strangled him without giving it a second thought."

William's head came up, though he did not turn to face Richard. "Elizabeth is as important as the air I breathe. I know it sounds foolish, but should something separate us again, I do not know how I could carry on."

"Do not worry, Cousin! After we locate the miscreants who helped Howton, and we recover the money, you shall return to Pemberley and marry the woman you love. Nothing will ever separate you again."

By his reflection in the glass, Richard could see his words made William smile; thus, when he turned, the colonel was not surprised his cousin's mood had improved.

"You are correct. I must keep a positive outlook, or I shall go mad. Besides, it is time Kronos had a workout. With any luck, perhaps when we return, a good report will await us."

Pemberley

Well aware of how protective Mrs. Reynolds was of Fitzwilliam's privacy, Millicent had no intention of asking her to open the art gallery in order to show Elizabeth the portrait. However, since this was the day the housekeeper normally went into Lambton to visit an ill friend, the countess decided to use that to her advantage. Consequently, by the time she, Elizabeth and the children were making their way back to the manor from the stables, she was already devising a plan.

Approaching the terrace where Mrs. Reynolds was pouring Lady Foggett a glass of lemonade, she whispered to Elizabeth. "Help me encourage the children to finish their refreshments quickly; I wish to be in the conservatory before Mrs. Reynolds leaves for Lambton."

"What about your aunt?"

"She will go back to her room to read and rest, anyway."

"Do you not want the children to rest as well?"

"Painting is not strenuous, and they will have all afternoon to rest." Millicent glanced to the housekeeper, who was pouring lemonade for Emily. "Once we are in the conservatory, no matter how outlandish, agree with whatever I say."

Elizabeth was amused. "What mischief are you up to?"

The countess' eyes twinkled. "Never you mind; just follow my lead."

The conservatory

The moment they entered the conservatory, while the maids

were assisting the children, Millicent grabbed the paintbrushes from a jar next to her easel and quickly confiscated Elizabeth's, too. She secreted them amongst several pots nearby which contained flowering shrubs. As Elizabeth's brows knit at her actions, the countess winked before addressing the youngest maid.

"Clara, what have you done with my brushes?" Before the baffled maid could answer, she turned to Elizabeth. "Are your brushes where you left them?"

Elizabeth tried not to smile as she answered. "They seem to have disappeared."

"I...I have no idea where they might be, my lady," Clara offered. She glanced at the other maid. "Did you move them, Martha?"

"I did not! Surely they are in here somewhere." Nevertheless, a thorough search of the room did not uncover the brushes.

"Well, you simply must go back to the art studio and get more!" Millicent demanded indignantly.

"But Mrs. Reynolds has the key, and this is the day she goes into Lambton," Martha answered, her voice getting higher as she realised the predicament the lost brushes had created.

"Then I suggest you get the key before she leaves," Millicent replied.

The maid nodded, then practically ran from the room. Praying that the housekeeper would give Martha the key and not open the art studio herself, Millicent waited for a few minutes before announcing, "I think I shall check on Martha's progress."

Slipping out of the conservatory, she found the room across from the art studio was unlocked. Cracking the door only enough to see across the hall, Millicent waited. When at last the maid approached, key in hand, she rushed to follow Martha into the room.

"What are you doing, my lady?" the maid exclaimed. "You are not supposed to be in here."

"Oh, but I already have been. Remember when you brought

the easels to the conservatory for Mrs. Gardiner and me? You left the door unlocked then, and I went inside. Now, the question is this. Do you want Mrs. Reynolds to learn you left it open, or would you rather it remains our little secret?"

"I would rather it be our secret, my lady."

"Good. Then go back to the conservatory and tell Clara to stay with the children whilst you spirit Mrs. Gardiner here. Do not offer your friend any explanation; the fewer who know about this the better."

Martha did not look happy, but she went to carry out the order. In a short while, she returned with Elizabeth, and once all three were inside the studio, the door was shut.

"Give me the key and return to the conservatory to keep Clara occupied," Millicent instructed the maid. "We will not be in here long. I will lock the door and return the key to you when we are done."

As soon as Martha left, Millicent addressed Elizabeth. "What I want you to see is in this room."

Elizabeth looked befuddled as she surveyed the disarray. "Here?"

"Close your eyes."

A bemused smile crossed Elizabeth's face as she complied. "Will this involve a secret tunnel?"

Millicent took her hand and began to lead her behind the free-standing bookcase. "No. But I dare say you will not be disappointed."

Stopping at the covered easel, the countess pulled the muslin drape off the charcoal drawing and let it float to the floor. "Now you may look."

Confronted by the portrait William had drawn so long ago, a half-breathless murmur of amazement and incredulity slipped from Elizabeth's lips.

Frozen in place, her hands flew to her mouth as tears blurred her vision. Mutely she analysed every nuance of her likeness, whilst a rush of emotions filled her heart. William had not missed a single trait which made her unique, even capturing the small scar under her eye.

"When Fitzwilliam drew this portrait of you, he unconsciously provided me—well, the entire world—a window into his heart. Once I saw it, I knew he could never love any woman save you," Millicent whispered.

Surrendering to years of pent-up emotions, Elizabeth sobbed. "I...I had no idea. When we parted at Kent, I truly believed he hated me." Trembling, her hand came to rest over her throbbing heart. "All these years—"

Millicent turned Elizabeth so they faced one another. "I did not show you the portrait to upset you, but to show you how blessed you are. It is every woman's dream to have a man who loves her this fiercely."

"Though William said he never stopped loving me, seeing this makes his confession so much sweeter." Elizabeth sniffled. "How can I thank you for revealing it to me?"

"By loving Fitzwilliam as he deserves to be loved."

"I will. Never doubt it."

Pulling out a handkerchief, Millicent dabbed at Elizabeth's eyes. "Try to compose yourself. We do not want to raise suspicions." Then, assuming a cheerful disposition, she said, "Martha is probably close to having an apoplexy, so we must hurry."

As they neared the conservatory, Elizabeth whispered, "I believe I am inspired to paint more than trees."

"If that drawing does not inspire you, my friend, nothing will."

Lambton
Three days later
The inn at Lambton was not as grand as those to which Lord

Van Lynden was accustomed; still, he had no plans to stay more than one night. After paying the innkeeper, he followed the maid to his room. As the young woman opened the curtains, he began questioning her innocuously.

"Miss, could you tell me which road leads to Pemberley?" The servant looked proud to have been asked. "I can, sir. If you turn right just past the livery stables, you will be on the road to that grand estate."

"Thank you. I plan to call on Mr. Darcy tomorrow."

"Oh, I do not think he is in residence at present. Talk is, he is in London."

"Well, then, I shall call and leave my card."

"I can tell you that presently there are two widows and their children visiting Pemberley—and neither accompanied him to London. It has been the talk of the village, Mr. Darcy hosting both women at his estate at the same time."

"I can only imagine," Van Lynden said, giving the maid one of his rare smiles. "Thank you. You have been most helpful."

She bobbed a curtsey. "Glad to be of service, sir."

She exited the room, just as Carney entered. That man stepped back to the doorway to watch her leave.

"Mr. Carney, I need you to deliver a letter."

"Now? We just got here, and I am tired. Can it not wait until tomorrow?"

"No. Mrs. Gardiner must get this today in order to meet me tomorrow."

The miscreant sighed. "Then at least let me have a pint of ale before I go. The dust has settled in my throat, and I need to wash it down."

"Ale comes later. For now, you will wash your face and change into your cleanest clothes. I am certain Mr. Darcy's servants are used to seeing sober express riders who are not too filthy."

Carney glared at his benefactor. "It had better be worth it."

"It will be," Lord Van Lynden said, pulling a shilling from his pocket. "You will deliver the missive and wait for a reply. After you return with her reply, you may buy all the ale you want with this." He tossed the coin to Carney. "Just do not get drunk. As long as you work for me, I need to be able to count on your services."

"As you say."

Pemberley

Mrs. Reynolds was in her private office, working on the household accounts, when a footman appeared in the open door.

"Yes, Mr. Cyril?"

"There is an express rider at the door, ma'am. He has a post for Mrs. Gardiner and said he is to await her reply."

"Thank you. I shall finish this entry and then speak to him. Tell him I will only be a minute." She went back to her work, but the footman did not leave. Looking up, she asked, "Is there something else you wish to say?"

"Perhaps I am wrong, but he does not look like an express rider."

Mrs. Reynolds stood. "Then let us have a look at him."

As she entered the foyer, she knew exactly what the footman meant. The man standing before her looked more like a thief than an express rider. And, from the way he surveyed the house, it looked as though he was deciding what to steal first. Nonetheless, when he heard her footsteps, he stopped his inspection and smiled, displaying most of his decaying teeth.

"I understand you have a letter for Mrs. Gardiner."

"Yes, ma'am." Carney held the missive out, and the housekeeper took it, turning it over as she inspected it.

"There is no return address."

"I just deliver them. I picked this up in London and was told to bring it here immediately."

"Who sent you?"

"I am not at liberty to say. You will have to ask the person to whom it is addressed."

Incensed by his answer, Mrs. Reynolds huffed and turned to the footman who had taken a position right behind her. "See that he waits right here!"

That being said, she went in search of Elizabeth.

Elizabeth was in the library reading a book to Emily when the housekeeper found her.

"The rider said he was told to await a reply," Mrs. Reynolds said.

When she noticed there was no return address, a confused look crossed Elizabeth's face. The only letters she got at Pemberley were from Jane, and they always had her address at the top. Immediately, she thought of William and found herself smiling widely as she hurriedly broke the seal.

Miss Bennet,

You have my daughter, and I want her back. Meet me early tomorrow in the park next to the confectioner's shop in Lambton. Come alone if you wish to resolve this between the two of us. Otherwise, I shall have no choice but to have you charged with kidnapping.

Lord Van Lynden

As fear gripped Elizabeth, she felt the blood drain from her face. Hoping the servant had not noticed, she smiled at Mrs. Reynolds. "Would you mind watching Emily while I compose an answer for the rider?"

"Certainly, Mrs. Gardiner. If you like, there is a small writing desk across from the sofa closest to the hearth. It has plenty of paper, pens and ink."

"That will be most helpful," Elizabeth replied. Then, she turned to her daughter. "Emily, darling, please stay with Mrs. Reynolds until I am finished."

The child looked up from the picture in a book she was holding. "Yes, Mama."

Rushing to the desk, Elizabeth quickly scribbled a one-sentence reply.

Chapter 17

Lambton
The next day

Lord Van Lynden's letter effectively put an end to Elizabeth's dreams. If he was in Lambton, he knew his daughter was there, and Emily favoured her father so keenly that there could be no doubt of her parentage, ensuring any court would rule in his favour. And, in all likelihood, if Van Lynden wanted to prosecute, she could hang for kidnapping. Dying would have been easier than being parted from either Emily or William; nonetheless, if Elizabeth had to choose only one, she knew which one that would be. In time, William would understand; Emily would not.

Having spent all night concocting a way to meet with Van Lynden, as well as a credible excuse for leaving Pemberley, Elizabeth was well prepared when she encountered the countess in the hallway that morning.

"There you are!" Millicent said. "When you did not come to the dining room, I thought you might have overslept."

"Actually, I have a miserable headache. I feel I must return to bed, but I hate that Emily will not be able to ride. She dearly loves being with Snow."

"You poor dear," the countess said, patting Elizabeth's hand.

"I shall be glad to escort Miss Emily to her lesson and watch her while she rides." She smiled knowingly. "I am acquainted with how much you hate to ask Mr. Wilson to watch over her."

"He is busy enough with all he has to do, but I also hate that you will miss your ride," Elizabeth responded. "Unfortunately, Cora is still in Lambton visiting her cousin. She should be back this afternoon, though that will be too late."

"I do not mind in the least, but what about you? Should I have Mrs. Reynolds concoct one of her headache remedies?"

"If I lie down for a while longer, that should suffice."

"Then I shall see you after you have had your rest."

As the countess and the children walked towards the stables, Elizabeth watched from her balcony. Unbidden, a dozen memories of happy moments spent here with William overwhelmed her, and for an instant, she believed he could put everything to right if only he knew. Then, reality interceded. Van Lynden was capable of great evil, and she could not live with herself if William were harmed because of her. Closing the door to what she desired, she hurried to find Mrs. Reynolds.

Learning from a maid that the housekeeper was in her office, Elizabeth headed in that direction. As she approached the room, she noticed that the door was open, and having no time to waste, she stuck her head inside. "Please excuse me, Mrs. Reynolds, but might I be provided with a ride into Lambton at once?"

The servant looked up, confused. "I understood you had a headache. Are you certain you feel up to it?"

"Actually, the headache was just an excuse to fool the countess. I will be returning to my sister's estate sooner than I had anticipated, and I wish to procure a gift for Lady Markham and her children. However, I want it to be a surprise; otherwise, she will insist on buying me something in return."

"Oh? Pardon my curiosity, but is your sister well? I ask only because you mentioned she is expecting a child."

"Jane is well, thank you. Still, I know she would like for me to return to Richmond before the child is born."

"That is understandable."

"Then may I count on your help to surprise the countess?"

Mrs. Reynolds stood. "Let me see if we can get you there and back before Lady Markham returns from the stables. Follow me."

In no time at all, Elizabeth was on her way into Lambton in a curricle driven by a groom. Now the only thing left was to pray that the early hour would ensure she did not draw undue attention. It would never do for anyone to see her with Lord Van Lynden.

The servant stopped in front of the confectioner's shop. "Please wait here," Elizabeth said. The groom nodded.

Picking out a decorative jar and two bags of sweets, she asked the proprietor to add her purchase to the jar and wrap it. As she waited, she pondered how she could escape the groom's watch. Then, surprisingly, someone entered the shop through a door on the side of the building.

As the clerk finished his task, Elizabeth said, "Please hold it for me. I shall pay you when I return. I will not be long."

"Yes, ma'am."

Elizabeth slipped out the side door and, spying the park not a hundred feet away, hurried in that direction. Once under a large canopy of trees, she turned in a circle. Disappointed to see no one, she began to wonder if Van Lynden had gotten her short reply.

"It has been a long time, Miss Bennet."

Recognising that wicked voice, Elizabeth found herself trembling. Still, she did not spy Lord Van Lynden until he stepped from behind a large tree. His blank expression chilled her to the bone, and she shivered even more.

"Or should I call you Mrs. Gardiner?"

"Mrs. Gardiner."

"You have a husband then? Might I ask where he is? My sources say he did not accompany you to Pemberley?"

Elizabeth answered as calmly as she could. "I am a widow. My husband perished during the influenza epidemic of two years ago."

Van Lynden's shrewd gaze fixed appraisingly upon her, lingering a little too long on her bosom. Feeling unnerved, when he spoke again, she jumped. "What have you done with Ingrid, Mrs. Gardiner?"

Elizabeth's mouth went dry. "I have been taking care of her for the last three years. You never returned, so—"

Lord Van Lynden raised a silencing hand. "I do not care to hear *why* you decided to abscond with my daughter; I am here to reclaim her."

Elizabeth's heart pounded in her throat. "But Ingrid believes I am her mother. It would break her heart—and mine—if you were to take her from me. Can we not act like adults and do what is best for her?"

His impatient scorn expired, and Van Lynden's eyes narrowed. "You dare tell me what is best for my child?"

"Forgive me, but for all practical purposes, you abandoned her and your wife when you sent them to Scotland. And when Lady Van Lynden was certain of her death, she asked me to take the baby. I was simply following her wishes."

"You have no idea what circumstances transpired to keep me away! And if my wife asked you to take our daughter, she was a bigger fool than I thought. The child should have been sent to her grandparents at Eagleton Park. They could have reared her in the manner in which she should have been raised. I dare say you cannot support yourself, much less a child."

"My family has helped me with Emily."

Lord Van Lynden scowled perplexedly. "And just *who* is Emily?"

"I...I call her that."

His eyes blazed. "No doubt in hopes of keeping me from finding her."

"I thought you were dead."

"Well, I am not! And you, Mrs. Gardiner, if that is your name, are as foolish as my late wife if you think I believe your tale."

Elizabeth stiffened, her eyes filling with tears. "Can we not come to an arrangement for Emily's sake? I love her as though she were my own child."

As his eyes roamed over her body again, a slight smirk lifted the corners of his lips. "I suppose if you acted as her governess, it would make Ingrid's transition easier."

Elizabeth's eyes dilated with pain and fear. "Is there no other way?"

"There is not."

Swallowing past the large knot in her throat, she murmured, "Then I will be Emily's governess."

"Excellent! Now, all that remains is to spirit you both from Pemberley without involving Fitzwilliam Darcy in my business. I do not take kindly to anyone interfering in my affairs."

Elizabeth could not keep the anguish from her expression at the mention of Mr. Darcy.

"What is this?" Van Lynden stepped closer, lifting her chin so as to look into her eyes. Unhappy with what he found, his tone grew more ominous. "If Darcy is more to you than a friend, tell me now. I do not wish to be challenged over a mere governess. I can always take my child and leave; the law is on my side."

"Mr. Darcy and I have become friends," Elizabeth lied. "Still, I would rather he believe I am simply returning to my sister's estate in Richmond, for he cares deeply for Emily."

"That is wise. Do you have funds enough to purchase tickets on the post coach out of Lambton tomorrow morning?"

"I...I am not certain of the cost, and a maid will be returning to Richmond with us. She is employed by my brother."

Van Lynden reached into his pocket and brought out several coins. Wrapping them in a handkerchief, he held it out. "Have someone bring you into Lambton in the morning and purchase passage only as far as the post inn at Belper. You, Ingrid and the maid will ride in my coach once you reach there."

Elizabeth took the handkerchief and nodded.

"There is one other thing. My uncle gave Ingrid a money box when she was born. It has sentimental value, as he has since died. Do you know where it is?"

"Lady Van Lynden packed two trunks for Emi...Ingrid that are presently at my sister's estate in Richmond. After she outgrew the clothes inside them, I had no need to disturb the contents. The last time I saw the box, it was in one of the trunks."

"Excellent."

A great gust of wind came from out of nowhere, almost re-moving Elizabeth's bonnet and, in the process, blew several curls about. Arrogantly, Van Lynden reached out to brush a wayward tendril from Elizabeth's forehead. Repulsed, she shrank back. For an instant his eyes burned with offence; then he smiled sardon-ically.

"After we collect my daughter's trunks, we will head to Lon-don, staying there only long enough to sell my estate in Scotland. Afterward, we sail for Rotterdam."

"Rotterdam?"

"Yes, Mrs. Gardiner. I plan to live in my native land for the rest of my life. Will that present a problem for you?"

A sense of desolation overwhelmed her. There would be no chance of ever seeing William again if they were in Rotterdam.

"No," she managed to murmur.

"Good."

With a heart heavier than ever, Elizabeth turned to leave.

"*Miss Bennet*." She stopped. "Do not think of defying me. Were that to happen, it would be very dangerous for you and for those you care about most. I am not a man to be trifled with. For your sake, I hope you understand my meaning?"

Leaving Emily's father standing in the middle of the park without so much as a goodbye, Elizabeth stoically returned to the confectionary shop. Entering through the side door, she paid for her purchases and went out the front entrance.

"Are you ready to go home?" the groom said. Then he quickly corrected himself. "Excuse me. I meant to say, go back to Pemberley?"

"Yes," Elizabeth replied softly. *I want to go home more than anything in the world.*

Crying silently all the way back to Pemberley, she had no more tears left by the time the groom helped her from the vehicle. Entering the manor house, Elizabeth wore a mask of stony acceptance as she headed straight to her rooms.

Elizabeth's bedroom
Later

Elizabeth was taking a last look at the splendour that was Pemberley when Millicent opened the door. Hurrying to the balcony where she stood, the countess began talking.

"Do not blame Cora for telling me you were awake. I just had to see for myself how you were faring. I do not recall you ever keeping to your rooms for so long a time, and I feared your headache must have worsened."

Elizabeth was glad her friend believed she had a headache, for she was incapable of pretending she was well. A slight smile was all she could offer in reply.

"I dare say you look worse than this morning. You must allow me fetch Mrs. Reynolds, so she can create one of her potions."

Elizabeth held a hand out to Millicent, and she took it. "It is not the headache which pains me now."

"Then what?"

"I...I must go back home tomorrow."

"Home?"

"To Richmond."

"You cannot leave now. Fitzwilliam will be returning soon, and I know how devastated he will be if you are not here."

"I must. Jane is due to have her child soon, and I know she wants me with her. Besides, the threats which sent me here in the first place no longer exist."

Millicent studied Elizabeth sombrely. "You would leave Fitzwilliam now, knowing how much he loves you?"

"I am not leaving him," she countered weakly, "for I will be nearer to William in Richmond than here."

"But he could be on his way home as we speak. You might pass along the way."

"I doubt that. Still, I shall send an express in the morning, telling him where I shall be." Elizabeth squeezed Millicent's hand. "All will be well. You shall see."

Though still dismayed, Millicent relented. "If you must, you must, but know that not only will Fitzwilliam miss you, I shall as well. You have become the sister I never had, and Emily like my own child." She started to cry. "I...I do not think I have ever felt this much kinship with a woman. My closest friends have always been Fitzwilliam and Richard."

"You were kind to Emily and me, even when you suspected the truth of my relationship with William," Elizabeth said. "And once you learned the truth, you put his happiness ahead of your own. How can I not love you as a sister, as well?" She hugged

Millicent, then quickly stepped back. "I must compose myself, so I can explain to Emily that we are leaving. I know she will be upset, for she has come to think of William as the father she never had."

"Fitzwilliam has always been good with children. As godfather to Hugh and Kathy, he could not have been more attentive. And I have seen him treat Emily with the same affection, so it is normal she should love him. If you are in Richmond and he in London, make sure he sees her often. That should assuage her fears."

"I...I will," Elizabeth stammered, appalled at having to lie. "Now, I must send for Cora to begin packing."

"Emily is having refreshments on the terrace with Hugh and Kathy. I will join them for tea and wait for you."

"I will be down as soon as I speak with Cora."

Lambton Inn

"Why do I have to ride next to the driver?"

"Because, Mr. Carney, there will be no room in the carriage."

"Humph! What if it rains? I have no great coat like your fancy servants."

"In that case, I shall lend you mine. Now, go to the stables and have them ready my coach. I wish to leave as soon as possible in order to reach Belper well ahead of the post coach."

"How do you know Mrs. Gardiner will do as she was told? She might head in another direction after we leave."

"She now knows she cannot hide. I found her once; I can find her again. And I made certain she knows what will happen to her loved ones if she decides not to cooperate."

Carney studied the man carefully. Though he might have the appearance of a gentleman, Van Lynden was as cold-hearted as any killer he had ever known.

"I will need funds to pay the livery."

Lord Van Lynden reached into a pocket and tossed Carney a shilling. "Tell him to send a man ahead to make certain we have fresh horses at every stop. I do not want to be stranded waiting for our horses to rest."

"It is your money," Carney replied.

Richmond
Canfield Manor

After walking all over the house, Kitty finally checked the gardens, where she found Jane sitting in a swing under a large tree with her hand on her protruding stomach and her eyes closed. The look of serenity on her face made Kitty smile, and not wishing to disturb her, she turned to leave. As she did, she stepped on a twig, and it snapped.

"Kitty! You startled me," Jane said, her hand covering her heart.

Kitty walked over to sit beside her. "I apologise. I just came to tell you that the girls are taking a nap, and I will be in the sewing room working on the baby clothes I started. When I saw your eyes were closed, I hoped to leave without disturbing you. Lord knows you need your rest."

"I am so large and uncomfortable that I never really rest well. Moreover, the baby kicks so often, I am blessed if I can close my eyes for a few minutes without being reminded he is there." She smiled. "But do not think I am complaining. I am thrilled for the reminder he is well."

"So you believe you are carrying a boy?"

"I do, though I would not be disappointed if *he* turned out to be another daughter. I would love to give Charles a son, though, for men want a son to carry on their name. Nevertheless, he has said as long as the child is healthy, he cares not whether it is a boy or a girl."

"That sounds like my amiable brother! You are blessed to have such a husband, and I am so pleased he will be coming home soon. Still, I do not understand why Mr. Grantham cannot get him back before the baby is born."

"From the beginning, Mr. Grantham set a goal which Charles must reach before he considers him well enough to come home. You will never hear me complain about his reasoning, for that man has worked a miracle, as far as I am concerned."

"I can only agree," Kitty said. "By the way, have you heard from Lizzy?"

"Not since the day before yesterday, but I am certain I shall hear from her again soon."

"I hope so. I see the worry in your eyes whenever you do not get a letter."

"I have gotten in the habit of worrying about her and Emily so much that I find it a hard custom to break."

Kitty giggled. "Before long, Mr. Darcy will marry her, and then she will be his to worry about."

"Please do not tell Lizzy I told you that they were in love! I should not have shared her secret, but I was so happy I could not keep it to myself."

"I do not know why she does not tell everyone. Though I well remember how much she disliked Mr. Darcy when he was at Netherfield, if they have come to an understanding, then I wish them only joy."

"I suppose she wants to wait until she is sure everything will work out. And Lizzy has confessed she never hated Mr. Darcy. It is my belief she was in love with him all along, but tried to convince herself otherwise."

"That makes perfect sense. Before Mr. Darcy came along, if Lizzy had no use for someone, she ignored him. Not Mr. Darcy! She went on and on for months about his faults."

"I do not know why I did not realise that earlier. Instead, when she returned from Kent the summer Charles and I married, I made him break all ties with Mr. Darcy. I thought she hated him, and I did not want to subject her to his company. Seeing the kindness he has shown my family, I know now he is an honourable man and incapable of being unkind to anyone, most especially Lizzy."

"It is good to know he will be taking care of her and Emily from now on. Lizzy deserves to be happy."

"Yes, she does."

Suddenly Jane winced. "Are you all right? Should I send for the physician?" Kitty asked.

"I am well. I fear my ribs are just tender from being kicked so heartily." She smiled wanly. "I believe I shall go upstairs and lie down. At least he is calmer when I am lying on my back."

Kitty stood and helped Jane to her feet. "I shall walk with you. You are not too steady on your feet of late."

"I shall not argue with you. By the way, if a letter comes while I am resting, can I count on you to bring it up to me? I confess I am anxious to hear from Lizzy today.

"You may."

Chapter 18

Belper
Two days later

The post inn at Belper was finer than most, so Lord and Lady Matlock utilised it whenever they travelled to and from London. This morning it was so busy as they descended the narrow stairs to the main room that they were forced to rub elbows with a contingent of less affluent guests, which irritated the earl.

"Why must I come downstairs at this hour? I prefer to take my leave after the rabble has gone on. Besides, you could easily have been mistaken."

"Shhh! She might hear you," Lady Matlock said. Then she leaned in to whisper, "I know it was Mrs. Gardiner. I have a good memory for faces."

"Still, I do not see the importance of sorting this out, Eleanor."

"It is important because Lady Markham introduced her as a widow. Look, there she is now!" Lady Matlock nodded in the direction of a dark-haired woman with a little girl holding to her skirts, standing before the innkeeper. At that exact moment, a tall man joined them. "And that is the man I was telling you about. He has the same flaxen hair as the little girl."

Sighing, Lord Matlock glanced in that direction. "I know what you are implying, my dear, but he could be a relative and not necessarily the girl's father. Besides, since Fitzwilliam has no attachment to this woman, what does it matter?"

"After seeing how attentive our nephew was to her during the ball, I am not convinced that he is not involved with her. That is precisely why it matters!"

"Well I, for one, am not going to borrow trouble by worrying about your assumptions; they may very well be wrong."

"Humph!" Lady Matlock said, turning to confront him. "I suppose you would agree with Fitzwilliam's choice if he were to decide to marry Mrs. Gardiner and not Lady Markham?"

"Fitzwilliam is his own man. I have finally accepted that, and you should, too. Now, I am returning to the room to finish dressing. My cravat is a mess, though I cannot blame Barkley. He was rushed because you were so anxious for me to get a glimpse of that woman."

As he started to leave, Lady Matlock caught his arm. "Now see what you have done! They have disappeared whilst you and I were quarrelling."

"There they are," Lord Matlock said, nodding in the direction of the large front window.

Through this portal both watched as the gentleman handed Elizabeth into a private coach and then entered the vehicle behind her. "It is just as I thought, they are travelling together! If you had not delayed me, I would have greeted Mrs. Gardiner and forced an introduction. Then I would know who he is."

"If you simply must know, ask the proprietor." With that the earl shook his head, bewildered by her curiosity, and went back up the stairs.

Immediately Lady Matlock approached the innkeeper. "Excuse me, but could you tell me the name of that gentleman—the one to whom you were just speaking?"

"The tall one with very light hair?" the proprietor asked. "That would be Lord Van Lynden, my lady."

Abruptly someone interrupted him, asking about the accommodations, and Lady Matlock stepped back. Pleased to know the man's name, she hurried back to their rooms to share the news with her husband.

"Lord Vanderhayden?" Lord Matlock repeated. "That is an unusual name. Are you sure you heard correctly?"

"Of course, I am," Lady Matlock retorted sharply. "All I ask is that, once we are back in Town, you query your friends to see if they know anything about him. And, since it is obvious Mrs. Gardiner knows him well, I think Fitzwilliam should be informed."

"I suppose you will tell him if I do not?"

"I will. He is my nephew, and I care about his reputation. If he has any foolish ideas about Mrs. Gardiner, he needs to know about her travelling companion."

Lord Matlock sighed and turned back to the mirror. Admiring his cravat, he said, "You have done well this time, Barkley."

His valet smiled.

London
Guthrie's townhouse

All of the men involved in the assassination plot, except for Lord Van Lynden and Carney, were assembled in the parlour. John Guthrie had called the meeting after receipt of the latest express from Van Lynden. After refreshments were served, he stood to address the others.

"Lord Van Lynden, Mrs. Gardiner and the child are on their way to Richmond as we speak. His Lordship is optimistic that the money box will be at Canfield Manor, the home of Mrs. Gardiner's sister. As soon as he finds the box, he will send another ex-press. He wants us to be ready to put our plan into action soon after he arrives."

There were nods of agreement amongst the foreigners, who were enthusiastically devouring the cakes and biscuits as though they had not eaten in days. Guthrie found their common man-ners amusing. Being a member of the *ton,* he never had reason to mingle with the working classes. Still, he relished being in com-mand. He was in his element.

"As we discussed at our last meeting, we will carry out our plan regardless of whether the money box is found. Though Lord Van Lynden believes having the map of the floors of Castlere-agh's townhouse and the key to the side door a great asset, the lack of them will not deter us."

Still busy eating, Van Lynden's three countrymen did not re-ply, so Guthrie added, "Since we are so close to implementing the plan, I wish to go over the details." Turning to the handsomest member of the group, he asked, "Mr. Bakker, were you able to charm Castlereagh's new cook?"

Jann Bakker smiled widely. "Was there ever any doubt?" All the Dutchmen laughed. "It was as easy as taking sweets from a child. I have been calling on her almost every day with flowers and such. Yesterday, she even slipped me into the kitchen unno-ticed to sample her apple tart."

"And did you sample it?" Peter Visser said suggestively, mak-ing them chuckle again.

"I had a piece of the tart, but we were interrupted before I could sample anything else," Bakker boasted.

A new round of guffaws was met by a warning from Guthrie. "Just remember what you are there for—to learn the design of the house in case we do not have the map."

"I know my duty," Bakker said irritably. "But I cannot just walk in the door and ask where the man sleeps, can I?"

Ignoring the comment, Guthrie continued. "Having seen the map before, Lord Van Lynden is fairly certain that the viscount's quarters are on the east hall of the second floor."

Then he addressed Mr. Visser. "Were you able to find the tools to pick the lock if it becomes necessary?"

"I met a fellow in a pub at Cheapside and traded him a pair of boots for his tools. Though I have not used my skills in years, I have been practicing. It may take longer without the key, but I will get us in."

"That is good to know. Once Castlereagh is dead, you are to leave through that same door. Mr. Carney will be waiting with a coach on the street bordering that side of the house. Just go through the shrubs and over the fence."

"Why should we trust that man?" Bakker asked. "He has no allegiance to Holland; he is only along for the money."

"You are in good company, then. Lord Van Lynden and I do not trust him, either," Guthrie declared. "Carney is merely the dupe who will take the blame. Whoever reaches the coach first will shoot him. His body will be left behind for the magistrate to find. It is Van Lynden's supposition they will be so pleased to have a suspect, even a dead one, they will not be in too big a rush to look for his accomplices"

"Let us hope that is the case," Klaus Jansen replied.

"Remember, you are to abandon the coach somewhere in the Mint and scatter in different directions."

"When do we get paid?"

"Before you leave the coach, look in the storage compartments under the seats. A package for each of you will be inside."

When no one said anything more, he added, "I trust you all have a plan to leave England as soon as possible. The magistrate's discovery of Carney's body may buy you some time, but I would not depend on it."

Guthrie raised his glass. "A toast, gentlemen: to sending Castlereagh back to Hades where he belongs!"

One and all raised their glasses. "Hear! Hear!"

London

Darcy House

The dining room

"What do you mean the magistrate cannot search John Guthrie's townhouse?" William asked angrily. "Cannot or will not?"

Having arrived long after William sat down to dinner, Richard hoped to forestall discussing the business at hand until he had caught up with the courses that had already been served. As usual, Darcy was too impatient to wait, forcing him to explain whilst he was eating.

"*Will not* at this point."

"I thought the red-haired man Charles' butler identified as one of Howton's thieves was seen at a pub with Guthrie shortly before the murder."

Richard took another sip of his cousin's expensive wine to wash down a bite of pheasant. "That is true. An informant saw Guthrie and another gentleman with Carney at a pub in the warehouse district the morning of the very day Howton was killed."

Angrily, William threw his serviette down on the table. "Then what is their justification for waiting?"

Defeated, Richard lay down his fork. "If you will cease with the interrogation, I shall explain."

Looking very irritated, William nodded.

"This case goes much higher than the magistrate's office now. The Prime Minister has more nefarious criminals in his sights than those who killed Howton."

"I do not follow."

"I was not called back into service merely to fill in for Colonel

Seeger, as my orders stated. Once I arrived at my office, General Lassiter briefed me on a matter of great consequence—a supposed plot to kill the Foreign Minister."

"Viscount Castlereagh?"

"Yes. Please remember that all of this is confidential. For now, watch what you say, especially in front of Browning and Whitaker. I do not think even the Bow Street Runners have been apprised of it."

William moaned, rubbing his eyes. "This disaster gets more complicated by the hour." Then he stood and began to pace. "So, Guthrie may also be involved in a plot to kill Castlereagh."

"At this point, the plot against the Foreign Minister is still speculation. However, Liverpool[14] is determined to treat it as though it is real. As I understand it, Castlereagh is now being guarded day and night, howbeit covertly. I doubt if even his servants are aware of who is truly a servant and who is a spy."

"So, if we are not allowed to pursue leads to locate Howton's murderer, what are we to do?"

"Wait. If the rumours are correct, the assassination attempt is to take place within the next week or two. If nothing happens, then Guthrie will be ours to question."

William sat back down despairingly. "What am I supposed to tell Elizabeth—that I have no earthly idea when I will see her again?"

"If she loves you, Darcy, she will understand that none of this is your fault."

"No woman will understand being forsaken forever."

"It is not forever. It is only two more weeks."

"When you love someone as I love Elizabeth, two weeks is forever."

Pemberley

One day later

As Mrs. Reynolds went in search of the countess, she prayed that what she had discovered in Mrs. Gardiner's bedroom might be easily explained. Knowing how close the countess was to their former houseguest, she hoped the lady would have an explanation which might assuage her suspicions.

Approaching the part of the gardens which contained a small goldfish pond, she stopped to smile at the scene playing out just ahead. Lady Foggett and Lady Markham were both sitting on a stone bench, cheering on Hugh and Kathy. Always competitive, the twins were vying to see which one could get a homemade boat across the pond first.

Suddenly, Kathy jumped up. "I won! I won!"

"By only an inch!" Hugh added, good-naturedly.

"I think you are both splendid sailors," Millicent exclaimed, clapping her hands. "With two very different designs, you almost managed to tie."

Just then she noticed the housekeeper and greeted her. "Mrs. Reynolds, do you need to speak to me?"

"For only a minute, if you please, my lady."

The countess addressed Lady Foggett, "Aunt, will you excuse me?" With the woman's nod, she turned to her children. "Hugh, Kathy, why not take the crumbs we brought and feed the fish?"

As the children hurried to get the bags of breadcrumbs, Millicent walked towards Fitzwilliam's servant. Seeing the concern in the housekeeper's expression, her brows knit. "What is wrong?"

Sighing heavily, Mrs. Reynolds reached into a pocket of her gown and brought out a cloth. Unfolding it, she handed it to the countess. "A maid was cleaning Mrs. Gardiner's room and found this on the floor of the closet."

Millicent took what was obviously a man's handkerchief and read aloud the initials embroidered on the corner. "V L."

"Could this have been in the room before Elizabeth arrived at

Pemberley?"

"No. I personally inspect all the rooms before and after use. Besides, no one with those initials has ever been a guest here."

"Hmm. Obviously, it belongs to a man."

"I agree."

"V L." Millicent repeated the initials several times. Out of the blue the surname of Emily's family came to mind. "Van Lynden," she murmured, her expression changing to one of concern.

"Do you know the man?"

"Please do not say that I told you, but Emily's father was, or perhaps I should say is, Lord Van Lynden. Elizabeth thought him dead, for he never returned to the estate in Scotland where he had banished his wife and child after Emily's birth. In fact, he did not return even after his wife died."

"What can this mean in regards to Mrs. Gardiner?"

"If this handkerchief does belong to him, then the reason Elizabeth left Pemberley may not be as harmless as wishing to be with her sister when the child is born."

Pacing as though she could not decide what to do next, the countess abruptly halted. "Do you remember the name and location of the Bingleys' estate?"

"Canfield Manor in Richmond."

"Yes, that is it. Would it be possible to leave my children here in the care of Lady Foggett whilst I travel to Richmond?"

"They are most welcome to stay. But why go to Richmond?"

"I intend to follow the same route in hopes of finding Elizabeth safe and sound. If I do not, then I shall know she left Pemberley under duress and raise the alarm."

"When will you be leaving?"

"Tomorrow. At first light."

Richmond
Canfield Manor
Two days later

As the large coach came to a stop at the front entrance to Canfield Manor, the two guards William had posted there, Hartley and Boggus, walked down the steps to examine the occupants. Dressed in the same livery as Bingley's footmen, Lord Van Lynden had no way of knowing that he was being assessed the moment he stepped out of the coach.

As Hartley helped Elizabeth from the coach, the front door opened, and Kitty came rushing down the steps. "Lizzy!" she exclaimed, hugging her sister tightly. "I had no idea you were coming, and I do not think Jane did, either. If she did, she said not a word to me."

Having already convinced Van Lynden to let her handle her family's questions, Elizabeth put on a brave face and hugged Kitty in return. "I...I wanted it to be a surprise."

By then Boggus had helped Cora and Emily from the coach, and Kitty stooped to greet her niece. "Miss Emily, how you have grown!"

A shy child, Emily had withdrawn even further after being forced to share a coach with her intimidating father, who made no effort to engage the child in conversation or to reveal his paternity. Quite traumatised by being plucked from the familiarity of Pemberley, she had spent the whole trip clinging to Elizabeth.

Noting her niece's discomfort, Kitty whispered to Elizabeth, "Emily appears to be upset about something."

"She is only tired," Elizabeth said, praying Van Lynden would keep his part of the bargain and be silent. "Is Jane well? I need to ask her where Emily's trunks are—the ones I brought back from Scotland." She motioned to Van Lynden. "Emily's father wishes to claim them."

Kitty's face went white. Edging closer to Elizabeth, she whispered, "We have protection. Two of our footmen are guards sent by Mr. Darcy. Just say the word, and he will be captured and held."

"Please, no! I have no choice but to abide by his wishes, or he will take Emily away from me. I have agreed to go with him as her governess."

"You...you have what?"

"He has the law on his side, so please do not make him angry."

Kitty nodded, and Elizabeth performed a short introduction. "Lord Van Lynden, allow me to introduce my sister, Catherine. Catherine, this is Emily's father, Lord Van Lynden."

Both parties nodded warily. Then, meeting the uneasy eyes of the two former Bow Street Runners, Kitty smiled. She knew they would assume all was well since that was their signal. Next, she addressed the maid who had been silently observing.

"I know that Gracie and Marianne will be glad that you are home, Cora."

A faux smile flashed across the servant's face and just as quickly disappeared. Picking up Emily, Kitty started up the steps beside Elizabeth while Van Lynden trailed behind.

"I just left Jane, so she should still be in the drawing room." More quietly, she said to Elizabeth, "This may be more of a shock than Jane can handle in her condition."

"Then you must help me to convince her that it is for the best."

When they entered the drawing room, Jane was lying on a sofa with her eyes closed. Seeing this, Elizabeth whispered, "Let her sleep."

"She naps constantly now," Kitty replied. "If you wish to speak to her, there is no convenient time."

Kitty handed Emily to her mother and walked over to Jane, softly calling her name. Jane awoke and tried to sit up, rising onto her elbows.

"Wha...what? Are the children—" Seeing Elizabeth, she smiled and held out her hand. "Oh, Lizzy! I was beginning to worry since I had not heard from you in several—"

Van Lynden approached, and Jane locked eyes with the villain standing right behind Elizabeth. A look of recognition and horror crossed her face before she fainted, falling back onto the sofa.

Jane's bedroom

When Jane regained consciousness, she was in her own bed, with Kitty on one side of her and Elizabeth on the other. Almost at once she remembered the sinister visage of Lord Van Lynden in her own home and reached out to Elizabeth with pleading eyes. "Tell me I did not see him. He cannot be here!"

Elizabeth swallowed hard. "Jane, please try to stay calm. All is well. Lord Van Lynden returned to England to find Emily and... and he has offered me a position as her governess so that we will not be parted."

"Lizzy, you cannot," Jane said, beginning to cry. "He is an evil man. You cannot think of going with him."

"I will not be parted from my child. Besides," Elizabeth said, crossing her fingers surreptitiously, "I never felt he was a threat to me. In fact, I imagine he could have already had me charged with kidnapping, but he has not."

"I beg you, tell Mr. Darcy! I know he is in love with you, Lizzy, and he will stop that man from taking Emily and gaining you as a bonus."

"Jane, Mr. Darcy has been far too kind—"

"Do you not love him?" Jane interrupted.

"It is because I love him that I will not put him in jeopardy with the law. Lord Van Lynden is within his rights to take custody of his own child, whether I agree or not."

"But, Mr. Darcy—"

"If Mr. Darcy were to interfere, he could be challenged to a duel or, at the least, arrested for interfering with Lord Van Lynden's custody of Emily. So, you see, her father is trying to be reasonable."

"Reasonable?" Jane sobbed. "Emily does not know him, and she believes you are her mother. If he were a reasonable man, he would leave her with you and support her financially."

"To men of his station, it is about status; he wants her raised in his sphere, not mine."

"Still—"

"Please, Jane." Seeing the pleading in Elizabeth's eyes, Jane went silent. "I will keep in touch, I promise," Elizabeth continued. "That way you will know all is well."

"Will you be staying tonight?" Kitty asked.

"No. As soon as we find Emily's trunks, Lord Van Lynden plans to leave for London."

"Where will you go from there?"

"I...I am not certain. He still has the estate in Scotland. In any case, I will write you every day no matter where I am."

Jane nodded, closing her eyes in resignation and sending the tears pooled there down her face. Then she reached for Elizabeth, who fell into her embrace.

"I shall pray God's protection on you both every day, and should I ever feel you are in harm's way, I shall not hesitate to send Mr. Darcy after you."

Elizabeth nodded against her sister's chest, then pulled back to look into Jane's eyes with fresh tears of her own. "I shall rely upon it."

The trunks Van Lynden wanted were easily found in the attic, and he opened them straightaway. Pleased to see the money box in the bottom of one, he ordered them closed and taken to the coach.

Jane was too upset to watch Elizabeth and Emily leave; thus, Kitty, who was equally broken-hearted, saw her and Emily off with plenty of hugs and kisses for both of them. Then, she stood on the portico and waved until the ominous black coach was completely out of sight.

London
Darcy House
Unable to spend the night, Richard had no idea that by the time dinner was over and he had left for a meeting with General Lassiter, William had become utterly despondent. The prospect of being separated even longer from Elizabeth was almost more disappointment than he could endure; thus, he decided to do something he had been contemplating for days.

Taking a candelabrum from a sideboard, he made his way to his study. Once inside, he locked the door and crossed to a large bookcase in a corner behind his desk. Moving one book, he pulled a lever that caused the entire bookcase to swivel open, revealing a secret room. Only Mr. and Mrs. Barnes were aware of its existence, as there was no door to the hallway. This small area, no more than twelve feet wide, had been used by Darcys for centuries to store personal and household ledgers. It also had a safe in the wall for storing valuables when the family was in Town.

Years ago, William had placed a table of art supplies, blank canvases and an easel near the natural light of the windows, so he could draw undisturbed while in town. He had not utilised that section of the room since starting the portrait of Elizabeth that now resided at Pemberley. Tonight, unable to put off his yearning, he was determined to draw her again, even if only by candlelight. The last portrait he had done was five long years ago, and Elizabeth was no longer that young girl. No, she was now a vibrant woman, and he hoped to capture her essence in a portrait meant for his eyes only.

Eager to get started, he found an appropriate canvas, selected two charcoal pencils, and placed the canvas on the easel. Closing his eyes, he tried to recall exactly how Elizabeth had looked on the balcony at Pemberley. Then, he opened them and began.

Chapter 19

London
Darcy House
The library

With Richard ordered back to headquarters, William was at loose ends. Having long since given up spending his days at White's while in London, he was not about to take up that habit again. Still, with the issue of finding Howton's killer deferred because of a dubious plot against Viscount Castlereagh, William was at a loss to know how to keep his mind off Elizabeth. Even the concerns his steward brought to his attention took second place to thoughts of her, and against decorum he had written a letter to Mrs. Reynolds, enclosing a letter to Elizabeth inside. He prayed that when she got it, Elizabeth would not only forgive his audacity, but also be inspired to answer. Now, all he could do was wait.

Though listless, he had heeded his livery manager's advice to take Kronos for a ride in the park, for the stallion was harder to handle when he was not ridden routinely. Afterward, William made his way to the library intent on reading the newspapers he had neglected since his arrival. An hour later, as he unfolded yet another paper, Mr. Barnes appeared at the open door.

"Lord Matlock, sir."

The earl, who had followed the butler, walked right past Barnes. As his uncle came towards him, William let the paper he was holding drop, and he began to rise. Lord Matlock motioned for him to stay seated.

"Do not trouble yourself, Fitzwilliam. I shall only take a minute of your time."

"I had no idea you had returned to London, Uncle."

"Yes, well, Edgar and I do not get on long under one roof."

"Has he improved?"

"He has stopped drinking, though that has his temper even more on edge." The earl shook his head in despair. "Hence, I am here, and he is there. Still, I am pleased that he is at least trying to get his demons under regulation. I believe the influence of liquor was the main cause of his debauchery."

"I agree. You know that I never held him in high regard, but I want to see him take control of his life and do well."

"I know you do, Nephew, and I appreciate it."

"In any case, I do not think you are here to give me a report on Leighton."

The earl laughed. "That is one of the things I admire most about you, Fitzwilliam; you never beat about the bush. So, I shall not either. First, let me say that I hope you realise I try never to meddle in your business; however, your aunt is not of the same mind, especially when it comes to eligible women. She is concerned you may have feelings for the widow you were hosting at Pemberley, Mrs. Gardiner. Thus, she insisted I hurry here to tell you what happened on our way back to Town."

William was irritated. "And?"

"We were at the post inn in Belper when we saw her." William's brows knit in question, so he continued. "Mrs. Gardiner was with a man. She and a little girl boarded a private coach with him."

William stood, his face falling into stern lines. "Are you certain it was Eliz...Mrs. Gardiner?"

"Frankly, I did not get a good look at her, but Evelyn is quite certain."

William's heart began to flutter with vague terror. Seeing his expression darken, Lord Matlock went on. "Evelyn enquired the man's name from the innkeeper and was told it was Lord Vanderhayden."

"Vanderhayden," William repeated. "That is not a name with which I am familiar."

"Nor am I. Moreover, you know how stubborn my wife can be when she thinks she is right. I have been ordered to enquire of all my acquaintances if they have heard of him."

"If...if you learn anything about this Vanderhayden, I should like to know."

Assuming his nephew would either dismiss their encounter with Mrs. Gardiner or be angry with his wife for being meddlesome, Lord Matlock was taken aback. "If that is your wish."

William rose from his chair and walked to the windows. The earl took the opportunity to change the subject.

"Have you seen Richard lately? My housekeeper said he has not been by the house in days."

"He was called back to duty several days ago."

"Oh? Is there something amiss?"

"I am afraid it is confidential; he would not tell me."

Lord Matlock nodded. "Well, if you should see him, say that his mother and I would love to have him dine with us soon. And, of course, you are always welcome."

William displayed a wan smile. "I hope to dine with you before long, and should I see Richard, I shall give him your message."

"Good! Now, my boy, I shall let you get back to whatever you were doing."

William walked his uncle to the library door, and Mr. Barnes escorted the earl to his coach.

Canfield Manor

Hartley and Boggus received regular updates from William, so they knew the man suspected of frightening Mrs. Bingley's relatives in Meryton had apparently killed Howton and was now evading them. Since William hoped he might ultimately lead them to the other thieves, Mr. Carney was not to be detained if he arrived in Richmond, unless they felt he was a threat to the family. Consequently, when he arrived on Lord Van Lynden's coach, he was recognised immediately and kept under careful observation.

Moreover, they were also watching three footmen who might have had opportunity to help Howton continue to poison Charles Bingley when he was at home. Though they had not previously determined exactly who it was, when Mr. Percival was seen conversing covertly with Carney, the connection became obvious. Searching that footman's room whilst he was occupied elsewhere, they found remnants of the same green-tinged powder Howton had kept in his bedroom and at his office, as well as a piece of paper giving the address of the warehouse where the stolen goods were kept. As a consequence, the retired Bow Street Runners waited only until after Van Lynden's coach had disappeared down the drive to act.

As Percival walked up the steps to the portico, Mr. Boggus grabbed him from behind and, with Hartley's help, forced him around to the side of the house. They marched him directly towards the stables where they planned to hold him in a cleaned-out tack room, courtesy of the livery manager. That man was the only other servant who knew about their search for the culprit who had helped to poison Bingley.

All the while, Percival protested. "Let go of me! You have no right to manhandle me like a criminal! What have I done?"

"I think you know full well what you did, Mr. Percival. You seem well acquainted with two other willing murderers," Hartley declared, shoving the footman into the empty room and securing the padlock.

"Who might they be?" Percival cried from within the tack room.

"The red-haired man on the last coach, Mr. Carney, and Mr. Bingley's cousin, David Howton."

At the mention of those names, Percival became silent. Hartley gave Boggus a satisfied smile. "I feel better now that we have this miscreant locked up."

"Aye. As long as he was free, I feared for Mrs. Bingley and the children."

"As did I. At least now we have something good to report. I shall write Mr. Darcy about Percival and warn him that Carney is on his way back to London."

"With all the disappointments Mr. Darcy has had of late, this should be welcome news," Boggus replied."

"I am sure it will. I shall also ask if he wants one of us to bring Percival into Town, since the local magistrate has recently died, and we have no idea how long it will take to appoint a new one."

"I hope we hear soon," Boggus said. "We cannot keep Percival in that room forever."

"He may not like it, but with food and water he will survive. That is more consideration than he gave Mr. Bingley."

"True."

London
Darcy House
    After his uncle departed, one thought hounded William. Could

the woman in Belper have been Elizabeth? Heart now beating like a drum, he crossed the library to a small desk, sat down and dashed off a quick note to Mrs. Reynolds, asking if Elizabeth was still at Pemberley. Afterward, he rang for Barnes.

Soon the butler appeared in the doorway. William held out the letter. "Send this by express rider, please."

The butler took it, gazed at the address, bowed and rushed to do as asked.

Alone once more, the idea that Elizabeth might have left him was so overwhelming that, for a moment, William felt he could not breathe. He had experienced the same effect the night he arrived in London from Kent five years before. Yearning for Elizabeth, instinctively his hand sought the only tangible connection that he possessed—her hair ribbon. Slipping his hand into his pocket, his fingers glided over the satiny finish. Still unsatisfied, he rose and walked to his study.

When he had finally finished the portrait the night before, he had been pleased at the contrast between the innocent young woman in the portrait at Pemberley and this one, which portrayed Elizabeth in all her womanly glory. He had drawn her as she looked that night on the balcony, her long hair tousled by the wind whilst she wore nothing save a thin, silk nightgown that clung to every feminine curve. Though she had pulled a lacy shawl over her shoulders and bodice the moment she noticed him, the image was already seared in his memory—a memory now captured on canvas.

Reaching the study, he rushed to the bookcase and opened the secret room. Once inside, he went straight to the drawing. As he removed the muslin cloth draped over it, unexpectedly he recognised something he had not seen last night. In depicting Elizabeth exactly as she looked the last time they were together, unconsciously he had included the love that shone in her eyes.

Oh, Elizabeth! Reaching to touch her, the hard canvas beneath his fingers caused his eyes to close in agony. *How long must I be parted from you, my love?*

Regaining his composure, he picked up the canvas and walked back into his study. Propping it against a row of books on a shelf, he poured a large glass of brandy and sat down on a sofa opposite the drawing. Had not Mrs. Barnes knocked on the door to announce dinner, he might have remained until the next morning, staring at Elizabeth's image as though she were there. Instead, he reluctantly returned the portrait to the secret room and made his way to his lonely dining room.

London
Guthrie's townhouse

Elizabeth was drained by the time they reached London, for not staying at Canfield Manor meant that they had stopped at an inn between there and Town. That inn had been so small and uncomfortable that she and Emily were forced to share one small bed. She had gotten little sleep, and by the time the coach pulled up to the rear of John Guthrie's townhouse in London, she was too weary to be afraid.

As Lord Van Lynden helped her from the coach, a gentleman came forward, removing his hat. Elizabeth thought he looked much too genial to be associated with Emily's father. Still, she was instantly wary of him.

"Mr. Guthrie, this is my daughter's governess, Mrs. Gardiner," Van Lynden said.

Guthrie smiled and nodded like an imbecile. "Mrs. Gardiner," he said with a slight bow. Elizabeth did not return his smile or his greeting.

Meanwhile, Emily had been helped from the coach by a footman, and she ran to Elizabeth, grabbing her skirt. Elizabeth picked her up and placed a kiss on her forehead. Guthrie looked between the girl and Lord Van Lynden. If he thought the man would acknowledge the child, he was mistaken, for Van Lynden immediately began to instruct the servants on which trunks to take to his rooms. Once he was finished, he again addressed Guthrie.

"Have you a room prepared for the girl and her governess?"

"We do."

"Good. Then, let us get inside before we are seen."

With his statement, Elizabeth's face clouded, for she wondered from whom Van Lynden might wish to hide. Still, she had no choice but to follow the men into the manor house.

Once inside, a woman Elizabeth assumed was the housekeeper stepped forward and asked her to follow her.

After they had gone up two flights of stairs, the older woman turned to look at Elizabeth. "I am Mrs. Southard, the housekeeper. I understand that you are the governess and the child is—"

Afraid of what she might say in front of Emily, Elizabeth interrupted. "Yes, I am Mrs. Gardiner, and this is Emily."

The housekeeper looked at her quizzically then continued on her way. Going down a long hallway, she stopped in front of a door. It opened instantly at her touch, revealing a suite of rooms which included a bedroom, a dressing room and a sitting area. After Elizabeth set Emily on her feet, she looked around the elegantly decorated space.

Mrs. Southard looked at the child. "The Master had a bed added to the sitting room for the girl. There is warm water in the pitcher in the dressing room, if you wish to wash. Should you need anything...anything at all, you may ring the bell, and I will answer." Resignedly, Elizabeth nodded. "I imagine it has been quite some time since you have eaten. Would you like me to send up tea or lemonade and some small sandwiches?"

"Lemonade and sandwiches would be wonderful," Elizabeth replied, giving the servant a slight smile. Immediately, the house-keeper exited the room.

Afterward, Elizabeth heard a key turn in the lock, and waiting a few seconds to be certain the woman had left, she tried the door knob. It was indeed locked. Putting on a cheerful face, she turned to her daughter.

"Why do we not wash our faces and change clothes? Then, when the refreshments come, we shall be ready to eat."

Emily nodded but did not smile. Elizabeth sat down and drew her onto her lap. "Do not be afraid, dearest. As I told you, we are going to have a great adventure, seeing places we have never seen before and meeting new people."

"But I do not want to, Mama. I want to see Mr. Darcy."

It took all of Elizabeth's strength not to cry, for that was her dearest desire, too. "We shall, love. After we are all done with our trip, then we shall go back to visit Pemberley."

Emily began to cry. "I...I want to go now. I miss Snow and Hugh and Kathy."

"Now, what did I tell you about Lord Van Lynden?"

"He is family," she murmured quietly.

"Yes. Lord Van Lynden is part of your father's family, and he wants to get to know you. That is why he has asked us to join him on this trip. It would hurt his feelings if we were to leave. You would not want to hurt his feelings would you?"

The child's light blue eyes filled with tears, and Elizabeth could tell Emily was struggling between what she desired and pleasing her. It broke her heart to use guilt to force her daugh-ter's cooperation, but fearing what might happen if Lord Van Lynden realised that his daughter had no desire to know him, Elizabeth had no choice. Beyond that, she had no earthly idea what she would do if Emily's father suddenly told her the truth. The fact that he had basically ignored the child thus far gave Elizabeth hope that he had decided to let Emily get to know him before revealing his paternity. She prayed he would continue in that vein for a long time.

In the kitchen, Agatha Grinder, Guthrie's cook, was creating a tray for the new occupants of the otherwise empty third floor. As she worked, she listened to the only other long-time employee, Mrs. Southard.

"I tell you, Agatha, something is not right about this. It was as though the governess did not want me to mention that Lord Van Lynden was the child's father."

"Perhaps you were mistaken."

"I could well be, but there are plenty of other odd things happening. For instance, why was I instructed to lock them in the room? I have never locked a guest in their room in all the years I have worked for the Guthrie family. Moreover, they are not to be let out unless the father wishes it. What kind of man treats his own child or the child's governess like a prisoner?"

Agatha nodded her head. "I agree with you on that. Many strange things are going on now that the master has befriended Lord *Whoever he is!*"

"Lord *Van Lynden,*" Mrs. Southard answered.

"That man makes me shudder every time he looks at me with those devil eyes."

"He does have an evil look about him; I will give you that," Mrs. Southard said. "And now that the mistress is too addled to control her son, Mr. Guthrie seems to have gone mad by inviting questionable men into the house for food and drink. He acts as though he has not a care in the world, though, from what you have said, he may be spending more than the household can afford."

The cook added, "Indeed! I received another note from the

butcher yesterday stating that I cannot order anything more until the bill is paid. Old Mr. Guthrie would turn over in his grave if
he knew!"

"If not for my loyalty to the mistress, I would have left long
ago."

"As would I," the cook said. "Do you think the master told her
about the governess and child now under her roof?"

"Not likely! Now that she cannot remember anything from
one day to the next, he hardly ever stops in to see her. I never
thought I would say this, but he has turned out to be a sorry man
and an even sorrier son. It is my opinion that he is just waiting
for her to die."

"I agree," Agatha said decidedly. "I think he is taking her to
Ireland in hopes that the arduous journey will kill her."

"Whenever I am with her, I make sure to hint that if she wishes to stay in good health, she should remain here at home," Mrs.
Southard said.

"Do you think she understands or will even remember?"

The housekeeper sighed. "I have no idea, but I pray she will,
for if she leaves, most likely we will never see her again."

"I believe you are right." Then, adding a pitcher of lemonade to
the tray, the cook continued. "Do you want me to take this upstairs?"

"No. There is another order. Only I am allowed to converse
with them."

"Stranger still."

"Indeed. Now that I think of it, I suspect that Van Lynden fellow is involved in some kind of trouble. Perhaps it would be wise
to contact my late friend Bertha's nephew."

"The one who works for the Bow Street Runners? What was
his name?"

"Whitaker. We have not spoken in a while—in fact, not since
my friend passed last year."

"You had better be careful. If Mr. Guthrie were to find out—"

"I shall be. I fear Lord Van Lynden learning of it even more than the master."

Canfield Manor
The next day

As Lady Markham prepared to depart for London, Kitty saw her to her coach. "I am so pleased to have met you, Lady Markham, and to know that Lizzy has an ally in you. Please send word the moment you learn anything. I have not been easy since Lizzy left here with that man. Just to know that she and Emily are safe will be a blessing."

Millicent stopped at the door to the coach to give Kitty an encouraging smile. "I shall write to you the moment I learn something. I am determined to find your sister and free her and Emily from *that* man's influence. I pray I did the right thing by making the situation seem trifling to Mrs. Bingley. In her condition, I did not think it wise to upset her. That is why I acted as though I only stopped on my way to London in hopes of finding Elizabeth here."

"I appreciate your concern for Jane. She has been upset enough and needs nothing else to add to her worries."

"Let me be off, then. I need to gain Town by dark if I wish to see Fitzwilliam today."

The countess took the hand offered by a footman; he helped her into the coach and shut the door. As it began to roll down the drive, both women waved until the coach was out of sight.

Kitty took a moment to consider all that she had heard; then, raising her eyes to heaven, she prayed.

"Lord, I ask for your protection over Lizzy, Emily, Mr. Darcy and Lady Markham, for I fear they are confronting a man who will stop at nothing to have his way." She started to go inside, but stopped. "Oh, and Lord, will you please send Charles home soon?"

Kitty was at peace when she went back inside to find Jane.

Chapter 20

London

Matlock House

Unable to sleep, William had been fully dressed long before daylight and eager to visit his relations to clarify some details about the lady they had seen in Belper. However, now that his carriage was coming to a stop in front of the imposing facade of the Earl of Matlock's townhouse, he began to wonder if they would be awake. He need not have worried, however, for just as a footman opened the carriage door, Lord Matlock stepped out the front door.

William exited the carriage just as his uncle began down the steps. "Uncle!"

"Fitzwilliam! What in the world has you out so early? I was just on my way to meet with my solicitor, but I can postpone the meeting."

"There is no need. I had a few questions about the man and woman at Belper, and since my aunt was the one who pointed them out, I believe she is the one I should ask."

"I shall be on my way, then. Hopefully, I shall see you across the dinner table soon."

"Of course," William said, giving him a quick smile before

continuing up the steps.

Seeing the master's nephew, the butler, who had been watching the exchange from the doorway, stood aside to allow William to enter.

"Mr. Darcy, what a pleasure to see you again, sir."

"Thank you, Soames. Is Lady Matlock available?"

"I believe that she is, sir. Please allow me to tell her that you are here."

The butler hastened up the grand staircase and vanished. In what seemed only seconds, his aunt appeared on the landing.

"Fitzwilliam, my dear boy!" she declared, beginning down the stairs. "Edward told me he talked with you yesterday, and I had hoped to hear you would be dining with us soon, but this is totally unexpected."

"In point of fact, I am here in regards to what my uncle had to say."

"Come," she said turning. "Let us speak privately in the drawing room." After William followed her into that room, she asked, "Would you like some tea?"

"No, thank you. If you do not mind, will you please answer a few questions regarding the woman you saw at Belper?"

Her expression grew wary. "Oh? What do you wish to know about *that* woman?"

"Are you certain the woman you saw was Mrs. Gardiner?"

"I am positive."

"Can you describe those with her?"

One hand came up to pinch her chin as she sought to remember. "The child, a little girl, looked to be about three years of age. The man was tall." She examined William. "About your size, I would say, and very well-dressed. As for whether or not he was handsome or plain, I cannot say, for he was facing away from me."

William's spirits sank, though his aunt was too busy trying to recall more details to notice.

Suddenly, her face lit up. "I do remember now that he had very light hair. I glimpsed it when he donned his hat, and I remember thinking that he must be a relation of the child, for her hair was the same shade. That was why I went to fetch Edward—I believed that Mrs. Gardiner must be travelling with the child's father."

William's pulse began to race. "And the clerk said his name was Lord Vanderhayden. Are you absolutely certain of that?"

"I...I believe that was what he said, but you know how Edward likes to tease me about my hearing."

William leaned in to give his aunt a kiss on the cheek. "Thank you. You have been most helpful. Now, I really must go; please excuse me."

As he began walking away, she called, "Come for dinner this Friday."

Almost as an afterthought, William replied, "I shall try."

Guthrie's townhouse
Elizabeth's bedroom

Mrs. Southard had always unlocked the door, then knocked quietly before entering without waiting for a reply; thus, when Elizabeth heard the key turn, followed by a loud knock and the door remained shut, the hair on the back of her neck stood up.

"Enter."

The door opened, and Van Lynden walked in. His face was as blank as a canvas, and Elizabeth grew anxious waiting for him to speak.

"Mrs. Gardiner, there are things we need to discuss." As he talked, he looked about the room. "Where is the girl?"

Incensed that he always addressed his daughter in that manner, boldly Elizabeth lifted her chin. "Emily is taking a nap."

"That is just as well. I do not discuss business in front of children. They are too impressionable. Do you not agree?"

Astounded at this statement, Elizabeth could only nod. His stare was unnerving, and she began to study her shoes. However, when he remained silent, she stole a glance, only to find that he was still staring at her, though now his expression was uncomfortably amenable.

"It is not unreasonable to assume Mr. Darcy has learned by now that you have left Pemberley to become my daughter's governess. Rumour has it he is in London. It follows that he may learn you are here and arrive to confront you...or me."

"I do not comprehend how he would know I am here."

"Oh, come now, Mrs. Gardiner. The wealthy have ways of finding anything they wish. Did I not find you?" When she did not answer, he continued. "In any case, you should know that if he does come, he will be allowed to speak with you alone. For our arrangement to work, Darcy must understand you took the position of Emily's governess of your own free will. As I said in Lambton, I will not be forced into a duel over a governess. You are free to leave. If he should come, it falls to you to convince him of that, not I."

"I...I understand."

His eyes fixed on the swell of her breasts and he stepped closer. "In this country, I fear for my daughter's safety; that is why your rooms are locked. But everything will be entirely different once we are in Rotterdam. There we shall become one happy family."

A stray curl had escaped from Elizabeth's bun, and he reached to push it behind her ear. She recoiled, and his aloofness instantly returned. "You will learn I can be very amiable and generous if I am accorded due respect. It is not out of the realm of possibility that, should I choose to marry again, I may give consideration to you. After all, my child is accustomed to your company."

Taken aback, Elizabeth could not answer. "I have business which demands my attention, so I will leave you to ponder what we have discussed." He went towards the door, stopping just before he exited. "A final word of caution: if you have any concern for Mr. Darcy, you will make certain he does nothing foolish."

With that, he left the room. Elizabeth shivered and sank into a chair, completely spent. She had never considered that William might find her before they left the country, and the thought of seeing him again left her emotions at odds. Though she would dearly love to see him one last time, she feared what might happen if he and Van Lynden met.

Please, Lord, do not let him find me!

Guthrie's study

John Guthrie wished to talk privately, so Lord Van Lynden joined him in his study for a glass of brandy. Having earlier warned his host that Fitzwilliam Darcy might appear on his doorstep demanding to see Mrs. Gardiner, he was surprised Guthrie seemed intrigued by the idea.

"I cannot fathom Fitzwilliam Darcy coming here. Though we are acquainted, he has never seemed cordial. In fact, I doubt he would remember my name."

"There is no guarantee that he will come, but I want us to be prepared if he does. He will be allowed to speak to Mrs. Gardiner privately if he wishes. As I told the lady, it is up to her to convince Mr. Darcy, should he come, that she is here because she is very devoted to my daughter and wishes to remain with her."

"And since Mrs. Gardiner is very pretty, I do not suppose you mind."

Van Lynden gave Guthrie an angry look. "That is not why she is employed."

Guthrie chuckled. "Of course not." Seeing that Van Lynden

had grown more enraged, he changed the subject. "But that is not what we are here to discuss. What do you suppose happened to Mr. Carney? Did I not hear you tell him to be here yesterday?"

"I did tell him, and it makes me very uneasy that he did not do as I asked. He knows too much to just let him disappear."

Suddenly, there was a knock on the door. Guthrie sighed, whispering, "It is always something." Louder, he said, "Come in."

Mr. Haggard opened the door and stepped forward to hand him a paper. "Sir, this note was just presented at the front door by one of the children from the neighbourhood. As soon as he handed it to a footman, he ran off like a frightened deer."

Exchanging a worried look with Van Lynden, Guthrie took the note. "Thank you, Haggard."

When the elderly butler disappeared, Van Lynden hissed, "Is it Carney?"

Reading the hastily scribbled message, Guthrie replied, "It is from his wife. She says Carney is drinking in the pub near their home and spouting off things best left unsaid. She begs us to come and get him before he gets into trouble."

Van Lynden stood, slamming his glass down on the table. "Bloody hell! Must we lock him away until he is needed?"

"Do you think it wise for us to be seen again with him?"

"What choice do we have? We must act quickly, and you and I are the only ones on hand."

"I see your point. I shall order my carriage be readied straightaway."

As Guthrie and Lord Van Lynden left the study, they encountered Mrs. Southard in the hallway. "Mrs. Southard, I see you have returned from your errand," Guthrie said.

"Yes, sir. It did not take long. I hope that all was quiet while I was away."

"It was. Lord Van Lynden and I are on our way to the warehouse district. We should return in about an hour or so."

"Very well, sir."

As she watched the two men walk away, Mrs. Southard pondered whether she had done the right thing. Suspicious of the situation involving the governess and the child, she had delivered a note to the Bow Street Runners' office asking Mr. Whitaker to contact her. Those in the office had related he was working for a private citizen at present, but they would see he received her missive.

Moreover, Southard had decided she needed to be more observant, trusting that by the time Mr. Whitaker contacted her, she could offer him more than her suspicions. For that reason, she had written down descriptions of the men who had been meeting with her employer and Lord Van Lynden, noting that all had light blond hair, one was tall and handsome, another was average in height and appearance and the last was shorter and had a scar on his forehead. She had even heard his name mentioned—Jansen.

Perhaps, she thought, *if they are up to no good, the information I provide will be of some use in identifying them.*

Then the housekeeper walked towards the kitchen to talk with Agatha, knowing her fellow servant would inform her of anything she needed to know.

Darcy House

Two hours had passed by the time Richard got the summons from his cousin and arrived at the townhouse. If William's cryptic note saying, "Come at once" had not been enough to concern him, Mr. Barnes' expression when he opened the door would have.

"I got a note from my cousin asking me to come straightaway, Barnes. Has someone died?"

"Not that I know of, Colonel Fitzwilliam."

"Then why the urgency?"

"I cannot rightly say. All I know is that Mr. Darcy was dressed at the crack of dawn and anxious to visit your parents. When he returned, he was in a lather—pacing the floor and drinking far too many glasses of brandy." Barnes then sighed heavily. "I speak in confidence, Colonel. Please, do not repeat what I just said."

"I assure you our discussion will go no further. I appreciate that you have always been forthright, even if Darcy would not approve."

As they conversed, Richard was discarding his outer garments. "No need to announce me."

Not stopping until he stood at the open door to his cousin's study, Richard took a look inside. Catching sight of William pouring himself yet another glass of liquor, he took a deep breath and assumed a cheery expression before entering.

"Cousin! What is so awful that you sent for me straightaway? Has your supplier of French brandy been caught and hanged?"

The scowl William gave him was not a hopeful sign. "This is not the time for levity, Richard."

"Then, suppose you tell me why not?"

"Yesterday I had a visit from your father. It seems that on the trip into Town, he and your mother saw Elizabeth and a child being helped into a private coach at Belper. The clerk identified the owner of the coach as Lord Vanderhayden."

Richard became guarded. "Were they certain? You know my mother's penchant for finding a scandal where there is none."

"Your father did not get a good look at them, so I spoke to your mother this morning. She is positive that it was Elizabeth. After further questioning, she recalled that the man had the same hair colour as the child, and her impression was that he was the girl's father."

"Vanderhayden, you say? That is not Emily's surname is it?"

"No. Her father was Lord Van Lynden. But, your mother could have misunderstood."

"Given my mother's poor hearing, that is certainly possible." Richard looked even more puzzled. "But if the woman at Belper was Mrs. Gardiner, why would she leave Pemberley without telling you?"

"Because she knows I would not stand for it, and all Van Lynden would have to do is threaten to take Emily away—"

"And she would go with him without a fight."

"Precisely."

"I can understand why you are upset, Cousin. From all you have told me about the man, he is not a pleasant fellow. Still, you do realise that claiming one's child is not a crime. And Mrs. Gardiner may have gone with him of her own free will."

William downed the contents of his glass in one swallow. "Van Lynden cares nothing for that child," he said angrily. "He has not bothered to see her since she was born. And while I know that Elizabeth would not allow Emily to return to him alone, I am equally certain that she loves me. She would not leave if she had a choice."

"Have you written Mrs. Reynolds to ask if Mrs. Gardiner is still at Pemberley?"

"I have, but it will take too long to receive an answer. In any case, from your mother's recollections, I am convinced that it was her. Very few people have hair that colour."

"If she and the child are with this Van Lynden fellow, what are you plans?"

"I have been considering that all morning. My only chance is to provide an incentive to make Van Lynden want to leave Emily in Elizabeth's care."

"What do you have in mind? Offer him a fortune to disappear?"

"I will do whatever it takes, but first I must find them! They could be anywhere by now—even in Scotland."

"But were they not on the route to London?"

"They could have changed routes, though I pray they did not. I have decided to offer a substantial reward for information leading to their whereabouts, in hopes of finding them quickly."

"How substantial?"

"What do you suggest?"

"A hundred pounds will be incentive enough. Any more than that would induce the gutter snipes to lie. You would spend all your time investigating leads."

"A hundred pounds it is."

"I shall have my associates pass this along. If the lowlife in London have any knowledge of Van Lynden, you can expect to hear about it soon."

William sank into his chair. "I pray that I do. I shall not sleep again until I am certain Elizabeth and Emily are safe."

Richard walked over to place a comforting hand on William's shoulder. "Do not lose heart! Given his looks, Van Lynden will be conspicuous. Now, I shall return to my office and summon Whitaker and Browning. They will be useful in passing along the information regarding the reward."

"There is nothing to keep me here. I will accompany you."

"That is not wise."

"But I cannot—"

"Darcy, I know waiting is torture, but you must let me go alone. If General Lassiter thinks I have shared classified intelligence with you, I will be disciplined. You do not want that, do you?"

"Certainly not."

Suddenly the door flew open, hitting the wall, and Millicent rushed in, with Mr. Barnes right on her heels.

"I am sorry, Mr. Darcy," the butler began to say at the same time that Lady Markham spoke.

"What are the two of you doing here when Elizabeth and Emily have been kidnapped by that blackguard?"

William dismissed Barnes with a wave of his hand, and the butler left the room.

"Do you mean that for once Mother's instincts were right?" Richard asked.

A half-hour later, Richard and William had explained to Millicent that, thanks to Lady Matlock's curiosity, they had just learned that Elizabeth had left with Lord Van Lynden. She calmed down considerably, though she grew emotional describing how Mrs. Reynolds found Van Lynden's handkerchief at Pemberley, and how she herself had rushed to Canfield Manor only to learn that Elizabeth had already left.

"If only one of the horses had not had to be replaced between Richmond and Town, you would have known yesterday."

"That was certainly not your fault," Richard replied.

"Still, each day that goes by is a day wasted." Millicent turned and addressed William. "I cannot believe Elizabeth did not tell you she was leaving. Just before she left Pemberley, she promised me she would."

Richard noted the pained expression on his cousin's face. "Obviously, she would not want Darcy to know, because he would try to stop her."

"Obviously," Millicent repeated. "I was such a fool not to see what was happening. I know how much in love you and she are, and it made absolutely no sense that she would not wait at Pemberley for you to return."

"You know?" William said incredulously.

Millicent looked sheepish. "I have known for some time, though I would not admit it to myself. It is no secret that you have been pining over someone these last five years. Fortunately, I got to know and admire Elizabeth before I found the drawing of her in your art studio. Seeing the passion evident in that portrayal was what convinced me you and she belong together."

Richard's ears perked up. "A passionate drawing? Tell me more!"

"It is not what you think, Richard," William said with a cross look.

"It was the most intimate likeness I have ever seen, though Elizabeth was clothed, I assure you. I could see every aspect of her in such detail—even the slight scar beneath one eye. No man would be able to paint a woman that intimately unless he was deeply in love with her."

"That is quite enough, my dear," William said.

Richard smirked. "Millie, remind me to ask about the portrait when we are next at Pemberley."

"Can we stop talking foolishness and speak of what is most important: finding Elizabeth?"

Knowing that William was right, Richard stood. "I shall leave now and pass on the word regarding the reward."

"Let me know the moment you hear something," William said.

"I came straight here, but I plan to stay at your parents' house." Millicent winked at William. "If I were to stay here, the gossips would have Fitzwilliam and I engaged before morning."

"We certainly cannot have that!" Richard said, chuckling. Then, he turned to leave. "Do not look for me again today. I have much to do before dark."

After the colonel exited the room, for the first time in their lives there was an awkward silence between the two friends. Finally, William spoke.

"Forgive me for not telling you about Elizabeth myself. To be honest, I was called into Town the night before I intended to confess. I vowed to tell you the moment I returned to Pemberley." William sighed, waving his hand about the room. "And you can see how well that worked."

Millie smiled. "As you are fond of saying: 'the best-laid plans of mice and men.'"

"You are very generous. Still, I feel it is important you understand what happened and in what order. When Elizabeth first came to Pemberley, I had vowed not to fall in love with her again. And I did try. It was only later that I realised I had never stopped loving her in the first place."

"I know that you did not mean for me to be hurt, Fitzwilliam. It is not in your nature. And I came to understand that it is not in Elizabeth's nature, either. I have learned to care for her like a sister. Knowing you both as well as I do, I can accept that you and she were meant for each other."

William stood and walked over to where Millicent sat. Taking her hands in his, he said, "You have always been one of my best friends; that shall never change. It is my hope that you and Elizabeth will become good friends, too."

She stood and kissed William's cheek. "We already are. Now, I shall go on to the earl's townhouse. I am tired and would like a hot bath. Promise me you will send word the minute you hear anything about Elizabeth."

"I promise."

Chapter 21

Darcy House
The next day

Mr. Barnes was always apprehensive when responding to knocks on the front door in the early morning hours, and today was no exception. Surreptitiously peeking through one of the etched glass windows beside the entrance, he was relieved to see William's cousin and threw open the door.

"Colonel Fitzwilliam! You certainly got an early start today."

"A bit too early, I fear," Richard said, suppressing a yawn. "Still, I suspect that Darcy did not get much sleep, either. He is awake, is he not?"

"He is, and you are correct in your assumption. Mr. Darcy walked the floors most of the night. I know, for I stayed awake in case I was needed."

"You are a good man, Barnes. Now, where did you say I would find him?"

Barnes smiled. "I did not say, sir; however, he is presently in the dining room." Knowing Richard's fondness for surprising his cousin, he placed Richard's hat and gloves on the foyer table. "Do you wish to be announced?"

Richard chuckled. "There is no need."

When Richard reached the dining room, he found the door open. William remained seated at the table, though obviously he was done eating, for he was reading a newspaper whilst a footman poured him another cup of tea.

Entering nonchalantly, Richard declared, "Have I made the society columns again, Cousin? I can just see the headline now: Handsome Army Officer Thrills All of London with His Attendance at Lady Cornwall's Ball."

The top-half of the paper dropped, and William smiled in spite of himself. "There is no lady in London by that name."

"Well, that explains why there was no one at the ball but the two of us! I have been duped by yet another admirer, intent on possessing my body."

"What a pity! I do hope you are here for more important matters than seeing if your name is in the society pages."

"I am. I could barely sleep last night for want of telling you what I learned."

"I was up most of the night anyway. You would have been welcomed with open arms."

"A cup of tea, please," Richard said to the footman before taking the chair on William's right.

Once he was seated, he continued. "Yesterday, one of the men watching Guthrie's house saw him leave with someone who matched the description of Lord Van Lynden—tall fellow, flaxen hair and all!"

"Van Lynden is staying with Guthrie?"

"It certainly looks that way, and there is more. As per our instructions, he followed them. They went directly to a pub in the warehouse district where they collected Mr. Carney, who was falling down drunk, and transported him back to Guthrie's livery stable."

"I would never have figured Van Lynden to be a part of that gang of miscreants."

"We are not sure he is. When we enquired around town about Lord Van Lynden, it came to light that his father and Guthrie's were acquainted. It was not unusual for the Van Lyndens to call on the Guthries when the diplomat was in town. So he could merely be a visitor whom Guthrie called upon to help him retrieve Carney. There is no evidence at present linking Van Lynden to Howton's death or the plot against Castlereagh."

"His choice of friends does not speak well of his character."

"Until now, despite some of his hare-brained theories, John Guthrie was considered a proper gentleman."

"Humph! I always considered him a fool."

"In any event, now that we know where Mrs. Gardiner and Emily are as soon as the government lifts the ban on interrogating those congregating at Guthrie's house, you may speak to her."

"No," William said quietly. "I will speak to Elizabeth now."

"I understand your position, Darcy; however, going there at this point could sabotage the entire investigation."

"Devil take the investigation!" William said, tossing the newspaper on the table. "I am not sure you do understand." He stood and began to pace. "Certainly I want to see Elizabeth. I am dying to see Elizabeth! I want to ascertain that she and Emily are well. But more importantly, I must forewarn her that she is in the midst of a nest of vipers. What if they decide to raid the house and shots are fired?"

"I would be apprised beforehand."

"You cannot guarantee I would have time to safeguard them! At this point, no one expects me to appear on Guthrie's doorstep. After I have spoken to Elizabeth, you can explain my reason for going there."

"As if they would listen! See here, Darcy, they are after those who are a threat to Castlereagh and, to a much lesser extent, those who murdered Howton. They watch that house religiously, and you could be arrested before you reach the front door."

"I doubt they will arrest me, for it would expose their surveillance. If they arrest me after I leave, then so be it."

"You mean *if* Van Lynden lets you leave," Richard said, sighing. "I do not suppose I can talk you out of this."

"No."

"If that is the case, then I insist on going with you."

"No. Too much depends on you. I will not risk your being in trouble with your superiors. It must appear I am there simply because I am in love with Elizabeth, which is the truth. You will be at your office when I confront Van Lynden, and if questioned, you will feign ignorance of my actions."

"It is too dangerous."

"Richard, I have to know if Elizabeth is there of her own volition."

Pondering his cousin's argument, Richard dropped his head. Finally, he looked up. "I may not agree with your timing, but I understand why you feel you must go now. Moreover, I agree to remain at my office, but only if you allow Whitaker and Browning to hide in your carriage. You can always keep the shades drawn. If they hear anything improper—gun shots, shouting or anything that sounds ominous—they will storm Guthrie's house immediately. Agreed?"

At last William cracked a smile. "Yes, Mother."

"Good! Now, what will we do about Millie? She will be livid if you do this without first telling her."

"And you know exactly what she would do if she knew."

Richard sighed. "She would go through the door right behind you."

"Precisely. So, I shall suffer her wrath and tell her after the fact."

"I hope that she blames you and not me. That woman has a

wicked temper!"

"I thought you admired her temperament."

"I do. But, I am smart enough not to come between Millie and those she cares about."

"You know her well," William said, before a totally different expression crossed his face. "In fact, now that I think of it, you and she would make the ideal match. Have you ever considered that?"

Richard smiled to himself. "No, and I am too occupied to give it proper consideration now. When are you planning to go?"

"There is no time like the present."

Richard stood. "Give me time to locate Whitaker and Browning. Promise me that you will not leave until they arrive."

"Richard, I am not a child!" At his cousin's glare, William sighed. "I promise."

Walking over to give his cousin a brotherly hug, Richard cautioned, "Be careful, Darcy." Removing a small pistol from an inside pocket, he handed it to him. "They may search your coat, so slip this in your boot." Then reaching into his boot, he pulled out a knife. "This always comes in handy."

"What? No sword?" Seeing irritation flick across Richard's face, William became serious. "I appreciate your concern; truly, I do."

Richard clasped his shoulder. "Godspeed, Darcy."

Guthrie's townhouse

Lord Van Lynden and John Guthrie had barely gotten Carney settled under guard in the carriage house at the back of the property, when Mr. Haggard came rushing down the path to the stables. He stopped in front of Guthrie's guest.

"Sir, the gentleman you said might call on Mrs. Gardiner is here!" Haggard held out a card, and Van Lynden took it. "I was told your carriage had returned just before I heard him knock on the door. Thinking you might wish that gentleman to wait, I directed him to the front drawing room."

As Van Lynden stared at the card, Guthrie asked, "Mr. Darcy?"

"Yes. He wasted no time." Then assuming his usual business-like mien, he said to Haggard, "You were correct. Please tell Mr. Darcy we shall be there shortly."

As the butler hurried back to the house, Van Lynden turned to Guthrie. "Let me do the talking."

The drawing room

Surprised that the butler acted as though he were expected, William was pacing the drawing room when the door opened to admit John Guthrie and Lord Van Lynden. Guthrie looked to Van Lynden as though expecting him to speak, though all the gentleman did was to coldly study William.

"Mr. Darcy, may I introduce my old friend, Lord Van Lynden? He is visiting from the Netherlands." At William's slight nod, Guthrie continued. "Lord Van Lynden, may I present Fitzwilliam Darcy of Pemberley in Derbyshire."

Van Lynden spoke first. "Mr. Darcy, I was expecting you."

"Why is that, sir?"

A small smirk lifted the corners of Van Lynden's mouth. "It was a conclusion I made based on the fact that while you were entertaining Mrs. Gardiner and my daughter at Pemberley, you likely became enamoured of my child's governess. And, once you learned that she had left your estate, you would search for her."

"I would be interested in learning how you knew Mrs. Gardiner was at Pemberley."

"Just as I would be interested in knowing how you knew she was here." At William's glare, he added, "We all have our ways, do we not?"

"I wish to speak to Mrs. Gardiner."

"You will get no argument from me." Van Lynden turned to Guthrie. "Please escort Mrs. Gardiner to the library and ask her to wait there for Mr. Darcy."

Guthrie seemed eager to please and rushed from the room.

"If I did not know better, I would think you were the master and Mr. Guthrie your servant," William remarked.

"It is not like that at all. Guthrie and I are old friends, and I asked him to let me address you because your visit concerns my daughter. She is very fond of her governess, and I do not wish her to be disappointed by losing Mrs. Gardiner's services."

"You did not appear concerned about your child during the time that Mrs. Gardiner cared for her alone."

Van Lynden's voice rose. "You know nothing about my concerns or my reasons for being absent. Once I was able, I began a search for her."

"Your daughter considers Mrs. Gardiner her mother. It would be cruel to separate them."

"This is precisely why I offered to allow Mrs. Gardiner to remain as her governess and, I might add, she accepted the position of her own free will."

"If Mrs. Gardiner had her way, you would leave the child and disappear."

"I believe that is your wish, not hers."

"How many pounds would it take to change your mind?"

"You may be one of the wealthiest men in Britain, but your money is of no use to you in this matter. My daughter is not for sale and, to be honest, I am quite fond of Mrs. Gardiner myself." Delighted to see William's eyes narrow, Van Lynden did not hesitate to add, "She has a way with my daughter I greatly admire. You are free, however, to try to convince her to go with you."

"You know she will not abandon her child!" William said angrily.

"We both know that, Mr. Darcy. If by chance your concern is for Mrs. Gardiner's future, you should know that I recently made it clear to her that I will consider her should I ever decide to marry again."

William's hands formed fists as he walked towards his nemesis.

"Now, Mr. Darcy," Van Lynden said, smiling confidently. "You would not want to jeopardise Mrs. Gardiner's position, would you? I do not think she will appreciate it if you are responsible for separating her from the child, and I have no intention of fighting over a governess."

William halted just as Guthrie opened the door. "Mrs. Gardiner is in the library."

The library

Fear held Elizabeth in a vice as she stood at the windows along the west side of the library. The thing she dreaded most had come true. William had found her! Now a myriad of worries swirled in her head.

If he and Van Lynden argued, would William be killed? If they did not come to blows, would Van Lynden keep his word and let her speak to him privately? If so, and William insisted that she go with him, what would she do? Loving him so deeply, Elizabeth feared she might not be strong enough to refuse.

She heard the door open and held her breath, not daring to look. When the latch clicked, signalling that the door had closed again, she steeled herself not to cry and turned. At the sight of the man she loved with all her heart, hope of maintaining control shredded, and a sob escaped her throat as she ran to him.

William's heart was beating wildly, and tears filled his eyes as he met Elizabeth halfway across the room. She slammed into him with such force it took all his strength to keep them both from falling. Still, holding in his arms the deepest desire of his soul, every fibre of his body cried out not to let go.

His hands roamed over her back. "Oh, Elizabeth. I have been so lost without you." She sobbed even harder, and he placed soft kisses in her hair. "Do not cry, my love. All will be well. Wait and see."

One hand slid to the small of her back, pulling her closer, while the other cradled the back of her head. Entwining his fingers in her hair, he tipped her head back to peer into a pair of dark eyes. In their ebony depths he found the reassurance of her love, and it banished any doubts about why she had left Pemberley. He proceeded to kiss every inch of her tearstained face before his mouth claimed hers. At the feel of her soft lips surrendering to his, he was lost.

Only when Elizabeth's knees began to buckle did reality return. Picking her up, he carried her to a sofa, where he sat down with her in his lap. Curbing his desire was difficult, but as she laid her head against his chest, he rested his head atop hers. They sat in this manner for some time whilst their breathing returned to normal.

At last able to speak, Elizabeth murmured, "I love you, Fitzwilliam Darcy. Please believe that. No matter what might happen, I will love you forever."

He knew the motivation for such a pronouncement. "I would rather die than to leave you and Emily under Van Lynden's control. Still, I understand why you feel you must stay with your daughter."

Reaching to cradle his face, love hovered in Elizabeth's gaze. "I knew you would understand. It is agony to be parted from you, but I cannot leave her."

"I know." He lowered his voice. "I am here not only because I had to see you, but to warn you. You cannot breathe a word of what I am about to say. It could be a matter of life or death."

Elizabeth's expression grew even more uneasy. "I will not."

William explained how Guthrie and his group were being watched, beginning with Howton's death and increasing after the threats against Castlereagh. He made it clear that a raid on the premises by lawful forces could happen at any time, and the occupants of the house might suddenly decide to vacate the premises if they suspected they had been found out.

Elizabeth stood, saying quietly. "You...you believe Emily's father is involved?"

"Some are not convinced, but I think he would not be here otherwise. If he is connected to the group, it will ensure he hangs." William stood, taking her back into his arms. "You must be aware of what is happening under this roof in order to protect yourself and Emily. Watch the streets when you have opportunity and listen for loud sounds, shouts or gunshots. Should the house be raided, be prepared to hide somewhere safe. You would do well to search for such a place now."

Elizabeth looked so vulnerable. He framed her face with his hands and gave her another quick kiss. "Have faith, my darling. I will find a way for us to be together. You have my promise." Then William's expression softened, and his voice suddenly sounded more hopeful. "Please forgive me. This is not how I envisioned asking, but—" Going down on one knee, he continued. "Will you do me the honour of accepting my hand in marriage, Elizabeth Bennet?"

Tears rolled down her face anew—tears of joy. "Yes! As soon as it is possible, I will marry you whenever and wherever you say."

Another deep kiss sealed their engagement before he broke away to pull a gold ring from a pocket of his coat. It was a delicately-braided ring, depicting roses on a vine. "This was one of my mother's favourites." He slipped it on her left hand. "Will you wear it until I can free you and Emily from this blackguard and replace it with a wedding band?"

"Oh, William," Elizabeth managed to say as she nodded her consent.

A passionate kiss was interrupted by a loud knock on the door. "Time is up, Mr. Darcy."

Recognising Guthrie's voice, William answered. "One moment, please."

Taking Richard's pistol from his boot, he placed it in Elizabeth's hand and folded her fingers over it. "Just in case."

Elizabeth dropped the gun in the pocket of her skirt, and William tried to smile reassuringly. "Whilst we are apart, remember that I love you."

She touched his face tenderly. "I shall always love you."

Pulling his mouth to hers, she kissed him ardently. Then, upon hearing the door open, Elizabeth rushed from the room. The sounds of weeping followed her down the hall.

John Guthrie watched her leave from his perch in the doorway. "Did something upset Mrs. Gardiner?"

Face set like flint, William stalked past Guthrie. With that man on his heels babbling more nonsense, he exited the house without ever bothering to reply.

Guthrie's townhouse

Mr. Darcy's appearance right on the heels of Carney's drunken pronouncements in public unsettled Lord Van Lynden greatly. So uneasy was he that he decided to move the plan to assassinate the viscount to the next day. Having made up his mind, he located Guthrie to tell him.

"Tomorrow? It was my wish to be on the way to Ireland with Mother before it was carried out."

"You said yourself that she is too ill to travel. Better to leave her in the care of loyal servants whilst you visit your relations." When he did not reply, Van Lynden continued. "I plan to leave for Scotland today, right after we meet with the others. I have farther to travel, and you can leave for Portsmouth in the morning, sailing to Ireland from there."

"I suppose that will work."

"It will, and here is what you are to do. When I leave, tell your servants that I am headed to Brighton. That way, if Mr. Darcy hears any gossip from your servants, he will think I am going south, instead of in the opposite direction. I fear he may try to follow Mrs. Gardiner."

"Certainly. Now, if we are to carry this out, we must get all the men together quickly. I shall send footmen after each of them. Meanwhile, my servants will start packing our trunks while I instruct the liveryman to ready our coaches."

Lord Van Lynden did something he rarely did: he smiled. "We have planned well. The men will be able to carry this out; you shall see. And while Castlereagh is being killed, we will have the perfect alibis. We will be out of Town."

John Guthrie nodded. "I cannot wait until that traitor is dead."

"Nor can I."

In mere hours, Visser, Jansen and Bakker were in the library with Guthrie and Van Lynden. The only member of the group missing was Carney, who was considered merely the sacrificial lamb and not really needed. Now sober and being held in one of the guest rooms until the plan was put in action, Carney was being kept happy with plenty of food and a small amount of liquor. The only restrictions were that he could not leave the room until the time came to carry out the plan.

Klaus Jansen asked about Carney's absence.

"Because of his propensity to get drunk, he is presently in the carriage house, under watch. We do not think it necessary for him to be included."

Suddenly noticing Mrs. Southard was still in the room, Van Lynden turned to John Guthrie and tilted his head towards the housekeeper.

Guthrie addressed his servant. "That will be all, Mrs. Southard."

Nodding in compliance, the housekeeper quickly finished setting out the refreshments before leaving the room. Once she did, though, she left the door slightly ajar. Surreptitiously placing her ear at the opening, she kept her eyes on the hallway to make sure no one caught her eavesdropping. Luckily, she was able to hear most of what was being said.

"Now, the reason we called you here today is to inform you our plan will be carried out tomorrow."

"Tomorrow is short notice," Bakker said.

"I have always said that you would be told the day before. Are you saying you are not ready?" Van Lynden asked.

"I am not saying that."

"Excellent. For it is to be tomorrow."

"Were the key and the map still inside the money box?" Bakker continued.

"Just as I thought they would be," Lord Van Lynden replied, taking the key from his pocket and holding it up for all to see before handing it to Visser.

"You do know that the locks could have been changed," Visser declared as he examined the key. "It is not unheard of for a man of Castlereagh's stature to change the door locks on a regular basis for security purposes."

"That may well be," Lord Van Lynden replied acerbically, "but since you are an expert at picking locks, it should not be an insurmountable problem."

Visser shrugged. "Still, depending on the difficulty, picking the lock could add anywhere from a few minutes to an hour to the plan."

Seeing the tension between the two, John Guthrie held up the map. "It was just as Lord Van Lynden thought. The map shows that Castlereagh's bedroom is on the east hall of the second floor."

With that, Van Lynden aimed a barb at Visser. "Assuming he has not also moved his bedroom for *security* reasons." Pulling four envelopes from inside his coat, he continued, "These are advances on what you are due. The rest will be in the coach that Carney will station on the street alongside the foreign minister's house. And this—" Van Lynden said, handing one last envelope to Jansen, "is the evidence that you will plant on Mr. Carney's body. It will tie him to the crime."

Jann Bakker tried to lighten the mood. "I, for one, will miss all those sweets from Castlereagh's kitchen. Perhaps I should ask the cook to marry me and accompany me back to Holland."

Laughter filled the room before Van Lynden replied sourly, "It is that way of thinking that gets one hanged."

"I...I was only teasing," Bakker sputtered.

"If you think hanging is something to tease about, then, please, go right ahead." When the room went silent, he added, "You are being paid well to avenge your homeland, gentlemen. Try not to fail."

Instantly Mrs. Southard eased the door shut and rushed to her office to send an urgent note to Mr. Whitaker.

Darcy House
The library

That evening found William attempting to read. Having stared at Elizabeth's portrait so long he feared he might go mad, he had vacated his study in favour of the library and something technical. It was not a solution, however, for he had read the last paragraph four times and still could not attest to what it said. Tossing the journal aside, he went to the double doors that led to the terrace. Though it was full dark already, he threw the doors open and went out. A clear sky the colour of blue velvet sparkled with stars too numerous to count. While he watched, one shot across the heavens, and he followed its path until it was out of sight.

How odd, he thought. *My entire world has been turned on its head, yet the universe carries on as though nothing has changed.*

Faint footsteps could be heard crossing the terrace, and before he could turn, an arm slipped through his. Millicent leaned her head against his shoulder. "Richard told me everything that happened. I am so very sorry." William nodded. "Tell me, what are you thinking?"

He took a ragged breath, willing his voice not to break. "I am thinking how useless my wealth and connections are when I need them most. Van Lynden's rights as Emily's father has Elizabeth terrified to challenge him. He has the right, and any court would side with him regarding Emily."

"I know. I was so angry; I was determined to go there and talk to Elizabeth before Richard explained what you and she were facing."

"As it is, I am reduced to a bystander. All I can do is pray that he, Guthrie and the others are actually planning to kill Castlereagh. Involvement in something of that magnitude would guarantee those involved will be brought to justice."

"I cannot stomach the thought of Elizabeth or Emily being under that man's control. And being so well acquainted with you, I know how it is tearing you apart."

William closed his eyes. "I will not deny it."

Millicent walked around to face him, taking both his hands. "Listen to me. If it turns out that they are not plotting against the foreign minister, then we shall think of another way to free Elizabeth and Emily. Do not give up! Truth and justice will prevail. Hold to that."

William tried to smile. "I am doing my best."

"That is all one can ask." She pasted on a smile. "Now, why do we not do what we used to when we were upset as children?"

At William's puzzled expression, she laughed. "No! I am not suggesting we put jam on the servants' doorknobs again! I am speaking of looking for something humorous to read aloud. As I recall, 'Much Ado About Nothing' used to make you laugh. Perhaps it will again."

"I fear nothing can make me laugh tonight. Still, I appreciate the thought."

"Well, if I cannot brighten your mood, I suppose I shall have to return to Matlock House before the earl sends someone to fetch me."

William embraced Millicent. "Thank you for coming."

Millicent nodded against his chest, holding back her tears. "Send for me if something happens and you need my help, or should you simply want to talk."

"I will."

Chapter 22

Darcy House

Having ridden his stallion to Darcy House, Richard trotted towards the back entrance just as William was preparing to take Kronos for a ride.

"I am glad I caught you," Richard said, throwing a leg over the saddle and jumping to the ground. "Dismount and let us go back inside. You need to be sitting for what I have to tell you."

William's brows furrowed; but instead of asking questions in front of the servants, he dismounted and threw the reins to a groom. "Unsaddle him."

As he started towards the house, Richard tossed his reins to another groom. "See that Titan is watered."

Both grooms watched the cousins walk away. When they were out of hearing, one said, "I do not think I shall ever understand gentlemen. Saddle my horse! Unsaddle my horse! They never know what they want."

Mr. Saulder, the livery manager, was standing not twenty feet away. "It is not for you to understand, boy! It is for you to obey!"

Startled, the grooms dropped their heads and hurried inside the stables with the horses. After they were out of sight, Saulder laughed and resumed what he was doing.

William's study

Sitting in the chair behind his desk, William absentmindedly slapped the riding crop he was still holding against his other hand. "And this woman—Mrs. Southard—just happened to know Mr. Whitaker?"

"Strange as it seems, this is true," Richard said, as he brought his feet up to prop on the corner of his cousin's desk. "She and Whitaker's late aunt were fast friends, and she has been the Guthries' housekeeper for over twenty years. Already suspicious of what she saw happening at the house, she tried to contact Whitaker several days ago, only to be told that he was working for a private client. Though the Bow Street Runners promised to pass her note along to him, once she overheard the plot to kill Castlereagh, she felt that she had no choice but to talk to him straightaway."

"What exactly did she hear?"

"John Guthrie, Lord Van Lynden and the men who usually meet at the house were discussing the assassination of Viscount Castlereagh. Perhaps your visit spurred them to action, for they decided it should be carried out tonight. My superiors have been informed, and we have doubled the number of men watching Castlereagh's home. There are men inside and out, ready to catch them in the act. Naturally, the viscount has been moved to safer quarters."

"Thank God Van Lynden is involved!" William said, throwing his riding crop down on the desk. "Once he is caught, he will be left with no argument in regards to keeping Emily."

"When he is hanged, he will have no legs to stand on—*period!*"

At that moment, there was a knock on the door. "Come," William called.

Mr. Barnes opened the door, though Mr. Whitaker stood right

behind him, looking very impatient. William waved to the Bow Street Runner. "Come in, Mr. Whitaker. Thank you, Barnes. That will be all."

Before the butler was completely out of sight, Whitaker was speaking. "I thought you should know that Mrs. Southard brought me more news this morning. John Guthrie is planning on leaving for Portsmouth this afternoon."

"Sounds like he wants to be out of Town before the assassination is set in motion," Richard said.

"Will he actually be allowed to leave London?" William asked.

"Since it is best that we catch them in the act, for now he can come and go as he pleases. We cannot take a chance on showing our hand. Guthrie will be allowed to travel a full day's journey towards Portsmouth, though we will trail him. At that point, he will be seized and returned to London. With any luck, by then his lackeys will have carried out their plan, been apprehended and implicated both Guthrie and Van Lynden. Even if they do not follow through with an assassination attempt, we believe we have enough evidence to convict all of them."

"There is more," Whitaker said, throwing an anxious look in William's direction. "While Mrs. Southard was out yesterday, a coach left the house carrying Lord Van Lynden, the woman and the child. Mrs. Southard did not realise they were gone until too late to inform me last night."

William stood, his eyes flashing with anger. "Did she say where they were headed?"

"That is the peculiar part. John Guthrie told her Lord Van Lynden was headed to Brighton; however, the butler distinctly heard the driver tell a groom they were headed to Annan, Scotland."

"It sounds as though he is trying to throw us off the trail," Richard said.

"Do either of you know where Annan is?" William asked.

"I once had to track a young man who was transporting a

maiden over the border to be married," Whitaker replied. "At Gretna Green, I was told they had already married and were off to Annan. According to them, it was a little further north. Since they were already married, I did not travel to Annan."

William turned to open a tall, mahogany cabinet behind his desk and began to lay several rifles and other weapons on his desk. "I am going after them."

"You cannot go alone, and I am expected to protect the foreign minister. Van Lynden is dangerous, and we have no idea how many men he has in total," Richard protested.

"I will take only my men who are crack shots."

"I hate that I cannot accompany you, for we have more than enough men to protect Castlereagh."

"It is better that you are here to capture the plotters and force a confession. With any luck, Van Lynden will be implicated."

"And if he is not?" Richard asked.

"I pray he is, but no matter the outcome, I will not let him take Elizabeth or Emily."

William rang for Barnes, who appeared again in the doorway within minutes. "Tell Mr. Saulder to ready my coach. I will be leaving immediately. Also, tell him I need a driver and three grooms who are all skilled with rifles. I shall leave it to you to select four footmen who can shoot accurately. Tell them when they report for duty that they will be provided with weapons and ammunition."

Barnes started to do as asked, but William continued. "Barnes!" The butler stopped and turned. "First, tell Mr. Martin to pack my trunks."

Nodding, the servant was quickly out of sight. As he and Whitaker prepared to leave, Richard said, "Try to let Mr. Barnes know where you are at all times. I shall keep in touch with him."

"I shall do my best."

Richard stuck out his hand. "Take care, Darcy. Godspeed."

William shook the proffered hand. "And to you, my friend."

Van Lynden's coach

Ushered into the coach late the day before and travelling a long way before stopping for the night, Elizabeth and Emily were still exhausted when awakened before dawn to continue their trip. Lord Van Lynden had offered no explanation for their quick departure and gruelling schedule, but Elizabeth assumed it had to do with William's appearance at Guthrie's house. She knew that when William learned they had left London he would follow, but she prayed for his safety and that God would allow him to find them quickly.

Furious with her for not speaking to him after William's departure, Van Lynden said nothing to Elizabeth when they were leaving Guthrie's house. He did, however, tell their host he would write once he reached his estate in Scotland and again when he was safely in Holland. Guthrie replied that his staff would forward the mail to him in Ireland. Meanwhile, Elizabeth prayed the plot against the foreign minister would ensnare both men.

Emily, who was asleep in her lap, suddenly began to squirm. As she reached to straighten the blanket covering her, Van Lynden spoke at last. "What is that you are wearing?"

Realising that he was staring at the ring William had given her, instantly an explanation came to mind. "It is my wedding ring. I had lost weight and it would not stay on my finger. Now that it fits perfectly again, I resumed wearing it."

She could tell from his expression that he was not convinced. Not caring, she stared at him defiantly.

"I find it odd that you decided to wear it only after Mr. Darcy visited you."

"He had nothing to do with it. I am a widow, and I see no reason not to wear my ring now that it fits."

Lord Van Lynden waved his hand as if dismissing her argument. "It is of no consequence. I plan to replace it with something more appropriate when we are married."

Astonished, Elizabeth sputtered, "Surely you jest! You have not asked, nor have I consented to marry you."

"I thought it unnecessary to belabour the point. You wish to stay close to my daughter, and that is the best way to accomplish it."

"That is preposterous! I am not a suitable wife for you. I am not of your sphere. I am content to continue as Emily's governess."

"Her name is Ingrid! It is time you accepted that."

"She will always be Emily to me, but unless we are alone, it will be as you wish."

"I do wish it! And if I wanted a woman like my late wife, I would have chosen one. It is my desire that you become my wife as soon as we are settled in Rotterdam. The sooner Ingrid has a mother, the better."

When she did not reply, his expression grew harsher. "You will learn it is best not to cross me, Mrs. Gardiner. A single woman left on her own in a foreign country can be at great peril."

"Are you threatening to dismiss me if I do not agree to the marriage?"

"If I were to marry someone else, she might not approve of you. After all, it is conceivable that another woman might be jealous of a handsome governess, and I would have no choice but to dismiss you."

"I see."

"I hope you do see, Mrs. Gardiner. It will be best for all concerned."

Sensing that it would do no good to argue, Elizabeth said no more. Instead, she shut her eyes and leaned into the corner as though trying to rest. Lord Van Lynden must have concluded she needed time to become accustomed to the idea, for he said no more. He had no way of knowing her mind was occupied with thoughts of how she and Emily might escape the moment they reached Scotland.

London
Viscount Castlereagh's residence
That night

The light rain of the afternoon had turned into a deluge, effectively hiding the coach bearing no crest, which was parked on a street adjacent to the foreign minister's house. Mr. Carney, unaware of his fate, had driven the coach there and then joined the others inside to wait until the rain lightened enough to begin. Having met a couple of hours ago at Guthrie's house, they had bidden their farewells to that man and watched as his coach rolled out of the yard before boarding this vehicle. Guthrie, who was likely several miles down the road by now, meant to travel as far as the first decent inn before stopping for the night, which meant that they were now completely on their own.

The humidity, coupled with such close quarters, made the inside of the coach almost unbearable, and Jansen pushed aside the window shade to stare into the blackness and complain. "Will this rain never let up? The longer we sit here, the more suspicious we become!"

"You had better thank your lucky stars it is raining," Carney said. "No one will be on the streets in this weather, and if they travel by coach, they will have the windows closed."

Since none of the men liked Carney, no one replied. At length the steady beat of rain on the roof stopped, and Bakker opened the door slightly. "It has slowed to a mist. Now is our chance."

Everyone except Carney exited the coach and ran to the wall of dense shrubbery on the east side of Castlereagh's house and began to work their way through it. Once they had reached the lawn on the other side, Visser pointed towards the door he meant to breech. As he bounded in that direction, the others followed. Fortuitously, that entrance was shielded on either side by large shrubs, and all three crouched behind them. Taking from his pocket the key Lord Van Lynden had retrieved from the money box, Visser inserted it into the lock. He was surprised and pleased that it fit perfectly, and with only a twist of his wrist, the door opened. Carefully pushing it back, he noted that sconces were lit along the hallway.

"What luck!" he whispered. "There are candles lit. Do your best, men, and I will guard the door."

Bakker and Jansen pulled pistols from their coats and crept down the hall. Once they were completely out of sight, time seemed to stand still. When, at long last, Visser heard a gunshot, he was relieved. The numerous shots which soon followed, however, made him instantly conscious of the fact that they had been found out. Panicking, he ran across the lawn and entered the shrubbery, intent on reaching the coach.

Almost falling on his face as he cleared the wall of vegetation, he noticed Carney sitting atop the vehicle, nervously looking about. Following instructions, Visser pulled a gun from his coat and fired when he got near. Carney fell to the ground, and Visser quickly hid the evidence on his body. Shouts were coming from the viscount's lawn, and without thinking, Visser immediately climbed inside the coach. Praying that it was Bakker and Jansen coming through the hedges, he opened a window and prepared to defend them. Oddly, something caused him to glance to the ground where Carney had been lying. The body was gone!

Giving him no time to ponder that curiosity, several red-coated figures came through the shrubs and rushed the coach. Voices called for his surrender. As he levelled his gun to fire, however, a blow to the back of his head left him senseless. Slumping to the floor, the last thing Visser recalled was hearing someone say, "Do not kill him! We need him alive!"

"You captured him, Colonel Seeger!" one redcoat shouted, as several came up behind him, peering over his shoulder at the men inside the coach.

Having sneaked inside the coach while Visser was distracted, Seeger barked instructions. "Sergeant Combs, help me carry this blackguard into the house. Sergeant Tiller, take your men and scour the grounds for more!"

While they rushed to do as ordered, Sergeant Combs picked up Visser's legs, and Colonel Seeger lifted his head and shoulders. Once at the house, they were met by others who took over, carrying the unconscious man to the room his cohorts now occupied. Combs and Seeger followed, only to find that one man was dead and the other secured by ropes. Visser was laid on the floor beside him.

"Is everyone inside the house?" Colonel Seeger asked.

"Yes, sir," one of the men guarding the prisoners answered. Then he added, "How are Colonel Fitzwilliam and Sergeant Hannah faring?"

"Were they hurt? I had no idea."

Yet another soldier interrupted, "Thanks to Colonel Fitzwilliam, Hannah took only a bullet to his calf. The colonel was more seriously injured with a wound to his shoulder."

"Where are they?"

"Upstairs. First two bedrooms on the right."

"I want no less than two men watching each of these blackguards at all times."

"Yes, Colonel!"

Once he reached the landing, a soldier informed Colonel Seeger that Sergeant Hannah was doing well enough to sit up. Relieved at the news, he hurried to check on Colonel Fitzwilliam, whose bedroom was marked by the number of men crowding the open door. Seeger joined his colleagues to watch the physician, and he did not speak until that gentleman finally stood.

Quickly walking forward, he asked quietly, "Mr. Colpack, should I send for the colonel's father?"

Without looking at him, the physician took a weary breath before he answered. "I think that may be wise. He lost a lot of blood before I could seal the wound. He is somewhat stable now; nevertheless, these injuries can get serious very quickly."

"I shall send someone right away."

"Are there men left to be treated?"

"We have a prisoner with a bullet in his arm and one who is unconscious. We would like to interrogate both once you deem them able to talk."

"Have them brought up here and put in one of the guest rooms. I shall look at them, but I want to stay close to the colonel...just in case."

"Whatever you say."

Matlock House

The loud banging on the front door could be heard clearly in the library, causing Lady Matlock to exclaim, "My goodness, who could be demanding entrance at this hour?"

Her guest, Lady Markham, who had been embroidering a pillowcase, stood cautiously. Intuition told her that this intrusion was more than just an inconvenience. Not wishing to alarm her hosts, she said calmly, "I think I shall return to my room to find my lavender embroidery thread. I forgot to put it in my sewing bag."

As she headed towards the foyer, she met Mr. Soames rushing towards the library, a soldier right on his heels. Strangely, the butler did not bother to stop or speak, making Millicent halt in her tracks. *A soldier... Richard!*

Aware that Richard was involved in Castlereagh's protection, her heart almost stopped. It took all her effort not to run after them. She arrived at the library door just in time to hear the redcoat say, "Viscount Castlereagh's house."

Lady Matlock began to cry, and Lord Matlock pulled her into his arms. "Now, now, Evelyn. Richard is a strong young man and has suffered worse wounds fighting on the continent."

"Wha...what has happened?" Millicent heard herself ask.

"Richard has been shot," Lord Matlock said matter-of-factly, though his eyes were full of anxiety. "Please stay with Evelyn while I go to him." The earl turned to the soldier. "Did you arrive on horseback?"

"No, sir! There is a carriage waiting for you on the pavement."

Placing a kiss on his wife's forehead, the Earl of Matlock pleaded, "Stay strong, my dear. I shall see about having him brought here, so please begin preparing a room."

The countess nodded, drying her eyes with a handkerchief pulled from her pocket. "Go and bring our son home." As he started to leave, she caught his arm. "Edward, if he is alert, tell him that I love him."

His voice almost broke with his answer. "I will."

Millicent knew what she must do and as soon as Lord Matlock and the messenger disappeared, she took Lady Matlock's hand. "Come. Let us figure out which room will best accommodate Richard's recovery."

As she led her hostess towards the foyer, Millicent appeared unperturbed; inside, she was filled with dread. *Oh, Richard! How shall I live if you do not survive?* This heartfelt cry of her soul surprised Millie, and instantly she stopped walking.

She had never considered how empty her life would be without Richard. Out of the blue, the inner voice spoke again. *You love Richard; you always have. Had you not been so focused on Fitzwilliam, you might have seen that already.* Confused, Millicent pushed those thoughts to the back of her mind. *I cannot dwell on this now. I must be strong for Richard.*

Reminded of her duty, she looked to Lady Matlock. That lady was studying her with a puzzled expression, so she gave her a slight smile. Then, without a word of explanation, she began to lead her towards the foyer once more.

Millicent had no way of knowing that it would be several days before she fully understood the meaning of the turmoil besetting her heart.

Chapter 23

On the road to Scotland

Intent on catching Lord Van Lynden, William pushed his men and horses to their limits. Nonetheless, on the morning of the second day, after having turned at Boroughbridge in Yorkshire onto a road which crossed England from east to west, extremely bad weather set in. Unfortunately, he had no way of knowing that the terrible weather had not delayed Lord Van Lynden, who then took an even larger lead.

After several miles, the driver, Mr. Crawford, pulled the Darcy coach into the open doors of a stable at the next inn. While the footmen and the assistant driver climbed down from the coach, Crawford leapt to the ground and was headed towards the coach door, but a footman was already pulling it open, and its owner stepped out.

"Why are we stopping, Crawford?"

"Sir, the horses are having trouble standing their ground in the mud. Two nearly fell during the last mile, and I am almost certain that—" Seeing irritation cross his employer's face, Crawford hesitated.

"Feel free to speak your mind," William instructed.

"I know it is your wish to catch the other coach, but if we keep to this pace, under the current conditions, we will lose one or more of the horses. I enquired about extra animals at the last inn, and they had all been taken due to the rain. I doubt the situation will be any different here or at future stops."

William was never one to put his men in jeopardy, and he knew the dangers of having an animal take a fall. "I wonder how far it is to Penrith. I recall the innkeeper in York saying it is not far from there to Carlisle. And Carlisle is the last stop before Gretna Green."

Mr. Crawford tilted his head towards the livery manager coming down the stairs from the rooms overhead. "I shall ask him."

William waited while Crawford spoke with that gentleman. When the driver returned, he reported. "We are half-way between York and Penrith, and just as I thought, he has no extra animals. He says that most patrons are not taking a chance by continuing in this deluge, and should we wait too long, all available rooms will be taken."

William winced. "I was hoping to make Penrith today." Then he shrugged. "It seems I am to be thwarted. See to the horses while I arrange accommodations."

That night

William had little appetite and requested that only tea, bread and cheese be sent to his room; however, he arranged for Crawford and the others to eat downstairs and have lodging in the rooms over the stables.

Late that night as he watched the storm's fury through a window, William could think of naught but Elizabeth. Instinctively, his hand went to the pocket where her ribbon resided, and he removed it. A faint scent of lavender still lingered, and it increased his longing. Closing his eyes, he pictured her.

Oh, Elizabeth, you must wonder why I have not come already.

Please do not despair, my love. Look to the ring, and remember my vow to replace it with a wedding band. Nothing shall keep us apart ever again—nothing.

Suddenly, the incessant sound of pounding rain on the roof quieted. William approached a door that led to a small balcony. Throwing it open, he stepped into the now misting rain and studied the sky. In the distance, the clouds were breaking. *Perhaps if it rains no more tonight, we can make up the lost time tomorrow.*

With renewed hope, William closed the door, removed his coat and shoes, and lay down on the bed, still dressed in the rest of his clothes. He had taken little time to look presentable during this trip. In fact, because he had not shaved since leaving London, he now sported a beard. Fingering the course stubble, he wondered what Elizabeth's opinion of it would be.

It was his last coherent thought before falling into a restless sleep.

Annan, Scotland
Sagewood Manor

Wilhelm Lothar had laboured as a man possessed ever since receiving the express stating Lord Van Lynden was on his way back. Having hired servants with the funds the master had left with him, Lothar was exceedingly proud of how much better the house and grounds looked. Moreover, he was eager to give his employer the good news. Having heard the master express a wish to sell the house, Lothar had passed the word around Annan. Subsequently, a gentleman had come forward who seemed eager to purchase the estate if an agreement on price could be made.

As Lothar entered the manor that morning, he noticed the housekeeper on the landing and motioned for her to come downstairs. "Mrs. O'Malley, did you inspect the rooms for Lord Van

Lynden's child and her governess as I asked?"

"I have," the housekeeper replied. "Twice, in fact."

Lothar nodded. "Excellent. I want everything as it should be when Lord Van Lynden arrives."

"It will be."

"Good! Then please see if Cook needs your assistance."

Mrs. O'Malley nodded and headed in the direction of the kitchen. As she did, she murmured, "Lord forbid I should have time to catch my breath."

Kathleen O'Malley, five and thirty, had raised her six-year old-daughter alone for the last year due to her husband's unexpected death. If not for that necessity, she doubted she would have taken the housekeeper position, in spite of Mr. Lothar's pleading.

Having worked as an upstairs maid at Sagewood Manor shortly before Lady Van Lynden's death, she vividly recalled how cruel Lord Van Lynden had been to his family, forsaking them without a word. No, she had no love for that gentleman or for Mr. Lothar, who was clearly more loyal to the master than he had ever been to the mistress.

Reaching the kitchen, Mrs. Stuart was nowhere in sight. Hurrying into the large pantry, Kathleen found the old cook spooning flour into a wooden bowl. "Do you need my help?"

The older woman stopped to smile; then she stretched her back as she wiped her brow. "You have been at work since daylight. I think you should sit down, prop your feet up and have a hot cup of tea. I am making Prince of Wales biscuits, and when it comes time to stamp them, you may help me if you wish."

Kathleen smiled, grateful for the kindness. "I will take my tea at the table, Aggie. That way I shall be ready when you are."

A half-hour later, the biscuits were rolled out, cut and ready to be stamped. As they worked, the women discussed the expected arrival of Lord Van Lynden.

"According to old Lothar, Lord Van Lynden is returning to Holland as soon as possible," Aggie said. "Do you suppose he will sell the house?"

"Rumours are that the manor is to be sold. Hopefully, if it is true, the new owners will keep the servants on," Kathleen replied. "That would please me. I need the work, though I do not care to be around Lord Van Lynden."

"I feel the same. I suppose we shall just have to wait and see what happens."

The sound of a coach upon the newly-gravelled drive caught their attention. Both women raced to the windows to peer out. Lord Van Lynden was already exiting the coach.

"That is him!" Kathleen exclaimed. She wiped her hands on her apron, removed it and hung it over a chair. "I must hurry. If I am not in the foyer when they enter, Mr. Lothar will never let me hear the end of it. I do hope the master is pleased with the house."

"The house is in good order."

Kathleen grimaced. "Let us hope he thinks so."

London
Matlock House

For the first two days after being wounded, Richard lay unconscious, mainly due to the medication used to control his pain. Mr. Colpack had to probe very deeply to find and remove the bullet in his shoulder, and the throbbing could only be relieved by the strongest of sedatives—laudanum. Still, the physician did not want to use that addictive formula for too long, so he began weaning him off the pain reliever that morning. The result was a patient who was not only suffering, but also ill-tempered. Nonetheless, his chief caregiver, Lady Markham, was undaunted. Being a mother had taught her a thing or two about uncooperative patients.

"Just one more spoonful of soup, Richard," Millicent said, coaxing her irritable patient with beef broth. "You will not heal if you do not eat."

"Broth is not soup!" Richard said testily. "And just so you understand, sitting up to eat causes excruciating pain!"

"Do not be such a baby," she replied. "Neither Hugh nor Kathy ever grumbled this much when either of them was ill or hurt."

"I dare say that neither has taken a bullet."

"Thank God that is true. Still, you are a decorated officer and no stranger to wounds. And, if you do not start cooperating, I shall bring in your batman to spoon-feed you. I doubt you would whine if he were your nurse."

"You would not dare!"

"Keep trying my patience, and you shall see."

"Many times I have told Darcy you were merciless," Richard croaked, his voice rough from neglect. "One would think we were married, the way you badger me, Millie." Then something came to his mind. "In fact, why are you here? Where is Mother?"

"Your mother is too distraught to do what is necessary; thus, I convinced her to let me take charge."

"At least she would have been kind."

Millicent smiled. "You need someone strong, not one to bow to your every complaint." She tilted her head mischievously. "If you and I were to marry, you would soon learn just how tenacious I can be."

"As Sergeant Murray used to say, 'Saints preserve us!'"

"Saints cannot help you now," she said, smiling. "Open wide."

Millicent guided another spoonful of broth into his mouth and gently blotted his lips with a serviette. "There. That did not hurt, did it?"

Surreptitiously watching from the doorway, his mother was astounded at how thoroughly Millicent had taken over her son's care. Though improper to have her care for Richard, it had also been a blessing. And Lady Matlock reasoned that the few servants who knew about what was taking place would never gossip; therefore, no one would ever know.

Millicent could cajole him to eat and take his medication when no one else could, by smiling and laughing to keep up his spirits. Still, she had also seen that lady weep bitterly when she thought no one was around. If any good had come from her son's injury, it was that it convinced Lady Matlock that Millicent loved Richard as much more than a friend. Obviously, his near death had awakened feelings of which she herself might not yet be fully aware.

For that reason, the countess was very concerned at how the young woman would respond to the physician's newest report. According to him, in spite of using the latest poultices and remedies, Richard's wound had developed an infection, and his condition was worsening. Left unsaid was that the infection would lead to death, if it was not controlled.

She waited at the door until her son was sleeping again. Once Millicent stood and reached to smooth the hair from Richard's forehead, Lady Matlock pasted on a faux smile. Thus, when the young woman turned to find her watching, she was fully prepared.

As Millicent neared, the countess reached for her hand. "Will you join me in the drawing room for tea?"

Millicent froze, studying her face. "I...I will."

Entering the drawing room, Millicent was surprised to see Lord Matlock come forward to offer her his arm. "Come, my dear," he said, softly patting her hand. "We have talked with Mr.

Colpack and wish to bring you up to date on what he had to say about Richard's progress."

The drawing room

"But...but we have done everything he instructed us to do! Why is it not working?" Millicent cried, leaping up from the sofa.

"He has no idea," Lady Matlock said, glancing to her husband for support.

Lord Matlock added, "Mr. Colpack is still hopeful Richard will improve if we keep to the present course of therapy."

"Then why is he preparing you to lose him?" Millicent asked, her voice rising in fear. "No! There must be something we have not tried!" She began to pace. "Fitzwilliam once said that Mrs. Barnes has several journals full of remedies that were written by a healer who lived in the last century. According to him, his housekeeper has used that man's remedies often and swears by them. Perhaps she and I can find something in them that would help Richard."

Lord and Lady Matlock exchanged worried looks before she spoke. "If you think it would help—"

"I do!" Millicent interrupted. "Will you make certain that someone sits with Richard while I confer with Mrs. Barnes?"

Lady Matlock walked over to take her hand. "You have been with our son almost continually since he was brought home. You really should rest. I can go."

"If you do not mind, I would rather do this myself. Besides, I cannot rest until he is on the mend." Withdrawing her hand, she rushed towards the door, calling over her shoulder. "Please have a carriage readied whilst I change clothes."

"Of course," Lord Matlock replied. With that, Millicent disappeared. "Evelyn, do you think it wise to go against the physician's instructions?"

"I cannot disagree with anything that may help Richard. If Mr. Colpack were to object, it would cause me to trust him less. Surely he would welcome a better remedy if one were found."

"I cannot disagree."

Annan, Scotland
Sagewood Manor

"Lord Van Lynden, this is our housekeeper, Mrs. O'Malley," Mr. Lothar said as he waved Kathleen forward.

Kathleen O'Malley curtseyed under the critical eye of her employer. Rising, she showed no fear as she met and held his gaze. After an awkward pause, Lord Van Lynden spoke.

"I am pleased to have you working for us. I hope you have found Sagewood welcoming."

Taking notice that he did not remember her, Kathleen replied curtly, "I have, sir."

Van Lynden stepped aside, exposing the woman and child hidden behind his large frame. "Mrs. Gardiner, this is our housekeeper, Mrs. O'Malley. She will show you to your rooms. I am certain you would like to wash off the dust and change clothes, perhaps even have a nap before tea."

Kathleen immediately recognised Elizabeth, but pretended otherwise. "Please follow me, ma'am."

She began up the grand staircase with Elizabeth and Emily following. In the foyer below, Lord Van Lynden watched until they were completely out of sight. Then he turned to Mr. Lothar. "Make certain they are watched day and night."

"As you wish."

"I am going to my room. Call me when tea is served." Without waiting for a reply, Van Lynden started to walk away.

"But...but, sir?" Wilhelm Lothar stuttered. Lord Van Lynden halted and turned to face him. "You said nothing about the house.

Do you not think it much improved since you were here last?"

Dispassionately, Van Lynden looked about. "It is. You have done well." With that, he ascended the stairs.

Lothar's spirits fell. Still, he hoped the news of a prospective buyer would gain the master's admiration. Deciding not to say anything until Lord Van Lynden had rested, he hurried to his office to have a small glass of brandy; it always calmed his nerves.

Above stairs, Kathleen and her charges had reached the bedrooms. She opened an elaborately carved door. "This is your bedroom, Mrs. Gardiner." She walked across that room to open another door. "And this leads directly into Miss Ingrid's bedroom."

Emily whispered to her mother, "She does not know my name."

Elizabeth brought a finger to her lips to silence her. "Thank you, Mrs. O'Malley. I am sure they will do admirably."

Suddenly looking sombre, Kathleen stepped closer to Elizabeth. "If you need anything...anything at all, I will be only too glad to be of service."

With those words, the housekeeper rushed from the room, leaving Elizabeth confounded. *What did she mean by that, and how does she know Emily's given name?*

Darcy House

The servants at Darcy House had been kept apprised of the colonel's condition by the Matlocks' staff and were praying daily for his recovery; consequently, Mrs. Barnes was taken aback to find Lady Markham on her doorstep with the news that an infection had set in, and Richard was not responding to the medications the physician had prescribed. Moreover, the countess wanted to read the journals given to her by a former apothecary.

"I shall be pleased to help you search the journals, but the best treatment for infection that I discovered inside them is the honey[15] that comes from New Zealand and parts of Australia. In fact, when I was given these journals, I was also given a trunk full of remedies, some of which were described in the journals. Among its contents was a jar of this honey."

"Honey?" Millicent repeated. "For infection?"

"Yes, my lady. When the Master was a boy, he cut himself severely, and it became infected. Nothing seemed to help until I recalled the journals, read them and discovered the honey. It was applied and destroyed the infection almost overnight. That was my first experience using that remedy, though definitely not my last. I have used it repeatedly throughout the years and tried to keep a supply on hand ever since."

"That sounds like the very thing we need. Would you share the honey and show me how to apply it?"

"Certainly. And if needed, I would be glad to assist."

Millicent smiled. "Please do not tell a soul, but I have been serving as Richard's nurse, and I am very protective of him. I am certain I can do justice to the job."

"Your secret is safe with me," Mrs. Barnes replied. "And I am certain that you will do well. After all, the majority of being a good nurse is caring about the person who is ill."

"No one can doubt that I care for Richard," Millicent answered. *More than I ever realised.*

Chapter 24

Gretna Green

It so happened that just as William's coach was passing the blacksmith shop at Gretna Green, a smiling couple walked out. Straining to watch as they walked towards a waiting coach, he was surprised to discover that the woman favoured Elizabeth in height and colouring. The happiness on her face, as well as the groom's, tugged at his heartstrings, and William contemplated the future wistfully. That establishment's reputation as the place to marry without having to wait tempted him to try to convince Elizabeth to marry him before returning to England. Suddenly, however, bitter reality intervened. Unless he found her and Emily, his future held nothing but emptiness. Therefore, forcing everything else from his mind, he focused anew on how he might locate them whilst the driver hurried past the infamous site.

In a few hundred feet, they arrived at the local inn. The vehicle had barely halted when William exited the coach to enter the already crowded establishment, intending to question the proprietor. An imposing figure, as well as a handsome man, William caused heads to turn as he strode purposefully towards the counter.

When the man behind it looked up, William enquired, "Can

you tell me how much farther it is to Annan?"

"Fourteen miles, give or take, sir. You will turn left at the crossroads ahead, and Annan is the next village on that road."

"May I ask you if you are familiar with a Lord Van Lynden? I understand he has an estate in Annan."

The man clasped his chin with one hand, rubbing his thumb across it as he repeated the name. "Van Lynden...Van Lynden. It does sound familiar, but I cannot say that I remember him."

Suddenly, a gentleman who had been listening to the conversation stepped forward, silencing the owner. "Darcy? My word! With that beard I barely recognised you."

William stoked his newly-acquired whiskers uneasily whilst Lord Atchley, a fellow classmate from university who had always been quite the talker, continued. "I do not think we have crossed paths since Lady Matlock's Christmas ball three years past. What could possibly bring you to Gretna Green?"

"I am here on business."

"I would have wagered that you were here to be married," Atchley said, chuckling at the look now on Darcy's face. "And what better way to avoid all the falderal surrounding that noble institution than to do it quickly and without much fanfare."

Atchley had no idea how much William wished he could do just that.

"I am trying to locate a Lord Van Lynden, whom I believe has an estate in Annan. Do you know the man?"

"This is your lucky day, old boy!" Atchley exclaimed, grinning widely. "When her grandmother died, my wife inherited a small estate in Annan called Breconrae. I am only in Gretna Green today because we are having it renovated, and I need to hire more labourers than Annan can provide."

William nodded, wondering what this story had to do with his quest.

"Much of the estate had been sold to pay the taxes, so I decided to purchase more land. While enquiring hereabouts I learned that the estate next to mine, Sagewood Manor, is for sale. Oddly enough, it is owned by Lord Van Lynden. Though I have never met the man, I have met the caretaker, and I just received word this morning that Lord Van Lynden is now in residence. I am to meet with him tomorrow to discuss buying the property."

William turned to the proprietor. "Do you have a private room where we may talk?"

"Of course." He walked around from behind the counter. "Follow me."

Lord Atchley looked puzzled. "I have never heard of a plot to kill Castlereagh."

"It would have been carried out the day I left London, and you are well aware of how long it takes for news to travel the length and breadth of England."

"And you say that this villain fled Town, taking the woman you love with him?"

"Yes. Elizabeth has raised Van Lynden's daughter from infancy and had no choice but to stay with her. It is my intention to rescue both her and the child and to take him back to London to face charges."

"Then allow me to assist you, Darcy. Come with me to Breconrae, and we shall devise a plan to save them and capture Lord Van Lynden."

"While I truly appreciate your willingness to help, this is not your obligation. I have no idea how many men I will have to face, and there is always the possibility of being killed."

"Do you remember when you came to my defence that summer at Cambridge?"

"It was nothing. You could have whipped that braggart with one hand behind your back."

"But I could not have whipped his friends as well. Without your intervention, I might have had to face every single one of them. Do you really think I would let you take on this blackguard alone?"

William stretched out his hand, and Atchley shook it. "I am proud to call you friend, and I gladly accept your help."

London
Matlock House

The Bow Street Runners, Mr. Whitaker and Mr. Browning, could not wait to share with Richard the news that one of the anarchists, Peter Visser, had confessed the fact that John Guthrie and Lord Van Lynden had planned and financed the attempt on Castlereagh's life. Guthrie had already been arrested, and a warrant had been issued for the other gentleman.

At first the Runners had trouble getting in to see the colonel. However, knowing he would want to be apprised of the situation, they had persevered day after day until they were shown into his room by Lady Matlock. Not wishing her son to tire, as she left to order a fresh pot of tea that imposing lady had warned them not to stay long.

When the countess re-entered the bedroom, she stopped in her tracks at the sight. Having arranged the pillows to prop himself up, Richard looked as though he was sitting at the desk in his office as he read whatever was in his hand, whilst more papers were strewn all over the counterpane. Worst of all, on either side of the bed stood the Bow Street Runners she assumed had left long ago.

Glaring at the visitors, she chided her child. "Mr. Colpack only agreed that you could sit up if you felt well enough. He did not say you could resume work."

Richard directed an apologising smile to the men. "How can I rest if I ponder repeatedly what is happening in this case? Surely you realise I have to know the latest information in order to have peace of mind."

Whitaker stepped back to allow the countess access to the bedside table, and she instructed her maid to set the tray down. "Well, I hope that you have learned all you need to know today about that horrible event, for I insist that these men leave."

"Thank you for not only thwarting the assassination, but for braving my mother's ire to bring me this report, gentlemen," Richard said with a smirk. Trying not to smile in return, Lady Matlock playfully tossed a serviette at her son. "Please continue to keep me informed, and let me know the second you hear from Mr. Darcy," Richard added.

"We will," Browning replied.

In only seconds, both men had disappeared, and his mother poured a cup of tea which she handed to him.

"Mother, I love that you are concerned about my welfare, but please bear in mind that I must handle business when I feel able, and I am greatly concerned about Darcy. I want to know the minute we hear from him."

"Mrs. Barnes promised to send over any correspondence from Fitzwilliam just as soon as it arrives. And, as for the rogues who tried to kill the foreign minister, it is my belief there are enough people handling that case to allow you to rest a while longer."

Setting her own cup down on the tray, she sat on the bed and caressed Richard's cheek. "Forgive me for worrying so much. No matter how old you may be, you will always be my baby."

"Mother!" Richard protested, glancing to the door to see if anyone was listening.

Lady Matlock smiled. "And, I might add, I have come to realise that there is someone else who thinks very highly of you."

At Richard's puzzled look, she continued. "I have marvelled at the way Millicent took control of your care. It was she who searched out the honey to control the infection that threatened your life. Furthermore, she would not rest until Mr. Colpack tried the remedy and then declared you were on the mend. The poor girl hardly slept for the first two days you were here. She is in love with you; of that I am certain."

Richard shook his head. "I fear you are wrong. Though she cares for me, Millie sees me as nothing more than a friend. It is Darcy she has loved most of her life."

"Until this happened, I would have agreed. But I am a woman, and I can tell when another woman is in love."

"Why are you telling me this?"

"Because it has broken my heart to watch you pine for her all these years, never saying a word because you love both her and your cousin. It is time for you to declare yourself...that is, if you still love her."

Richard's head dropped, and he appeared to be studying the tea in his cup. "Do you really believe that she is in love with me?"

"You may rely upon it. She is."

He could not hold back a smile. "Then I had best strike while the iron is hot."

The countess stood, leaning down to kiss his forehead. "Should I tell her you wish to speak with her?"

"First, would you retrieve the ring?"

"I had forgotten Mother's amethyst was promised for your future wife."

"Millicent once told me that she loves amethysts, and when we marry, I shall have a wedding band designed to complement it."

Lady Matlock smiled. "Though she may not be aware of it just yet, she is a very fortunate woman. You are an honourable man, my son, and I love you."

"I love you, too, Mother. And I consider myself the fortunate one, for I have you as my mother, and God willing, I will have

Millicent as my wife."

She beamed. "Let me make haste. I cannot wait until you are engaged and all of England knows. What festivities we shall have—balls, suppers, all manner of soirées..." Lady Matlock was still chattering as she hurried out the door.

Richard looked dazed. *Balls...suppers...soirées? I had forgotten the many ways Mother can think of to celebrate.*

Annan, Scotland
Sagewood Manor

As Kathleen O'Malley ascended the back stairs to the family quarters with a tray of tea and biscuits, she pondered what had happened between the period of time when Elizabeth Bennet left Sagewood and now. Whatever it was, from that lady's expression, she was clearly not pleased to be back at Sagewood, and, for that matter, neither was the child. There had been no time to speak privately with the governess since her arrival, but she hoped to learn today what lay behind her decision to return to this dreadful place.

At last standing before the bedroom door, Kathleen knocked before turning the knob and entering. Seeing and hearing no one, she set the tray down on a table and walked towards the next room. Sunlight filtered through an open door to the balcony, and she could see the governess and the child through the opening. The girl was nestled in Elizabeth's lap, and though they were talking, she was unable to hear the conversation. As silently as possible, she crept closer.

"But, Mama, when will Mr. Darcy come? I miss him and Snow so much."

Elizabeth smiled. "And I am certain he and Snow miss you very much, too, but we must be patient. He will come for us as soon as he discovers where we are."

I was right! She truly does not wish to be here! The housekeeper stepped from behind the curtain, startling Elizabeth. "Forgive me if I alarmed you, ma'am, but I feel I must speak with you."

Elizabeth addressed Emily. "It is time to take your nap, dearest."

"I am not sleepy."

"You do not have to sleep. You have only to rest."

Ever the obedient child, Emily kissed Elizabeth's cheek and slipped from her lap.

Elizabeth stood, addressing Kathleen. "Let me get Emily to bed, and then we will talk."

Emily? Kathleen thought as she watched the two disappear into the other room. In a few seconds, Elizabeth came back through the door.

As she approached, she offered a wan smile. "Now we may talk freely."

"I fear you do not remember me, but my name is Kathleen. I was employed as an upstairs maid when Lady Van Lynden returned from London with her newborn. You accompanied her as the child's nanny."

"You look familiar. However, you are correct. I do not remember you."

"That is because you had little dealings with me, and as I recall, your hands were full taking care of the mistress as well as the baby."

"The house was understaffed. I did my best to tend to her and Emily."

Looking about cautiously, Kathleen lowered her voice. "I know you have no reason to trust me, but what if I told you I know about the letter slipped under your bedroom door the day before you left Sagewood with the baby?"

Elizabeth looked shocked. "How do you know about that?"

"I wrote it."

As Elizabeth's expression grew more puzzled, she began to explain. "I was chosen to help the mistress decide what to put in the trunks she sent to Eagleton Park in the weeks before she died. During that time, she spoke often of Ingrid—how she prayed you would take her with you once she was...well, no longer here. The last day I packed the trunks, she begged me to help you escape with her child. I felt terrible what with that horrible man having left them both here to die, so I promised Lady Van Lynden I would do what I could."

"Then you were responsible for the carpenter who just happened to arrive with a wagon full of furniture, so I could slip inside it and escape?"

"That is my cousin, John Reilly. He builds and repairs furniture and comes by here often. I knew his presence would not raise any suspicions. And, since he routinely travels from here to York on his route, it was no trouble for him to escort you that far."

"He and his wife were so kind. We stayed in their home in Gretna Green the first night. She provided me with extra blankets and clothes from her own children."

"Colleen is a good woman."

"You could have been in great trouble had you been found out. Why did you help me?"

"After she died, I could still hear Lady Van Lynden's pleas. That is why I despise Lord Van Lynden...and Mr. Lothar, too, for that matter. There are a few good people working here, such as Aggie Stuart, the cook. Like me, she is only here because she needs the pay. But the rest I would not trust if I were you."

"I understand."

"May I ask why you call the child Emily and how you came to be Mrs. Gardiner?"

"I left here believing that Lord Van Lynden would never return for his daughter, so I renamed her. And I was never married. Mrs. Gardiner is a fictitious name I created to fend off questions in regards to Emily."

Kathleen nodded. "What brought you and the child back?"

"Her father returned to England with a plan to execute the British foreign minister, supposedly to avenge a treaty the minister arranged. While he was here, he intended to retrieve his daughter."

"Was the foreign minister killed?"

"I do not know. It was planned for the day we left London. I imagine, whether he was successful or not, the news will be slow to reach here."

"This is true. But what has that to do with his daughter? Why would he take her from you? He never showed any interest in her when Lady Van Lynden was alive."

"From what little I overheard, she is only a pawn to appease his relations in South Holland. Apparently, they put more stock in family than he, so bringing her back could influence them to hide him from the authorities."

"Poor little girl! She must have been shocked to learn that Lord Van Lynden is her father."

"He has not bothered to tell her, and I would not know where to begin. When he appeared out of the blue, I had no choice but to go with Emily as her governess, but now he insists I must marry him when we reach Rotterdam."

"How horrid!" Kathleen said. "If he is talking of Rotterdam, then this confirms he is planning on leaving the country. Aggie and I wondered if he would."

"Last evening I overheard him tell Mr. Lothar that in three days' time we will sail from Gatehouse of Fleet north to Glasgow. From there, we will cross the country to Edinburgh and board a ship to South Holland. He believes no one would expect us to take that route."

Suddenly, Kathleen remembered. "Just before I announced myself on the balcony, I heard you mention a Mr. Darcy. I got the impression that he is coming for you."

For the first time a genuinely happy smile graced Elizabeth's face. "I have faith he is searching, and hopefully, he will find us before we leave here. If not, he will keep looking until he does. Of this I am certain. He is the most honourable man I have ever known."

"Then, let us give this honourable man more time to find you by devising a plan to delay your departure."

Elizabeth brightened. "I should be ever so grateful, and so will he. In fact, I have no doubt you will be richly rewarded for your help."

"My reward will be seeing the master's face when Mr. Darcy comes to take you back. Now, let me and Aggie put our heads together and see what we can come up with. I shall let you know as soon as we agree on a plan."

Matlock House
Richard's Bedroom
Millicent stuck her head in the door and, seeing Richard awake, hurried to the bed where he lay. All the while, she anxiously searched his face for signs of something wrong.

"Your mother said that you wished to speak to me. Is your wound beginning to ache again? "

"There is nothing amiss," Richard said with a smile. "In fact, I feel very well." Millicent's brows knit in puzzlement. Seeing her expression, he added teasingly, "By the way, you look so much better than when last I saw you."

Becoming annoyed, she replied testily, "I imagine I do. The last time you saw me I had not slept for two days."

"Then that explains the dishevelled hair and the dark circles under your eyes."

Defiantly, Millicent's hands came to rest on her hips. "Did you send for me just to berate me?"

Richard laughed aloud. "Do not be so quick to anger. I was only teasing. I sent for you because I wished to tell you how grateful I am for your care. Mother told me how diligently you have tended me since I was brought home."

Instantly Millicent calmed and looked a bit sheepish. "I am sorry. I thought perhaps your wound was troubling you again, which put me on edge. As for what I did, I would do the same for anyone in your condition."

"Oh? Then you did not do it because you cared for me in particular?"

"Do not twist my words. Of course, I care for you."

"Ah, but the question is: Do you care *more* for me than you would for just 'anyone in my condition?'"

"Richard, you never talk in riddles! Please just say what you mean."

Now it was Richard's turn to look sheepish. "I...I was hoping that your care had a deeper motivation. I love you, Millicent, and I wish to know..." He took a deep breath to steel himself and reached to take her hand. "If you are in love with me."

For the longest time Millicent stood rooted to the spot, unable to speak. Then her eyes began to fill with tears. "You love me?"

"I have loved you most of my life. I believe I fell in love with you the day we met, yet I soon realised you had your heart set on my taciturn cousin; therefore, I said not a word. I kept hoping that at some point you would realise Darcy was not the man for you, and once that happened, I planned to reveal my true feelings. Only, you met Henry before that came about. After your marriage, I shuttered my heart against the pain of it, prepared never to marry if I could not have the woman I loved. And if it were not for Mother insisting today that you are in love with me, we would not be having this conversation now."

She began to cry in earnest, and Richard pulled Millicent to sit down on the bed. Sniffling, she began to explain. "What you said is true. I was so fixed on winning Fitzwilliam's love before I married and then again after Henry died, that I never considered how I felt about you. It was not until you were injured—when I thought I might lose you—that I realised how empty my life would be if you were not in it. You have always been my rock, and knowing that you could die without hearing me say—" She could no longer hold back a heartfelt sob. "That was when I realised I am in love with you."

Beaming, Richard cupped the back of her head and guided her lips to meet his. The kiss began innocently, but quickly intensified until, at length, he reluctantly quit the kiss to frame her face with both hands. "I have never loved another. Millie, will you consent to be my wife?"

Tears rolling down her face, she nodded fervently. "Yes, Richard, I will marry you."

Pulling a small blue box from under his pillow, he opened it to reveal his grandmother's amethyst ring. As he slipped it on her finger, she whispered, "It is so beautiful."

"*You* are beautiful," Richard murmured, pulling her into another passionate kiss. It was quite some time before they broke apart to let their rapidly beating hearts calm.

"I cannot wait to see Mother's face when she learns we are engaged. She will be so delighted to spread the news that she may bankrupt Father in the process. But perhaps she will allow us to contribute in some small measure to the wedding plans."

"We *are* speaking of your Mother," Millicent said with a wide grin.

"Forgive me. I had a moment of insanity."

Millie laughed. "Knowing her as well as I do, she will insist on having her way, and to be truthful, I would not deny her that pleasure."

Millicent and Richard had no way of knowing that his mother

was so certain of the outcome of his proposal that she was already planning an intimate dinner celebration for just the two of them—one that would be served in his room that evening. A family celebration would have to wait until after William returned safe and sound from Scotland.

Chapter 25

Richmond
Canfield Manor

Having finally gotten Grace and Marianne to lie down for a nap, Kitty realised it was past time for the post to arrive if there was to be any today. Rushing down the hall towards the landing, she whispered a prayer that Lizzy had had the opportunity to send word of her situation. As she arrived at the head of the stairs, she realised the housekeeper was halfway up them, and in her hands was a silver salver holding several letters. Kitty waited until Mrs. Watkins stepped onto the landing and handed the salver to her.

The old servant smiled at her mistress' sister and then proceeded to go back down the stairs whilst Kitty walked slowly towards Jane's suite of rooms. As she walked, she looked through the stack of letters. On top of the pile was one from Charles' solicitor, Mr. Smith. Beneath it was one from their sister Mary and another from Jane's nearest neighbour, Lady Needham. She breathed a sigh of relief, however, upon finding a letter from Charles beneath them all.

Just the thing to keep Jane from worrying about why we have not heard from Lizzy!

Kitty had last heard about Lizzy from Lady Markham, the countess having informed her that her sister and niece had been spirited away from London by Lord Van Lynden, with Mr. Darcy in pursuit. However, she had left it up to Kitty whether to tell Jane or to spare her the worry. Kitty had been reluctant to share the whole truth, praying Mr. Darcy would be able to recover Lizzy and Emily before any explanation might become necessary. Thus, Jane only knew they were travelling with Lord Van Lynden to his estate in Scotland.

Reaching her sister's sitting room, Kitty took a deep breath and pasted on a faux smile. Opening the door, she spied Jane sitting on the balcony with her feet propped up on a stool, a spot she occupied more and more of late. Seeing Kitty, Jane waved her forward.

"Kitty, do not keep me in suspense. Have we heard from Lizzy or Charles?"

Kitty waved the letter from her brother and ignored the question about Lizzy. "Your husband has written you yet another letter this week!" Smiling to see her eldest sister's eyes light up like a child's, she handed the letter to Jane.

For some time, Jane read in silence, though her face began to glow with happiness. Once she began to speak, however, it was as though she could not talk fast enough.

"Charles is coming home, Kitty! Mr. Grantham allows that his stomach ailment is completely healed and his lungs nearly so. He writes that if he agrees to keep to the regimen prescribed, the physician says he is free to come home immediately."

Jane began to cry, and Kitty sat down on a nearby chair. "This is wonderful news, Jane. With any luck, Charles may be safely home before the baby is born."

"I had not allowed myself to hope he might be home in time for that. If only he would come straightaway!" She pulled a handkerchief from her pocket and dabbed at her eyes. "I would be so relieved if he were holding my hand when the time comes."

"Then, let us pray that that is the case. Has he already purchased passages for himself and his valet?"

"No. Just after hearing that he is free to come home, he decided to write. He said he will write again as soon as he knows the name of the ship and the day it sails."

"Well then, my dear sister, I think we have much to do if you wish to complete the shirt you began as a homecoming present for your husband."

Jane beamed. "I have only to attach the sleeves and embroider his initials and mine beside the collar on the inside. I have always added our initials as a token of my love, and he will look for them."

"That is so romantic," Kitty said with a smile. "My poor husband is happy just to receive a shirt once a year and without any initials!" Chuckling, she added, "Now, do you wish to read the rest of the letters, or shall I read them aloud as I did yesterday?"

"Please read them to me. I am so deliriously happy that I do not think I am capable of making sense of them."

"Delighted to be of service, *your ladyship*," Kitty said, teasingly dropping a curtsy.

After all the letters were read, Jane's expression grew solemn. "Another day with no word from Lizzy."

"We must keep the faith, Jane. Lizzy is nobody's fool, and she is capable of taking care of herself and Emily. Besides, Lady Markham said that Mr. Darcy is staying apprised of their situation."

"That is my only consolation."

"What say I fetch the sewing box and our projects? You can work on Charles' shirt whilst I finish embroidering bluebells on the baby's gown. After all, Charles would not want his son dressed in Marianne's rose embroidered gown, now would he?"

Jane's quick smile boosted Kitty's spirits.

"No, he definitely would not."

Annan, Scotland
Breconrae

Lord Atchley convinced William to pay for lodging at the inn and to leave his coach in the nearby stable. In that way, Atchley argued, William could slip into Atchley's own coach for the trip to Breconrae, leaving any who might be interested to assume he was in his room at the inn. William's servants were instructed to stay out of sight and later join them by means of a rented, unmarked coach. While agreeing it was a brilliant ploy, William was still so anxious to find Elizabeth that he found it difficult to relax, even after entering his friend's coach. Consequently, by the time Atchley's coach finally entered the gates to Breconrae, he had to force himself to pay attention as his host pointed out the features of his estate.

Despite being a little larger than Rosehill, his mother's respite, Breconrae looked more like a cottage than a manor. Made of red sandstone, it boasted two stories covered in copious vines, some of which were flowering. Atchley pointed out that the areas next to the house were planted with a combination of herbs and flowers, whilst the majority of the lawn had been absorbed by the wilderness which surrounded the house. In that area, wildflowers grew in abundance. Any further observations were cut short when the coach abruptly halted and the vehicle rocked as a footman climbed down to unfold the steps and open the door.

The instant Atchley stepped out, he continued his assessment. "It is as I said. Most of the land was sold to pay the taxes, and in the last decade, the house and lawns were neglected. There is much work yet to be done."

"It is still lovely," William stated.

"That is exactly what my wife said," Atchley replied with a

chuckle.

Suddenly an older couple appeared in the now open front door. "Allow me to apologise for the lack of maids and footmen. While we have a good many grooms, carpenters, and gardeners, we have hired few house servants thus far. We plan to add more once the renovation is complete. As for now, Lady Atchley simply brings an entourage with her whenever she visits. Since she did not accompany me this time, you and I shall have to make do with the ones available."

"That will not inconvenience me. I no longer travel with a valet, and at times I find it quite agreeable to be left on my own."

"So do I!"

When they reached the front door, Lord Atchley began introductions. "Darcy, allow me to introduce Mr. and Mrs. Kelley, my butler and housekeeper."

William nodded as Atchley addressed the servants. "This is Mr. Fitzwilliam Darcy of Pemberley in Derbyshire. He is to be our guest for the next few days. Please see that his trunks are taken to the blue room."

The servants welcomed William to Breconrae, and stepping aside so that the gentlemen could enter the house, they began taking their coats, hats and gloves.

Atchley noted that William was examining the house. "We renovated this portion first, so do not be discouraged when you first see the remainder."

"You shall not hear me complain," William replied. "It is kind of you to ask me to stay here."

"Not at all," Atchley replied. "Is a half-hour enough time for you to meet me in the library to formulate a plan, or would an hour be better?"

"Even sooner would suit me. Knowing the people I love are only a few miles away makes me eager to act."

"I can only imagine," Lord Atchley said. Then he turned to

Mrs. Kelly. "Please bring refreshments to the library."

As the woman rushed towards the kitchen, Atchley motioned for William to precede him up the stairs.

"Come. Due to the lack of help, Mrs. Kelly always assists the cook; thus, it is left to me to show you to your room."

Sagewood Manor
Elizabeth's bedroom

Kathleen was animated as she described the plan that she and Aggie had concocted. "Using heated rocks and plenty of quilts, we can make it appear that Emily has a high fever. Hopefully, that will be enough to convince Lord Van Lynden she is too ill to travel. If we can delay the trip, even by a day, it will give Mr. Darcy more time to find you."

"I am not certain that will work," Elizabeth said. "Emily's father cares not a whit about her. Why should he be concerned if she is ill?"

"He may not, but a proper captain would never allow an obviously sick person, be it child or adult, to board his vessel. They might infect the entire crew as well as the other passengers. And the ships that sail from Gatehouse of Fleet north to Glasgow are not very large vessels. Lord Van Lynden must realise how difficult it would be to hide a sick child on so small a ship."

"Of course, you are right," Elizabeth said wearily. She appeared to be considering the consequences. "Lord Van Lynden is so unpredictable that he could decide to leave here at any moment. We had better arrange the hoax this evening."

"I foresee only one problem," the housekeeper said. "Can the child be convinced to play along? After all, she will be very uncomfortable under all those quilts, and her father could decide to come upstairs and question her."

"If I explain the reason why, she will cooperate," Elizabeth answered. Then a small smile crossed her face. "And she can be quite the little actress when she wishes."

"Good! I shall inform Aggie you agreed with our plan. We shall bring up lots of quilts and several heated rocks right after tea. Once she begins to perspire, we can remove the evidence and send for her father."

Elizabeth took a deep breath and let it go. "Let us pray it works."

Lord Van Lynden's study

Holding up the note which had been delivered to Sagewood Manor only moments before, Lord Van Lynden declared, "Stationing a man in Gretna Green to watch for Mr. Darcy's coach was an excellent idea, my friend. This confirms the gentleman reached Gretna Green today and is staying at the inn."

Wilhelm Lothar beamed. "I strive to think of ways to be helpful, my lord."

Van Lynden rose and turned to stare out a window. "His search will lead him to Sagewood eventually, which is why I must leave directly after I meet with the prospective buyer in the morning. What did you say his name was?"

"Lord Atchley."

Van Lynden sighed. "An Englishman—yet, what do I care? His money is as good as a Scots'. The moment he is out of sight, I mean to leave for Gatehouse of Fleet. I wish to board a ship for Glasgow this week."

"For the most part, your trunks are packed. I shall instruct the housekeeper to see that Mrs. Gardiner and the child's trunks are packed this evening."

"You have been a valuable asset, Lothar, and the minute I reach Holland, I shall send for you. Once I have my full inheritance, you will be richly rewarded for your loyalty."

"But...but you said I was to sail with you."

"That was before Mr. Darcy insinuated himself into my business. I must leave right away, and you must remain to make certain Sagewood Manor is sold. And, if need be, you will point Mr. Darcy in a different direction—tell him I set out for Dundee. That should distract him until I can reach Edinburgh and sail from this miserable country forever."

"What if he arrives before you leave?"

"Then I shall have no choice but to confront him. Are any of the men you hired handy with weapons?"

"Yes. I made certain they understood they would be expected to defend the estate, and you, if need be."

"Hopefully, I will not need their assistance. Still, I am pleased I can count on a show of force, should it be necessary. Now, be off with you. I want to know everything is ready before I lay my head down tonight."

"Yes, sir."

Mr. Lothar hurried from the room, totally unaware of what was transpiring upstairs.

Breconrae library

"I am not sure you should go with me tomorrow, Darcy. If Lord Van Lynden were to see you, the situation could get unpleasant very quickly. After I return, we will have a better idea of how many men he has employed, and at that point, we can come up with a plan."

"People I love are being held against their will, and I cannot take a chance that Lord Van Lynden will leave directly after meeting with you."

"I agree that it would be easier to confront him at his estate than once he is on the road, but how do you suggest we do that?"

"I propose the men and I follow your coach and wait in the

woods near the entrance to Sagewood. You will meet with Van Lynden to assess the number of servants he has and learn what you can about Elizabeth and Emily and his future plans. Once you leave the estate, you will join us. At that point, we will make a decision on how to proceed."

Lord Atchley stood. "And if I learn that he is leaving straight-away?"

"We shall immediately return to the house in force, stopping where the drive ends near the manor and fanning out, so that it is obvious we have a large number of men."

"You *do* know someone is likely to be killed. Are you not worried about the woman and child?"

"I think constantly of their safety. I had considered slipping into the house whilst you talk with Emily's father. But if I were seen, Lord Van Lynden would realise that you had brought me there. Without all the men standing with us, you and I would likely be killed. Where would that leave Elizabeth and Emily?"

Atchley replied resignedly, "Where, indeed? I suppose we will not know exactly how to proceed until the time comes."

"Those were my thoughts exactly."

Atchley took a deep breath. "If we are to do this, we need to address the men. Stay seated, and I shall have Mr. Kelly fetch them."

His host walked out of the library, leaving William to his thoughts, which, as always, were of Elizabeth. Just the idea of seeing her again caused his pulse to race. Yet at the same time, he could not shake a spirit of dread. Elizabeth's own words reflected the fact Lord Van Lynden was not a man to be thwarted, and he wondered what the cad would do when he was cornered. Realising it would serve no purpose to dwell on something beyond his control, William closed his eyes.

Instantly, he was riding in his coach accompanied by Elizabeth and Emily. They were on the drive leading to Pemberley when the vehicle halted at the highest point. This setting provided the best view of his ancestral home, and the driver knew to pause whenever they reached it and to wait until ordered to go on. Daylight was waning as he exited the coach, picked up Emily and glanced to see Elizabeth's beautiful eyes sparkling with tears of happiness. He was leaning in to place a kiss on her forehead when Atchley walked back into the room. His voice broke the spell.

"They will be here shortly," Lord Atchley said as he walked over to a liquor cabinet. Holding up a decanter filled with amber liquid, he continued. "Until they arrive, I am going to have a glass of French brandy. My father always said it is good for whatever ails you. May I offer you one, too?"

Very disappointed to be jarred from his daydream, William said, "Please do." Silently he added, *though I doubt it can help with what ails me.*

Sagewood Manor
Elizabeth's bedroom

The minute Lord Van Lynden walked into the room, Emily's smile disappeared, and fright filled her eyes. Never expecting that man to come upstairs to examine her child, Elizabeth instantly wondered if she had made a mistake in agreeing to Kathleen's plan.

Uncommonly silent, she watched as he walked straight to the bed and peered unfeelingly at the tiny child lying in the middle of the large mattress. Emily's face was flush from the heat of the rocks, and there was a thin layer of sweat on her forehead. Elizabeth prayed that would be sufficient to convince him she was too ill to travel. For her part, Emily was so scared that she appeared paler than normal.

At length, Van Lynden pressed his hand to her daughter's

forehead. Drawing it back, he declared, "I shall have Mrs. O'Malley fetch the local physician. Ingrid must be ready to leave by the day after tomorrow at the latest."

"But...but if she is not—"

"I will hear no further arguments, Mrs. Gardiner. We will leave the day after tomorrow. Is that clear?"

"It is."

Lord Van Lynden marched out of the room, slamming the door behind him. Emily began to cry, and Elizabeth rushed to cradle her in her arms. "Hush, dearest, all is well. He is gone."

"Was I a good actress, Mama?"

"You were perfect, sweetheart. He is convinced you are ill."

Kathleen slipped out of the closet where she had hidden and tiptoed to the door. Opening it, she peered both ways down the hall. Convinced he was gone, she closed the door and locked it. Then she let go the breath she had been holding. "At least we have bought another day."

"That is better than nothing," Elizabeth answered. "But what will you do about fetching the physician?"

"That is no problem. We have not had a physician in the area for many years. The nearest one is in Gretna Green, and it is hard to find him at home. He is usually in another part of the county whenever we need him. I shall tell Lord Van Lynden he was not at home, but I left a message for him to come as soon as he returns. Of course, I shall do no such thing."

Elizabeth reached out to take Kathleen's hand and gave it a squeeze. "I have no idea what I would have done without you."

"I am just glad to be of service."

Chapter 26

Sagewood Manor
The next day

As Lord Atchley's coach came to a stop in front of Sagewood Manor, he pulled aside the curtain to see who might be waiting. A footman came rushing down the steps and he braced himself and stepped from the vehicle. Once he was on solid ground, Mr. Lothar hurried out of the house.

"Lord Atchley! So good to see you again, Sir. Lord Van Lynden is expecting you; however, we expected you much later. I am uncertain of his whereabouts at this moment. If you will follow me, I will show you to the library where you may wait whilst I locate him."

Atchley nodded and followed the man inside the house, across the foyer and down a hallway. Stopping in front of two ornate doors, Mr. Lothar opened both to reveal a well-appointed library.

"Make yourself comfortable, and I shall return shortly." Hurrying back the way he had come, Lothar left the doors open.

With the servant gone, Lord Atchley walked around the elegant room, hoping to gain some insight into the man who owned Sagewood. He was disappointed to find the room apparently held nothing personal, as even the paintings on the walls were of landscapes, not portraits. As he was completing his trip around the room, Lord Atchley heard raised voices coming from the hallway. Easing stealthily to the door, he tried to overhear what was being said.

"I do not care to hear any excuses, Mrs. O'Malley! Find a physician or at the very least an apothecary. We leave tomorrow, even if Ingrid is sick."

"This is not London, sir. I cannot promise to locate the physician quickly, and we have no apothecary."

"That is your problem, not mine! Now, send someone to Gretna Green immediately, and report to me as soon as you have an answer."

Hearing footsteps coming in his direction, Atchley quickly stepped over to a bookcase and grabbed a book. Sitting down on the nearest sofa, he opened it just as a tall, flaxen-haired man stepped into the room. That gentleman, evidently Lord Van Lynden, hesitated only a moment before coming towards him. Though he feigned a smile, it never reached his eyes.

"Lord Atchley?" Atchley stood. "It is a pleasure to meet you," Van Lynden added, extending a hand. "I was just informed that you had arrived. I apologise for not being available to greet you."

Atchley shook his hand. "The pleasure is mine I assure you, Lord Van Lynden."

"It is my understanding that you seek an estate to purchase."

"I am considering enlarging my estate which is situated next to yours."

"That is good to hear. My wish is to sell Sagewood Manor as soon as possible. I am open to any reasonable offer."

Suddenly, Lothar rushed into the room. "I am sorry, my lord. I have been looking for you. We must have crossed paths."

"No need to apologise, Mr. Lothar. Lord Atchley and I have introduced ourselves. Please resume your duties."

Looking very flustered, the butler immediately disappeared,

leaving them alone again.

"Please, sit down so we may discuss this matter," Van Lynden said motioning to a nearby sofa.

Atchley did as asked, and his host took the sofa directly across from him. Eager to know how many men Lord Van Lynden might have, Atchley brought up the subject of servants.

"I am in the middle of renovating Breconrae, and while I wish to add more land, I am not necessarily in need of another house. The purchase of a house would require a good deal more servants. If you do not mind my asking, how many people do you employ?"

Perturbed, Van Lynden leaned forward, speaking in a clipped manner. "At present we have twelve men employed as grooms, gardeners and footmen. Some can fill more than one position as needed. Other than the housekeeper and cook, we have four maids."

"So many? That is only a few less than the number I employ at Breconrae."

Van Lynden's expression hardened. "I was led to believe that you wanted to purchase Sagewood Manor in its entirety."

"I am sorry if I gave your man the wrong impression."

"If the price for the entire estate is acceptable to you, why would you not take it all? You can always divide the property and dispose of what you do not want later."

"I will have to confer with my solicitor before making such a commitment."

"And I suppose your solicitor is in London?"

"He is, but it would take no more than three weeks to—"

Van Lynden stood, cutting short his remarks. "Do what you think is best. I have other things occupying my mind at present. Mr. Lothar serves as my steward, as well as my butler, and he is able to act on my behalf. I have a solicitor in Edinburgh who will handle the sale, should I receive a realistic offer."

"Oh? Then I will not be dealing directly with you in the future?"

"No."

"Surely, if you actually wish to sell Sagewood, you would—"

Losing his patience, Van Lynden interrupted, declaring, "I plan to sail for my homeland as soon as I can arrange it. I will leave the sale of the estate in Mr. Lothar's capable hands." Without further niceties, he said, "If you will wait here, someone will show you out."

Van Lynden disappeared before Atchley could ask more questions. Walking to the door, he looked both ways down the hall. Seeing no servants, for a brief moment he considered heading in the opposite direction to see how many servants he might encounter. That idea was instantly quelled when Mr. Lothar appeared at the end of the hallway.

"This way, Lord Atchley."

In the woods

William paced in front of Lord Atchley's coach for a time before stopping to address his friend.

"With Emily ill, I cannot justify waiting any longer. Besides, we are here now. Why should we take a chance he will leave before we can be in place again?"

"You will get no argument from me. After hearing how callously he spoke of his daughter, I understand why you would not wish to wait."

"Van Lynden is heartless."

Atchley nodded. "I was relieved to learn he apparently does not have a great number of men. We are closely matched, it seems."

"I would rather not fight man-to-man. Too many could get hurt."

"What do you propose?"

"As I said yesterday, we approach the manor on horseback, lined on either side of your coach. Fanned out in that manner, we will look imposing. Once we reach the circular drive, one of my footmen will deliver my challenge." William patted his coat. "In this pocket is a letter I wrote last night, offering Van Lynden a way out. I will propose we settle this like gentlemen, on the field of honour. In that manner we can best avoid others being hurt or killed. I believe that his pride will force him to accept."

"You trust that blackguard to agree to your terms without using treachery? I would never trust Van Lynden to fight fairly."

"If he follows the rules, I will not lose, and if he cheats, it will be left to you to stop him. I want you as my second."

"I think you are taking an incredible risk; nevertheless, I will abide by your wishes."

William patted Lord Atchley on the back. "Thank you, my friend." Then, motioning for a servant to bring his horse forward, William checked his pistol to make certain it was loaded. "Let us pray Lord Van Lynden is vain enough to accept my offer."

Atchley watched Darcy mount his stallion before turning to the others. "Check your weapons, men; then mount up, and follow us."

Van Lynden's study

As Lord Van Lynden and Wilhelm Lothar were going through the items to be shipped to Rotterdam, a servant practically barrelled into the room.

"Sir, this was just delivered!"

Both turned to see that the footman was white as a sheet. When he offered the letter in his hand to the master, Van Lynden snatched it from him. Quickly opening it, he began to read, and the longer he did so, the more crimson his face became.

At last he ordered, "Fetch all the men, Hannigan! Tell them to come straight to the house and bring their weapons."

Though shaking furiously, the footman stayed in place. "There is more."

"What now?"

"As the messenger was leaving, I noticed a large number of men assembled on the drive."

Van Lynden and Mr. Lothar flew to the windows. Feeling fearful for the first time, Van Lynden shouted, "GO, NOW!" That order sent Hannigan scurrying out the door.

"What do they want?" Mr. Lothar whispered as though the intruders could hear.

"It is that fool Darcy. He is here after Mrs. Gardiner and my child."

"Surely, they are not worth your life. Why not let him have them?"

Lord Van Lynden grabbed Mr. Lothar by the collar, lifting him to his toes. "NO MAN will take what is mine! Ingrid is my daughter, and I will make Mrs. Gardiner my wife. Besides, it is evident now that only death will stop a man like Darcy. I have no doubt that if I do not kill him now, he will follow me to Rotterdam."

Lothar nodded, so Van Lynden released him. "Find my duelling pistols."

"Sir, what if he is a better shot? Have you considered the sword?"

"I have not fenced in years. Besides, swords will not afford me the chances a pistol will. Or, perhaps I should say *pistols*. While Darcy will no doubt follow the rules of the duel, I have no intention of being that honourable."

Walking over to his desk, Van Lynden opened a drawer and removed an ivory-handled pistol. Checking to make certain it was loaded, he shoved it into the waistband of his breeches. Then he covered it with his coat.

"Instruct all the men to wait until I have killed Mr. Darcy to begin firing."

Lothar watched, opened-mouthed, as his employer walked to the door. Just before he exited, Van Lynden said, "Fetch Mrs. Gardiner. Having her watch the duel will make Darcy more nervous. Assign one man to physically restrain her, if necessary. Then tell everyone to wait for me in the library."

"Where are you going?"

Van Lynden laughed. "I am going to speak to my opponent."

If William was surprised when Lord Van Lynden walked out of the front entrance alone, he showed no sign of it. He glanced at Lord Atchley. "Wait here."

All the while Darcy approached his adversary across the middle of the circular drive, Lord Atchley and the men kept their hands on their weapons.

Van Lynden acted unaffected as William approached. "I thought better of you, Darcy. Why would a man of your station chase after a woman he knows is here of her own free will? Surely, you can accept that Mrs. Gardiner does not love you."

"We both know that is a lie." The only indication William had hit his mark was a slight narrowing of his opponent's eyes.

Van Lynden then studied the group of men who had accompanied William. "Is that Lord Atchley?"

"It is."

"I should have known. You Britons always stand together. Well, Darcy, it seems my best option is to take up your challenge. And I will, but only if you agree to one condition."

"Which is?"

"When I win, all of those on your side will leave Sagewood, and I will be free to go wherever I please without further interference."

Knowing Atchley would take care of Van Lynden and free Elizabeth and Emily if anything happened to him, William agreed.

Van Lynden pointed to a level area of lawn to his left. "Does that field suit you?"

"It does."

"Fine. Select a second from your group. I shall have mine bring the duelling pistols, and both our seconds will inspect the weapons before we begin. The balance of your men and mine will stay where they are. Does this meet with your approval?"

"Yes."

"Then let us begin." As William turned to leave, Van Lynden exclaimed smugly, "I am going to enjoy *taking* Mrs. Gardiner as my wife."

Whipping around, William struggled to keep control of his temper. In the end, he settled for taunting his adversary with the truth. "I can safely say that Mrs. Gardiner would NEVER have you. Not even if you were the last man in the world."

Upstairs

While William and Van Lynden were meeting, a tough-looking bounder who worked as a groomsman was sent to fetch Elizabeth. Using brute force he dragged her from the room under protest from Emily and Kathleen. Powerless to help when she was locked inside the room with Emily, Kathleen found that the girl was so upset by the sight of her mother being treated so shamefully that she had her hands full consoling her.

Elizabeth realised that whatever was transpiring was likely in response to William's arrival. Therefore, whilst being taken to the library, she prayed God would keep him safe. Even so, once she was shoved into the room, the number of men and guns assembled caused her heart to sink. There was no time to dwell on the danger, though, because Lord Van Lynden chose that moment to enter.

"Thank you for not shirking your duty to Sagewood Manor or to me, men. An enemy has come to my door, one who intends to take my daughter and her governess away by force. I have challenged him to a duel in hopes of settling this without involving you." Van Lynden pointed to the French doors, which led from the library onto a huge terrace. "He agreed to meet me on the lawn just beyond those doors. However, I do ask, that you take up positions at the windows and doors, and on the lawn if you can do so stealthily. If it becomes necessary, I will call for your assistance."

Glancing at Elizabeth, he continued. "Since this gentleman is obsessed with Mrs. Gardiner, I intend to have her stand on the lawn near me. Perhaps her presence will hamper his aim." He then looked to his friend. "Did you find the duelling pistols, Mr. Lothar?"

Lothar held out an elegantly-carved mahogany box. "I did."

"Excellent." Addressing the blackguard who held tightly to Elizabeth's arm, he said, "Follow me, and keep a good grip on her."

The man nodded.

"You do know Van Lynden's men have plenty of places to hide in and around the house, while ours have none?" Lord Atchley cautioned William. "Should this evolve into an all-out battle, our men will have to advance across an open field."

"I realise that. And if something happens to me, you will have to hold off Van Lynden until our men can advance to help you. Are you still willing to do this?"

Atchley smiled. "I must be mad, but I am." He opened his jacket to show he had two pistols inside his waistband.

William smiled, opening his own coat to show the same. "Let us just hope that neither of us wastes a shot."

"Are you ready?" Atchley asked.

Taking a deep breath, William answered. "I am."

As she was being dragged onto the lawn, Elizabeth was surprised to see a large number of men congregated at the end of the drive. Trying hard not to panic, she spied William standing not a hundred feet away. Though he now sported a beard she knew him instantly, and tears filled her eyes. His hair was blowing in the wind, and he looked so handsome she ached to fly into his embrace. At that exact moment he turned, and their eyes met. She mouthed, "I love you."

He smiled, nodding ever so slightly, and said the same.

Mr. Lothar walked past her then, carrying the mahogany box. A well-dressed gentleman standing next to William headed towards Lothar, and they met half-way. It appeared as though each was examining the pistols before William's second selected one. Lothar lifted the other from the box and motioned for Lord Van Lynden to approach. William followed suit, and soon all four men were standing in the middle of the grassy field.

"Shall we draw straws to see if your man or mine counts the paces?"

William stooped to pick up a piece of straw and handed it to Lord Van Lynden. Immediately he broke it in half. "Your call. Long or short?"

"Whoever picks the longest straw will call the paces," William stated.

Lothar and Lord Atchley each drew a stick, with Atchley taking the longer one. William and Van Lynden walked a few feet away before turning to stand back to back.

Lord Atchley shouted, "Gentlemen, I will count to forty. At

'forty' you are free to turn and fire at will. Are you ready?"

Both men nodded, so the count began. While Atchley was still in the twenties, a man on horseback rode out of the woods adjacent to the field. This distracted Lord Atchley, keeping him from realising that Lord Van Lynden had already turned and was aiming at William's back.

Seeing what was taking place, Elizabeth screamed, "William! Watch out!"

Van Lynden managed to get off a shot just as the man guarding Elizabeth slapped a hand over her mouth. Still, her shout was enough to alert William. He stepped to one side and began to turn. Not able to evade the bullet entirely, it grazed his right shoulder. The impact made him drop his weapon, and though he stooped to pick it up, he found it difficult to use his shooting arm.

Seeing that he had failed, Van Lynden quickly dropped that weapon and pulled another from beneath his coat. Lord Atchley already had Van Lynden in his sights when the sound of a rifle being fired cracked the air.

For a second, all eyes save Atchley's flew to the man on horseback who was placing a rifle back in its sheath. Atchley, however, kept his eyes trained on Lord Van Lynden, who suddenly pitched forward, landing flat on his face. Mr. Lothar ran to his employer and, seeing he was dead, picked up the still-loaded gun. When he aimed it at William, Lord Atchley shot him.

Seeing that both Lord Van Lynden and Mr. Lothar were dead, the blackguard who restrained Elizabeth shoved her aside and ran towards the back of the house. His desertion was apparently enough incentive to cause the rest of Lord Van Lynden's men to flee as well.

Elizabeth immediately rushed towards William, who had ripped off his cravat to use as a bandage. When she reached him, he instantly pulled her into an embrace. Sinking his hand deep into her hair, he directed her lips to his, and for a brief moment all was right with the world.

Remembering his wound, Elizabeth broke the kiss and began to examine his shoulder. "Let me see to that, William!"

Taking the cravat from his hand, she began to work the coat off of his arm, exposing his injury. On that side his shirt was soaked with blood.

"Oh, William! You need help at once!"

Lord Atchley hurried to stand beside them, along with another man. "This is Mr. Douglas, Darcy. Before he retired and came to work for me, he was a surgeon in the navy. Let him see your wound."

Aggie, who had slipped out of the house to check on Elizabeth when the guns went silent, stepped forward. "I am certain that the house is safe. There are no men left—only a few women. If you will follow me into the kitchen, I will lay a blanket on the table so that you may tend to his injury."

The wound, though deep in places, proved easier to treat than Elizabeth had feared, since the bullet doing the damage had not lodged in William's shoulder; however, the former navy surgeon warned that an infection could prove the main reason for concern. Mr. Douglas worked with surprising calm though Elizabeth was not as composed.

From the moment she and Kathleen were freed from the bedroom, Emily had insisted upon seeing her mother. Then, after learning William was there, she was adamant about seeing him as well. Not wishing the child to be traumatised by the sight of William's injury, Elizabeth insisted on removing her daughter to the drawing room to wait. Trying to concentrate on the book she had chosen to read to a fretful Emily, a sudden slam of a door caused both to jump.

Soon afterward, Kathleen came into the room, smiling from

ear to ear. "Mr. Douglas has finished, and Mr. Darcy came through it splendidly."

Elizabeth closed her eyes in relief. "Thank God."

"Lord Atchley's men are moving him upstairs to one of the bedrooms. I will notify you as soon as we get him settled."

"Does Lord Atchley think it safe for us to remain here?"

"After he conducted a thorough search, he assured us that all of the men who worked here have fled. He thinks it best not to move Mr. Darcy tonight, so he and a majority of the men plan to stay, just in case. I find it hard to believe any of the lowlifes Mr. Lothar hired will show their faces again after seeing what happened to him and Lord Van Lynden. Most of the lot were petty thieves and wastrels, not mercenaries."

Elizabeth sighed. "I have not had time to digest the fact that Emily and I are finally free."

Kathleen patted her shoulder. "You will in time, my dear."

"I must see William. I have missed him so much and so has Emily." The child nodded vigorously.

"Well, be forewarned. Mr. Douglas gave Mr. Darcy some laudanum to ease the pain before stitching his shoulder. He may not be entirely himself until it wears off."

"I think I will ask Aggie to make a pot of tea and bring it up when we are allowed to see him, just in case he should want some."

Emily slid off her mother's lap. "Let us hurry, Mama. I want to tell Mr. Darcy that I have missed him very much."

As soon as William was settled in a bedroom, Lord Atchley pulled a chair to one side of the bed whilst Mr. Douglas checked his patient's bandages from the other.

"Darcy, do you know the identity of the man who shot Lord Van Lynden—the chap who rode out of the woods on horseback?"

Though already a bit woozy, William was able to reply. "My guess is it was Carney."

"The man who killed Howton and then joined Van Lynden's plot against Castlereagh?"

"The same. His hat fell off when he rode back into the woods. That was when I noticed he had red hair."

"Providing it was him, what do you make of it?"

"If Lord Van Lynden did anything to cross him, he is the type of man who would exact revenge."

"But why not take a shot at *you* while he was here? After all, you and Richard had been tracking him for weeks with regards to Howton."

"Richard has been front and centre in the investigation, and if Carney *was* looking for me, the beard might have thrown him off. In any case, it appears that Van Lynden was his target."

"Well, I am taking no chances. All our men are armed, and if he shows up again, they have orders to kill him."

William nodded.

"I cannot wait to read what the London papers say about the attempt on Castlereagh. Perhaps a copy will make it this far north tomorrow."

After he finished inspecting William's dressings, a knock on the door brought Mr. Douglas around the bed. Opening it to find Elizabeth and Emily waiting, he stepped aside to let them enter.

Elizabeth was straining to see William, so Atchley said, "I must go look after the men. I shall check on you in the morning, Darcy. Mr. Douglas, would you care to join me?"

Instantly catching his meaning, Douglas said, "I would."

Both nodded at Elizabeth and immediately vacated the room.

Chapter 27

London
Matlock House

Tired of lying in bed all day, Richard had become an irritable patient in spite of Millicent's best efforts, and today would prove no different. Knocking on the bedroom door, she entered without waiting for consent—her normal routine of late—and found an empty bed. At once her eyes flew to the door which led to a small balcony. Seeing that it was ajar, she cried, "Richard, what have you done?"

"I have escaped!"

Already rushing in that direction, she was on the balcony by the time he finished speaking. Lying on a chaise in the sun, his colour was still pale and her heart clenched with concern.

Instantly, her hands found her hips. "What did the physician say when you asked about getting out of bed?"

"I know what he said. I just chose not to listen."

"Are you going to be this much trouble after we marry?"

"Oh, no! I plan to be much more trouble then."

The smirk on her beloved's face was a reminder of how charming he could be and caused most of Millicent's anger to dissipate. She walked over to sit in a chair beside him. "I imagine being married to you will be like having a third child to rear."

Richard took her hand and pulled her onto his lap. "I can assure you, madam, that I am a fully grown man."

He cupped the back of her head and brought her lips to meet his. Lost in delectable passion, neither heard Lady Matlock walk onto the balcony. Only her deliberate cough broke through the trance that had befallen them, abruptly ending the kiss as each pulled back to see the source.

"Mother! In the future if you enter my bedroom unannounced, you had better make your presence known straightaway, else you could find yourself embarrassed."

"I knocked loudly several times," Lady Matlock replied with a knowing smile. "You were merely too *involved* to notice. Besides, I assure you there is nothing you could be doing that I have not seen before."

Holding back a laugh, Millicent removed herself from Richard's lap, taking a place in the chair once again. Meanwhile, the countess walked over to hand her son a letter. "I thought you might want to read this now."

Seeing William's distinctive handwriting, Richard ripped open the seal and began to read it aloud. At length, he addressed Millicent. "I must get back on my feet. Now that Darcy is closing in on Van Lynden, he will need my help."

"You are in no condition to go anywhere," his mother stated.

"Fitzwilliam is no man's fool, Richard," Millicent added. "He will take every precaution."

Richard stared transfixed at the letter. "I need to warn him about Carney."

"Do you still think that blackguard followed Lord Van Lynden?" Millicent asked.

"What other explanation could there be? He was seen heading north out of London, leaving the money he stole from Howton behind. That he did not bother to stop for Howton's bag tells me he left in a rage, likely to exact revenge. After all, Visser confessed to taking a shot at Carney, only to find he had vanished seconds later."

Lady Matlock spoke up. "How do you know this man Carney left the money here?"

"Browning told me last evening. He and Whitaker searched the house where Mrs. Graham's daughter and her children live. They found Howton's bag hidden in the roof of an attached shed."

"Richard, you cannot help Fitzwilliam. He is already too far ahead of you," Millicent said.

At last, he acquiesced. "I...I suppose you are right. Still, should something happen—"

Millicent reached to clasp his hand, giving it a comforting squeeze. "To speculate now is only borrowing trouble."

Lady Matlock chimed in. "It is likely my nephew will return to Pemberley once leaving Scotland. Do you wish to address a letter to him there?"

"I do," Richard replied. "I have much to tell him about the whole debacle regarding Castlereagh."

"I shall tell Soames to have the small writing desk in the library brought up here. Then you will be able to keep up with your correspondence without leaving the room."

"One would think you were conspiring with Millicent to keep me contained."

"One would be right."

With that, Lady Matlock swept back into the bedroom, leaving Richard and Millicent staring after her.

"I admire your mother."

"For her sharp tongue?"

Millicent laughed. "No. I admire that she is not afraid to speak her mind."

"I am not surprised. You are much like her in that regard."

Pinning Richard with her emerald eyes, Millicent said, "Will that present a problem?"

"On the contrary, I relish your candour. I never liked to be flattered with insincere avowals. You, my dear, are perfect for me."

Settling into Richard's lap again, she slipped her hands into his hair and purred in his ear. "Do not tell me, dearest—show me."

And Richard proceeded to do just that.

Scotland
Sagewood Manor

For Elizabeth, the night had been torturously long. She and Emily had seen William, but by the time they were shown into his room, the laudanum had taken effect, and he could not carry on a conversation. In fact, whilst she was speaking to him, he had drifted to sleep. Moreover, though she dearly wished to sit with him, Mr. Douglas insisted he would be the one to stay with his patient. Sorely disappointed, Elizabeth had put on a pleasant expression and acquiesced when it was suggested she and Emily get some rest.

Afterward, repeated night terrors consumed her dreams, resulting in no sleep at all. In each instance, she was incapable of speaking and was forced to watch mutely as Lord Van Lynden brought the gun from under his coat and fired at William's back. As a result, she had witnessed the man she loved fall to the ground mortally wounded time and again, and now her emotions were raw.

Determined to see William early in the morning, she had prevailed upon Kathleen to sleep in the room with Emily, which left her free to put to rest her fears. Dawn found her creeping stealthily down the hallway whilst most of the household was still in bed. Reaching the bedroom where he lay, she turned the doorknob, held her breath and stepped inside.

Mr. Douglas, who had slept sprawled across a small settee,

immediately sat up, causing Elizabeth to jump.

"How is he?" she asked quietly.

"He is as well as can be expected. He suffered with a slight fever by midnight, but that is nothing remarkable given the severity of his wounds."

"Would you mind if I sat with him today?"

Mr. Douglas acquiesced. "First, let me ascertain he has not been overtaken by a fever since last I checked."

Walking directly to the bed, he placed a hand on William's forehead and turned to smile at her. At his return he whispered, "His fever has not increased. If he should waken, tell him that he needs to lie still. The stitches could loosen with too much activity, and I do not want him to lose any more blood. If he is in a great deal of pain, I have a bit of laudanum left, and I could send someone to Breconrae to fetch more. Now, I believe I shall go to my room and catch a bit of sleep. Feel free to send for me if I am needed."

Once she was alone, Elizabeth rushed to the bed and sat down beside William. The sight of his unclothed neck and shoulders were an instant reminder of the night at Pemberley when he appeared on the balcony to declare he had always loved her, while the bandages covering his wound spoke of how close she had come to losing him. She reached to brush a lock of hair from his eyes and was surprised when he opened them.

Her carefully constructed facade began to crumble. "Oh, William," she sobbed, resting her head on his chest. "I was so frightened. When I saw you fall, I thought..." She could not continue.

William slid his uninjured arm around her and patted her back. "Hush, sweetheart. I am here, and we are together. That is all that matters."

Sniffling, Elizabeth sat up. "You are right. We are, and I thank

God that you are alive."

Trying to raise his head, William moaned and fell back on the pillow.

"Are you in pain? Mr. Douglas has more laudanum if you need relief."

"I feel as though I was thrown from a horse and trampled, but I would rather suffer the pain than be in a stupor. Will you slide another pillow under my head when I try again?"

"But Mr. Douglas warned that you should lie still. The stitches could loosen if you move."

"If I am to return to Pemberley, I must get back on my feet, and I am determined to go home soon. Pray do as I ask."

Grabbing the pillow lying on the other side of the bed, she placed it behind him as he struggled to sit up, grimacing in pain the whole time.

Fresh tears pooled in Elizabeth's eyes. "You are much too stubborn for your own good. Your wounds are serious and—"

William reached out to caress her cheek, instantly silencing her. "I love when you show concern for my welfare."

Closing her eyes, she leaned into his hand. "I have been so worried that I feel sick."

"I know the feeling, my love."

"*My love.* To hear you say that...I am amazed that you love me—that you would risk your life for me."

"I love you with all my heart and soul, Elizabeth. Kiss me."

Elizabeth poured her heart and soul into the kiss, and William responded just as fervently. Suddenly, he broke away and moaned. "Oh, Elizabeth! Relieve me of my agony. Say that you will marry me whilst we are in Scotland, and let us return to Pemberley as man and wife."

Instantly her expression changed, causing him to grow sombre. "You do not wish to marry me?"

Seeing the pain in his eyes, she kissed him quickly. "No, never say that! What I desire is completely the opposite. I wish to be your wife so desperately I can think of nothing else. If I did not have Emily, I would marry you this very hour. However, I need her to understand that marriage is sacred and not to be taken lightly."

"Do you believe just because I wish to marry you right away I am not taking marriage seriously?"

"Oh, darling, if any couple deserves to marry straightaway, we do. We have wasted so many precious years because of foolish misunderstandings, and we both know what it is to truly love another even when there appears to be no hope of reconciliation. Still, we must set an example for Emily, as well as any future children we may have. What argument could we use to dissuade one of them from eloping if they have only to remind us of our own hasty wedding?"

At the mention of *their* children, William acquiesced. "Though my treacherous body betrays my desire to make you mine now, I see your point. I would hope that our children would wish to marry with their family surrounding them."

"I knew you would understand."

Instantly pulled into another feverish kiss, Elizabeth was breathless by the time William murmured passionately in her ear, "Just keep this in mind, my love. I have longed for you the better part of five years, and I am desperate to make you my wife. Plan the wedding swiftly, for I wish to marry you within a month of our return to Pemberley. Will you agree?"

In a daze from his kiss, she did not answer right away, so he repeated, "Do you agree, Elizabeth?"

"I...I do."

A blissful expression crossed his face. "I am pleased we are in agreement."

Suddenly, her expression became concerned. "I just thought of something dreadful. Might there be consequences as a result of

Van Lynden's death?"

"Atchley is familiar with the local constable and plans to inform him of what happened, as well as Lord Van Lynden's involvement in the plot against Viscount Castlereagh. Hopefully, the London papers will have already arrived, supporting my report. Atchley is certain there will be no consequences. Nonetheless, I hope to be in England before any objections could be raised."

"I pray that is so." She laid her head back on his chest. "I never want to be parted from you again."

The door opened before they could part, and Lord Atchley walked towards them with a big grin. "To think I was worried about you. It seems my fears have been misplaced."

Blushing, Elizabeth stood and stepped aside, though William refused to let go of her hand.

"Do not leave on my account, Mrs. Gardiner."

"She will not," William said, giving her a loving look. "What is the matter, Atchley?"

"I see that you are as eager for me to disappear as I am to be off, so I shall state my business and leave the two of you alone. I came to see how you were faring this morning, Darcy."

"My shoulder is intolerably sore, which makes it nearly impossible to use my right arm. Otherwise, I am well."

"According to Mr. Douglas, your wound is still grave enough to warrant taking no chances. Nonetheless, I must ask if you feel well enough to let us transport you to Breconrae. Douglas thinks if we keep you lying on your back, we can safely move you tomorrow. I have a wagon that can be filled with quilts to make the road less brutal. Do you agree, or would you rather wait?"

"The sooner we are away from here, the better I will like it."

"Good. Though the men employed by Van Lynden are unlikely to return, and a good number of our men will stay until we can move you, Mrs. Gardiner and the child, I would feel more at ease if we were at my home."

"I agree. And, Atchley, please accept my gratitude for your help. I could not have freed Elizabeth and Emily without you."

Atchley smiled. "I am glad I could be of service." Glancing at Elizabeth, he said, "You are blessed that Fitzwilliam holds you in such high regard."

"I am well aware of that," she said, giving William a smile. "Please let me add my gratitude for your assistance."

"You are most welcome." Addressing William, he added, "If you need anything, you have only to ask. The cook already has the dining room table groaning under the weight of all the food she has prepared. I shall remind her to bring up a tray for you and Mrs. Gardiner." Lord Atchley performed a slight bow and walked out of the room.

Still holding her hand, William drew Elizabeth back to his side. "I thought he would never leave. I need to taste your lips again."

At once, his hand entwined with her hair, drawing her mouth back to his. The kiss began slowly, with the passion building until they were unaware of anything save the desires coursing through them.

A closing door caused both to startle, and they watched as Aggie set a tray of food down on the only table. When she turned to see Elizabeth in William's arms, the cook blushed.

"I apologise for disturbing you." Hastily, she bobbed a curtsey. "I shall leave you to...to carry on with—" Suddenly realising what she was saying, she ran from the room.

"Now," William said dreamily. "Where were we?"

Richmond
Canfield Manor

As Kitty was going down the hall towards Jane's rooms, she heard a cry. Breaking into a run, she was inside her sister's bedroom in seconds. Relieved to find that she was not in labour, Kitty brought her hands to her heart.

"Jane! You scared me half to death." Swiftly crossing to where she was standing, Kitty gripped both her shoulders. "The physician said that you must not get excited. Sit down and tell me what has happened."

Jane held out a letter. "It is Charles! He is already aboard a ship. He is truly on his way home!"

Kitty could not help but smile at Jane's enthusiasm, though she cautioned, "You do remember that you wanted Charles to be here when the child is born. If you do not calm down, you might have it today."

Jane took several deep breaths, trying to still her wildly beating heart. "You are right. I must not get overly excited." Then she giggled, grabbing Kitty's hand to give it a squeeze. "But, he is on his way home, Kitty! Is that not an answer to my prayers?"

"It is." Suddenly, Kitty's expression changed to one of annoyance. "How did you get the letter before I saw it?"

"Please do not blame Mrs. Watkins. The post was early. When I noticed the express rider coming down the drive, the children were still involved with their lessons. So, I opened my door and just happened to see her in the hallway. I asked her to bring any letters to me right away."

"And I suppose you dismissed her immediately?"

"Of course. She has other things to attend."

So much for trying to keep you safe, Kitty thought. "Well, I wish she had informed me after she delivered it to you. I have tried to make her understand that I worry you will faint with no one around to notice."

"I know you do, and I appreciate your concern. But pray do not stay upset. I want everyone to be as happy as I am today."

At Jane's pleading look, Kitty acquiesced. "I am elated to hear that my brother is on his way. Will you tell Grace and Marianne?"

Jane looked thoughtful. "I think not. They are too young to understand and will ask continuously where he is."

"Then you will let it come as a complete surprise?"

"I will," Jane said, then she sighed. "I cannot help but believe that Mr. Darcy will bring Lizzy and Emily safely home soon. Lady Markham's last letter said he was close behind Lord Van Lynden's coach."

"Knowing how many years he and Lizzy were in love, despite being separated by cruel circumstances, I pray this is so. They, and Emily, deserve as much happiness as each of us have found in our marriages."

"I could not agree more."

Jane's expression turned wistful. "Would it not be perfect if Charles arrived home before the baby decides it is time to be born?"

"I could not think of a more perfect ending to all the madness of the last few months."

"Nor could I."

Chapter 28

On the road to Pemberley
Six days later

Against William's wishes, they did not leave Annan until a full three days after he was wounded. Mr. Douglas and Lord Atchley were only able to convince him to wait that long by insisting that if he did not take time to recuperate, he would not be able to protect Elizabeth once they were on the road. Still, on the fourth day Darcy declared himself fit to travel.

Now that they were on the last leg of their trip back to Pemberley, Elizabeth's nerves were completely on edge. Having watched William's pain increase with each passing mile, she found herself praying constantly that nothing would delay them further.

An unexpected dip in the road brought another groan from William, and Elizabeth's eyes flew to him. Having fallen into a restless sleep, he lay curled upon the makeshift bed on one side of the coach. The bed—nothing more than a wooden box built to bridge the gap between the seats and topped with a small mattress—had proved too small and unforgiving to be comfortable. It had also required Emily and those accompanying them, Kathleen and her six-year-old daughter Colleen, to follow in a hired vehicle.

All Elizabeth could do to provide some relief for William was to rub his neck, arms and uninjured shoulder each night with the salve Mr. Douglas had sent along and to add the tiniest drop of laudanum to his evening tea. Satisfied that the small amount allowed him some rest, she kept the addition to herself, just as Mr. Douglas had advised. Since the surgeon had schooled her on the addictive nature of the drug, she was determined not to give him a drop more than was necessary.

After the wheels found another large hole in the road, William turned so that he now faced her, his clean-shaven face so very handsome her breath caught at the sight. The realisation that this complex man was hers—heart, body and soul—made her heart soar. However, that sensation was short-lived as the abundance of silver in his hair again triggered her sense of guilt.

Oh, William! How much of the silver is my fault? If only I had accepted your proposal at Kent! I was such a fool!

An inner voice quickly reminded her that where William was concerned, to live in the past would simply be unbearable. Vowing to dwell on more pleasant things, Elizabeth's thoughts turned to their wedding.

I cannot believe we are to be married in four weeks! As she listed in her head all that had to be accomplished in that brief period of time, Jane came to mind. *I cannot imagine marrying without Jane present, but it is impossible to predict when the baby will be born.*

Abruptly, the coach made a swing to the left, and Elizabeth pushed aside the window curtain to see what was happening. They had pulled into a post inn, presumably to change the horses. Aware that William did not wish to appear frail in front of the others, she attempted to wake him by calling his name. When he did not respond, she leaned over to whisper in his ear. "My darling, we have stopped to change horses."

At once his eyes flew open, and he sat up. Whilst he rubbed his eyes, she watched as he grimaced silently—a practice he had begun, she supposed, to keep her from knowing how much he was suffering. It had not worked.

"My hat," he managed to murmur.

Elizabeth reached to her left, where she had kept it safe, and brought it forth. "Here it is, but you need not leave the coach for my sake. Emily and Kathleen will be here at any second. I shall not be alone in the inn if you would rather stay here and rest."

"It is my duty to protect you."

Realising to argue would be futile, she helped to straighten his cravat. "I do not see how you can stand to wear this. Surely, it does not help the pain and soreness in your neck."

"The pain is not unbearable," he answered unconvincingly.

A footman opened the coach door, and the moment he pulled down the steps, Emily stepped onto the bottom one and peered inside. "Mr. Darcy! Did you miss me?"

William could not help but smile. "Terribly. But tell me, have you enjoyed your trip thus far?"

"Oh, Colleen is such fun. We have been playing a game. We each try to find a cow, and the first to find five wins. Then we start over."

"And are you winning?"

Emily looked thoughtful. "I do not know. I keep forgetting how many I have found."

As William and Elizabeth laughed, suddenly Kathleen appeared behind Emily. "Step down, Miss Emily, so that your mother and Mr. Darcy may exit the coach."

Emily did as instructed, and soon the entire party was entering the inn. The proprietor, a man very familiar with the Master of Pemberley, rushed in their direction.

"Mr. Darcy, sir. What a pleasure to have you here again. What is it that you require?"

"Is a private dining room available?"

"For you it is! Follow me."

Crossing the common room to a door, the proprietor opened it and waved them inside. "I hope you will find this satisfactory."

Seeing the upholstered chairs, William said, "It will do nicely."

Elizabeth could almost hear William's groan of relief when he sank into a comfortable chair at the head of a large, cloth-covered table.

"What can I get for you, sir?"

"Tea and biscuits for the ladies and brandy for me."

"Right away."

When they resumed their journey, William chose to sit upright across from Elizabeth. Though he winced every time one of the coach wheels found another hole, he refused her entreaties to lie down.

"Elizabeth, have you said anything to Emily about our wedding?"

"No. I wished for her to be at home—I mean, at Pemberley, before I broke the news. She has been tossed from pillar to post for so long that I would like her to feel more secure before I tell her."

"You were right the first time, my love. Pemberley is her home as well as yours. I understand your misgivings about breaking the news during all the upheaval, but I have a request. If you do not mind, I would like to be the first to tell her. I wish to ask if she will be my daughter."

Tears filled Elizabeth's eyes. "That is so dear of you."

"I love Emily, and I want her to feel just as much my child as any born of our union."

Elizabeth beamed. "I could not love you any more than I do at this moment. If you were any more perfect, I would be forced to nominate you for sainthood."

William laughed. "Rest assured that will never happen. Besides, being a saint is not my idea of true happiness."

"Then what is?"

William reached for her hand. "Being married to you."

"If you keep saying such things, I shall be forced to sit in your lap and kiss you, and that will not be good for your shoulder."

Pulling her onto his lap, he growled, "Let me be the judge of that."

An innocent kiss rapidly transformed into a more passionate one, and William tightened his grip around her waist; however, the instant he moaned in satisfaction, Elizabeth leapt from his lap and sat in her former seat.

"Why did you move?"

"You moaned. I feared you were in pain."

William sighed. "I cannot wait until we are home. Perhaps then you will allow me to kiss you properly without fearing for my life."

Elizabeth chuckled. "Perhaps. Now, is there anything else we should discuss before we reach Pemberley?"

"Have you decided what position Mrs. O'Malley will have? I would like to inform Mrs. Reynolds the moment we arrive, so she can place her in the appropriate quarters."

"I thought that since Cora returned to Canfield Manor, she could serve as Emily's maid. Would it pose a problem for Colleen to live in the servants' quarters with her?"

"It is not unheard of to have servants' children live in their quarters. And now that I know your wishes, I can instruct Mrs. Reynolds to assign her a small apartment in lieu of a single room."

Elizabeth reached for his hand. "You are so kind to help her and Mrs. Stuart—Aggie. She told me it was you who suggested to Lord Atchley that she would make an excellent addition to his staff."

"Knowing how much help she and Mrs. O'Malley were to you

and of her wish to stay in Scotland, I could do no less. In truth, Atchley was eager to employ her after he had sampled her cooking."

Elizabeth laughed. "Then it is a good thing she is a fine cook."

"Rest assured, she will be well situated with Atchley. I do not know a kinder or more honest person. Moreover, I intend to gift her and Mrs. O'Malley five hundred pounds each, to be placed in an account at the Bank of London. That amount should generate sufficient interest to allow them to save for the future. As for Colleen, I plan to improve her prospects with an education and an appropriate dowry."

Elizabeth brought his hand to her lips, placing a kiss on the back. "One of the reasons that I love you is your thoughtfulness."

William smiled. "Perhaps my thoughtfulness will inspire yours."

"Are you speaking of our wedding?"

"I am."

"I *have* been thinking about it. I am wondering how we will ever gather everyone in one place that quickly."

"And have you a solution?"

"I thought that after you have sufficiently recovered, we would visit Canfield Manor. Jane should be close to her lying in, or the baby may have already been born by that time, and I truly wish to see how she is faring. Once there, we can begin planning a wedding for London. If you still intend to marry so hurriedly, that location would be central to most of our family."

William's brows knit. "The only people I have to consider are the Earl and Countess of Matlock and Richard and Millicent. Georgiana cannot possibly return from Ireland in time."

Elizabeth brought her hand to her mouth. "I completely forgot about Georgiana. Millicent mentioned your sister had married and moved to Ireland, but with all that has transpired, she never crossed my mind."

"Do not let it trouble you. When I made the decision to marry right away, I had no intention of waiting for her to sail back to England. We shall just have to visit her and Lord Charlton in the near future."

"Then that leaves only my sisters and the Gardiners."

"Will you be disappointed if the wedding is somewhat private?" When Elizabeth's lips curled in a smile, he hurried to explain. "I would gladly place an announcement in every paper in England, Scotland and Wales to ensure the whole world knows you are to be mine, but I shall be satisfied if only the mothers of the *ton* are enlightened. A small service at St. George's will ensure that, for all the weddings at that venue are published in the papers. Nevertheless, I will defer to your wishes."

Elizabeth's right eyebrow rose teasingly. "So you wish for the mothers of the *ton* to know you are off the market?"

"Exactly!"

"It is my recollection that you never enjoyed participating in society, so how did they manage to become the target of your resentment? One would think you were hardly ever in their daughters' company."

"You forget I have a formidable family and equally formidable friends who coaxed me from Pemberley on occasion. In fact, I had just returned from a fox hunt and ball at Hudson Hall when I arrived at Canfield Manor."

Elizabeth smiled. "I remember the way you acted when we met at Netherfield Park, so I shall have to ask Millicent if you performed any better while you were at her home."

William grinned, both dimples flashing. "You will be delighted to know I did not! However, I am resigned that once we are married, I must participate in a few of the activities of the *ton* for the sake of our children. At some point they will have to navigate society, and I intend to make their passage smoother than my own."

"Oh? You are willing to attend balls and soirées, but only for the sake of our children?" William nodded. "And do you intend to dance at those events?"

"Only with you." As the corners of her mouth began to lift, he added, "Or those with whom I am well acquainted."

Elizabeth chuckled. "I imagine that will break many a heart."

William sobered. "My only concern is your heart."

"Saint Fitzwilliam Darcy. How does that sound?"

"Come here!"

William pulled her back onto his lap, and the next few miles were spent without a word spoken...except by their hearts.

Pemberley

It was late afternoon by the time they reached Pemberley, and William was exhausted. Immediately after laying eyes upon him, Mrs. Reynolds nodded at one of the footmen, which was his signal to fetch the local physician, Mr. Camryn. As he rushed towards the stables, she proceeded to greet Mr. Darcy, Elizabeth and Emily before turning to smile at the unknown newcomers.

"Mrs. Reynolds," William said. "This is Mrs. O'Malley. She is Emily's new maid." As the housekeeper nodded, he motioned for Colleen to come forward. "And this is her daughter, Colleen. Please arrange for them to have one of the empty apartments."

"Yes, sir." To Kathleen, she said, "We are pleased to have you with us."

"I am surprised that Hugh and Kathy are not here to greet us," William said, glancing at the front door. "Surely they missed Emily as much as she missed them."

"I am sorry, sir. You had no way of knowing, but they accompanied Lady Foggett when she left for London."

Surprised, William asked, "When was this?"

"Two days past."

"And they travelled without an escort?"

"An old acquaintance of Lady Foggett's happened to be in Lambton and called on her. The next thing I knew, he was escorting them to Town."

William looked perplexed. "Did anything happen to disturb her?"

"All I know is that after she received a letter from Lady Markham, she seemed eager to leave."

"I see."

William glanced to where Elizabeth stood chatting with Kathleen, whilst Emily and Colleen carried on a similar conversation.

"You must all be tired. Shall we go inside?"

Once in the foyer, the housekeeper instructed a maid to direct Kathleen and her daughter below stairs and to bring them a tray of tea and biscuits once they were settled in their rooms. Then she instructed a footman to carry a bucket of hot water there. Another maid was sent to locate Mr. Adams, whom she felt certain Mr. Darcy would need.

By the time that was done, Mrs. Reynolds turned to find her employer halfway up the stairs, escorting Elizabeth and Emily to their rooms. Shaking her head at his ability to function even when he was clearly in pain, she went in search of Mr. Walker, who had been supervising the unloading of the coaches.

"Please send for me the minute Mr. Camryn arrives. I have not told Mr. Darcy that he is coming."

Mr. Walker smiled. "Only you could get away with calling the physician without asking the master's permission."

"If I ask his permission, he will not allow it."

Walker laughed as he watched her go back into the house. *You are a formidable woman, Agnes Reynolds!* Then he turned to resume his task.

When William opened the sitting room door, Emily rushed straight to the window seat. Climbing onto it, she looked towards the stables. "We are home, Snow!"

William and Elizabeth exchanged smiles. "I do not think she can hear you," Elizabeth said.

"Then I shall have to go and tell her," Emily said, slipping to the floor.

Winking at Elizabeth, William squatted to stop her as she ran towards the door. "At this hour, Snow is likely in the barn getting ready for bed. But you can tell her in the morning."

Emily looked as though she was pondering his words. "In that case, I will just have to get up very early."

"As long as you wait until daylight," Elizabeth replied. "Ponies need their rest, too."

"I am never leaving Pemberley again," Emily proclaimed.

Amused, William asked, "Not even to visit your cousins?"

"Gracie and Marianne will just have to visit me here!"

Suddenly, an upstairs maid walked into the room. "Begging your pardon, sir, but Mrs. Reynolds wanted me to ask if I may be of service to Mrs. Gardiner."

"You may," Elizabeth answered. "Would you help Emily wash her face and hands and change into clean clothes? Afterwards she needs to take a nap before dinner."

"Oh, Mama! I do not feel tired."

"You will once you lie down," Elizabeth replied. "Now, do as I ask."

"Yes, ma'am."

As Emily followed the maid, Elizabeth's gaze stayed fixed on the child. Wishing to gain her attention, William ran a finger gently down her cheek. She turned, smiling.

"I shall retire to my room. Mrs. Reynolds will be anxious for

Adams to change the bandages so that she may have a look."

Elizabeth smiled knowingly. "After all these years, the mother lion still takes care of her charge?"

"It may seem amusing, but I trust her with my life. Over the years she has saved me from mishaps and illnesses too numerous to mention. In fact, I trust her instincts more than I do most physicians."

"I am glad for that. I would not want anything to happen to you."

William pulled her into an embrace, kissing her softly before resting his head atop hers. "You have nothing to fear, my darling. You will never be rid of me."

"Do you promise?"

"I do. Now I shall leave, so you may rest before dinner."

After another quick kiss, he disappeared, closing the door behind him.

Though it was quickly getting dark, Elizabeth opened the door which led to the balcony and walked out. When the coach had halted on the highest point in the drive so that William could show her and Emily the view of Pemberley from afar, she had been overwhelmed with how perfectly it was placed amongst the landscape. Now, viewing the estate close up, her heart swelled.

I never dreamed that I could love any place as much as I love Pemberley, or any man the way I love William. Thank you, Lord, for keeping our love alive all these years.

Stars were already appearing on the horizon, and one large one in particular twinkled brightly the moment she finished speaking. Pleased, Elizabeth went back into her bedroom just as a maid walked in from the sitting room.

"Mrs. Reynolds asked me to deliver this to you. It is the post that came for you while you were away."

William's dressing room

William was not surprised when Mr. Camryn appeared at his dressing room door before Adams was done removing the last of the bandages. Having seen Mrs. Reynolds nod to the footman who immediately rushed towards the stables, he was only surprised it had taken so long for the physician to arrive.

As soon as Camryn entered the room, Mrs. Reynolds addressed him. "Mr. Camryn, I placed a jar of the medicinal honey on the dresser should you think it warranted. Now, if you will excuse me, I shall look in on Mrs. O'Malley to see if she needs anything."

Camryn set his bag on the dresser and washed his hands. As he turned towards William, Adams stepped back to allow him access. Noting that the bandages Adams had just removed were stained with blood and that the flesh surrounding the stitches was inflamed, the physician heaved a loud sigh.

"Whoever decided you were able to travel so soon after your injury is a fool."

"I decided that," William declared.

"I stand by my assessment! And I am convinced you will not listen to me any more than you listened to the physician in Scotland. Should I just gather my things and leave?"

The physician's irreverence made the quick retort on William's tongue vanish. "I have an estate to run and business which needs my attention in London, but I will try to comply as best I can."

"London should be the last thing on your mind. These stitches should not be strained. If you will heed my advice and rest for the next week—better yet two—we may be able to prevent a serious infection." To emphasise his point, Camryn pressed one of the worst spots.

William groaned in spite of himself. "Point taken."

"Excellent! Now, I am going to apply the honey, which should help to halt further spread of the infection, and I will leave a draught with Mrs. Reynolds. You must drink it twice a day, morning and evening. It may make you a little drowsy, so be prepared to lie down if you feel tired."

"But I—"

Camryn shook his head. "No excuses! If you do not wish to die of infection, you will adhere to my advice."

William decided to remain silent. As Mr. Camryn began to bandage his shoulder once again, he reached for the personal letters that had arrived whilst he was on the road. Noting that there were two from his Aunt Evelyn, he began with those.

Elizabeth's bedroom

The more she read of Millicent's correspondence, the more anxious Elizabeth became. Learning that Richard had been shot, she opened all the letters and scanned each for news of his progress. Relieved to find in the last letter that he was recovering more quickly than expected, she was nevertheless apprehensive about how William would respond.

Well aware that news of Colonel Fitzwilliam's injury would devastate the man she loved, Elizabeth hoped against hope that he would stay at Pemberley long enough for his own wounds to heal. Still, she knew he would not consider his needs when anyone he loved was in peril. Having just read of Millicent's engagement, the door to her sitting room flew open, and William walked in, startling her.

As he headed straight to where she sat on the edge of the bed, she stood up. Instead of speaking, he pulled her into his arms, burying his face in her hair.

"What is the matter?" she managed to murmur.

"I cannot bear to leave you."

"I do not understand."

"Richard has been hurt."

Elizabeth pulled back to look into his eyes. "I know, sweetheart. Millicent was kind enough to write to me." Seeing fear in his eyes, she added, "But in her last letter she said Richard is doing so much better. He is able to sit up now for hours at a time."

"You do not understand. For my cousin to be bedridden still, his injury must have been grave."

"Still you are not in any condition to go to him. You, too, must recover or else you will be of no use to him. At least agree to delay for a week."

William sighed uneasily. "I shall wait to see what news the next letter brings. In his present condition, Richard cannot possibly handle the business with Charles' cousin, nor would I expect it. As soon as it is practical, I must go to London to see how he is faring and to conclude the investigation."

"If you will wait one week, I shall not complain."

He kissed her forehead. "The thought of leaving you again after..." He could not continue.

"Now that Emily is entirely mine, and she and I are yours, we will never leave again."

William captured her lips in a torrid kiss, breaking away only to whisper in her ear, "You *are* mine, Elizabeth; just as I am yours."

Walking her backwards until they reached the edge of the bed, he gently laid her down. Quickly divesting himself of his jacket, he joined her. One kiss led to another, kindling desires long restrained. Elizabeth's hands found his back, her fingers pleading for him to come even closer. Slowly his kisses moved across her face to the tender skin of her earlobe, which he suckled. Continuing, he kissed every inch of her neck as he sought the softness of her décolletage. Her breasts, easily accessible in the low-cut gown, grew taut when his hand came up to caress them. Elizabeth threaded her fingers through his hair before gripping the back of his head, urging him to continue.

A knock on the door broke the spell. "Mrs. Gardiner?"

Recognising the voice of a maid, Elizabeth called out, "Just a moment."

William rolled over to his good side, moaning with the effort. Then he whispered, "Forgive me."

Elizabeth had already stood, and she leaned down to whisper her reply. "There is nothing to forgive."

She answered the door, opening it wide enough to address the servant whilst remaining hidden behind it. "Yes?"

Unbeknownst to her, William had followed, and he chose that moment to wrap his arms around her.

It took all of her strength not to react as the maid replied, "Dinner will be in half an hour, ma'am."

"Thank you."

Before the maid could curtsey, Elizabeth had shut the door.

Luxuriating in William's touch, she let her head rest against his chest. He murmured, "I love you so much, Elizabeth. It frightens me how much I want you."

She turned, their mouths coming together in an ardent kiss. At first his hands were content to roam over her back, but soon they sought the firmness of her bottom. Still, it was when he pulled her against the evidence of his desire that both became lost. Feeling her body trembling, William abruptly stepped away. He was breathless, his eyes as dark as coal.

"Promise me, Elizabeth," he said, his voice husky with need, "from now until the day we are married, you will lock your doors. And you will not let me in if you are alone. Do you understand?"

Equally affected, Elizabeth could only nod. Following another quick kiss, William walked out into the hallway. She watched until he entered his bedroom, and then she closed the door and locked it. Shaken, she hurried to the balcony, where she sank into a chair, still trembling.

Considering how rapidly desire had overwhelmed her good judgment, she did not hold William's ardour against him. He had expressed himself as sensibly and as warmly as a man violently in love could be expected to do.

Now I understand how a woman can be so in love that she may throw caution to the wind.

Chapter 29

London
Matlock House
Days later

The earl and countess had just sat down to eat when Richard walked into the dining room dressed in his uniform. Stunned, Lady Matlock managed to ask, "Richard, why are you up and dressed so early?"

"To be truthful, Mother, I thought it might scandalise London if I were to go into my office wearing only my nightshirt."

"That is not amusing, Son," Lord Matlock interjected. "Your mother is just voicing what we are both thinking. Mr. Colpack's instructions were that you were not to leave the house until he gave permission."

"Had I been on the field of battle, I would have been back in the fight days ago."

"But you are not in a battle!" Lord Matlock declared. "And there is no need for you to push yourself to return so quickly. General Lassiter told me that you should rest until the physician feels you are fully healed. Now sit down and have something to eat."

"I ate earlier, thank you. And with all due respect, I am a better judge of how I feel than General Lassiter or Mr. Colpack."

When his mother began to raise more objections, Richard cut her short. "Please remember that I am a man, not a child." Seeing his mother's wounded expression, he added more tenderly, "I do appreciate that you have my best interests at heart, and I promise to conserve my energy and not to keep long hours for a while. However, there are things I wish to handle instead of having Lassiter turn them over to someone not as familiar with the circumstances."

"I suppose you are talking about the assassination attempt on Castlereagh," his father said.

"That and the investigation into the murder of Mr. Howton. Besides which, I would like to see the monies recovered from Carney returned to Charles Bingley. And that brings up another matter—where is Carney? Darcy's last letter said he believed it was he who killed Lord Van Lynden. I do not like the idea that Carney has not yet been found, and someone with knowledge of the whole sordid business needs to make certain all that can be done is being done. Since Darcy cannot travel yet, that leaves me."

"What of Millicent?" the countess asked. "Should she come by, what shall I tell her?"

"Tell her I will be at my office if she needs me. In any case, seeing as how she abandoned me, she may not notice my absence at all."

"She did no such thing!" the countess retorted. "Millicent simply felt that since you were recuperating so well, it was best that she move back into her own home until the wedding. You do remember she needed to prepare for the arrival of her children and Lady Foggett."

Richard murmured sullenly, "The least she could have done is stay here with me until the children arrived."

Lord Matlock chuckled. "Is this the same person who just

boasted he is a man and not a child?"

Looking sheepish, Richard changed the subject. "Bingley's footman is to be charged with helping his cousin administer the poison, and Whitaker and Browning need my testimony. After I am done with that, I shall go over the case against those who conspired with Lord Van Lynden against Castlereagh."

"That is all the talk at White's," Lord Matlock said. "Rumour has it that Castlereagh's cook had a part in the plot to kill him."

Richard was aware that Viscount Castlereagh's cook was actually a spy planted by the Bow Street Runners, but he was unable to say anything until she testified at the trial. "It amazes me how things get misconstrued. I can say categorically the cook was not helping Lord Van Lynden."

"How can you be so certain?" the earl asked.

"I am afraid I cannot tell you the particulars just yet, but trust me. She will be vindicated."

"Well," said Lady Matlock, "that makes me rest easier. Who wants to think that their cook could be conspiring to kill them?"

Lord Matlock lowered his voice. "A time or two I suspected ours was up to the same thing." Suppressing a smile when Richard's eyes met his, he added, "Though I suspected she was only trying to poison *me*."

As father and son guffawed, Lady Matlock looked around, making certain that no servants had heard. "Edward! Please do not say such things. This is the third cook we have hired this year, and it becomes more difficult to replace them because your reputation of being hard to please precedes you. It makes it challenging to hire good people."

"Then we shall search outside of London for the next!" her husband declared.

"I shall leave you two to settle this argument. I have much to accomplish today," Richard said.

After giving his mother a kiss on the cheek and his father a pat on the shoulder, he quit the room.

"I have never seen Richard so moody," the countess said. "He has been sulking like a little boy since Millicent announced she was moving back to her townhouse."

"I told you that having a long engagement would not work, Evelyn."

"I fear you were right. Still, I wished to celebrate their engagement by having several soirées this winter. After all, when does a mother get to honour her children but on such occasions?"

"I never thought I would say this, but given a choice, I believe I would choose Matlock Manor and Leighton's belligerence over staying here and watching Richard brood."

"Given how you and Leighton get along, that *is* a surprise," Lady Matlock said, sighing heavily. "There is nothing else to do but speak to Millicent. I shall determine her opinion on a shorter engagement."

Elsewhere in London

Mrs. Graham's daughter slipped into the run-down pub, praying that the Bow Street Runners watching her house had not discovered that the man who left it a short while ago had actually been she. Having summoned one of Carney's friends, she had persuaded him to wait at the house whilst she donned his clothes. It was the only hope she had of seeing Carney without his being arrested.

As her eyes adjusted to the dingy, dark establishment, Bess Graham found it empty, save for a man with black hair and a beard sitting alone in one corner. Convinced that he was not Carney, she stepped back out into the sunlight. Suddenly, that same man rushed from the pub. Grabbing her arm, he pulled her into an alley nearby.

"Do you not know me?" Carney asked, pulling off his cap to show that his hair was red except for the black around the edges.

"How was I to know it was you? You do not look the same."

He replaced the cap. "I let my beard grow and used boot polish to cover it and the hair near my face to dodge the law." At her nod, he continued. "Rumour is that the men who helped Lord Van Lynden are all dead or in jail."

"That is what the papers say."

"An old friend also told me that the Bow Street Runners found my money."

"If you mean the package you hid in the roof of the shed, they did."

"Blast those devils! Now I will have to figure out another way to get what I deserve."

"If you are smart, you will get out of Town. The authorities are vowing to find everyone involved."

"Ha! Do you think I would leave with nothing to show for my trouble?" Carney raised his sleeve to expose a scar. "I took a bullet helping that blackguard Van Lynden. I will not leave empty-handed."

"What do you plan to do now?"

"I will find out who is behind the investigation and target them."

"The papers say that a Colonel Fitzwilliam is in charge."

"If I remember correctly, he is a cousin of Fitzwilliam Darcy. That is the man that Howton said was handling the investigation into Bingley's warehouses. And I overheard Van Lynden tell Guthrie that Darcy was in love with Mrs. Gardiner." Scratching his prickly chin, Carney smiled knowingly. "This is going to be easier than I thought."

Canfield Manor

The return trip from Spain had gone much more smoothly than the one to the Continent, and Charles Bingley could not have been more pleased. During the first trip, he had been too ill to worry about the ship being tossed to and fro during the storms they had encountered; now that he was in better health, he appreciated the tranquil sail back home. Never one to enjoy sailing because of a fear of drowning, he thanked God, too, that the winds were in their favour, which made their homecoming voyage even faster.

Afraid the news of his arrival in England might send Jane into labour, Charles decided against sending word when he reached the docks of London. Instead, the minute his feet were on English soil, he hired a coach and struck out for Richmond. By the time the coach was nearing the gate to Canfield Manor, his heart was beating wildly.

If it were not so undignified, I would leap from the coach the moment we stop and kiss the ground.

When the coach finally came to a stop, however, he stepped serenely from the vehicle as two footmen he did not recognise came down the steps.

The one who reached him first said, "Mr. Bingley, I presume?"

"Yes, and you are?"

"I am Robert Hartley, sir." He gestured towards the other man. "And this is my colleague, Theodore Boggus. Mr. Darcy hired us to protect your family."

"That sounds like Darcy."

"If you do not mind, we would like to make certain that you are Charles Bingley before you enter the house."

Charles was impressed with their conduct, though his valet, Mr. Bartlett, was not. The servant had just begun to defend his employer when Kitty ran out the front door.

Upon seeing her brother, she cried, "Charles! You are home!"

Both Bow Street Runners stepped aside as she ran towards Bingley. After they had embraced, she said, "I am so relieved that you are here. Jane has been grimacing with pain off and on all day, but she refuses to send for the physician."

"Janie is having the baby?"

"She says not, but I disagree."

Bingley turned to Hartley. "Do you know where Mr. Clark lives?"

"I do."

"Please fetch him, and if he is not at home, bring Mrs. Jimmerson, who lives next door. She is a midwife."

Hartley immediately headed to the stables for a horse, whilst Charles and Mr. Bartlett followed Kitty into the house. Mr. Mercer was coming from the direction of the kitchen just as the housekeeper was hurrying down the grand staircase. They all congregated in the foyer.

"Oh, Mr. Bingley!" Mrs. Watkins exclaimed. "We are so happy you are home, sir. And, what good fortune that you arrived today, for Mrs. Bingley is about to have the baby."

"Are you certain?"

"Her water just broke. That is why I came down—to alert Mrs. Thomas."

"I was just in the kitchen, and the water is already boiling," Mr. Mercer said to no one in particular.

Charles addressed Kitty. "Where are the girls?"

"I had them lie down for a nap a half-hour ago. Jenny is watching them."

Charles began up the stairs, taking two at a time. Kitty followed, trying her best to keep up. When he reached the landing, he hesitated. "Kitty, tell the servants not to say anything to the children about my return. I will greet them after this child is born."

"Whatever you think is best, Charles."

Jane's bedroom
Hours later

Fortuitously, Jane's fourth child was in a hurry to be born. In fact, it was only two hours after Mr. Clark's arrival that Master Charles Bennet Darcy Bingley made his entrance into the world. A healthy eight pounds plus, he let his frustrations at being forced from the safe haven of his mother's womb be known by crying vociferously. Only after he was washed and settled at his mother's breast did his loud protestations cease.

Bingley was beside himself with joy, and when Mr. Clark clapped him on the back in congratulation, the tears in his eyes began to roll down his cheeks. Kitty was crying openly, just as she had when Marianne was born, and Mrs. Watkins surreptitiously wiped her eyes with the handkerchief she kept hidden in her sleeve. To say that the whole household was jubilant would be an understatement. Downstairs, Mr. Mercer had already opened the second of several bottles of vintage wine that Bingley set aside for the servants to celebrate with on such occasions, and most of the staff had already toasted the heir at least once.

After Clark determined that Jane was doing very well, Bingley requested that Grace and Marianne be brought to the bedroom. Not long afterward, Jenny appeared in the doorway holding each girl by the hand. The moment they saw their father, they pulled free and ran to him.

As Charles stooped to receive them, excited cries filled the air. "Papa! Papa!"

Copious hugs and kisses were exchanged before Charles pulled back to ask, "Would you like to meet your new brother?"

Ginger curls bobbed up and down, so picking up Marianne and taking Grace's hand, Charles walked to the bed where Jane lay with the baby in the crook of her arm. Placing Marianne on the unoccupied side, he picked up Grace and set her next to her sister. Their eyes grew as large as saucers, though neither spoke.

Jane said serenely, "You may touch him if you wish."

Being the oldest, Grace leaned forward to rub a single finger down his arm. "He is very soft."

"Yes, he is," Jane replied.

Marianne tried to do the same; however, when she touched the baby, he stretched and yawned, causing her to quickly withdraw her finger.

"He is just sleepy," Charles reassured her. "Everyone stretches and yawns when they are sleepy."

"What is his name?" Grace asked.

"Charles Bennet Darcy Bingley," Charles replied. "But he shall be called Ben."

"When can he play with us?" Marianne asked.

"When he is older," Jane replied. "For a while he will mainly sleep and eat so that he can grow big like you."

Grace's forehead furrowed as she studied her new sibling. "I think he will not be as big as me."

"Or me!" Marianne parroted.

Charles had come around the bed to sit beside Jane, so she turned to him. As their eyes met, silent words said all that either needed to hear. Heart full, Charles leaned in to give the woman he loved a tender kiss. It did not take long for the girls to begin giggling, prompting Charles to quit the kiss.

"It was so much simpler before we had the children," he said chuckling.

"But not nearly as fulfilling," Jane countered.

Charles brought her hand to his lips. "I could not agree more. Have I told you how much I love and adore you, Janie? For I cannot help but love you more with each passing day."

Tears filled Jane's eyes. "You have, Charles, and I love you in just the same way."

Grace and Marianne were obliged to watch as their parents shared another kiss.

Pemberley

Due to the remedy prescribed by Mr. Camryn, William spent the better part of the next several days in bed. Full of natural sleep inducers, the draughts kept his wits too muddled to think clearly and that, along with the toll taken by the trip from Scotland, made sleep hard to resist. Fortuitously, during this time, word also came from London that Colonel Fitzwilliam was back on his feet, effectively putting an end to the excuse William had for going to Town straightaway. Nevertheless, when Mrs. Reynolds appeared in his room that morning, she was shocked to find Mr. Adams helping William dress.

"What is this?" she asked.

"I refuse to lie in bed another day."

"But Mr. Camryn said—"

"I will handle Mr. Camryn," William replied decidedly, motioning for the valet to continue with his cravat. "Is Mrs. Gardiner awake yet?"

"Yes. She and Miss Emily are breaking their fast in their sitting room."

"Excellent!"

Eager to join them, William stood and held out his arms for the valet to help him with his coat, then surveyed his image in the mirror. "Thank you, Adams. That will be all."

The servant nodded and picked up William's banyan in order to return it to his closet. As he disappeared into the bedroom, Mrs. Reynolds followed her employer into the hallway.

"What shall I say to Mr. Camryn when he arrives?"

"Tell him to wait in the drawing room while you fetch me." William walked over and knocked on the door of Elizabeth's sitting room.

"Come," Elizabeth called.

Smiling, William opened the door.

Leading Emily through the gardens on one of several gravel paths which led to the stables, William marvelled at how talkative she was—a stark contrast to her early days at Pemberley. Though Elizabeth had walked ahead to the stables to give them time alone, he was beginning to fear they would reach the paddock before Emily stopped speaking. Hence, spying a concrete bench, he interrupted her chatter.

"Miss Emily, would you mind sitting down a moment? I fear I stayed in bed so long that my energy is lagging."

Emily peered up at him, her blue eyes clouding with concern. "I do not mind." As William helped her onto the bench and sat down beside her, she added, "I wish you had not been hurt helping me and Mama."

William patted her tiny hand. "Do not worry, Poppet. My injury was not serious, and I am getting better each day."

"I am glad."

"And I am glad that we are alone, for to tell the truth, I wish to discuss something very important with you." Curiosity replaced the anxious look on her face. "The day we returned to Pemberley you said you never wanted to leave again. Do you remember that?"

Blond curls bounced up and down.

"Well, I do not wish for you to leave, either; however, it is not proper for a single man like me to live in a house with an unmarried lady, such as your mother. If unmarried men and women share a house without being chaperoned, they should get married. So, I thought—if you did not object—your mother and I would marry in the next few weeks."

When Emily did not answer, he became concerned. Leaning over to look into her troubled eyes, he asked, "Emily, is something wrong? Do you not wish for me to marry your mother?"

Her voice grew quieter with her reply. "I...I think it would be good for Mama. She likes you a lot."

"But how do you feel about it? Would it be good for you?"

Emily stuttered, "You...you want me, too?"

With his good arm William pulled the child into his lap, placing a kiss atop her flaxen hair. "Of course, I want you, too. Are we not the best of friends?"

Emily's head bobbed up and down. "And I picked you flowers."

"True, you are the only one who has ever given me flowers." Seeing the pride in her face, he added, "The day that your mother becomes my wife, the law says that you will become my daughter. But I want you to know I have thought of you as my daughter for a long time."

Emily twisted so that she could look up at William. "You have?"

"I have. It began the first time you rode with me on Zeus. You were so brave that I thought I should like to have you for a daughter."

"After you marry Mama, can I call you Papa like Gracie and Marianne call Uncle Charles?"

"If that is what you wish to call me."

Emily beamed. "It is!"

William gave her a hug, then let her slide from his lap. He stood and held out a hand, which she accepted. "Well, now that all of that is settled, what say we find your mother and inform her that we are all getting married?"

"If you tell Mama, may I tell Snow?"

"You certainly may!"

Later that night

After the incident in Elizabeth's bedroom, William had kept his word and was never alone with her. Though intellectually she accepted his logic, in truth Elizabeth missed his kisses and the feel of his embrace. Consequently, after they had eaten dinner and William had once more excused himself to work on business in his study, Elizabeth found herself dressed for bed but pacing the balcony in misery.

After having fretted for nearly an hour, she went into her bedroom, intending to crawl into bed and read until she fell asleep. However, upon picking up the book of poems lying on the bedside table, she told herself that she needed something more tedious to read; thus, donning her dressing gown, she picked up the chamber candlestick and opened the door. Looking in both directions, the sconces with lit candles strategically placed along the hall provided evidence that no servants were about. Slipping into the hall, Elizabeth hurried towards the landing and, once there, peered over the railings. Seeing no one downstairs, either, she hurried down the staircase and in the direction of the library. However, once she was standing outside that room, she could not help but glance down the hall to where a light from William's study was visible.

Tiptoeing down the hallway until she stood outside the partially open door, she took a deep breath and peered inside. Unable to see William from that angle, she decided to open the door a bit more. Unbeknownst to her, Mr. Walker was approaching with a carafe of coffee at just that moment.

"Mrs. Gardiner," he said much too loudly for Elizabeth's taste, "may I be of service?"

Hearing her name, William hurried to the door, opening it just as Elizabeth was trying to decide how to answer Mr Walker. Noting that her face had turned crimson, he answered instead.

"Please set the tray on my desk, Walker. I shall help Mrs. Gardiner." The butler did as he was told and hurried from the room. "You may go to bed now. I will not need you again tonight."

"Yes, sir."

Walker disappeared down the hall, leaving Elizabeth and William facing each other at the door. Embarrassed to be found out, she motioned towards the library.

"I was on my way to the library when I saw your light. I...I thought I would see if you had fallen asleep at your desk. You have done that many times of late."

Noting how beautiful Elizabeth looked with her hair down, William took the chamber candle from her hand and set it on a nearby table. "And for what reason were you going to the library at this late hour?"

"I...I hoped to find a book that might bore me."

William fingered a lock of Elizabeth's hair that hung over her décolletage. "Is that because you are having trouble falling asleep?" Mesmerised, she could only nod. "That is why I am in this study and not my bed."

A hand surreptitiously slipped around her waist and pulled her closer. "Whenever I close my eyes, I find myself reliving the way you feel in my arms and the softness of your lips."

Unconsciously, Elizabeth nodded, which made William smile. "Do you find yourself thinking such thoughts?"

"Constantly."

Framing her face, William captured her mouth with unrestrained desire. Before long, both were transported to a time and place where nothing mattered except the giving and receiving of love. Suddenly, Elizabeth's dressing gown was discarded, and she found herself backed against the wall. While she moaned her approval, William's large hands began to explore every womanly curve. Then, just as abruptly, he stopped.

With his forehead touching hers, he whispered, "If we continue, you know what will happen." Elizabeth nodded. "And if we were to make love now, I could not look you in the eye in the morning. Moreover, I could not possibly ask our future sons to act honourably if I do not."

"I understand."

Immediately released, she stood still as William replaced her dressing gown. Then he swept her into his arms and began carrying her towards the family quarters. Once they reached her bedroom door, he set her on her feet, turned the knob and pushed the door open.

Tears pooled in Elizabeth's eyes as he pulled her once more into his arms, murmuring in her hair, "Do you believe that we can share one kiss at this door each night and go no further?"

"I...I do."

Kissing her soundly once more, William stepped back. "This is just a foretaste of how it will be once we are married, my love. Sleep if you can, for I fear I will not sleep again until we are one."

With that, William returned to his study.

Chapter 30

Canfield Manor
One week later

The Darcy carriage had just come to a stop when Charles Bingley walked out the front door of Canfield Manor, looking remarkably like he had years before. He had gained weight, and the pallor of months past had been replaced by rosy cheeks and a fuller face. As he hurried down the steps towards William, who was now helping Elizabeth and Emily from the coach, Kitty appeared in the doorway and, seeing who had arrived, followed her brother.

"Darcy!" Charles exclaimed, clasping William's hand and pumping it continuously. "I cannot tell you how grateful Jane and I are that you agreed to help us during our hour of need. If not for you, I do not know what would have happened to me, my family or my business."

William noted the renewed strength in Charles' grip. "My reward is seeing you returned to health, and I have no doubt you would have done the same for me."

"In a heartbeat! If you should ever need me, I shall move heaven and earth to be at your side." Overwhelmed with gratitude, Charles impulsively embraced William before quickly stepping back. "You look so well that I completely forgot about your shoulder. Forgive me if I hurt you."

"You did not, though I admit that it is still quite sore. According to my physician, it will be for some time. Nonetheless, it has improved immensely in the last week. The trip here was no more unbearable than those of the past."

"That is good to know. I was worried sick when Jane told me you had been shot rescuing Elizabeth and Emily."

"Fortunately, I was merely grazed by the bullet. However, let us speak of more pleasant things, such as your new son."

"Oh, I forgot to tell you! Jane and I decided to name him Charles Bennet Darcy Bingley as a small token of our gratitude. And, if you will agree, we would like you to be Ben's godfather."

"I am humbled, Charles, and proud to accept."

"Excellent!"

Kitty had walked past the gentlemen to embrace Elizabeth. After a brief re-union, she released her sister to pick up Emily. "And how is my beautiful niece?"

As Kitty conversed with Emily, Elizabeth took the opportunity to greet Charles, enfolding him in her arms.

"You have no idea how many prayers went up for your recovery and then for a safe and swift journey home."

"I appreciate all your prayers. I truly believe it is only by the grace of God that I am here today. Only He could have moved Darcy to keep his promise after all those years."

"Promise?" Elizabeth repeated, turning to look at William, who sheepishly dropped his head. "William never mentioned a promise."

"It was nothing," William murmured.

"I must disagree!" Charles declared. "After Jane and I married, she feared that being in Darcy's company might make you feel uncomfortable; therefore, I informed him it would be best if he stayed away from my family."

Ashamed, Elizabeth looked down. "After William and I met again on this very spot, Jane told me of that."

"At any rate, Darcy's response to my unkindness was to take the high road. He promised that he would help me if I was ever in need. A lesser man might have turned his back after five years with no contact, but not Darcy. His word is his bond."

Elizabeth smiled adoringly at William. "I am not surprised; he is the most honourable man of my acquaintance."

"Now we must hurry. Janie knows your coach has arrived, and if we do not go up quickly, she will insist on coming downstairs to find you."

"I am so excited to see Jane and the baby," Elizabeth said. "I pray they are still doing well."

"More than well. Mr. Clark says that they are both in excellent health."

As Charles and Elizabeth linked arms and started up the steps, Kitty, who was holding Emily, walked over to William.

"Charles is right. You have been a godsend, Mr. Darcy. Thank you for stepping in when you were asked to help." Not surprised to see William's unease at her praise, Kitty added, "And I want to thank you for saving my sister. Lizzy is a remarkable woman, but I am certain by now you have noticed her flaw."

"I cannot say that I have."

"Stubbornness. Even when we were children, Lizzy was very independent. After our parents died and Mary and I accepted offers of marriage, she refused John Lucas, declaring she would never marry merely for security. Later, when Emily came into her life, she was more determined than ever to rear her alone."

"That does not surprise me."

"Nor did it surprise me. Still, I truly believe it was only after you and she met again that she realised how much she wanted— no, she *needed* to be loved."

"I do love her...very much."

"After all you went through to bring her home, no one could doubt that." Emily learned towards William, so he took her from Kitty. "Now, we need to heed Charles' advice. Jane dotes on you now, and she will worry if you are missing. In fact, she could not stop talking about the wedding and how delighted she is that you are to become our brother. We all are."

"No more delighted than I am to become a part of your family."

Suddenly Charles popped his head out of the doorway. "Do not dawdle, Darcy!"

Just as swiftly, he disappeared.

William held his free arm out for his future sister, and Kitty laid her hand atop it. As they began up the stairs, she began to laugh.

"If someone had told me after the ball at Netherfield that one day you would be my brother, I would have said they were mad, for back then none of the Bennets liked you, least of all Lizzy."

William winced. "I know. Elizabeth made that very clear in Kent."

London
Matlock House
A drawing room

Whilst she waited for her fiancé to return from his office, Millicent visited with Lady Matlock. It was during that time that her future mother shared that she and the earl felt the wedding date should be moved forward. In truth, Millicent had never seen any reason to postpone the event, except to indulge the countess' love of entertaining, and now that they were in agreement, she was eager to inform Richard that they could have an autumn wedding.

As it happened, just as two maids brought trays of fresh tea and small cakes into the room, Richard walked in behind them.

He went unnoticed by Millicent, who sat with her back to the door, until Lady Matlock smiled in his direction. Turning to follow the countess' line of sight, she was thrilled to discover he was home. Standing, she rushed to him, and they embraced.

"Richard, dearest, I hoped you would be here before I had to leave. I have missed you dearly, and so have the children. We wish you to dine with us tonight. Cook is making a roasted pheasant, and I know it is one of your favourites."

"All I need do is change clothes, and we can be off. That is, unless you wish to go ahead and have me follow later."

"She will wait!" his mother interjected with certainty. "Run along and change whilst we conclude our conversation. We still have many things to decide in regards to your wedding."

"Ah, the wedding," Richard said. "I hope you both remember I wish it to be a small family affair."

"Hearing you talk like that, one would think you were Fitzwilliam," Millicent teased.

"There is something to be said for Darcy's penchant to keep his private life private."

"This is no time to turn into your sombre cousin," his mother declared. "I have many friends, and I wish to invite them all. Unfortunately, you shall just have to accommodate my wishes with a smile."

"That is where you are wrong, Mother," Richard teased. "I may have to accommodate your wishes, but no one said I had to smile."

"Nonsense!" Millicent declared. "A man who does not smile on his wedding day cannot possibly be in love with his bride."

"I beg to differ. You may not see Darcy smile when he and Elizabeth wed, but I can assure you his heart will be beaming."

"With regard to Fitzwilliam, I would have to agree," Millicent said. "But I am pleased that you are a more demonstrative man. And, I expect you to be smiling on our wedding day."

Richard performed a deep bow. "Your wish is my command,

my lady. Now, if you will allow me, I will change clothes."

As Richard exited the room, Lady Matlock watched Millicent follow him with her eyes. "When will you tell him the wedding will be sooner rather than later?"

Millicent turned to smile at her. "After the children have retired tonight."

"I have never seen my son so happy. To think that I thought you the best match for my nephew only months ago."

"What was your reason?"

"I knew that Richard cared more for you than he would admit, but he would never try to come between you and Fitzwilliam. And I was convinced that you would never see the virtues of the one you had always overlooked."

"You were wiser than I. It was not until I was confronted with the possibility of life without Richard that I realised how much I loved him."

"And are the children satisfied that you are marrying Richard and not Fitzwilliam?"

"I never gave them any reason to think that Fitzwilliam would ever be more than their godfather. And, while Hugh and Kathy love them both, I think Richard has the advantage. He is so animated when he is with them, whereas Fitzwilliam is naturally more restrained—or, I should say he *was* restrained before Elizabeth came back into his life. And gaining Emily in the bargain, I am sure Fitzwilliam will learn very quickly how to interact with children."

"I agree. There is nothing like being thrown into the pond to learn how to swim," Lady Matlock said.

"Indeed!"

"Did Elizabeth write to you of their wedding plans?"

"I understand they want a private ceremony at St. George's,

and the wedding breakfast is to be held afterwards at Darcy House."

"That is what I was told; however, I plan to suggest that Edward and I host the wedding breakfast. The servants at Darcy House are not accustomed to entertaining the numbers who will attend the breakfast. They have hosted no balls or large soirées since Lady Anne's death. Other than a few family dinners, Fitzwilliam has hardly entertained at all."

"I imagine Elizabeth will appreciate your offer, for it will allow her to concentrate her efforts on the wedding. I wonder if she has even considered what to wear. One cannot have a wedding gown designed and created overnight."

"If the gown she wore when she accompanied you to the ball at Matlock Manor is any indication, she does not appear to be interested in clothes."

"Given that she had to raise Emily alone, I am not surprised she is disinterested in fashion. However, I mean to take her under my wing and make certain she understands that most of the *ton* will be hoping to find fault with the woman who has captured Fitzwilliam Darcy's heart. Any *faux pas* will reflect badly on him and their future family. A wedding day is the time to put one's best foot forward."

"Let us hope she listens."

"She will. We are friends, and she knows I have her best interests at heart."

"I am amazed that you and she are even cordial. I thought you might be resentful that Fitzwilliam chose her over you, and I feared she might resent your place in his life."

"To own the truth, I was always aware he was not *in love* with me, but I thought if he was determined to settle for a marriage of convenience, our friendship would make our union work well. There was only one thing wrong with my supposition."

"What was that?"

"It was what Richard tried to tell me all along. If Fitzwilliam and I married, I would be settling for a man who considered me his only option when what I really wanted was a man who considered me his whole world."

Lady Matlock reached to pat her hand. "I am glad that you determined that before you and my nephew made an irreversible mistake."

"So am I."

Suddenly, Richard appeared in the doorway. "Are you ready, my dear?"

"My goodness, that was fast," his mother said.

"I am not one to waste time when an excellent meal is waiting."

Richard and his intended paid little attention to the fact that Lady Matlock had followed them to the front door. The countess found it amusing that it was only when they started to enter the waiting carriage that they stopped to look back at the portico.

"Enjoy the evening, Mother," Richard called. "Tell Father not to wait up tonight. I shall not be home until late."

Tears of joy filled the countess' eyes as the carriage rolled slowly down the street. In the not too distant past, Edward would often stay awake until Richard got home, just in case he wished to talk.

At last Millicent has taken your place and mine, Edward, and all is as it should be.

Quickly composing herself, the countess straightened to her full height and walked regally back inside the house, across the marble foyer and up the grand staircase.

Canfield Manor
Later that day

When Elizabeth first saw her new nephew, he was asleep, so she asked one of Jane's maids to fetch her the next time Ben was awake. Therefore, the moment the newborn heir decided he needed more nourishment, she found herself summoned to her sister's bedroom. Slipping quietly inside, she was full of expectation as she neared the bed where Jane was staring at her son adoringly whilst he nursed.

Jane looked up. "I apologise for falling asleep and staying in bed all day, Lizzy."

"Nonsense. You need your rest. Besides, we have no plans to leave in the foreseeable future, so I shall be happy to visit any time you wish before I do." Elizabeth sat down beside her sister and reached out to run a hand over the baby's fine hair. "Ben is the image of his father; he looks just like Charles."

Jane smiled. "All the children do. I fear I am not represented in any of them."

"Yes, you are. Gracie may have his colouring, but she has your eyes and nose. And her hair is getting lighter each year. I expect by the time she is twelve, her hair will be more blonde than red."

"Do you really think so?"

"I do." As further encouragement, Elizabeth added, "And Marianne definitely has your disposition."

Elizabeth watched Jane's smile vanish. "Do you think she will have a propensity to like everyone as I once did?"

"Oh, Jane. I have learned you were right to give people the benefit of the doubt—at least at first. Had I been more like you and found less fault—"

Jane captured her sister's hand and gave it a squeeze. "You are remembering how you misjudged Mr. Darcy."

"I was so mistaken. William is so kind and honest and caring—"

"Just what a gentleman ought to be," Jane teased. "I give you leave to like him, for he is also sensible and good-humoured—as well as devastatingly handsome."

Recognising her words from the night of the Meryton assembly, Elizabeth made a face. "How humbling to have my own words used against me."

"I am teasing. Besides, you were merely imitating Papa. He loved mocking people's faults, and he was proud when you did the same."

"But he was wrong, and so was I. That first impressions are often erroneous was a hard lesson to learn."

"At least you *did* learn the truth about Mr. Darcy." Jane smiled. "Charles says he has never seen him besotted before—even when they were at Cambridge."

Elizabeth blushed. "We are both besotted. That is why we wish to be married as soon as possible. William wants to wed at St. George's in two weeks."

"That is understandable. I have learned that men are impatient creatures." Jane grinned. "But what about the banns?"

"William has already obtained a special license."

"My goodness! He *is* in a hurry!"

Trying not to blush anew, Elizabeth changed the subject. "My concern is for you. I want you to stand up with me, but I will not have you overtaxed."

"I should be recovered by then. Besides, it is only an hour's ride. We can stay at our townhouse for a few days before making the return trip. I foresee no problems."

"Then shall I tell William to set the date?"

"By all means, and once you have, inform Mary. Kitty has only to send for Harvey, while Mary must make plans to bring her husband and children. They can all stay at our townhouse. It will be enjoyable to have our family together for such a happy occasion."

"I cannot imagine how you will manage, now that you have Ben. Adding Mary's children to the family party could prove eventful, to say the least."

"John is three now and Philip almost two, so they should fit well with my girls. Will you leave Emily with us, too?"

"Millicent mentioned having Emily stay with her since Hugh and Kathy have missed her so much. She will already have seen Gracie and Marianne."

"Whatever you decide, I approve." Ben had finished nursing but was still awake, so Jane asked, "Do you still wish to hold him?"

"I certainly do."

Taking her nephew from Jane, Elizabeth sat down in the upholstered chair next to the bed. For some time, Jane watched as her sister whispered to the baby, punctuating her words with kisses on his cheeks.

Eventually Jane said, "Charles is going to ask Mr. Darcy to be Ben's godfather, and we wish for you to be his godmother."

"I would be honoured." Elizabeth's expression grew more serious as she studied the baby. "After Papa and Mama died, I thought my life would be spent in service. Emily was a blessing I never expected, but she was also a reminder that I would never marry or experience the joy of giving birth. After all, few men would take on a woman of my age with no dowry, no connections and another man's child."

"You forget that you are intelligent, witty and kind. And it does not hurt that you are still beautiful."

"And you are prejudiced!"

"I may be, but you cannot lay that claim on Mr. Darcy."

Elizabeth sighed. "I cannot argue with that. For whatever reason, he fell in love with me."

"I like to think God has the right mate for every man and woman if only they will search for them with their hearts."

"Have I ever told you how wise you are?"

Jane chuckled. "I believe you were too busy telling me how naive I was."

"Never again, dear sister. Never again."

That evening

Hoping William would remember their midnight kiss, Elizabeth had been reluctant to retire; thus, she was reading by candlelight in the sitting room that divided her bedroom and Emily's. She was startled when the door to Emily's bedroom opened, and the child came into the room.

"Mama, I have another question."

Elizabeth held out her arms, and Emily rushed to her. She was quickly lifted into her mother's lap. "What is bothering you now, my darling?"

"You said I must stay with Hugh and Kathy for a week after you and Mr. Darcy marry."

"I did."

"But we have never been apart, and I shall miss you."

Elizabeth kissed the top of her head. "I shall miss you, too."

"Then take me with you. Mr. Darcy will not mind; he likes me."

Elizabeth smiled. "Mr. Darcy loves you, just as I do. Still, there are times when men and women need to be alone—such as when they marry."

"I heard Mr. Darcy tell Uncle Charles that he would like an heir."

"You did?"

Emily's head bobbed up and down. "What is an heir?"

"An heir is someone who will inherit property. In this case, Mr. Darcy was speaking of having a son."

"Why does he want a son? He will have me."

"Well, he and I love you so much that we want to have more

children. Would you not like to have a brother or a sister?"

"Sometimes Gracie complains that Marianne is a baby."

"That is natural, but she also enjoys playing with her."

"I suppose I might like a sister, but no brothers."

"Why do you say that?"

"Because Ben is a brother, and he has no hair."

Pursing her lips to keep from laughing, Elizabeth said, "His hair will grow."

A knock came at the door, so she stood, letting Emily slip to her feet. "Now, go back to bed and no more questions tonight."

As Elizabeth watched Emily disappear into her room, she heard another knock. Rushing to the door, the smile she wore instantly vanished the moment she discovered who was there.

Noting her sister's disappointment, Kitty said, "I was not certain you were still awake since you came upstairs hours ago, but Mr. Darcy asked me to relay a message. He and Charles are in the middle of another game of billiards, and he wanted you to know he would not see you again until morning." Trying not to smile, Kitty teased, "Whatever could he mean by that?"

"I...we...it is our custom to bid each other goodnight at my door."

"That explains why you both have such long faces. He looks miserable, poor man, but Charles will not let him stop playing. And *you* cannot sleep without your goodnight kiss. Oh, to be so in love!"

"Were you never in love with Harvey?"

"He is very good to me, and we are comfortable with one another. I am content. And whenever I encounter Charlotte and that horrid Mr. Collins, I am grateful for what I have." Kitty smiled. "Now I shall leave so you may get some sleep."

"Thank you for delivering the message. At least I will not lie awake thinking William forgot me."

"I do not think you will ever have that problem."

A quick embrace and Kitty walked down the hall towards her rooms. Elizabeth shut the sitting room door and leaned back against it. Try as she might, she could not imagine being married to a man she did not love beyond all reason. Sighing, she went into her bedroom, donned her gown and was soon fast asleep.

In fact, she slept so soundly that she did not hear two light raps on her bedroom door an hour later.

Chapter 31

London
St. George's Church
Two weeks later

As Elizabeth and Jane waited in the small antechamber of the church, Jane studied her sister.

"I am so thankful that Lady Markham lent you her lady's maid, Lizzy. I could never have styled your hair so beautifully, and your gown is exquisite. You look as though you just stepped out of the pages of **Ackermann's.**"

Elizabeth did indeed look radiant in a gown of white French gauze over a pink satin slip. Flounces of Brussels lace started halfway down the skirt of her gown and continued to the hem. Puffed sleeves, worn off the shoulders, were of satin, as was the bodice, and featured a pattern of pale pink roses. A narrow row of embroidered pink roses with green vines and leaves circled the gown underneath the bodice. She wore a white pearl necklace and earrings—a wedding gift from William. White kid gloves adorned her arms, and satin shoes completed her bridal ensemble.

Elizabeth walked over to peer once more in the mirror hanging on one wall. "I cannot believe how styling my hair in a different manner changed my appearance so greatly." She laughed. "I hope William recognises me."

"You need not worry about that and in that gown he will not be able to take his eyes off you."

Elizabeth ran her hands over the exquisite creation. "I would have settled for something far less intricate if not for Millie. She moved heaven and earth to have this gown finished in time. Her modiste brought in extra seamstresses and they worked day and night. I would hate to see the bill Madam Claire sent to William."

"Your Mr. Darcy will be pleased to pay any price when he sees you in this gown. It is perfect."

"Will you adjust the roses in my hair? I fear the maid may not have used enough pins. You know how hard it is to keep pins in my wayward curls."

"Turn around and let me look."

Elizabeth did as told, and Jane inspected the sprig of pink roses pinned at the base of her head, just above the curls that were left to hang down her back. She moved some of the pins declaring, "There! All is well."

Then out of the blue, Jane became teary eyed. "I cannot believe you are actually getting married."

"If you do not believe it, how do you think I feel?" Elizabeth said, laughing. "I was the one who swore I would never marry."

"I remember what you said, and let me correct you. You said 'only the deepest love will persuade me into matrimony, which is why I will end up an old maid.' Thank God you found that kind of love with Mr. Darcy."

"I did. Still, I cannot believe this is happening to me. It is as though I am in a dream, and I shall wake at any moment."

"Then let us pray you do not wake until after the ceremony," Jane added. "Now, let me see if I can find Charles. He should have been here by now. I would not be surprised to find him with your Mr. Darcy."

Exiting the room, Jane rushed down the hall to where William and Colonel Fitzwilliam were waiting to be summoned by the bishop. Even with the door closed, she could hear her husband's voice and it brought a smile to her face.

She rapped lightly. "Charles?"

The door opened just wide enough for her husband to peek out. "Janie, I was just telling Darcy I had to locate you and Elizabeth. After all, I am to walk the bride down the aisle!"

"That is why I am here. We all need to be in our places."

Without opening the door very wide, Charles turned to address those in the room. "I am off to do my duty! It is too late now to change your mind, Darcy."

Jane barely heard William's reply as the door closed behind her husband. "That will never happen!"

As Charles walked with her back down the hall, she slipped her arm through his. "Oh, Charles, this brings back so many memories of our wedding. I hope I do not cry."

"Crying is not permissible today, Janie. Only joy and happiness is allowed."

"But," Jane sniffled, "I *am* happy!"

In another part of St. George's, Whitaker and Browning, dressed in their best clothes, hoped they did not stand out too much amongst the guests. Asked to be in attendance by Colonel Fitzwilliam, last night they had received valid information that Carney had returned to Town. It was rumoured that he intended to recover the money confiscated from his shack and pay back those who had taken it. And what better chance could he have to even the score with Darcy or the colonel than during the wedding festivities?

The custom of allowing the lower classes—those who lined the pavement in front of the churches to witness the rituals of the wealthy— to slip into the back pews once the wedding party was seated, made it nearly impossible to guard against someone intent on doing harm. Consequently, since they had not had time to apprise Mr. Darcy or Colonel Fitzwilliam of the latest information, Whitaker and Browning had taken it upon themselves to recruit several of their associates to join them in case Carney was foolish enough to try anything.

In the rear of the sanctuary, Browning rose on tiptoes to look over the heads of those who were still standing. "Do you see Colonel Fitzwilliam?"

"No. But I imagine he is with Mr. Darcy waiting for the wedding to begin. Since our men are in place, I suggest we find them now. They need to be aware of Carney's boasts."

The knock on the door was answered by Richard. Expecting to see the bishop, he was taken aback to find Whitaker and Browning waiting without. Though they were scheduled to attend the wedding as a precaution, he knew something was amiss from the expressions on their faces.

Turning to William, who was trying to loosen his cravat, he said, "Darcy, I am going to see if the bishop requires anything. Wait right here."

"Where else would I wait?" William replied. As Richard closed the door, he heard him grumble, "This bloody cravat is too tight!"

Motioning for the men to follow, Richard walked several feet down the hall before stopping. "Please tell me your long faces are only because you are not fond of weddings."

Regrettably, that was not what they had to share. At first the colonel was silent, but when at last he spoke, it was clear he had been busy devising a plan.

"Carney would be a fool to try something today, but he has proved himself foolhardy often enough that we cannot take the chance. If he comes, we must do whatever is necessary to protect the family from danger."

"That is what we aim to do."

"I am grateful that you thought to bring more men. Since I will be at the front with Darcy, I should like the two of you, especially, to guard the rear. The others can take up positions wherever you decide. Should Carney appear, try to stop him without notice; however, do not hesitate to bring him down, spectacle or no." Both men nodded. "Take up your positions. I must return to Darcy."

"Will you tell him?"

Richard studied the floor. "No. I prefer his wedding day to be filled with thoughts of his bride and not that blackguard."

Minutes later

All of London had been captivated by the news of Mr. Darcy's upcoming nuptials, a fact not lost on Mr. Carney. Certain that an event of this nature would be the perfect chance to abscond with a member of Darcy's family—namely, his bride's daughter—Carney prepared for the day by shaving his beard and, knowing he would remove his cap, applying black boot polish to all of his hair.

Unfortunately, liquor had always been his undoing, as it proved to be that morning. Too inebriated to think rationally, when he applied the polish he neglected to check his work in a mirror. Unbeknownst to him, he had missed a small patch of red at the crown of his head. It did not help, either, that when he entered the church he chose to sit directly in front of where Mr. Whitaker happened to be standing.

Immediately noting that the late arrival's starched white collar sported splotches of black, Whitaker's eye travelled upward. Catching sight of sprigs of red hair, his heart began to race. Looking to Mr. Browning, who stood directly across the aisle, he tilted his head towards Carney. Browning nodded, instantly moving to a seat on the blackguard's right, whilst Whitaker claimed the place on his left.

Though at once apprehensive, Carney did not want to appear overly concerned; thus, he sat perfectly still. However, when he could bear it no longer, he grasped the back of the pew in front and started to stand. At once he was pulled back down, his rib cage accosted by the barrel of a pistol on his right, while the sharp tip of a knife bore into his neck on the left.

"I suggest you come along quietly," Whitaker whispered. "For if you decide to cause a scene I will be happy to cut your throat right here. You decide."

Having no alternative, Carney nodded. He was lifted from his seat and forced out of a side door. Bow Street Runners on that side of the building rushed forward to help, taking control of the blackguard and dragging him around to the back of the building where he was placed in a vehicle specially fitted with iron bars and locks to transport law-breakers.

Watching as Carney was dragged away, Browning asked, "When should we tell Colonel Fitzwilliam?"

"I shall tell him the minute the family gathers on the front steps to watch the Darcys leave."

Browning nodded, and they returned to the sanctuary to view the ceremony.

The wedding

The Master of Pemberley looked every inch the wealthy gentleman in his expensive black breeches, coat and shoes, white linen shirt and gold embroidered waistcoat. So handsome was he that a good many of the women in attendance could not take their eyes from him and spent the entire ceremony fantasising about how it would feel to be the bride.

Their husbands were not free from distraction, either. From the moment Elizabeth appeared—a vision of loveliness in her pale pink gown—many of Darcy's contemporaries were envious of his good fortune. Gossip in the men's clubs was that the reserved Mr. Darcy was marrying a woman with no connections, no dowry and no fortune; thus, curiosity compelled them to see the creature capable of accomplishing a *coup* of this magnitude. After seeing the bride and the expression on Darcy's face as she approached the altar, none would ever again harbour doubts that the gentleman from Derbyshire had married for love.

The ceremony was brief, but meaningful, in accordance with the groom's wishes. Nearing the end of the vows, Emily slipped out of her seat and ran to stand beside her mother. She was the only child at the ceremony and had been well behaved up to that point. As a quiet rumble of laughter filled the church, the bishop ignored the interruption and finished the ceremony, eventually declaring the couple man and wife. Instantly, William brought Elizabeth's left hand to his lips to kiss her ring and then stooped to take Emily into his arms. The trio faced the congregation together.

As quietly as a three-year-old could, Emily asked, "Are we married now?"

William whispered, "Yes."

Throwing her hands around his neck, she said, "Thank you, Papa, for marrying us. I love you."

A lump filled William's throat with his reply. "I love you, too, my dear."

Hearing the exchange, Elizabeth began to cry, but since it was not uncommon for a bride to cry on her wedding day, she did nothing to hide her tears.

The bishop stood beside William. "If you and your witnesses will follow me to the vestry, you need to sign the register."

The newlyweds and Emily, along with Richard and Jane, followed the bishop through a side door. As soon as this requirement was complete, Richard picked up the child and headed back into the sanctuary with her in one arm and Jane on the other. He proceeded towards Millicent, who was to keep Emily during his cousin's honeymoon.

It was obvious to the bishop that William was in no rush to join the throng in the sanctuary, so he said tactfully, "Mr. Darcy, please excuse me, for I must make entries in the church ledgers. You may have use of this room as long as you wish. Before I go, however, let me wish you and Mrs. Darcy a long and prosperous marriage, filled with joy."

After the door clicked shut behind the clergyman, William pulled Elizabeth into his arms, kissing her soundly. Then, resting his head atop hers, he let go a long sigh. "I thought this moment would never come. Not seeing you these past days has been maddening. I had to restrain myself from kissing you at the altar for fear my fervour would scandalise the *ton*."

"I missed you, too, but Millie kept me so busy with the gown—"

"You are not at fault. Selfishly, I desire all your time."

Elizabeth caressed his cheek. "I am glad you desire my time."

A longer, more ardent kiss ensued before he said, "*Mrs. Darcy*. I love the sound of that."

Elizabeth sank deeper into his arms. "Not as much as I love hearing you say it."

Suddenly he released her, clasped her hands and took a step back. "Let me look at you." It seemed that he took forever to examine her, and Elizabeth began to blush. "Make no mistake. Your gown is exquisite and your hair lovely in this style, but your beauty does not rely on such things."

"How do you always know what to say to make me love you more? I love you so much, William. Mere words can never express my devotion."

"Then let us not waste time talking."

And they did not.

A short time later the bride and groom re-entered the sanctuary and were immediately encircled by family and friends wishing them joy, which took a good bit more time than William desired. Consequently, when his aunt reminded him that they needed to leave for the wedding breakfast, he swiftly escorted Elizabeth out of the church and halted abruptly on the top step. The carriage which would take him and his bride to the Matlocks' townhouse waited on the street below, decorated from one end to the other with flowers and greenery. In fact, the decorations were so dense that one could no longer see the black finish of the vehicle.

As he and Elizabeth chuckled, a profusion of flower petals and seeds filled the air and followed them as they ran down the steps. The shower continued until the ground was thoroughly covered, and the vehicle began to roll away from St. George's. The newlyweds departed to the sight of Richard, with Emily in his arms, along with Millicent, the Earl and Countess of Matlock, the Bingleys and the Gardiners waving to them from the pavement, whilst Mary and Kitty, along with their husbands, waved from the first step. Their loved ones continued to wave until the carriage went around a corner.

At this point, William captured her hand and kissed it. "I hope the wedding was all your heart ever wished for, Elizabeth."

"All my heart ever wished for was you," she whispered.

Though they were in an open carriage and the streets were filled with onlookers, William kissed her.

Millicent continued to smile and wave, even while she leaned in to whisper to Richard, "I hope you are not labouring under the impression that you have kept me in the dark. I could tell from the look on your face when you entered the sanctuary that something was amiss, and after Mr. Whitaker stopped you on the portico to talk, I was certain."

"I would have been disappointed had you not figured it out."

"Is anyone in danger?"

"Not anymore. I shall tell you everything once we are alone." Then Richard smiled. "I see that my days of keeping secrets are numbered. They will end the minute we are married."

Taking Emily from his arms, Millicent begged to differ. "Those days were over the minute we became engaged."

"I cannot believe how quickly a woman can take control," he teased.

By now the rest of the family was listening, and Lord Matlock chuckled, saying, "You have seen nothing yet. Wait until you are married!"

Overhearing this, Lady Matlock interrupted. "Come now, Edward. One can hardly accuse you of not being in control." Without missing a beat, she commanded, "Now, we must leave if we wish to greet our guests before the breakfast begins."

As they walked towards their carriage, those around them chuckled at the irony.

Matlock House
The wedding breakfast

If Elizabeth and William were hungry, they did not act the part as they stood in the receiving line next to the Earl and Countess of Matlock for what seemed forever, greeting well-wishers. It had taken longer than William had expected for the ladies of the *ton* to scrutinize Elizabeth and, of course, to fawn over him, an opportunity they had seldom been afforded in the past. Stalwart as ever, Elizabeth bore their annoying questions and rude examinations admirably.

William's patience, however, had stretched thin by the time the third matriarch gushed over how handsome he looked in his wedding attire. It had taken a hidden pinch from his new bride to keep him from replying as he would have liked, and by the time everyone had taken their turn being insufferable and moved on, he was exhausted.

"Allow me to apologise for subjecting you to so many trying people," Lady Matlock whispered to William. "Still, they *are* part and parcel of the *ton,* and you may find that many of them can help or hinder your children's prospects in the future. There is no time like the present to begin engaging them in conversation. However, now that they are settled, please take the time to eat something. I had Cook create the dishes you used to favour when you were a boy."

William gave her a slight smile, and the countess and earl left to circulate among their guests. The moment they were out of hearing, William asked Elizabeth, "When would you like to slip away to Darcy House? I had Mrs. Colton cook, too, so I am certain she has plenty of food prepared should we desire it."

Elizabeth's eyes danced with happiness. "Your aunt and uncle went to the trouble and expense of hosting our breakfast. Should we not stay a bit longer to show our gratitude?"

William sighed. "One hour more."

Having already finished eating, Richard excused himself and left Millicent talking to Jane whilst he made his way to his cousin. Elizabeth was speaking to Kitty on her right, so he sat down in the chair vacated by his mother on Darcy's left.

"Tell me, Cousin. How does it feel to be an old married man?"

William smiled mischievously. "I believe you should ask me that question tomorrow."

To keep from laughing aloud, Richard pursed his lips. Once he had composed himself, he replied, "I see your point." Then, looking around to make sure his parents were not nearby, he said quietly, "Have you noticed that Leighton is not here?"

"Yes, and I do not mind saying I was relieved to find he was not."

"I do not blame you—not after the way he treated Elizabeth. However, Father said he has begun to see a change in him. Supposedly, my brother no longer drinks and is ashamed of his previous behaviour towards your new bride. Nothing kept him away today, but he thought it best not to come. Again, according to Father, Leighton feared it would not be fair to Elizabeth."

"That does not sound like the cousin I know."

"I thought the same." Richard sighed. "If he is sincere, it does show promise."

"I agree. But how will that affect your inheritance?"

"Father said he still intends to put more assets in Mother's name, which can only benefit me. And, if Leighton continues to improve, he will make certain my brother has enough funds to keep this house and the Matlock estate solvent and on the right track."

"I suppose that would only be fair if Leighton does reform."

"It would. Besides, when Millie and I marry, I will take on Hudson Hall to manage."

"My cousin, the gentleman farmer!"

"You have no idea! I have not told Millie yet, but I plan to resign from the army soon. Though campaigns on foreign soil used to interest me, that is no longer the case. Hugh and Kathy have lost one father, and I will do everything in my power to see they do not lose another."

"I am proud to hear it. The last time you were overseas, it was torture waiting from week to week for the reports of those dead or wounded."

"Try looking at it from the other side," Richard said with a hollow laugh. Then he grew sombre. "I lost many good friends in that campaign. It made me think long and hard about what I wanted to do with the rest of my life."

"Like get married and raise children?"

"You read my mind."

Chapter 32

London

Darcy House

Having resided with Millicent since her arrival in London, Elizabeth had never seen the inside of Darcy House; therefore, she was understandably nervous when the carriage came to a stop in front of her husband's London home. As she looked up at the imposing three-storey brick façade, one thought came to mind: *What will the servants think of me?*

There was no time to dwell on the subject, however, for William had already exited the vehicle and was reaching for her hand. As he helped her to the pavement, a smile crossed his face, and he kissed the hand he held. Then, threading his fingers through hers, he began to lead her up the steps. Just as they reached the portico, the front door opened, and Mr. and Mrs. Barnes stepped out.

"Welcome home, Mrs. Darcy," they said in unison. Then both stepped aside to allow William and Elizabeth to enter.

Though Elizabeth had worried only moments before about their acceptance, the kindly looks on the Barnes' faces dispelled her doubts. "I am so pleased to meet you," she replied. "Mr. Darcy has spoken often of his reliance upon the both of you to keep his home running smoothly."

If possible, Mr. Barnes stood even taller, though both servants appeared a bit embarrassed at the praise. Amused, William took the opportunity to speak.

"Elizabeth, I wish to explain why there are no other servants here to greet you. Since I wanted our arrival to be as private as possible, I asked Mr. and Mrs. Barnes to give everyone the week off, except for those essential to keeping the house open. You will meet all the servants when the rest return. No maids or footmen will be allowed upstairs this week unless absolutely necessary, so it is possible you may see no one all week except me."

Elizabeth's face grew hot, a certain sign that she was blushing, though William seemed not to notice, for he was already addressing the housekeeper.

"We shall dine early this evening, Mrs. Barnes; I think seven will do. Have a maid bring the meal to our sitting room. Mrs. Darcy and I will serve ourselves, and I will ring once we are finished."

Without missing a beat, William swept Elizabeth off her feet and began carrying her up the grand staircase. Mortified, she glanced over his shoulder to find the butler and housekeeper watching from the bottom of the stairs, their eyes full of merriment.

"William!" she whispered. "What will they think?"

"I imagine they will think I am a newly-married man who is very much in love with his wife."

When at last they were at the door to the sitting room between his suite and hers, William let Elizabeth slip to her feet. Placing a kiss on her forehead, he turned the knob and pushed the door open. When Elizabeth turned to look inside, she gasped. Walking to the middle of the room, she executed a complete circle before murmuring, "It is lovely."

Easily larger than any of the bedrooms at Longbourn, all the doors, windows and trim were white, as was the furniture. The carpet was mauve, and the walls were the same hue, though the paper-hangings also featured intermittent strips of white flowers and lattice borders. Beginning to inspect the items atop various tables, Elizabeth discovered statuettes of bone china, porcelain bowls filled with colourful balls, and crystal vases filled with red roses. She stopped at one vase to breathe in the fragrance of the flowers before noticing a row of books on the mantel above the hearth. Choosing one, she spied the window seat and rushed there to sit down. It was upholstered in white, and when she sat down, she arranged three well-padded mauve pillows behind her back. Once settled, she pulled aside the curtain to find a garden just below.

"Should you ever miss me on a rainy day," she teased, "you will find me right here reading this book on—" She looked at the title in her hand and then giggled. "Well, I do not think I shall be reading about crop rotations. More than likely, I will be reading a copy of **Irish Melodies** by Thomas Moore."

William, whose eyes had followed her around the room, chuckled. "That is good to know."

Crossing to the door on his right, he opened it. "This is my bedroom." When Elizabeth made no move to join him, he asked, "Would you like to look inside?"

Suddenly aware of her quickening heartbeat, Elizabeth stood, set down the book and walked across the room to stand in front of her husband. She leaned over to peer into his domain, taking great pains not to enter. The space, large enough to be a drawing room, held over-sized, mahogany furniture with fine gold trim, as well as equally dark doors, windows and borders. However, what quickly caught her eye were the flocked, blue and gold paper-hangings, for they spoke volumes about her new husband's wealth. The plush carpet featured a wide border of the same blue, whilst in the middle a cream-coloured square held overlapping circles of blue, green, crimson and gold. A striped satin counterpane in blue, crimson and gold adorned the bed and matched the canopy.

"It looks very..." Bringing one hand up to clasp her chin, Elizabeth tilted her head first one way then another, as though trying to think of the proper word. Then she smiled. "Masculine."

Laughing, William slipped a hand around her waist, pulled her against his chest and kissed the exposed skin of her neck. "I am glad you think so," he whispered against the softness. "After all, I *am*."

His kiss flooded her with warmth, and turning in his embrace, the look in his eyes caused her heart to flutter. "I...I know that very well, *Mr. Darcy*."

Cupping the back of her head, he brought her mouth to his. This kiss, unlike any other they had shared, was full of hunger and urgency. Then, as quickly as it began, it ended. Breathing heavily, William stepped back.

"You have not yet seen your bedroom."

A shiver passed through Elizabeth as William led her to a door on the opposite side of the sitting room. Opening it, he walked in, bringing her with him. If she had thought the other rooms were magnificent, she was astonished when she saw this one.

Like the sitting room, it was decorated with white furniture, only this was trimmed broadly in gold. The walls were papered with multi-coloured flowering trees, birds and butterflies on an ecru background. As with the sitting room, this room was filled with vases of red roses.

"Oh, William," Elizabeth said breathlessly. "I have never seen anything like this."

"My mother was fond of these paper-hangings. When she died, I left the room as it was, with the exception of replacing things as needed. I always hoped—"

The pain in his eyes drew her in, and Elizabeth caressed his cheek. "You hoped a new Mrs. Darcy would decide what would be changed."

He closed his eyes, and she could barely hear his reply. "Yes."

Standing on tiptoes, she brushed a kiss across her husband's perfect mouth. "I am here now, my darling, and I will never leave you."

Instantly clasped to a rock-hard chest by arms more akin to steel than flesh and bone, Elizabeth found herself kissed so fervently she barely realized when William's fingers began to struggle with the buttons on her gown.

"William, it...it is the middle of the day."

Desire hovered in his eyes. "We have waited years for this day, my love. When two people love as deeply as you and I, marital relations are a blessing not limited to the cover of darkness."

"Forgive your foolish wife, William. You are right. There should be no restrictions placed on our love. The appropriate time is whenever either of us desires the other." She turned. "Will you help me undress?"

William began unbuttoning her gown, and before long the elegant creation slipped to the floor, leaving her clad only in a satin corset, thin chemise, stockings and slippers. A tumult of emotion passed over William's face, and he hesitated.

Elizabeth asked nervously, "Does the corset present a problem?"

Shivers raced down her spine as he tasted the silky skin of her shoulder before whispering roughly, "Not for a man in love."

Soon the corset joined the dress on the floor. Unable to resist, William captured her breasts through the delicate chemise, her head falling back against his chest. Then both hands slid down to grab the hem of the garment and bring it up and over her head. Tossing it aside, he was instantly on his knees removing her slippers and the silky stockings.

As he stood, Elizabeth said, "I wish to see you, too, my husband."

He shed his coat and waistcoat swiftly, and by the time his cravat was tossed aside and he had begun to pull the expensive lawn shirt over his head, Elizabeth's eyes were wide and dark as coals.

His eyes held Elizabeth spellbound as she was swept off her feet and carried towards the bed. Once there, he set her down and kissed her with a fervour previously forbidden. Then, pulling aside the satin counterpane, he laid her on the silk sheets. Shedding his shoes and breeches quickly, he climbed into the bed beside her and rolled over, covering her body with his.

"I love you, Elizabeth Darcy. I shall until I draw my last breath, and if God is willing, I shall love you throughout eternity."

Elizabeth's fingers threaded through his hair as tears rolled down her face. "Throughout eternity, my love."

Drowning in passion, their lips met in an endless succession of fiery kisses as William began the slow, deliberate seduction of his wife. The freedom to love Elizabeth as he had on countless nights in his imagination was intoxicating, and he began to place hot, ravenous kisses over every part of the body he ached to explore. Elizabeth writhed beneath him, and her hands moved to his back, her fingers urging him closer with every moan of pleasure.

"Love me now, William. Love me."

And as blood rushed through William's veins like a torrent, Elizabeth gave herself to him—heart, body and soul.

Lying naked across William's sandalwood-scented torso, a feeling of elation overwhelmed Elizabeth. Through her husband's patience and expertise, she had experienced a level of ecstasy that made even Aunt Gardiner's reassuring account of the marriage bed pale by comparison. Moreover, the groans of pleasure he had made as he intensified the rhythm of their lovemaking before reaching his peak proved he had experienced the same euphoria as she.

Even now, his heart drumming against her breasts brought Elizabeth unimagined satisfaction. She was his now, truly and forever! And the realisation that a child might result from their union brought Elizabeth unspeakable joy. To give William a child and Emily a sibling was her dearest wish.

Her musings were interrupted by her husband, who began to bury the fingers of one hand in her lavender scented curls whilst stroking her back with the other. "Dearest, are you well?"

Lifting her head to look into his eyes, Elizabeth smiled. "I am, William."

"There is ample water heated—"

A dainty finger instantly sealed his lips. "That is thoughtful, but dinner is still hours away, is it not?"

"Elizabeth, I do not expect you to—"

"What if I have other hungers you need to fulfil? Must I beg you to love to me again, *Husband*?"

William smiled. "For that remark, *Wife*, you shall have to beg me to stop."

"I shall hold you to that promise."

William's answer was to kiss her again. This time their joining expressed all the pent-up passion of years of unrequited love. Carried once more to heights where no one existed save themselves, they did not hear the bell announcing that dinner had been delivered to the sitting room.

To Elizabeth's mortification, when they learned that their meal was cold, William insisted on ringing for Mrs. Barnes to have the food replaced. Whilst he spoke with the housekeeper, Elizabeth went to her dressing room to splash water on her crimsoning face. She was drying her face with a towel when he returned, so he embraced her from behind.

"William, please tell me that you did not *explain* to Mrs. Barnes why the food was cold?"

He laughed, turning her to face him. "Elizabeth, I think that goes without saying."

Elizabeth blushed anew, causing William to tease her. "I believe we may have enough time before the cook—"

Playfully she pushed at his chest. "I will never be able to face the servants if you send the food back again, but after we have eaten..."

"You are an amazing woman, Mrs. Darcy."

"I have just begun to amaze you, Mr. Darcy."

Instantly, she was pressed against the wall, her dressing gown untied and pushed aside. Teasing one generous breast and then the other with his tongue, he murmured, "If you keep saying such things, Elizabeth, neither of us will eat tonight."

Downstairs
Early the next day

Three upstairs maids were chosen to work the week of the Darcys' honeymoon—Edna, Sally and Jessie. Given their assignments because they were employees of long standing and not prone to gossip, the three were not immune to sharing each other's confidence.

Consequently, the instant Sally came downstairs holding the sheets removed from the mistress' bed, Edna, who was busy ironing another set, said, "Did you hear? The master asked for more food to be sent up after dinner was served last night." She grinned knowingly.

"Yes, that bodes well for a happy marriage," Sally replied, giving her co-worker a wink. Dropping the contents of her arms into a basket, she added, "You best be careful, though. I swear Mrs. Barnes can hear through the walls."

"I thought she was upstairs."

Having been up since dawn, Sally yawned before replying. "She was. Jessie was making the bed when I went into the hall with my arms full of bedclothes. I did not see her, and we ran right into one another. From the look on Mrs. Barnes' face, one would think St. Peter himself had summoned her, though I presume the master rang."

Edna chuckled at that image before remembering what she wanted to ask. "Tell me quickly, then. Did you see the mistress?"

"You do remember we were ordered to do our jobs without being nosey?"

"But surely you stole a glimpse?"

Wishing to brag about being the first to see the new Mrs. Darcy, Sally relented. "To tell the truth, out of the corner of my eye I saw movement on the balcony and glanced in that direction. Anyone would have done the same."

"Of course, they would. What did you see?"

Sally smiled unconsciously. "They were a sight to behold. Both were facing the stables—he with his arms around her from behind. She was in a nightgown, but he was dressed only in breeches." The maid pretended to fan her face. "I have to say Mr. Darcy looks very manly in just his breeches."

"What nonsense you spout!" Edna exclaimed, looking at the door to see if anyone was listening. "You are too old to be thinking such thoughts, especially about Mr. Darcy!"

"I am only one and forty, thank you. And I can still appreciate a handsome man with a fine body, no matter who he is."

"Please no more! Let us return to the subject at hand. Did you see the mistress? Is she beautiful? Surely only a beautiful woman would tempt Mr. Darcy to marry."

"I got only a brief glimpse of her face, but from what little I saw, she appears to be a natural beauty with dark hair and eyes."

"Is she tall like Miss Darcy?"

"When they were embracing I noted her head was several inches under the master's chin, so I would say she is shorter."

Meanwhile, Jessie had returned and was listening to Sally's descriptions with rapt attention. Once Sally was done speaking, she said, "I heard from one of the Matlocks' maids that our new mistress has no family connections and no dowry. I bring that up not to disparage Mrs. Darcy, but because it sheds light on Mr. Darcy's character, if you ask me."

"What do you mean?" Edna asked.

"Clearly the master could have married Lady Markham or someone like her. Yet he chose to marry a woman with nothing to recommend her. It must be a love match."

"After what I witnessed on the balcony today, I could not agree more," Sally concurred. "They were so enamoured of one another they never noticed me."

Long drawn-out sighs filled the air, whilst dreamy expressions settled on each face. It was this scene that greeted Mrs. Barnes upon her return.

Immediately her hands found her hips. "What is going on?"

Denials that anything was wrong ensued and quickly dissipated as the maids hurriedly resumed their duties. Satisfied, Mrs. Barnes walked towards the kitchen.

Lady Markham's townhouse
The music room
Three days later

Whilst her parents enjoyed their honeymoon, Emily seemed satisfied to join Hugh and Kathy in painting, drawing and playing the various games they devised to entertain her. There were times, however, when melancholy overcame her, and she sought the comfort of Millicent's lap, as she did that day.

Intending to listen to her twins practice the pianoforte, Millicent entered the music room, and Emily rushed to sit beside her—a sure sign that she wished to be held. As Millicent pulled the child onto her lap, she was not surprised to hear her ask the question she asked everyday: "Is it Sunday?"

"No, Poppet, it is Wednesday. There are four more days until your mother and Mr. Darcy come for you."

"He is my papa, now. You may call him that."

Millicent suppressed a laugh. "I apologise. I meant to say your papa." Hoping to distract her, she added, "I was thinking that since the rain has stopped, we could take a ride in the park after tea. I will rent a pony for the three of you. Or you may ride with me, if you wish. What do you say?"

"I want to ride Snow. I miss her."

"And I am certain that Snow misses you."

Emily crooked her neck to look up at Millicent. "When will I see Snow again?"

"It is my understanding that your papa wishes to return to Pemberley after the honeymoon. But keep in mind, his plans could change."

Emily's brows knit. "Honeymoon?"

"After a man and a woman marry, they wish to spend time alone. This time is called a honeymoon."

Emily looked as though she was considering the explanation. "I hope Mama and Papa get tired of their honeymoon and come get me."

Millicent hugged the child, chuckling. "What say we write them a letter telling them all that you have been doing while you have been here?"

Emily nodded. "And you can tell them to come and get me!"

"I can see that Fitzwilliam is going to have his hands full with you."

The little girl smiled. "Papa has big hands."

"That he does, Poppet, and a heart equally as big."

Suddenly, Kathy was standing before them. "Emily, would you like to practice the song I taught you?"

Immediately, Emily slid out of Millicent's lap to grasp Kathy's hand. Once at the pianoforte, Hugh helped her onto the bench, and soon Emily was playing a few notes under his sister's tutelage. Tired of it all, he took a seat in a nearby chair, where he began looking through the new sheet music Richard had brought the day before.

Just then, Richard walked quietly into the room. Seeing the children occupied, he sat down beside Millicent. As they watched the scene, Richard leaned in to ask, "How is Miss Emily today?"

"The same as every day; she misses her parents."

"Have you heard from them?"

"I have no expectation of hearing anything. Fitzwilliam and Elizabeth will contact us when they are ready and not a minute sooner."

Richard sighed. "Then I suppose I shall just have to wait to tell Darcy the good news."

"What news is so important you cannot wait until their honeymoon is over?"

"I want my cousin to know that Carney tried to escape when they were transporting him to Newgate prison. He was shot and killed. Bingley's money, which was being held for evidence, shall be returned since there will now be no trial. And the footman at Canfield Manor confessed. He was sentenced to hang and is now in prison awaiting his fate."

"That should give Fitzwilliam and Elizabeth peace of mind, but what about the others accused of trying to kill Castlereagh?"

"The foreigners confessed and implicated John Guthrie. He

denies everything, and given his station, he will have the chance to defend himself in court. Still, with the amount of evidence against him, I am certain he will be convicted."

"I still find it hard to fathom that Elizabeth was caught up in something of that magnitude, all due to that horrible Lord Van Lynden. She and Emily are lucky to have escaped with their lives."

"They have Darcy to thank for that."

"And you."

Richard shook his head. "I played no part in recovering them."

"Still, you were instrumental in finding their location in London and proving Van Lynden was involved in the assassination attempt, which meant that Emily would never be taken away from Elizabeth again." Millicent squeezed his hand. "In my eyes, you are a hero."

Richard's heart swelled. "While I may not agree, it is kind of you to say."

"I do not say it out of kindness or because I love you. It is the truth."

"Have I told you that I fall more in love with you each day?"

The corners of Millicent's mouth lifted in a wry smile. "You have, but I never tire of hearing it."

Richard attempted to steal a kiss, but Kathy interrupted. "Listen to Emily play, Mama!"

Stopping in mid-air as the first few notes of a simple song began, Richard wagged his brows at Millicent. She laughed.

"After the children are in bed, I shall kiss you as I wish to," Richard stated.

"And how do you *wish* to kiss me?"

"I will not spoil the surprise by telling. Might the children go to bed early tonight?"

Millicent chuckled. "I see no reason why not."

Chapter 33

Pemberley

August 1818 – Eleven months later

Lady Matlock's heart swelled with pride as she inspected the public rooms of Pemberley before the guests were to arrive for the ball welcoming Lord and Lady Charlton back to England. After all, impressing the *ton* was her forte, and the touches she had made to the rooms were subtle but effective. To her amazement, she encountered no objections from Elizabeth when Fitzwilliam suggested she step in to supervise last-minute preparations—most likely because her niece was only four weeks removed from having given birth to her first child and was preoccupied with him.

Alexander 'Alex' Fitzwilliam George Darcy was the spitting image of his father, with dark hair and eyes equally as light. Moreover, as young as he was, he possessed what Richard called the "Darcy glare" whenever his eyes focused on something or someone.

Lady Matlock laughed to recall the look. *You certainly cannot deny that he is yours, Fitzwilliam.* Not that her nephew would ever wish to do so. No, the Master of Pemberley was still walking on air and so focused on caring for his wife and child that he was more fastidious than ever, which was her reason for walking through the house one last time.

Presently on her way to the ballroom, the countess' thoughts turned to the circumstances surrounding Georgiana's return. Not only was her niece's husband sole heir to his father's estate, but he was also the sole heir of his mother's bachelor brother, Lord Charles. With that man's sudden death only months previously, Charlton had inherited Peabody Manor, a large estate in Cheshire on the border with Derbyshire, and they decided to make it their home. He had confided to Georgiana's brother that she missed England, and he hoped the move would lift her spirits. It had done that and more, for it had greatly pleased her family as well.

Turning into yet another hall, Lady Matlock spied William ahead, speaking to Mrs. Reynolds. They were standing before a set of double doors to the ballroom, and as she watched, the housekeeper nodded, dropped a small curtsey and hurried in another direction. Not noticing his aunt, William disappeared inside the ballroom.

She sighed. *I hope he has not found something else he wishes to change.*

Once she gained the door, she asked, "Do you approve, Nephew?"

William whirled around. "I did not hear you approach."

"You were preoccupied."

"Who would not be preoccupied after seeing this?" William asked, gesturing to the ceiling where eight chandeliers, newly polished and filled with hundreds of lit candles, swayed in response to a breeze wafting through the open doors to the terrace. Each move made the candles, which were reflected in the mirrored walls, fill the room with twinkling lights. The effect was magical.

"I am amazed how a thorough cleaning has brought this room back to its former glory. Seeing it now, I wonder why I ever ordered it closed."

"If I remember correctly, you closed the ballroom because you hate balls," his aunt answered, her eyes twinkling. "It was just as well. After your father died, you held a few dinner parties, but no balls."

William sighed. "I should have done better by Georgiana."

"Do not be so hard on yourself. You made certain she had ample opportunity to partake of society when she stayed with me during the season. How else could she have met her husband?" A slight smile crossed William's face. "Now, tell me. Why did you decide to host a ball for Georgiana when you dislike them so heartily?"

"Elizabeth thought my sister's return deserved more than a dinner party—which reminds me, I must thank you for answering my plea. When she planned the event, Elizabeth was under the impression Alex would make his debut weeks earlier. By coming to our rescue, you preserved my sanity. I am in your debt."

"I am pleased I could help. Now, correct me if I am wrong, but the older woman—Mrs. Grassley—seems to do nothing but sit in the nursery whilst Elizabeth takes care of the baby. And what happened to the maid from Scotland? I had the impression she was to be Alexander's nanny."

"Mrs. O'Malley's primary responsibility has always been Emily, though she was going to help with the baby. After Alex was born, however, Emily decided it was her duty to be his nanny." William's eyes crinkled with mirth. "It is touching to see how much she loves him, but she tries to take him from his bed whenever he cries, and that will not do. Since O'Malley has her hands full with Emily, I brought in Mrs. Grassley, who came highly recommended. Still, Elizabeth insists on caring for Alex as much as possible, leaving Mrs. Grassley with little to do."

"She looks exhausted. May I ask what the physician had to say about Elizabeth's recovery?"

"According to Mr. Camryn, Alexander was a large baby by any standards, and because Elizabeth is so petite, the birth took more of a toll on her. Still, he assures me that, given enough time and rest, she will recover fully. My dilemma is trying to get her to rest."

"Might I suggest you hire a wet nurse? At least Elizabeth could utilise the nurse at night and get more sleep."

"Elizabeth is of the opinion that God meant for mothers to feed their own children. Besides, she fears that she would miss too much of Alexander's formative months if she were to turn him over to another for nursing."

"All women of the *ton* have wet nurses."

"No offense intended, Aunt, but I thank God every day that my wife is not a woman of the *ton*. And as long as her health is not at risk, I will support her wishes."

"I may not agree, but I understand. Are any of Elizabeth's sisters staying after the ball? Perhaps she would let them lend a hand."

"Though Lord Charlton leaves tomorrow for Peabody Manor, Georgiana is staying another two weeks to get better acquainted with Elizabeth and Alexander, but she has no experience with children. Bingley's youngest child is cutting teeth and is not presently a very sociable young man," William said with a wry smile. "They are returning to Canfield Manor the day after tomorrow. I could ask Kitty to stay, but Mrs. Grassley is very willing to help if only she is allowed."

"I recall meeting another of Elizabeth's sisters. I believe she lives in Hertfordshire."

"Yes, Mary. She is expecting her third child any day, so they did not make the trip."

"With Millicent due to give birth in another month, there will be no shortage of babies in our circle this year."

"Millie looked very well when she and Richard arrived, but

when I tried to speak to her privately, she was resting. How is she faring?"

"I begged her not to come, but you know Millicent. She is as stubborn as ever." Lady Matlock's face softened and she smiled. "At least she had only to come from Hudson Hall and not London. And, while she may look well, her feet swell when she stands too long. In fact, she confided in me that she may not stay downstairs long tonight."

William pointed to an alcove were footmen were placing comfortable chairs in front of large pots containing small trees and greenery. "I am filling all the alcoves with comfortable chairs so Elizabeth and anyone who so desires may sit down and watch the festivities. Millie is welcome to join us."

"Us?"

"Naturally, I will be by Elizabeth's side."

The countess inspected William from head to toe, noting how splendid he looked in his formal attire. "Unfortunately, you are a handsome man, Nephew, and will be a sought-after partner. While you may refrain from dancing with this year's debutants, it will be considered rude if you do not humour their mothers."

"You flatter me. Still, I have danced very little since university, and I am not sure that I recall all the steps."

She patted his hand in a motherly fashion. "Your excuse is invalid. It is like riding a horse—you never forget."

Suddenly, the musicians, who had filled the balcony whist they talked, began to tune their instruments.

"Excuse me. I had better see if Elizabeth is ready," William said, hurrying towards the door.

"Send Edward, Lord Charlton and Georgiana down, too!" she called after him. "I shall be in the foyer in case of early arrivals."

Elizabeth's bedroom

Mrs. Grassley waited inconspicuously in a corner of the mistress' bedroom to take the heir of Pemberley, who was presently lying on his mother's bed, back to the nursery. In her years as a servant, she had perfected the art of keeping her emotions hidden, but as Elizabeth and Emily conversed while sitting beside Alex, she struggled to keep a straight face.

Elizabeth smoothed a few dark curls from Alexander's forehead. Upon observing her mother, Emily said, "Why does Brother have hair and Ben does not?"

"Some babies are born with lots of hair. Eventually those who do not have hair will catch up with the rest."

"Did I have lots of hair?"

"Not when you were as young as Alex."

"May I show Brother to Snow tomorrow?"

"I am afraid that he is still too young to visit the stables."

"Why does he sleep so much?"

"Babies need plenty of rest so they can grow big enough to play with their older brothers and sisters."

"Gracie said Ben does not play well. He cannot walk without falling."

"Ben is just learning to walk. He will get better."

Suddenly, Emily took note of the jewellery her mother was wearing—a choker consisting of four strands of brilliant diamonds that came to a point over her décolletage. At the point, a large ruby surrounded by smaller diamonds was suspended. A pair of matching ruby and diamond earrings completed the set.

The child timidly touched the ruby. "You look pretty, Mama. Are you going to dance? Gracie said her mother is going to dance."

"Thank you, sweetheart. And, yes, I plan to dance with your papa."

"I saw Papa. I think he looks pretty, too."

Elizabeth tried not to laugh. "I agree. Your papa looks very pretty."

Just then there was a knock on the door, and Kathleen stuck her head inside.

"Are you ready for Miss Emily to go to bed now, ma'am? I just came up from downstairs, and I heard the musicians tuning their instruments."

"Do I have to go to bed now, Mama?"

"Yes. I must attend the ball, and you must go to sleep. Now, say goodnight to your brother and go with Mrs. O'Malley."

Emily kissed the baby's forehead. "Good night, Brother."

Promptly she turned to give her mother a kiss. When Elizabeth helped her to the floor, she ran to Kathleen.

In mere minutes, Jane and Kitty entered the bedroom, taking up positions around the bed where Elizabeth still sat admiring Alexander.

Both looked lovely, and compliments were exchanged regarding their gowns including Elizabeth's choice of an ecru, bead-embroidered muslin. Then Georgiana entered the room and smiled.

"Elizabeth, you are wearing Mother's choker and earrings! I hoped you would like them. They were her favourite."

Unconsciously, Elizabeth's hand flew to the necklace. "William insisted I wear them, and they do suit this gown."

Suddenly, Alex stretched, yawned and opened his eyes. Instantly, Jane reached to capture one of her nephew's velvety feet. "Alexander is so beautiful. And he is such a big boy! Ben was not this big until he was two months old."

Kitty, who stood at the end of the bed, weighed in. "I beg to differ, Jane. Ben was not this large until he was four months old."

Everyone laughed when Georgiana added, "That is because Alex is the spitting image of his father—he has the same hair, same eyes and same glower."

Elizabeth planted a kiss on one of her son's chubby cheeks, declaring, "Alexander does not glower. He is just unsure how to react to silly women!"

"Just like his father!" Georgiana interjected, bringing a new round of laughter.

Then her eyes grew misty, and she ran a gentle hand over her nephew's head. "Mr. Camryn said that Alexander will be tall like my brother. That is why he is so long."

Picking up her baby, Elizabeth nuzzled his neck. "While at times you may look as serious as your father, fortunately your smile is just as beautiful as his, Alex."

The baby's arms flailed and he appeared to be trying to answer his mother when William appeared in the doorway.

"Ladies, the ball is about to begin, and my aunt requests everyone's presence downstairs."

All but Elizabeth hurried past him, with Jane and Georgiana murmuring something about finding their husbands. Mrs. Grassley walked into the sitting room and closed the door to give her employers privacy.

William sat next to Elizabeth and slipped his arm around her waist. As she leaned into him, he whispered in her ear. "Thank you for wearing the jewellery I selected. Mother designed this set, and she would be so proud to know you wore them."

"I am honoured to wear them."

William captured Elizabeth's lips in a soft kiss before she settled back into his arms again. As they admired their son, he touched one of Alex's small hands and was elated when the baby grasped his finger in a tight fist.

Flooded with love, he murmured, "Alexander is so perfect. At times he takes my breath away."

William gave his child a kiss, and upon drawing back, he watched as Alex made sucking motions with his mouth. "Everything reminds Alex of his mother's milk," he said chuckling.

Then William's eyes settled on Elizabeth's breasts. Since giving birth, all of her gowns strained to contain her bosom, including this one. Tempted, he placed a soft kiss on first one and then the other breast, teasing, "And everything reminds me of—"

"*William,*" Elizabeth said, her breath coming faster. "Mr. Camryn said we must wait at least another month."

William framed her face with his hands. "Forgive me. Just thinking of your body turns me into a schoolboy." He placed a chaste kiss on her lips. "Of course we must wait until you have fully recovered."

Elizabeth sighed. "Still, another month does seem forever."

"It is reassuring to know that you miss being with me, too."

"Oh, I do, William. Never think otherwise."

A more passionate kiss followed, only to be interrupted by a loud rapping on the door.

"Mother will be livid if you and Elizabeth are late," Richard declared. Ribald laughter filled the air while the sound of heavy boots vanished down the hall.

William stood, smiling wanly. "As much as I would love to stay here with you, we have a ball to attend."

Crossing to the sitting room door, he opened it and waved Mrs. Grassley inside. She went directly to Elizabeth, who kissed her son once more, then laid him gently in the nanny's arms.

"I shall take good care of Master Alexander. Please try not to worry, ma'am," Mrs. Grassley said. Instantly she disappeared with their son.

As they stood looking at the empty door through which she had gone, William held out an arm.

"Come, my love, it is time for all of Derbyshire, and I dare say half of London, to meet the beautiful woman who owns my heart."

If success was measured by the number of people in attendance, this ball was a coup. Since his aunt had taken it upon herself to add to the guest list he and Elizabeth had compiled, Pemberley was filled with dozens of people William did not recognise. And, much to his chagrin, they included plenty of single men.

Just as his aunt had predicted, after he danced with Elizabeth, he was cajoled into partnering one matron after another. Meanwhile, Elizabeth, who was still almost unknown to the *ton*, became the belle of the ball. Numerous men, at least those not aware of her husband's temperament, kept her busy on the dance floor. Snatching glances in her direction with every turn of the dance, William watched jealously as her partners changed with every set.

By the time the latest set had ended, William was fuming. Outwardly, he pleaded a stiff ankle and hurried in Elizabeth's direction. Not recognising the blond-haired Adonis now standing next to his wife, William stuck out a hand. His manner, nonetheless, was anything but friendly.

"Fitzwilliam Darcy," he said stiffly.

As he took the hand extended, the blond stranger said, "Darcy? Oh, Darcy! Then you are this lovely creature's husband?"

William's eyes narrowed and his grip tightened as they shook hands. "I am."

"Adamson, Lord Gravel's cousin, newly arrived from Bath," the gentleman said, struggling to remove his hand from William's grip. Once free, he quickly added, "If you and Mrs. Darcy will please excuse me. Someone I know from Sussex just walked onto the terrace, and I wish to greet him."

As the man hurried away, William followed him with his eyes.

"If you frighten away every gentleman who speaks to me,

there will be none left to partner me."

William's anger vanished at Elizabeth's tease, and he turned, smiling brilliantly. "*I* am your partner. Now, since this is the last set before supper, I suggest we get ahead of the crowd and go to the dining room." He held out his arm. "Shall we?"

The dining room

Pemberley's vast dining room was full of tables and chairs for their guests' use, while its sideboards were heaped high with food and drink. When William and Elizabeth entered, they found the room half full, with Richard and Millie already seated at a table for four.

Spying them, the colonel called, "Sit with us, Darcy." As they neared, Richard added, "If you and Elizabeth fill these chairs, it will save me the trouble of strangling the next person who sits here to ask a foolish question."

William tried not to smile at his usually good-natured cousin's irritability, for he fully understood how having a wife near her confinement made the slightest things seem a nuisance.

"Such as?"

"Hardly a minute passes that one of Mother's friends does not ask when our child is due. Obviously, the baby is due soon. Are they blind?"

Placing a hand on Richard's shoulder, he gave it a squeeze. "Perhaps their only motive is to show their concern."

Millie smiled. "I tried to tell him that, but Richard will not listen to me."

William turned to Elizabeth. "You need to sit down and rest. May I fill a plate and bring it to you?"

"That would be wonderful." Then she said to Millicent, "Would you like something more?"

"I would love another biscuit and a fresh cup of tea."

"Come, Cousin," William said, slapping Richard on his back. "Let us hurry. The music has stopped, and everyone will be here shortly."

As William filled a plate for Elizabeth, he glanced at Richard, who was filling another with biscuits. "Leighton surprised me by apologising to Elizabeth and me for his past behaviour. He did it privately, just before we formed the receiving line."

"Father was certain he would, though I was not as convinced. I am glad he did. What do you think of Miss Templeton? Mother believes they will be engaged soon."

"I suppose she is proper enough if Leighton brought her. Lord knows your mother would never allow him to escort someone unacceptable."

"You are right. She is nothing like the women he cavorted with in the past. Perhaps my brother has learned his lesson."

"Let us hope so." Richard looked as though he wished to say more. "Is there something else?"

Unexpectedly, what Richard feared came pouring out. "Darcy, tell me. How did you know when Elizabeth was about to give birth? I mean to say...is there a certain look or action that alerts you?"

William's expression darkened as he turned to face his cousin. "Do you believe Millicent is in labour?"

"I...I do not know!" Richard hissed as quietly as a man under strain could. "All I know is something seems to have changed between yesterday and today, though when I ask Millie how she is faring, she replies that she is well. It is driving me mad."

The moment she sat down, Elizabeth noticed a tight grimace cross her friend's face. "What is wrong, Millie?"

"Nothing is wrong. It is just that the baby is in a peculiar position today, and I am very uncomfortable."

Immediately, Elizabeth was on guard. "Are you having pains?"

"No, just an odd feeling on occasion."

"I think we should go upstairs. You may lie down whilst I have William send for Mr. Camryn—just to be certain all is well."

Millie started to protest, but another unusual sensation sealed her lips.

Seeing the look on her face, Elizabeth whispered, "I insist that you humour me. We are going upstairs."

Glancing about the room for William, Elizabeth found him looking at her with a quizzical brow. She motioned for him to return, and he leaned over to speak to Richard. When Richard turned around, his face was ashen, and by the time he and William were back at the table, Millicent was willing to see the physician.

Later

A footman was sent to Lambton to fetch the physician, and Mrs. Reynolds ordered maids to ready the guestroom furthest from the ballroom to serve as a birthing room. Pots of boiling water and stacks of sheets and towels were ready and waiting when Mr. Camryn's carriage stopped at the front door, and he was spirited upstairs with the guests none the wiser.

After examining Millicent, Mr. Camryn announced that she was indeed in labour, and since she had borne children before, he predicted the baby would arrive within a few hours. Millie insisted that the ball proceed, and Lady Matlock agreed. She declared that she and Lord Matlock, along with Lord and Lady Charlton and the Bingleys, would carry on downstairs as though nothing was amiss.

The only sign that things had changed, if one were clever

enough to notice, was that the band played naught but very lively country dances, Scottish reels and cotillions. Moreover, the time between the sets was shortened so that there was little time to change partners—all designed to cover any sounds that might come from the family quarters.

Upstairs, Elizabeth, Kitty and Mrs. Reynolds lent their support to Millicent while in the adjoining sitting room William was left to calm an increasingly fretful Richard. Though he poured his cousin glass after glass of brandy, it proved ineffective. Richard was too overwrought for the liquor to take effect, and after an hour had passed, his temper was getting the upper hand.

"Why have I not been told something?" Richard asked. "Surely the physician knows by now if the child will live or die."

"Camryn said only that the child might need to be turned."

"If something happens to Millie—"

William grabbed his cousin's arm. "Stop it! They are both in good hands. Just wait. You will—"

Slamming his empty glass on the table, Richard interrupted, "I cannot wait a minute longer." He stood up. "I will see my wife."

William stood, too. "Unless you calm down, your presence will do Millie more harm than good."

Suddenly the door opened to reveal Elizabeth. "You may come in now, Papa."

When Richard still did not move, William grasped his arm. "Millie needs you."

Suddenly, Richard shot through the door, and William walked over to join his wife. As he slipped an arm around her waist, they watched as two people they loved very much experienced the same wonderment they had only a month earlier.

William whispered, "Is everything well?"

"Yes. The baby did not have to be turned—I believe in answer to our prayers. And Millie must have miscalculated how far along she was, for the baby did not arrive early, according to Mr. Camryn."

As her husband's shoulders slumped with relief, she closed the door. Abruptly, she was pulled into William's embrace. As he rested his head on hers, he asked, "Boy or girl?"

"I am proud to say that Master Richard Edward Fitzwilliam has joined his parents as our guest."

William smiled. "I know my cousin is over the moon; I was when Mr. Camryn said I had a son. I dreamed of having an heir first, followed by many more beautiful daughters like Emily."

"Many more?" Elizabeth smiled. "How many more?"

"I was thinking four would be the right number."

"Four?" Elizabeth exclaimed.

Suddenly they were interrupted by Lady Matlock rushing into the room. She was followed by her husband, the Charltons and the Bingleys.

"Has Millie had the baby?" the countess asked, her worried eyes flicking from William to Elizabeth.

"She and your new grandson are doing very well," Elizabeth said. "Richard is with them now."

Chatter and laughter filled the room. Then Lady Matlock said, "I shall take over now, Elizabeth. I imagine Alexander will soon need his mother, and you need to rest."

"I agree," William said. "Why do we not all go to bed? There will be ample opportunity to see Millicent and the babe in the morning."

As the Charltons and Bingleys obediently left the room, the countess winked at William and Elizabeth. "I must get a glimpse of my grandchild tonight, or I shall not sleep at all."

Gingerly she opened the door, only to meet Kitty coming out. As she stepped aside to allow Elizabeth's sister to pass, she heard Richard call, "Come in, Mother and Father." The countess grabbed her husband's hand, and they reverently entered the bedroom.

As the door closed, Kitty turned to Elizabeth. "No matter how many times I witness a child come into this world, I am amazed at the miracle of life."

"I know how you feel," Elizabeth replied, taking her hands. "Thank you for helping me. I could not have been as strong had you not been with me."

"I was glad to be of service."

"Now, Mrs. Reynolds will make certain Millie and the child are well cared for tonight." Elizabeth chuckled. "I would not be surprised if Richard and Lady Matlock stay awake all night, so please go to bed. You deserve some rest."

"So do you," Kitty replied. Giving Elizabeth a hug and William a smile, she went out of the room.

Later
On a balcony

Alexander was soundly sleeping on his mother's breast as William and Elizabeth lay on a chaise on the balcony outside her bedroom. Elizabeth rested her back against her husband's chest, while his arms enveloped both her and the baby. They had lain this way since their child had had his fill over a quarter of an hour ago.

"We really should ring for Mrs. Grassley," William whispered, kissing the soft skin below one of her ears. "Let her take Alex back to the nursery so you can rest."

Elizabeth sighed. "I should, but this moment is so precious I hate to break the spell. It just occurred to me that this month one year ago, you and Richard were both badly injured. And now—"

"And now we each have all our hearts could desire?"

"Yes. I am overwhelmed with gratitude to God and love for you, Alex and Emily. Still, I admit that often I have imagined how different my life would be now had you not kept your promise to Charles."

"I have considered that as well. You and I learned a hard lesson—that one wrong choice can make the difference between happiness and despair."

Elizabeth brought his hand to her lips. Placing a kiss thereon, she said, "I thank God I was given another chance to choose you. Life could not possibly be any more perfect than it is at this moment."

"That is why I am determined to squeeze every ounce of joy from each day I am given with you and our children."

Elizabeth crooked her head to look at him, "I can face the future, as long as I face it with you, my darling William. I love you."

"And I promise to love you and never leave you for as long as God allows."

A soft, sweet kiss sealed their declarations.

Epilogue

The future was kind to the Darcys, and William's desire for four more daughters was almost prophetic. Ultimately, he and Elizabeth had three additional daughters and another son.

With each new addition to the family, Emily became more determined to mother her siblings and eventually presided over a makeshift school in the playroom where, at one time or another, each of her brothers and sisters were first exposed to their numbers and letters. It was a foreshadowing of things to come, for by the age of seventeen, Emily was tutoring those children who were delayed in their reading skills at Lambton's school and filling in whenever the teacher was taken ill. She, her sisters and brothers were educated by the same tutors, and for the rest of her life, Emily was a strong advocate of education for girls as well as boys.

By the time Alexander was a grown man, he was nearly an exact replica of his father. Tall and handsome, the sight of him walking from the stables to the house was often enough to make Elizabeth's heart skip a beat because he reminded her of the first time she had seen William in Meryton. A scholar, Alex finished at the top of his class at Cambridge, and upon his return to Pemberley, he instituted several new fertilisation techniques, which resulted in a two-fold increase in the yield per acre of their crops. Moreover, like his father, he was well-versed in investments, trade and new inventions, such as steam-powered railroads. Thanks to their shared interests, Fitzwilliam Darcy owned investments in textile mills, coal mines and railroads long before his peers, and in later years this would prove essential to Pemberley's survival.

Two years after Alexander was born, Elizabeth gave birth to their daughter Elizabeth Anne. Named after her mother and grandmother, Anne inherited her father's black hair and her Aunt Georgiana's dark-blue eyes. Sociable like her mother, Anne was a proficient at both pianoforte and harp, and under Georgiana's guidance, as well as several masters, she became an accomplished musician. Often asked to perform at prestigious events, she could have parlayed her talent into a profession had she wished for one; however, Anne loved her home too much to travel and preferred to reserve her talent for family and friends.

Their third child, George Fitzwilliam Bennet Darcy, arrived three years after Anne. Though he had his father's dark, good looks, his temperament matched his mother's. Moreover, the fact that he was two inches shorter than his father and brother also spoke of Elizabeth's influence. Still, at just over six feet tall, he could never be considered short. Given to a gregarious nature, George finished Cambridge with good grades, though without the honours Alex had accrued. Not having the responsibilities of the heir, he threw himself into his passion: horses. Being an excellent judge of horseflesh, George grew Pemberley's stables into one of the foremost horse-breeding establishments in the country. In addition, his animals began to participate in and win many prestigious events which contributed to both Pemberley's reputation and her coffers.

Due to a miscarriage, it was four years before another child was born. Of all his children, William thought Claire Jane most favoured Elizabeth in appearance and temperament, and that similarity never failed to make him smile. If Emily aspired to teach, Claire aspired to write. By the time she was one and twenty, she was writing a monthly article for a leading fashion magazine based in London. Even as she wrote for the magazine, she was secretly working on a novel, which was later published under a pseudonym. Her novel proved so popular that Claire's name was eventually exposed. By then, however, there was little stigma associated with novels or with the women who wrote them.

Just as she was certain that her child-bearing years were over, Elizabeth was stunned and delighted to discover she was pregnant again. Five years after Claire's birth, she was delivered of another daughter, Sophia Rose. Of all their daughters, Rose looked most like William, and by the age of twenty, she was the tallest daughter, at five feet and nine inches. After taking a tour of Kew Gardens as a child, Rose's aspiration was to learn all about flowers. In pursuit of that goal, she was given charge of a portion of Pemberley's gardens and put under the tutelage of their master gardener. The youngest Darcy quickly became an authority on the subject.

Autumn of 1842

Over the course of their marriage, Rosehill became a welcome respite for William and Elizabeth—a place to throw off the cares of parenthood, position and duty in order to rekindle their passion. Within her walls, promises to one another took priority; thus, when they returned to Pemberley, it was with a renewed commitment to their union and, on occasion, a newly conceived child.

As the Darcys completed their twenty-fifth year of marriage, Emily, now eight and twenty, had been married to the Earl of Hawthorn for six years. She and the earl lived in Liverpool with their children—William and Elizabeth's first grandchildren—five-year-old Will and two-year-old Eliza.

Having just graduated from Cambridge, Alexander had recently offered for Gwendolyn, the middle daughter of Lord and Lady Atchley, and their nuptials were scheduled for the spring of 1843. Anne, who would turn two and twenty in months, had accepted an offer from the Bingleys' son, Bennet, who had graduated from Cambridge the previous year. Wanting to distance her wedding from her brother's, Anne planned to marry at Christmas the following year.

George, Claire and Rose were still at home. Even so, William and Elizabeth realised that this was just the beginning, and at some point, all of their children would have families of their own. Already Charles and Jane's daughters were married, and Bennet, of course, was engaged to Anne. As for Richard and Millie's children, Hugh and Kathy had each married years before, while Richard Edward had just finished Cambridge with Alexander. Already married to his sweetheart, the daughter of Lord Claxton, his younger brother, John David, would begin his third year at Cambridge in the fall.

Georgiana gave Lord Charlton three children: Weston, Lavenia and Julia. Mary had three more children, and except for her two youngest, they had all left home to marry. Sadly, Harvey Thomas, Kitty's husband, died unexpectedly three years after Alexander's birth. Unhappy living alone, Kitty had sold all her property and moved in with the Bingleys at Canfield Manor, at Jane's insistence. Harold Smith, the solicitor who had once set his cap for Elizabeth, was still handling Charles' affairs, and after becoming reacquainted with Kitty, fell in love with her. Married two years later, they were blessed with a son and a daughter.

Through the years, the Darcys and their extended family added numerous sons and daughters. Afterwards, grandchildren began filling the empty places left by their parents' departures. Privileged to have had the greater part of their family for many unbroken years, William and Elizabeth considered themselves among the most fortunate of people.

In the winter of their days, they were just as much in love as the night they first declared their devotion on a balcony at Pemberley. Having once said that *only the deepest love will persuade me into matrimony*, Elizabeth had found that kind of love with Fitzwilliam Darcy. And it had made all the difference in the world.

Finis

Footnotes

1 *I imagine Chatsworth as a substitute for Pemberley. Richard is admiring the scenes from the life of Julius Caesar, painted from 1692-1694 by Louis Laguerre. http://pemberley-state-of-mind. tumblr.com/post/916446092/the-painted-hall-ceiling-chatsworth-house-scenes*

2 *"The best laid schemes o' mice an' men / Gang aft agley" (often paraphrased in English as "The best-laid plans of mice and men / Often go awry") is from,* **To A Mouse**, *a poem written by Robert Burns in 1785, and included in the Kilmarnock volume. http:// en.wikipedia.org/wiki/To_a_Mouse*

3 *I chose to use the proposal scene from the 2005 Pride and Prejudice movie for it works with the rain in this chapter.*

4 *Angelo's Haymarket Room – A fencing academy run by Henry Angelo and then his sons. In 1770, the salle d'armes was at Carlisle House, overlooking Soho-square; then it was moved to Opera House-buildings in Haymarket, next to Old Bond Street. The Regency Encyclopedia and www.georgianindex.net*

5 *Sarsenet -a fine, soft silk fabric used as a lining material and in dressmaking.*

6 *The Mint – The most notorious slum in London, a ten-minute stroll from London Bridge and home to the most desperate thieves and beggars. www.regencyassemblypress.com*

7 **Lavender's Blue** *(perhaps sometimes called* "**Lavender Blue**,") *is an English folk song and nursery rhyme dating to the 17th century, which has been recorded in various forms since the 20th century.*

It emerged as a children's song in Songs for the Nursery in 1805 in the form:

Lavender blue and Rosemary green,
When I am king you shall be queen;
Call up my maids at four o'clock,
Some to the wheel and some to the rock;
Some to make hay and some to shear corn,
And you and I will keep the bed warm.
http://en.wikipedia.org/wiki/Lavender's_Blue

8 Stillroom - a distillery room found in most great houses, castles or large establishments throughout Europe, dating back at least to medieval times. Medicines were prepared, cosmetics and many home cleaning products created, and home-brewed beer or wine was often made there. The still room was a working room: part science lab, part infirmary and part kitchen. http://en.wikipedia.org/wiki/Still_room

9 British Foreign Minister Robert Stewart, Viscount Castlereagh.

10 **The Eight Articles of London**, also known as the London Protocol of June 21, 1814, was a secret convention between the Great Powers: United Kingdom of Great Britain and Ireland, Prussia, Austria, and Russia to award the territory of current Belgium and the Netherlands to William I of the Netherlands, then "Sovereign Prince" of the United Netherlands. He accepted this award on July 21, 1814. **The Anglo-Dutch Treaty of 1814** (also known as the Convention of London) was signed between the United Kingdom and the Netherlands in London on 13 August 1814. It was signed by Robert Stewart, Viscount Castlereagh for the British, and Hendrik Fagel for the Dutch. The treaty noted a declaration of 15 June 1814 by the Dutch that ships for the slave trade were no longer permitted in British ports, and it agreed that this restriction would be extend-

ed to a ban on involvement in the slave trade by Dutch citizens.
https://en.wikipedia.org/wiki/Eight_Articles_of_London

11 *La Belle Assemblée (in full La Belle Assemblée or, Bell's*
Court and Fashionable Magazine Addressed Particularly to
the Ladies) was a British women's magazine published from 1806
to 1837, founded by John Bell (1745–1831). http://en.wikipedia.org/
wiki/La_Belle_Assembl%C3%A9e

12 *Money Boxes. Known in England from at least Tudor times,*
money boxes, sometimes called money jars since few of them were
actually square, were used by many working-class people to keep
their meagre savings. Though they were not especially glamorous,
these small vessels would have been present in a great many Regen-
cy households, and, despite their humble appearance, they would
have been very precious to their owners. Not entirely unheard of in
the upper classes, they were also purchased as gifts for babies and
young children, as it was customary for a parent or god-parent to
give a baby a money box, into which they placed a few coins to start
the child's savings. Typically, the money box was entrusted to the
child's mother, who would safeguard it and present it to the child
when they came of age. https://regencyredingote.wordpress.com

13 *Once upon a time green paint literally killed people. In 1814 in*
Schweinfurt, Germany, two men named Russ and Sattler tried to
improve on Scheele's green, a paint made with copper arsenide. The
result was a highly toxic pigment called emerald green. Made with
arsenic and verdigris, the bright green color became an instant fa-
vorite with painters, cloth makers, wall paper designers, and dyers.
https://janeaustensworld.wordpress.com/2010/03/05/emerald-
green-or-paris-green-the-deadly-regency-paint/

14 *Robert Banks Jenkinson, 2nd Earl of Liverpool KG PC (7 June*

1770 – 4 December 1828) was an English politician and both the youngest and longest-serving Prime Minister (1812–27) since 1806. He dealt smoothly with the Prince Regent when King George III was incapacitated.

15 *Mānuka honey is produced by introduced European honey bees feeding on the mānuka or tea tree (Leptospermum scoparium) which grows uncultivated throughout New Zealand and south-eastern Australia. At times, it has been touted for medicinal purposes, though lately those claims have been questioned. For the purposes of this story, I have overstated its reputation.*